SO-BZL-618

SPECIAL MESSAGE TO READERS

This book is published under the auspices of

THE ULVERSCROFT FOUNDATION

(registered charity No. 264873 UK)

Established in 1972 to provide funds for research, diagnosis and treatment of eye diseases. Examples of contributions made are: —

A Children's Assessment Unit at Moorfield's Hospital, London.

•

Twin operating theatres at the Western Ophthalmic Hospital, London.

•

A Chair of Ophthalmology at the Royal Australian College of Ophthalmologists.

•

The Ulverscroft Children's Eye Unit at the Great Ormond Street Hospital For Sick Children, London.

You can help further the work of the Foundation by making a donation or leaving a legacy. Every contribution, no matter how small, is received with gratitude. Please write for details to:

**THE ULVERSCROFT FOUNDATION,
The Green, Bradgate Road, Anstey,
Leicester LE7 7FU, England.
Telephone: (0116) 236 4325**

**In Australia write to:
THE ULVERSCROFT FOUNDATION,
c/o The Royal Australian College of
Ophthalmologists,
27, Commonwealth Street, Sydney,
N.S.W. 2010.**

Hilary Bonner is a former showbusiness editor of the *Mail on Sunday* and the *Daily Mirror*. She now lives in Somerset and continues to work as a freelance journalist, covering film, television and theatre. She is the author of five previous novels.

A KIND OF WILD JUSTICE

He's a barbaric killer. He abducted and tortured an innocent seventeen-year-old girl, brutally raped her, then left her to die. Yet when James Martin O'Donnell stood trial he was acquitted. Twenty years later a chance DNA test makes it clear that there has been a shocking miscarriage of justice. But the law of double jeopardy means O'Donnell cannot be tried again. And when Joanna Bartlett, the crime correspondent who covered the case two decades ago, starts to delve into the past, she is forced to revisit not only the crime she can't bear to remember but also the maverick police detective she has forced herself to forget . . .

Books by Hilary Bonner
Published by The House of Ulverscroft:

A FANCY TO KILL FOR
FOR DEATH COMES SOFTLY

HILARY BONNER

A KIND OF WILD JUSTICE

Complete and Unabridged

Jefferson-Madison
Regional Library
Charlottesville, Virginia

WITHDRAWN

ULVERSCROFT
Leicester

3028686656

First published in Great Britain in 2001 by
William Heinemann
London

First Large Print Edition
published 2002
by arrangement with
William Heinemann
The Random House Group Limited
London

The moral right of the author has been asserted

Copyright © 2001 by Hilary Bonner
All rights reserved

British Library CIP Data

Bonner, Hilary
  A kind of wild justice.—Large print ed.—
Ulverscroft large print series: mystery
1. Judicial error—Fiction
2. Suspense fiction
3. Large type books
I. Title
823.9′14 [F]

ISBN 0–7089–4703–4

Published by
F. A. Thorpe (Publishing)
Anstey, Leicestershire

Set by Words & Graphics Ltd.
Anstey, Leicestershire
Printed and bound in Great Britain by
T. J. International Ltd., Padstow, Cornwall

This book is printed on acid-free paper

This book is dedicated to the remains of
Fleet Street — wherever they may be

Acknowledgements

Grateful thanks are due to:

Detective Constable Phil Diss who put the original idea into my head; Sylvia Jones who really was Britain's first woman national newspaper crime correspondent, appointed by the *Daily Mirror* in 1980, (the same year as my fictional Joanna whom Sylvia would have left for dead should they ever have encountered each other on a story); Detective Sergeant Frank Waghorn whose endless patience and expertise in the trickiest areas of criminal law saved the day when I really thought I'd terminally lost the plot; Frank's son Dean Waghorn who knows absolutely everything about computers, Detective Constable Chris Webb whose local policing knowledge was invaluable; Chief Superintendent Steve Livings for sharing with me his rich fund of case histories; Billy who knows first hand about crime and punishment from the other side of the fence but has no wish to draw attention to himself so Billy's not his real name; civilian inquiry desk clerk Dave Jones of Okehampton Police Station and WO1 Stuart Woods and Col. Tony Clark of Okehampton Camp, without whom I would never have found my eerie Dartmoor crime scene; Richard Stott, former editor of the *Daily Mirror*, who forged a hole you could drive a truck through in my disgracefully sketchy knowledge of newspaper law and then bought me lunch while he filled it in, as it were; Mirror lawyer Charles Collier-Wright for his guidance and in the hope that he won't sue me for misusing his famous nickname; Phil Walker, former editor of the *Daily Star*; Larry Haley of L.A. for giving me the FBI angle on DNA; Simon Patterson and Brian Bourne, who know what banks and bankers get up to; Mike Milburn for telling me about guns; John Pullinger for telling me about maps; Graham Bartlett at the National Meteorological Library and Archive for ensuring I got the weather right; Samantha Fox of Vodafone and Ken Lennox super-snapper for advice on phones and photos; the nice lady at Okehampton Magistrates Court who let me snoop quietly around without filling in 16 forms in triplicate; Maggie for listening to my desperate and incoherent ramblings; Oscar and Sophie for silent companionship; Paul and Joan Smith for providing the place of inspiration (or as near as I can ever get to it.).

And last but not least all the characters of Fleet Street, the chauvinists, the drunks, and the deadbeats as well as the talented, the legendary and the near geniuses, who made up the crazy world in which I managed to survive, even very very occasionally flourish, for more than 20 extraordinary years, and without whom this book would not have been possible.

The bits I've got right are in no small way thanks to these guys — well, not really the drunks and deadbeats of Fleet Street, but the rest of them anyway — and, as they say, any mistakes are all my own work.

'Revenge is a kind of wild justice, which the more man's nature runs to, the more ought law to weed it out.'

Francis Bacon 1561–1626
(Essays — 'of revenge')

Prologue

Very, very carefully Detective Inspector Mike Fielding put the slim sheaf of papers back in their plastic folder. He placed it neatly to one side of his desk. Grey metal frame. Standard issue. No clutter. That was the kind of man Fielding was. He didn't like mess. And he was once again being confronted by the biggest mess of his life.

He noticed that the folder was not lined up precisely with the edge of the desk and shifted it slightly so that it did. Then, with a great effort of will, he turned his attention back to his computer screen.

For almost two and a half minutes he attempted to concentrate on the case he was supposed to be working on. Industrial theft. More than £100,000 worth of electronic equipment nicked from a warehouse on an Exeter industrial estate.

It really didn't seem to matter much, that was the problem. Nothing mattered much except what was in that plastic folder. He found himself picking it up again, and once more he removed the contents and spread them out before him.

There were just half a dozen or so sheets of printed foolscap paper, which basically contained two salient pieces of information.

One was a DNA sample taken from a young woman, kidnapped, raped and murdered twenty years previously.

The other was the DNA of the man who had stood trial for her murder and been acquitted.

The two sets matched. Exactly.

That meant there was around a ten million to one certainty that the acquitted man had been, after all, guilty of the murder. And of the other monstrous crimes committed against the teenager.

But he could not be tried again. Not for the same crime. Not for as long as he might live. That was British law. It was called double jeopardy and the new scientific evidence, irrefutable as it undoubtedly was, made not a jot of difference.

Ten million to one. Even the most astute of legal teams, and the bastard had always had access to those, would be hard-pushed to get around that bit of scientific truth. He'd been guilty as charged. And he'd got away with it. But then Fielding had never doubted that, really.

The policeman glowered at the damning information in front of him.

After the body had been found the murderer had been dubbed the Beast of Dartmoor, so horrific was the way in which he had tortured and killed that innocent young woman.

The law would change, of course, eventually. No doubt about it. Britain's double-jeopardy laws were 600 years old and, in view of the recent extraordinary advances in forensic science, the legal profession had already canvassed the Home Secretary. But the change would not come quickly enough. Not nearly quickly enough. Not for Mike Fielding.

So that was it, really. Over.

2

He opened the bottom drawer of his desk and took out the two photographs which lay there, easily to hand, right at the front. One was of the murdered girl, fresh-faced, dark-brown curly hair and matching eyes, averagely pretty, a sprinkling of freckles, smooth, creamy skin, uncertain smile, young-looking for her age. Seventeen years old. Still innocent. Unusually so, perhaps. She had been a virgin until the Beast had got his hands on her. Strange how you could somehow guess that just from the photograph. She looked slightly uncomfortable in a silky pale-pink dress, cut straight off the shoulders, hemline well below the knee. Obviously expensive, but far too old for her, almost frumpy. She had been a bridesmaid at her brother's wedding and she was carrying a posy of pale-pink rosebuds, which matched the colour of the dress. It was the last photograph taken of her, just four months before her disappearance.

Fielding placed it on his desk on top of the DNA reports and put the second photograph alongside it. This was the man he had always believed to be the Beast. A mugshot from when he had been arrested. Glowering at the camera. Arrogant. He had always been an arrogant bastard, but then, when you came from his family, that went with the territory. There he was, staring straight ahead with his mocking watery blue eyes, bleached-white blond hair shaved almost to a stubble, mouth set in a hard line, his chin, also stubbled but darker, tucked into a thick, fleshy neck, overly prominent forehead leaning towards the camera.

How Fielding would like to get his hands on him

in a locked room. Best that he never got the opportunity, though, because he doubted he would know how or when to stop.

Fielding had been the first police officer on the scene when they found the girl's body. It remained the worst moment of his twenty-eight-year career, and goodness knew, there had been some down times. He had been a high-flying young detective sergeant then, full of optimism and confidence. Tough, too. It hadn't occurred to him that he could ever be confronted by something that would really disturb him. And it certainly hadn't occurred to him that just one case would destroy so many of his aspirations and remain still, he fervently believed, the reason why he had not risen beyond detective inspector. The fact that a lot of it was probably his own fault did not help. Not when he thought about what he had seen up there on the moor. Not when he thought about what might have been for him had none of it ever happened.

He had learned to live with it all. That's what you did, wasn't it? That's what everybody did who wanted to survive. But now it had all returned to haunt him.

Abruptly pushing both photographs away, and turning them face down so he no longer had to look at them, Fielding consulted a note he had made on a message pad, picked up the telephone and dialled the first three digits of a London telephone number.

Then he stopped.

Then he began to dial again, this time a local Exeter number. His wife answered on the third ring.

'I'm going to be late,' he told her bluntly. She

4

registered no surprise. After nearly thirty years of marriage to a police detective who liked women almost as much as he liked whisky, there wasn't much he could do that would surprise her. Fielding replaced the receiver and studied the DNA reports once more. He picked up a red marker pen and encircled the damning data on both sets.

It had all happened by chance in the end. Not that there was anything strange about that. They only caught the Yorkshire Ripper because of a routine check by traffic cops. Mind you, the Ripper case had been one of the most incompetent criminal investigations of the twentieth century.

Fielding put the top of the marker pen in his mouth and began to chew it. It was a habit he had indulged in since he gave up smoking. That had been almost ten years ago and he had lapsed only briefly just a couple of times. For once in his life, he had shown some won't-power, he reflected wryly. Never short of will-power, it was just the won't-power he struggled with — his father had coined that one about him. His father, Jack Fielding — also in the job, retired as a uniformed superintendent — who had at first been so proud of the bright, intelligent son following in his footsteps, but then, Fielding suspected, by the time of his death three years previously, bitterly disappointed.

Anyway, Mike had always used the won't-power line as a kind of running joke, but there was, of course, a lot of truth in it. The top drawer of his desk was full of pens and pencils with chewed broken tops. Occasionally he ended up with ink all over his mouth. And he didn't work in the kind of environment where some kind soul was likely to obligingly point this out before he made a complete fool of himself. Remembering this, and that the marker pen was a particularly vivid red, he took it out of his mouth and replaced it with a pencil.

He didn't really like thinking about incompetent investigations. The whole Beast of Dartmoor operation had been deeply flawed. He knew that. A lot of it had been down to his governor — Parsons had been far too sure of himself, as indeed, Mike was aware, he himself had been back then. He was also certain that at least one of the mistakes which had been made could be laid at his own door. Perhaps the biggest mistake of all.

He reached behind the pile of files in the bottom drawer of his desk and retrieved a two-thirds empty bottle of supermarket Scotch. Then he rummaged around for the glass he was sure he had replaced there the previous day. He couldn't find it. In the end he just took a deep swig from the bottle.

The rough, cheap spirit hit the back of his throat and burned a little as he swallowed. First of the day. It felt good. It always did. Fielding rarely drank at lunchtimes. He didn't dare. He kidded himself that as long as he didn't drink till the evenings he didn't have a problem. Certainly he knew that the longer he could put off the first taste, the better chance he had of ending the day in a reasonable state.

He took a second welcome swig. Then he put the bottle back in the desk drawer and closed it. He leaned back in his chair, closed his eyes, still enjoying the warmth of the whisky, and, for just a few seconds, tried not to think. Not about anything.

It didn't work. He pulled open the desk drawer again, removed the bottle and took another deep drink. This time he didn't bother putting it away. Instead, he stood it on the floor next to his chair, where he could reach it easily but nobody coming into the room could see it.

The Beast of Dartmoor had been involved in a minor traffic accident in London. Proof yet again that even traffic cops had their uses. Mike allowed himself a wry smile at that. It hadn't even been the Beast's fault, and he certainly hadn't been drunk. Far too controlled for that. After all — although Mike didn't believe his habits would have changed much, and certainly not his sexual perversions — he'd kept out of trouble, somehow, for twenty years, albeit through nothing other than nifty footwork. But the Beast had been given a routine breath test, just standard procedure, and failed. It was also routine to do a DNA test, a buccul swab, a kind of toothbrush scrape of the inner mouth. It had all been routine, in fact. The DNA was run through the computer, standard practice again, and bingo, as Fielding's old adversary Todd Mallett — with whom he had attended police college, which was absolutely all the two of them had in common — would have said.

It came up the same as DNA taken from the dead girl's body, from the body fluids that could only have been deposited by her murderer.

DNA. Deoxyribonucleic acid. Minute threadlike molecules, each made up of two intertwined strands, which carry the unique genetic make-up of every human being. A sort of personal blueprint.

7

Strange how quickly such an extraordinary development in science had become taken for granted. DNA had transformed police work, no doubt about that. Except in this case it made no difference. Suddenly there was irrefutable evidence of the guilt of a vicious perverted murderer, but there was bugger all anybody could do with it. That was the law for you. And sometimes it seemed to have very little to do with justice.

After a few moments Fielding stood up and walked over to the window. It was Monday, 26 June 2000. A remarkable landmark day. Fielding had earlier watched the TV news and seen the announcement that scientists had cracked the DNA code. Soon they would be able to map out your body's future for you, predict what diseases you were likely to develop and maybe prevent them. Perhaps even predict that a particular human being was liable to turn into a perverted monster like the Beast of Dartmoor. Fielding didn't understand the half of it, but one thing he was damned sure of was that the law would get involved sooner or later, and would no doubt make an ass of itself as it had, in his opinion, with every other DNA development so far.

He checked his watch. It was just gone seven, his favourite time of day in the police station at Heavitree Road, Exeter's premier nick, which had been his base throughout the bulk of his service. Unless something really big was afoot, the evenings were usually quiet; he could clear his head, allow himself time to think. When he was alone like this at the end of the working day in the environment he was so familiar with, Fielding was inclined to feel as much at peace as he ever could. But not today. Today there could be no peace.

It was hot, too. In Devon it had been one of the best days of a so far disappointing summer. Too hot to work, though, and the temperature had yet to drop much. Fielding's first-floor office was small and airless. It looked over the car park and a broad patch of grass to the Heavitree Road beyond, one of the main arterials leading to and from the city centre. Exeter's workforce was still wending its way painfully home and the slow-moving vehicles seemed to be creating their own heat haze. Fielding half imagined he could see their passengers sweating. Too hot for driving as well. His office window was open although it brought scant relief. Fielding tugged at his already loosened tie. A trick of the evening sunlight caused him to be able to see his own reflection in the angled glass.

He was a big man, almost six feet three inches tall, but rangy rather than burly. He had thickened a little with the years, particularly round the waist, but had never had a weight problem and remained surprisingly trim and fit-looking for his age — which was knocking fifty now. It was a miracle, considering his lifestyle — and his drinking habits. He rubbed his chin reflectively, his fingers scratching over the stubble. By around sixish in the evening he could invariably do with another shave, really. He had always had a heavy beard, unusually so for a man with light sandy hair. Thinning hair, now, and greying. His beard would be grey too if he ever let it grow. Still, it could be worse. His father had been almost totally bald at his age. Thinking back twenty years made you wonder about ageing. Fielding knew he'd fared pretty well, certainly better than he deserved. He had retained the easy lopsided grin which, somewhat to his surprise nowadays, women still seemed to go for. He had never been a particularly handsome man but for some reason had always been attractive to women — and once he'd realised that, he had rarely been able to resist any opportunity that had come his way.

She'd been that, to begin with, just another opportunity, a quick lay. Sex had been like getting a fix for him back then. Mind you, it was much the same now except he didn't need it nearly so often. He'd rarely had much use for women other than sex.

He had married his wife when she was twenty and he was nineteen. She had been pregnant, of course, and it had been 1970, for God's sake. That was what you did in 1970. Ruth was all right. A pretty girl back then, with auburn hair so bright it made his look dull, the palest of skin and a ready smile. He had been at university when they'd had to get wed and she'd worked behind the bar in the pub they all went to. She'd carried on working, too, right up to and after their first child was born, getting her mum to mind the baby, all so that Fielding could finish his degree and fulfil his ambition of fast-track entry into the police force. That had been the plan, anyway. And whatever had gone wrong over the years had certainly never been Ruth's fault. She'd brought up his children, turned them into almost reasonable human beings, in fact. And she'd put up with him. Pretended not to notice the bulk of his indiscretions. He knew that and he loved her. He supposed that he'd always loved Ruth in his own way. But the other one. Well, they say everybody has a single great passion in his or her life. The other one, she had been his, no doubt about it. And it was inextricably connected in his mind with the Beast of Dartmoor case. Delve into any one area of that and all of it came back to him.

He could only think of one thing left to do about the Beast. And in a way this was a wonderful excuse to make the call he had half wanted to make for something like eighteen years. Half not. Certainly never had. Well, it wasn't an easy call to make.

Resolutely he squared his shoulders and walked back to his desk. 'Right,' he said out loud.

He sat down in his chair and, once again, picked up the phone and dialled the same three digits of the London number he had begun to call earlier. This time he continued with the call. It was to the switchboard of a national daily newspaper.

He could hear the tone clearly as an extension rang somewhere in a dockland building he had merely seen pictures of — not Fleet Street any more. He had had a sort of romantic affection for the Street of Shame, strange for a copper, but because of her, most likely. Impatiently he drummed the fingers of his free hand on his desk. He supposed he would end up with voice mail; that seemed to be the norm nowadays. He found himself rehearsing a message to leave and was mildly taken aback when a live human voice came on the line.

'Joanna Bartlett.'

Tones clear and precise. No nonsense. No 'hello'

or 'can I help you'. No embellishments at all. Fielding could not suppress a half-smile. It didn't sound as if she had changed a bit. But then, he wouldn't have expected her to.

'Hi, Jo,' he said quietly.

Part One

Part One

1

It began in the summer of 1980 on one of those rare warm and balmy English days when even on Dartmoor the midday heat had been stifling and only the cool of nightfall brought welcome relief. Nobody was grumbling, though. It had until then been another miserable summer and, in fact, the coldest July for fifteen years.

Angela Phillips lived with her parents, her brother Rob and his new wife Mary, at Five Tors Farm — so named, predictably enough, because, on a clear day, you could just see the rocky summits of five tors — on the edge of the moors not far from the lovely old granite-built village of Blackstone. Their home was a beautiful rambling Devon longhouse, one end of it converted to provide a more or less separate unit for Rob and Mary.

A smart new stable block had recently been built on to the rear wall of the main milking shed, and from it could be enjoyed as fine a view over the moors as from anywhere on the Phillipses' land. But during the late afternoon of that particular day, seventeen-year-old Angela noticed little of her surroundings as she fed her three horses, two hunters and a showjumper, and prepared to turn them out for the night in the adjoining paddock.

Angela was going to the village dance with, for the very first time, a boyfriend. Her casual friendship with Jeremy Thomas, her brother's best friend, had begun to turn into something else at the hunt ball the previous winter when he had unexpectedly kissed her during the last dance.

Feelings Angela did not know she possessed had overwhelmed her. And since then Jeremy, and their occasional heavy petting sessions, had become a major absorption for a young woman who had previously shown little interest in anything other than her beloved horses.

The sun was just beginning to drop in the sky and Dartmoor glowed gloriously before her as she shut the paddock gate and turned to walk back to the farmhouse. Angela remained totally preoccupied with the evening ahead. After all, she had made rather momentous plans for it.

In that very focused way teenage girls sometimes have, she had decided that the time had come to rid herself of the burden of her virginity, that she was going to do so in a proper bed and that tonight, as she knew Jeremy's parents were away, was the ideal opportunity.

So far Angela and Jeremy had conducted the physical side of their relationship almost entirely in the back of his car. Neither had parents of the modern liberated kind who would allow their young offspring to sleep with their girlfriend or boyfriend under their roof. An unfortunate attempt at a passionate encounter in one of Five Tors' more remote copses, which had ended abruptly with a number of ants finding their way into her underwear, had put Angela off the idea of outdoor venues. Jeremy had been unusually grumpy when she had stopped him from going any further that

16

day. She didn't really blame him, though, because she had already learned enough about sex to know that she had led him on shockingly.

Tonight she was not planning to stop him at all.

She glanced at her watch as she made her way across the farmyard. She'd better hurry. It was well gone five, Jeremy was picking her up at seven, she had yet to wash her hair, and as she intended this to be such a memorable night it would probably take her much longer than usual to get ready. She had some new make-up to experiment with, too, which would take her ages to put it on because she hardly ever wore the stuff.

She also had a new outfit, the most grown-up she had ever owned. Normally Angela was not particularly interested in clothes, favouring jeans and baggy shirts on the rare occasions she was not wearing either her school uniform or jodhpurs. But she had persuaded her mother to take her shopping in Exeter to buy something special for the dance, traditionally held after the fête on the final day of Blackstone's annual festival, which this year had fallen on the last Saturday in July and for which the weather had so mercifully cleared.

Angela broke into a trot, ran through the farmhouse kitchen, ignoring her mother's shouted protest when she failed to close the yard door behind her, and bounded up the stairs to her bedroom. She felt the excitement mount when she saw the black miniskirted shift dress spread on the bed waiting for her. A pair of very high-heeled black patent leather shoes stood on the carpet alongside. Angela had shiny dark-brown hair and smooth, creamy skin, but she thought her hair was too curly and judged, quite correctly, that she was fairly average-looking, facially anyway. She also knew she had a truly great figure, honed to super-fitness by her riding activities, and that her legs were her best feature. Although only five feet four inches, most of her height was in her legs which, because they were so slim and well-proportioned, succeeded in looking much longer than they really were — and the extravagantly expensive sheer black tights she had bought out of her own pocket money would be the final touch.

She bathed, and washed and dried her hair quickly, having decided not to attempt an elaborate new style and just to go for the clean, glossy look, but easing on the unfamiliarly sheer tights without ruining them took some time and she was as clumsy as she had expected to be with her make-up. However, after several attempts she eventually got it more or less right and regarded her appearance critically in the full-length mirror inside her wardrobe door.

She thought she looked pretty darned good, but so different that she hardly recognised herself. She just hoped Jeremy appreciated the transformation. She had done it for him, after all. She didn't know which she was looking forward to most, showing herself and Jeremy off to the village, or — whatever might happen afterwards. She gazed dreamily out of the window, again hardly seeing the view, and thought about her big, blond, handsome boyfriend, just two years her senior. She imagined them dancing the night away together, glowing warmly under the admiring glances of their friends and peers. Then she started to imagine what it would be like to 'go all the way' with him . . .

A familiar throaty engine roar interrupted her reverie and she watched the souped-up red Ford Escort, which was Jeremy's pride and joy, coast to a halt outside the kitchen door. He was clever with mechanical things and she knew that he had almost entirely rebuilt the car himself, painting a sporty gold flash down each side and adding oversized wheels.

Angela glanced at her watch. He was actually five minutes early — as keen as she was, apparently. She turned away from the window, hurried out of her room and, in spite of her high heels, ran down the stairs almost as quickly as she had earlier run up them.

Rushing through the kitchen, she called goodbye to her mother over her shoulder and was outside in the yard before Jeremy even had a chance to knock on the farmhouse door. Well aware that she was wearing rather more make-up than her mother would approve of, she didn't want anything to spoil the moment when her boyfriend was confronted with her new look for the first time.

Jeremy didn't disappoint her. As she emerged, his face broke into a big, crooked grin and he took an exaggerated step backwards. 'Wow!' he said, then followed that with a loudly approving wolf whistle.

Angela felt smug. So far everything was going according to plan. Jeremy knew nothing of his girlfriend's ulterior motive in choosing an outfit far sexier than anything he had ever seen her in before.

Nonetheless he beamed at her in that rather proprietorial way she found so disarming and escorted her to the car. Then, just as he started the engine, a waving figure emerged from the other end of the house.

'Hey, wait for me,' shouted her brother Rob.

Angela adored Rob and was normally delighted to have his company anywhere — but not on this particular night. 'I thought you were staying home with Mary,' she muttered in a not too friendly manner as Rob jogged across the yard towards them.

'Nope, she said I should go out and have some fun, bless her,' responded Rob with a big grin.

Angela didn't reply.

'Great, mate,' said Jeremy enthusiastically. He and her brother had been close friends before Rob's marriage. Since then, Rob had been completely preoccupied with his new bride and his achievement of making her pregnant almost certainly during their honeymoon. Indeed, it was this pregnancy which had kept both Mary and Rob more or less housebound, because Mary was not having an easy time of it and felt slightly sick almost non-stop — as she complained volubly.

No wonder Rob was excited about a night out, Angela thought, feeling selfish for a moment.

'C'mon, Ange, get in the back, I'll never fit in there.'

Instantly feeling irritable again Angela, in spite of her high heels and short, tight skirt, did as she was bid, somehow managing to manoeuvre her way through the gap between the two front seats. Her brother was exceptionally tall and gangly for a Phillips, a build inherited from their mother's side of the family.

'First night out with the lads since I got wed, no point in me driving as well,' chattered Rob as he settled into the front seat alongside Jeremy.

'I am not a lad,' muttered Angela tetchily from the back.

'I know that, you're my baby sister,' pronounced Rob mischievously, knowing full well how much it would annoy her.

Angela bristled in silence. Then Jeremy made it even worse by laughing loudly. Angela was used to being the centre of attention — with both her family and her boyfriend. She didn't like this at all. By the time they got to the village she was already in a thoroughly bad mood.

'How about one in the Blackstone Arms,' suggested Rob and, to her annoyance, Jeremy readily agreed. The boys were first out of the vehicle and headed straight for the bar, not even bothering to look over their shoulders to see if Angela was following them. As she climbed out of the car, hurrying in order not to be left behind, Angela caught the top of her right leg in the seat mechanism, snagging her tights. She cursed.

The scene at the Blackstone Arms was very old-fashioned. But then the village of Blackstone was an old-fashioned place. The men were all propping up the bar, some already in distinct disarray, and the women, of all ages, were sitting at the tables and chairs which lined the walls, giggling into glasses of gin and tonic, and white wine.

A group of local lads, apparently already well oiled, welcomed the newcomers noisily. Jeremy ordered himself and Rob a pint each, then finally seemed to remember Angela and offered her a drink too. She asked for a shandy. She occasionally drank wine or beer but, being only seventeen, the most she could get away with in her village pub was shandy — the low-alcohol kind, which was largely lemonade and came ready-mixed in a bottle.

'I'm going to have a bloody good night,' said Rob as he passed her the drink, which left Angela thinking gloomily that she doubted she would.

She was pleased when two friends called her over and asked her to join them. That would show Jeremy. But he appeared not even to notice as she sat down at their table, tugging at her skirt in an attempt to keep the snag in her tights covered. It was then she noticed there was a smear of blood on her leg as well. That depressed her even further. She had made such an effort with her appearance.

Morosely she stared at Rob and Jeremy over the too-fizzy weak shandy. Her two favourite men in all the world, apart, of course, from her father, and at that moment she thoroughly disliked both of them. They grew louder and louder, and the only attention they paid her was to offer periodically to replenish her drink and occasionally shout 'All right, Ange?' across the bar. She knew they hadn't had an opportunity for a drink together in a long while. But she was still angry. She made an effort to talk to her friends, mostly about horses, until, almost two hours and several pints later, she finally persuaded Rob and Jeremy to move on to the dance.

If she could just get Jeremy away from his cohorts, on to the dance floor and into her arms, her original plans for the evening might be resurrected. She was no longer so sure about ending up in his parents' bed, but perhaps a little romance could yet be injected into the evening.

However, at the village hall Rob and Jeremy again headed straight for the bar.

Angela sighed with frustration. 'Shouldn't you be careful? You are driving,' she said quietly to Jeremy. For a moment her boyfriend, who was usually a very sensible young man, looked uncertain.

But Rob had overheard her remark. 'Christ, henpecking him already,' her brother jeered. 'Stop being such a spoil-sport, Ange.'

Jeremy squeezed her arm. 'I'll be all right, honest,' he said. 'Just one more pint. And it's only the back lanes home, isn't it?'

Encouraged, she whispered, 'Can we have a dance, then?'

'Any minute,' said Jeremy.

But 'any minute' stretched on and on. The one pint became another and then another. Her two favourite young men were starting to look quite unsavoury. Stuck in the corner of the bar with them, she could only glance with envy at the couples gyrating on the floor. The village hall was packed and the air was heavy with cigarette smoke. The music was so loud she could hardly hear a word anybody was saying, which didn't actually matter much as there was nobody she wanted to have a conversation with. Certainly Rob and Jeremy were well past that, she reckoned. After a bit she even

23

began to think that the band, allegedly the best in the area, sounded pretty lousy and started to wonder why she had been so excited about the village dance in the first place. Suddenly everything seemed second-rate, particularly her two companions.

She glanced at her watch. It was almost 11.30 and so far her romantic night out had been a complete disaster.

She made one last attempt to rectify matters, although she knew it was too late. 'Come on, Jeremy, come and dance,' she coaxed, tugging on the sleeve of his jacket.

Again Rob interfered. 'Don't let her nag you, mate, she takes after her mother,' he said.

This time Angela felt the anger rise inside her. Her cheeks flushed. She was not used to being treated like this. She was accustomed to getting her own way, indeed to being spoiled rotten, by her father, her brother and, usually, her boyfriend.

Again Jeremy laughed loudly. Too loudly. It was probably rather a nervous laugh, but Angela was too angry by then to notice.

'Fuck you both,' she shouted at them, using the kind of language she hardly ever used. 'I'm going home. And Jeremy, I hope you crash your bloody silly car and get breathalysed . . . '

'Oh, go away,' murmured Rob conversationally.

'I'm going, don't worry, and I hate you,' she said, pushing aggressively past them and bumping into Jeremy so that beer spilled from his glass over his trousers and shoes.

Rob smiled and took a swig of his pint. 'Always

did have a temper on her,' he announced, slurring his words and swaying slightly as he spoke.

Jeremy giggled. This time he definitely sounded nervous. 'I'd better go after her,' he said, reaching to put his now almost empty glass on the bar.

'I'd let her cool off, if I were you, mate,' advised Rob.

'I suppose you're right, Rob, but it's a good two miles back to your place.' Jeremy was watching Angela's retreating back as, shoulders set in anger, she fought her way through the throng on her way to the door.

'Walk'll do her good,' said Rob resolutely. 'C'mon, Jer, it's your round.'

★ ★ ★

It was almost two in the morning before Lillian and Bill Phillips heard the unmistakable sound of Jeremy Thomas's customised Escort roaring into their farmyard, followed by the slamming of a car door and some loud laughter.

They even heard their son's voice: 'Some night, mate, aye, some bloody good night,' followed by more laughter.

'They're back,' whispered Lillian Phillips unnec- essarily. She knew it was silly, both their children were grown-up now and Rob was a married man, an expectant father even, but she could never sleep properly until they were home. And she was well aware that neither could her husband, though he denied it.

Bill Phillips grunted. 'Boy's drunk,' he stated.

25

'First time he's let his hair down since he was wed, bless him,' said his wife, her voice indulgent.

Bill Phillips grunted again. 'How come you're never that understanding when I've had a few?'

'Because you're my husband, of course,' replied his wife, offering no further explanation.

'And don't I know it,' he muttered, softening his words by reaching for her hand.

She sighed in the darkness. 'We're so lucky, aren't we? Two wonderful children, this place. And now we're going to be grandparents. Do you know, I just can't make up my mind whether I want it to be a little boy or a little girl. What about you, Bill? I suppose you want a boy, do you, make sure of the farm. Aye? Bill? Bill?'

This time the only reply was gentle snoring.

Carefully Lillian Phillips withdrew her hand from his and snuggled contentedly into the deep warmth of the bed. Within seconds she had fallen into an untroubled sleep.

★   ★   ★

In the morning, Bill Phillips was first up as usual. He didn't do the milking any more, hadn't for years, the Phillipses employed a dairyman for that, but old habits died hard. He liked to be up soon after five and settled by the Aga with his first cup of tea, listening to the farming programme on the radio.

Rob was usually up not long after him and would come down to his parent's part of the house for his first morning cuppa knowing that the tea would already be brewed. Bill didn't expect him very early that morning, though, not after the kind of night he'd apparently just enjoyed.

The farmer smiled to himself. Secretly he was as tolerant of his son's rare excess as was his wife. Rob was a good, hard-working boy. They could not have wished for a better son and, although Bill had always said that he wanted both his children to have choices and that no son of his would ever be forced into farming the way he had been, he was, of course, delighted when it became clear that all his only son wanted in life was to run Five Tors Farm one day. Rob would be the fourth generation of Phillipses' to do so.

Sometimes, particularly if the day were bright and sunny, Bill would go for an early inspection tour of his land. But the morning had dawned dull and drizzly, the previous day's sunshine already proven to have been just a brief respite in a terrible stretch of weather, and it was also Sunday. He poured a second cup of tea, settled himself more comfortably in his armchair and decided to stay where he was, enjoying the warmth and the radio for at least another hour or so.

Lillian was also an early riser and was up soon after six as usual. Normally, she took Angela a cup of tea in bed to soften the blow of having to get up. Angela liked her bed. The early-rising habit of her farming ancestors seemed somehow to be missing from her genes. On weekday mornings Lillian would wake her daughter at 6.30 in order for her to see to her horses before getting off to school. On Sundays Angela was still expected to be up at 7.30 for her stable chores. But remembering the late night and how much her daughter had been looking forward to the dance and to wearing her new dress, and being escorted there, for the first time, by her very own boyfriend, Lillian Phillips decided to let her have a rare lie-in. And an even rarer rest from her morning routine.

Lillian pulled on her boots and set off to bring in the horses herself. During the summer they were put out to grass only at night. They got too fat otherwise and the daytime flies bothered them.

The job did not take long. As soon as Lillian opened the paddock gate the animals came towards her, expecting their usual morning corn feed. Back in the house just a few minutes later, she made fresh tea and carried a mug of it up the stairs.

It was just before 8.30 a.m. when she paused and listened outside the door to her daughter's bedroom. Not a sound came from within. Smiling, she pushed the door open. 'C'mon, lazybones, I just hope you weren't in the same state as that brother . . . ' Lillian stopped in mid-sentence. Her daughter's bed had not been slept in. There was no sign that she had been in the room at all since the previous evening when she had been getting ready for the dance.

Startled, Lillian quickly put the mug of tea down on the landing floor and hurried into her son's and daughter-in-law's part of the house. Passing their bedroom, she knocked on the door and, receiving no reply, ran down the far staircase and into their kitchen.

Rob was sitting at his kitchen table with Mary. He

looked more than a little dishevelled and bleary-eyed, but he managed a wan smile as his mother entered the room.

'Hi, Mum,' he began. 'No point in asking you if you heard me come home, cos I know darned well you would have done . . . ' Seeing the expression on his mother's face, he too stopped in mid-sentence. 'W-what's wrong?' he asked uncertainly.

'Rob, where is your sister?' his mother asked.

'I dunno. In bed, I suppose. Late night, wasn't it? Why?'

'She did come home with you? Surely you brought your sister home with you, Rob?'

Rob was momentarily bewildered. After all, his head was not very clear. 'What? No. She'd had enough of Jer and me. Got in one of her tempers and stomped off; said she'd walk home. She should have been back more than an hour before us . . . '

He realised his mother was just staring at him, the shock in her eyes all too clear.

'Oh, my God, Mum, she's not here, is she?' he blurted out.

His mother just shook her head.

2

The desk clerk on front-office duty at Okehampton police station took the first call at 8.45 a.m.

The Phillips family had not waited to make any enquiries of their own. Instead, Rob Phillips looked up the number for their closest police station in the phone book. And when he made the call, although the panic was already rising inside him, not to mention the guilt at his own behaviour the previous evening, Rob spoke quietly and as calmly as he could. Nonetheless he had difficulty getting the words out in a lucid fashion.

In Okehampton, George Jarvis listened carefully. He was that kind of man, a civilian clerk but with a lifetime of policing behind him. And missing seventeen-year-old girls were every policeman's nightmare. They had minds of their own, did teenage girls. And bodies that were going through all kinds of metamorphoses their parents didn't usually want to know about. 'Our Doreen's not like that.' How often had George heard that one. He knew better. They were all like that, he had discovered over the years, even the most unlikely ones. Sometimes he was almost glad that he and his missus had never managed to produce any children. George knew more about the pain children caused their parents than he did about the pleasure, of course. That was a policeman's lot, really.

George had been the solid, old-fashioned sort of

copper. He even looked a bit like the actor who'd played George Dixon, Britain's first famous TV bobby, and he'd been teased a lot about that in his younger days: same Christian name, same looks, same build. He wished he had a quid for every time he'd walked into a pub to be greeted with 'evenin' all'. 'Course, it didn't happen very often nowadays. Nobody remembered George Dixon any more. Like Dixon, George Jarvis had been a uniformed sergeant when he'd retired four years earlier after completing his thirty years, always working a country beat. He'd signed on again immediately as a clerk. George liked being in police stations. His work had always been more of a way of life to him than just a job.

'Are you sure she didn't go home with her boyfriend for the night, Mr Phillips?' he asked, then, remembering himself and the offence such remarks could give, even at times like this when you'd think they had something more to worry about than appearances, 'I mean, to his family . . . '

'No,' said Rob. 'I told you. Jeremy gave me a lift back and went home on his own. We both thought Angela was already here at the farm.'

George wasn't at all sure he had told him that, but he didn't push the point. 'Is there any chance that she could have walked to his home and waited for him there, instead of going back to your place?'

'Well, I suppose she could've done. But no, she wouldn't have. I'm sure of it.'

'Is the Thomas place also within walking distance of the village?'

'About the same distance away as our farm, in the other direction,' said Rob. 'But I'm quite sure she

31

didn't go there. She was angry with Jeremy and, anyway, she wouldn't have done . . . '

George Jarvis sighed. 'Have you phoned the Thomases to check, sir?'

'No.'

More often than not the relatives of a missing kid would have done that before they called the police, thought George. This lot hadn't even thought about it, apparently, quite convinced their Angela must have come to harm not to have got home. He'd come across that sort of certainty in the past, only to find that it was misplaced.

He knew the Phillips family, of course, had seen Bill Phillips in Okehampton on market day only two or three weeks before. George had once been the village bobby at Blackstone in the days when villages had their own policemen instead of some anonymous car patrol passing through once a month — if you were lucky. George had known Rob Phillips when he was a nipper at the village primary school — Blackstone had had one of those too, once — but he didn't expect the lad to remember him. And the policeman had never known Angela at all. He was well enough aware, though, that parents also almost always thought their daughters were sensible. And all too often they were anything but.

'Right,' George began patiently. 'Then may I suggest you do so right away, sir. And try to think of any other friends she might have gone to and get in touch with them. Also, could she perhaps have fallen and hurt herself on the way home, and not been able to continue her journey?'

'W-w-ell, I don't know, I suppose she could have

done, but Angela knows the lane home from the village like the back of her hand . . . '

'You haven't checked her route?'

'No, but Jeremy and I came back that way last night . . . ' The young man sounded uncertain.

'It was dark, sir, wasn't it? You could have missed her easily enough. Did your sister have a torch?'

'N-n-no.'

George thought he detected something in Rob Phillips's voice. Was it guilt, perhaps? Nothing unusual about that in the case of a missing person. The family and those closest often felt guilty, and sometimes had good reason to. First thing any copper worth his salt checks out is the alleged nearest and dearest. George collected his thoughts. He was getting ahead of himself. There wasn't even a crime, not yet, anyway. Just a seventeen-year-old girl who hadn't come home from a dance.

'Right, sir, you may like to have a bit of a look around. And make those calls. If you find anything, get back to me at once. Meanwhile we'll start making some enquiries and I'll get a man over to you soon as I can.'

George Jarvis hung up the phone and sat staring at it for a moment or two. He wasn't sure how seriously he should take the call yet. But he knew what to do. Stick to procedure. Go by the book.

He entered the call meticulously in the message log. Then he used the radio to contact a constable he knew was not too far from the Phillips farm because he'd recently been despatched in his panda car across the moors to investigate a break-in at a garage near Moretonhampstead. George Jarvis was

33

used to making decisions and issuing instructions. He might be just a civilian desk clerk now, but he was still inclined to behave like the station sergeant he had once been. 'We've got a missing person, Pete,' he began, as he redirected the constable to Five Tors Farm.

Then he made himself a cup of tea. No point in notifying the top brass yet; see how it pans out, he told himself. But George had an uneasy feeling about this one, even this early on. The Phillips family weren't ones to panic. They were a pretty solid bunch. More than likely, the girl was of the same stock. And even if she were the daft, irresponsible sort, at seventeen she was highly vulnerable. Best to share the burden, George thought.

He checked his watch. Still not quite nine o'clock. He knew the recently promoted Detective Sergeant Todd Mallett was on duty in CID that day, but being a Sunday with nothing much on so far, he wouldn't expect Todd in before 9.30 or so. George liked Todd, one of the best of the younger chaps, he thought. He took a couple of sips of tea and considered his options for a moment or two more. Then he called Todd Mallett at his home in Sticklepath, just a few miles out of Okehampton on the Exeter road.

Todd listened just as carefully as George himself had done when Rob Phillips had called in. 'I think I'll take a run out there, then, George,' he said eventually. 'Not much point in coming in to the station first; it's quiet enough otherwise, isn't it? Young Pete Trescothwick could do with some moral support I reckon, if nothing else.'

Typical Mallett, thought George. Taking it calmly, step by step, but finger on the pulse already. There were those who regarded Todd as a bit old-fashioned and overly thorough. But George approved of qualities like that in a policeman.

★ ★ ★

At the farm, the whole family gathered in Rob's end of the big old house. They were unimpressed when Rob told them what George Jarvis had asked him to do.

'But she wouldn't . . . ' began his mother.

'I know, I know. But look, let's just do it, shall we?' Rob replied. His voice came out higher-pitched than usual with just a hint of hysteria in it now.

'I'll call Jeremy,' said his mother, still sounding tearful but also as if she were glad to have something to do.

'And didn't you say she was chatting to those riding chums of hers last night?' Mary enquired. 'I'll call them, and anyone else I can think of.'

'Good. And I'm going looking for her.' Rob's face was set.

'Where, where will you begin?' asked his father, the strain clear in his voice too.

'I'll walk the way she should have come home. I ought to have thought of that already. Maybe the policeman is right. Maybe she did fall and hurt herself, maybe she was taken ill, maybe she's lying in a hedge somewhere . . . '

Rob tried to sound optimistic. Any of those

possibilities was infinitely preferable to the one they were all dreading. But his voice tailed off almost plaintively. He didn't believe what he was suggesting and the rest of the family knew it. However, it was action of a sort, something to do. Anything was better than sitting around the house waiting. The guilt was like a dull pain nagging away in the pit of his stomach. He had got drunk, played the fool, not bothered to see that his sister got home safely. And now the potential consequences of his completely out-of-character bout of irresponsibility were too dire even to think about.

'I'll come with you, boy,' said his father. 'Let's take the Land Rover and walk it in stretches. Then we'll have a vehicle to bring her back in.'

But Rob didn't think his father sounded as if he believed he would be bringing Angela back. Nobody had criticised Rob. Not yet. But he knew that would come. He could hardly bear to think about what this would do to his family.

* * *

As soon as the men had departed, Lillian Phillips and her daughter-in-law started to telephone people: Jeremy Thomas and any other friends of Angela's whose homes she could possibly have reached on foot.

Jeremy answered the phone sleepily, as if he had been woken by it, even though it was mid-morning. No, Angela had not been to his house last night, he said. And then, as if the significance of what he was being asked had suddenly dawned on him he exclaimed abruptly, 'Oh, my God! I'll be right over.'

'No, Jeremy,' said Lillian at once. 'We couldn't cope with anybody else here right now. We'll call you as soon as we have any news.' Then she hung up before she had to explain or discuss the situation any further.

Her daughter-in-law had given up and Lillian was speaking to the final friend of Angela's she could think of when Constable Pete Trescothwick's panda car pulled into the yard. Mary, even more pale and drawn-looking than she had been throughout her troubled pregnancy, opened the door and ushered the constable in.

Pete Trescothwick was young and green. He was bright enough, though, and it didn't take him long with the two women to begin to fear, as they obviously did, that something very serious had happened to Angela. His instinct was to believe that he was being told the truth and that Angela had indeed never returned home from the dance. Nonetheless there were procedures to go through. 'Do you mind if I have a look around?' he asked.

Lillian Phillips appeared slightly bemused. 'She's not here, Constable, I told you. Do you think I wouldn't know if she were here?'

Trescothwick coughed to hide his embarrassment. A search of the home of a missing person or victim of a violent crime was standard procedure. So many crimes were committed within the family set-up. Where there should be the greatest safety there was so often the greatest danger. Everybody in the Devon and Cornwall Constabulary knew about the major hunt for a missing woman over in Plymouth that had gone on for several days and all the time she was in the garage wrapped up in a carpet. There were certain police officers involved in that one whose careers had come to a sudden dramatic halt. Pete Trescothwick had no intention of allowing that to happen to him, despite his gut reaction that the distress of the Phillips family was one hundred per cent genuine. But he did try to be as tactful as he could. 'Just routine,' he said in a casual voice.

Not casual enough to fool Lillian Phillips, it seemed. 'You're not suggesting that we've got her here somewhere, are you?' she asked sharply. 'You're surely not suggesting anyone in this house has hurt our Angela?'

'Of course not, Mrs Phillips, just routine, like I said. There's a way we have to go about things.'

But the distraught woman interrupted him and now she sounded close to breaking point. 'Just go and find her, find my Angela, please,' she screamed at him, her voice high-pitched, desperate, her tears suddenly flowing freely. 'Don't waste your time here. Go and find her. Something terrible has happened to her, I just know it . . . '

Pete Trescothwick shifted uncomfortably from foot to foot.

Mary Phillips came to his rescue. 'C'mon, Mum,' she said soothingly. 'Let me make you a cup of tea and we'll let the constable get on. He's only doing his job . . . '

'I don't want any tea . . . ' the older woman began, but she fell silent and let Mary lead her over to a chair.

Trescothwick slipped out of the room and began

his search. First he went through the bedrooms, looking in the wardrobes and under all the beds. Then he checked all the downstairs rooms before starting on the yard. He did his best to search the big cowshed, the stables and the barn where they kept the feed, all with no result as he had more or less expected. It was now gone 10 a.m. The girl had been missing for almost eleven hours. She was wearing party clothes, a skimpy black dress if Trescothwick had ascertained it correctly. The only money she had was a few pounds in a small handbag. She had no coat. All right, it was the end of July, but nonetheless she was hardly equipped to do a runner. Trescothwick had extremely bad vibes about this and decided he wanted to shift responsibility for it on to broader shoulders as soon as possible.

As he walked back to his car, intending to use the radio to call George Jarvis, a familiar dirty grey Ford Granada pulled into the yard and came to a halt alongside his blue and white panda. And it was with some relief that Trescothwick greeted Todd Mallett.

The two policemen stood for a few minutes while Trescothwick gave a report on his findings so far. 'Which amounts to bugger all, Sarge,' he admitted. 'Not sight nor hair of her, nor do I think there will be, not around here. Some toe-rag's had off with her. I reckon the family are dead right.'

'Yes, well, let's not jump to any conclusions,' instructed the detective sergeant coolly. 'Evidence, not hunches, eh, Pete? I'd like to talk to the family myself and the boyfriend, and then decide . . . '

He was interrupted by the noisy arrival of a Land

Rover. A young man leapt out of the driver's side and an older one opened the passenger door rather more slowly, his face quite grey. The younger man's eyes were unnaturally bright. He opened his mouth as if he were about to say something but seemed unable to find words. Instead, he managed only a sort of low-pitched moan.

'Mr Rob Phillips, I assume? I'm Constable Trescothwick and this is DS . . . ' began Pete, thinking a formal introduction might help.

'Yes, all right, Pete,' said Todd Mallett quietly and something in his voice stopped Trescothwick at once.

He glanced towards the DS and followed his eyes, which were fixed on the man Trescothwick took to be Angela Phillips's father. Tears were starting to run down Bill Phillips's face. In his right hand he carried a single stiletto-heeled black shoe.

★ ★ ★

The shoe changed everything. It was the same story when Jeanette Tate's bicycle had been found after the girl disappeared on her paper round two years earlier. Any slight chance that Angela Phillips might have taken off under her own steam had now been eradicated. Not with one shoe, she wouldn't have done.

Todd instructed Trescothwick to look after the family as best he could and got straight on his radio to HQ in Exeter. Within an hour of his call a major missing person's investigation, on the scale of a murder hunt, was under way.

Blackstone village hall was commandeered as the investigation centre, a senior investigation officer appointed, DCI Charlie Parsons out of Exeter, and a team of more than fifty officers, CID and uniform, swiftly drafted in. Parsons was a very modern policeman. He regarded himself as more of a manager than a cop. A neat, trim man with a neat, trim moustache, he was much better at planning and paperwork than he was with people. His favourite detective sergeant, Mike Fielding, a high-flyer who at twenty-nine had already passed his inspector's exams, would be Parsons's unofficial number two, in charge of far more of the on-the-scene policing than a DS really should be.

A search was launched that afternoon, in the usual fashion with officers beginning at the suspected scene of the crime, the stretch of lane where Angela Phillips's shoe had been found, and working progressively outwards, taking in an increasingly greater radius of territory. A team of scene of crime officers, SOCOs, cordoned off the suspected scene itself for more detailed examination. In the soft muddy ground of an adjacent gateway to a field they found a set of distinctive tracks, which one of the SOCOs, whose hobby happened to be Land Rover rallying, was able immediately to identify as being from Avon Traction Mileage tyres, a popular brand fitted almost exclusively to four-wheel drives. The clarity of the impressions left by their unique combination of wavy lines and knobs, designed to give maximum grip on and off the road, indicated that the tracks were almost certainly from the last vehicle parked

41

there. However, this did not take the investigation much further as there were probably almost as many four-wheel drives in the area, particularly Land Rovers, as there were ponies on the moor.

Then the search brought an early result. A customised red Ford Escort, equipped with overly large wheels bearing Avon Traction tyres, was found by the search team later that afternoon wrapped around a tree in the woodland to the west of Blackstone. The vehicle appeared to have careered off the road, and would have been easy for Rob and Bill Phillips to miss when they had walked and driven that way earlier in the day, because it had ended up surrounded by a dense tangle of shrubs and bushes. The car's unusual appearance enabled the briefest of enquiries to establish that its owner was Angela's boyfriend, Jeremy Thomas.

★　★　★

Joanna Bartlett had been chief crime correspondent of the *Comet* for only three weeks when Angela Phillips went missing. An appeal was almost instantly put out to the public on TV and in the press nationwide for anyone who might have seen Angela around the time of her disappearance, or anyone and anything else that might be relevant, to come forward. The press response was instant and across the board. Missing teenage girls were hot news. Good copy. Good TV. Photographs of Angela were issued and a press conference called at Okehampton police station for 5 p.m. It was clear that the case would make every TV news bulletin that night and was certain to be splashed all over the newspapers the next morning — apart from anything else, the story had broken on a Sunday, an invariably quiet news day, so a major crime yarn like this one would be pounced upon by every news desk in the land. Angela Phillips's innocent smiling face would soon be everywhere.

Jo had been at home with her husband, enjoying a Sunday off duty, when she received the call from the *Comet's* news editor that sent her hurrying down the M4 to Devon. She was the new girl on the block, a woman just twenty-seven years old. She had a lot to prove and she knew it. The knives were out in the *Comet's* office just off Fleet Street. The policemen and press officers at Scotland Yard with whom she had daily contact were not a lot better, Jo thought. She had entered an exclusive men's club, one of the last bastions of male chauvinism. She was Britain's first woman crime correspondent on a national newspaper, the first-ever woman member of the Crime Reporters Association. It seemed incredible to her that this could be so in 1980 but it was. In Margaret Thatcher the country had a woman prime minister of such force and magnitude that she dwarfed her entire Cabinet. Jo didn't like Thatcher's politics, but she could not help but admire her strength and tenacity in the face not only of small-mindedness but also open hostility.

The sadder elements of Westminster were known to try to make themselves feel better about their all-conquering woman prime minister by making silly jokes about her hitting people with her handbag. Whatever you thought of Margaret

43

Thatcher's politics, her exceptional ability could not really be questioned. But few men would ever allow that the success of any woman was down simply to merit. The *Comet's* two veteran crime boys, Frank Manners and Freddie Taylor, both approaching twice Joanna's age, had a wonderfully simplistic way, she knew, of explaining away her own appointment, which had been over both their heads. It was, of course, because she was sleeping with the editor. She had no idea whether or not the editor, Tom Mitchell, was aware of the mythology — because that was exactly what it was.

Jo straightened her shoulders in the driver's seat of her cherished MG roadster. Didn't the stupid bastards realise that their schoolboy attitudes just made her all the more determined to leave them for dead? In any case, she didn't have time to worry about them. She was a top crime reporter heading out on a top job: a missing teenage girl, quite probably a murder. Stories didn't come any bigger than that. She was excited.

She drove straight to the scene of the crime at Blackstone. There was plenty of activity and it wasn't difficult to find the spot where Angela Phillips was believed to have been abducted, but the area was cordoned off and there was little to see, so Jo drove on to the missing girl's farmhouse home. It was almost seven o'clock by the time she arrived, but the earlier rain had cleared, and it was a warm and pleasant evening. There was a single uniformed police officer standing at the end of the lane which led to Five Tors Farm. The pack were staked out all around him. With some difficulty Jo found enough of a grassy verge to park her car just about off the road. As she climbed out she narrowly avoided a rather large cowpat and wrinkled her nose with distaste. Sidestepping smartly, she was vaguely aware of admiring glances from one or two of the waiting journalists, not directed at her, she was quite sure, but at her car, which was an absolute beauty: British racing green with gleaming wire wheels.

Joanna was tall and slim, with mid-blonde hair that hung straight and sleek halfway down her back — a legacy from her teenage years during the hippy-influenced sixties and early seventies. However, she thought her hair was lank and boring, and was all too aware that her slim figure owed more to cigarettes and nervous tension than healthy diet and exercise. Although she wasn't pretty, she had a good strong face, high cheekbones, clear skin and nice eyes. And she certainly didn't have an inferiority complex, not about anything. But it simply did not occur to Joanna that her appearance was particularly attractive. And certainly the behaviour towards her of most of the men she had dealings with did nothing to alter that.

She picked her way carefully across the narrow road to the assembled group. The countryside was great when you were driving through it in a nice warm car or looking out of the picture window of a luxury hotel, Jo thought, as she glanced around her. However, though she might not be mad about it, unlike many city folk she did at least understand that the countryside did not look after itself. The big Devon hedges all around her had been freshly manicured, the farm lane was no rough track but a tarmac driveway flanked by imposing granite pillars, the gate, standing open, was painted immaculate white. The Phillipses obviously kept their land beautifully, and had the money and workforce to do so. Their farmhouse was hidden from the road, but Jo imagined that the family lived in some style. Through the gateway opposite she could see a sweeping view of Dartmoor, hazy and purple in the evening light, its unique tors, those piles of granite boulders at the summit of sharply pointed hillocks, piercing the skyline a bit like falling-down church spires. It was a lovely spot, Jo admitted grudgingly to herself.

There were about a dozen men standing around, talking and smoking, at the lane junction. Some were obviously camera crews and radio reporters; others, she guessed, were local reporters and regional men for the nationals, and there were already a couple of Scotland Yard press corps lads who had rather irritatingly got there before her. But then, she had wasted time trying to smooth things over with her husband before leaving. Chris had not been best pleased to have one of their rare Sundays together interrupted. Male hacks rarely seemed to have those kinds of problems with their wives.

Harry Fowler, the *Comet* area man, who she knew had covered the earlier press conference, was also already there, as she had expected him to be. She was the only woman, as she had also expected.

Harry looked across and gave her a slightly uncertain wave. Fortyish, a little on the plump side, pleasant-faced, you could tell almost by looking at him that here was a man who had found his niche in life in a part of the world he loved. She had met him before, of course, and he was a nice enough guy without any of the chips on his shoulder of the London crime lads she had to work most closely with. But he would be well aware of the furore her appointment had caused in Fleet Street.

The Scotland Yard reporters already at the scene, Nick Hewitt and Kenny Dewar, were two of the most contemptuous of her after her own alleged colleagues. They were watching her arrival with expressions of amusement and disdain. Patronising bastards, she thought. And, from the expression on his face, it was clear Harry Fowler didn't know quite how to deal with any of it. She decided to take the bull by the horns and strode towards him, trying hard to display a kind of confidence she was not really feeling.

She had to walk straight past Hewitt and Dewar, and she made sure her steps did not falter as she wished them a curt good evening.

'My God, the *Comet's* sent in the heavy brigade,' announced Hewitt with a derisive laugh.

And both quickly and loud enough to be sure she was still well within earshot, there followed Dewar's clear stage whisper: 'You know something, Nick, I'd like to give 'er one really hard and bite 'er lip till it bleeds.'

Joanna ignored both comments. Women who couldn't stand the jolts were not expected to join the Street of Shame. She knew the rules and how to live by them.

Harry Fowler, however, began to look even more ill at ease.

Joanna pretended nothing had happened. 'All right, Harry? Anything new?'

Harry smiled uncertainly. 'Hi, Joanna. Not a lot. I expect you know they've got the boyfriend in Okehampton nick.'

Joanna shook her head. That information was obviously too fresh to have made any of the radio news bulletins she had listened to on the way down. Harry would already have passed it on to the news desk, of course, but although the MG did have one of the new car phones, linked by radio to a Post Office operator, it was unreliable. The reception had proved to be almost non-existent outside the London area and she hadn't talked to her office since setting off.

'They say it's just routine,' said Harry. 'But he's been in there since three this afternoon apparently. The word is that they found the boy's motor near where the girl disappeared. I've got a stringer over there on a watching brief.'

Joanna felt her excitement wane a little. If the boyfriend was guilty this might not turn out to be quite as big a story as she had anticipated. It was certainly likely to be cleared up quickly.

'We might get something else soon,' Harry continued. 'Fielding's supposed to be coming out to speak to us any minute.'

Joanna nodded. She knew who Fielding was. She had already been given the names of the principal investigating officers when the news desk had called her at home. She took a packet of Marlboro from her jacket pocket and offered Harry one.

'No thanks, given it up.' He tapped his abundant

torso in the vague region of the heart.

Then she remembered. He'd been off work for six months following a bypass operation. Now back on the job on a story like this, something nice and stress-free, she thought wryly, lighting a cigarette as she leaned against the nearest parked car and settled in for a wait.

She hadn't even finished her smoke when a squad car approached from the direction of the farm and pulled to a halt at the end of the lane. Two large men climbed out of the back seat. Both were well over six feet tall, but while the first to emerge was thickset and fleshy with dark hair and a swarthy complexion, the second was long and lanky with light sandy hair, which flopped over his face as he moved. The dark swarthy one, who was wearing a particularly ill-fitting brown suit, looked as if there were a million other things he would rather be doing. The fair lanky one, snappily dressed in a trendy navy-blue linen jacket and immaculate dark-cream trousers with what looked terribly like Gucci loafers on his feet, gave the impression that he was thoroughly enjoying himself.

He strode straight into the gathering of hacks. 'For those who don't know me, I'm Detective Sergeant Mike Fielding and this is DS Todd Mallett,' he announced, waving his hand at his colleague, whose discomfiture seemed to increase. Then he made a brief statement. It was standard stuff, all about growing concern, no further development, a renewed appeal for anyone who might have witnessed anything suspicious to come forward. 'Also, I would like to ask on behalf of the

Phillips family that you respect their privacy at this difficult time,' he finished predictably. 'There's no point in hanging around here, lads, really there isn't. Nothing's going to happen at the farm. We're in the process of setting up an incident room in Blackstone village hall and I or one of the team will give a press briefing there tomorrow at 4 p.m. — and every day until we find Angela.'

As soon as he stopped talking the pack surged forward, surrounding him and Mallett, bombarding them with questions, almost all about Jeremy Thomas.

'We do have a man helping us with our inquiries, but it really is just routine at this stage,' said Fielding predictably. 'There is no more I can tell you today, lads, I'll see you tomorrow.' As he spoke he was trying to force a way through the throng back to the squad car, the completely silent Todd Mallett at his shoulder. But the pack continued to harangue the two policemen, pushing and shouting.

Joanna was in the thick of it. That was what she was paid for, after all. 'What about the car you found near the scene, Detective Sergeant?' she called and felt she could hear her own voice clearly above the chorus, perhaps because her pitch was higher.

Maybe she was right, because Fielding swivelled round to face her, his surprisingly soft grey eyes seeking her out in the crowd. 'And who are you?' he asked.

'Joanna Bartlett, the *Comet*.'

He flashed a lopsided grin at her. 'Thought so. The first woman in the Scotland Yard corps, eh?

Frank Manners has told me all about you.'

The bastard, thought Joanna. He's even warned off his contacts. 'I'll bet he has,' she said, half to herself.

Fielding heard her, though. 'Don't worry about it, darling, you can tell me all about Manners any time you like. And any place.' He looked her up and down appreciatively.

There was loud laughter from the throng, particularly, not at all to Jo's surprise, from Dewar and Hewitt. Another patronising sod, just like all the rest, thought Joanna, staring levelly back at the detective. She did not rise to him, choosing instead to remain silent.

'Honestly, lads, that's all for today,' he said then.

He did not attempt to answer her question, although she didn't blame him for that, but his eyes were fixed on hers. Suddenly his face broke into that lopsided grin again. It was actually quite an endearing grin, thought Joanna, and was instantly annoyed with herself.

Then the man winked.

Joanna felt an almost irresistible urge to slap his face. She was quite glad to be clutching a notebook and pencil in her hands. How could a policeman investigating a murder behave like that, she wondered.

3

Jeremy Thomas was detained at Okehampton police station all night. He claimed he had crashed his car driving home from Five Tors Farm after giving Rob Phillips a lift. He also claimed that the last time he saw Angela was when she had left the dance in a huff.

The previous afternoon Fielding, along with Todd Mallett, had conducted the first formal interview with Jeremy. There had been no solicitor present. The young man had turned down the offer of one. Fielding hoped that wasn't going to cause problems in the future in view of Jeremy's youth. But no policeman would turn down the chance of interviewing a suspect without the interference of lawyers.

The SOCOs had found strands of dark-brown hair, some attached to follicles of skin, in the Ford Escort and a small amount of fresh blood on the frame of the passenger seat.

Fair, crew-cut Jeremy had admitted at once that the dark hair could well have been Angela's. 'She's always in my car and well, you know, she's my girl and, well, we've only got the car . . . '

Fielding understood what the boy was trying to say clearly enough. If they'd been using the car for a kiss and a cuddle, and maybe more, you would expect some signs of that to remain. Hair, yes. But blood?

'I don't know,' said Jeremy. 'Maybe she knocked herself. Maybe somebody else did . . . ' Maybe, thought Fielding. Maybe not. 'Lead you on, did she?' he asked. 'Was that the problem? Things got out of hand . . . '

'No,' insisted Jeremy Thomas tearfully. 'Nothing like that happened, honestly. I'd never hurt Ange.'

The boy didn't seem all that bright and he was scared rigid. But his story never changed. Fielding's attention span was short. When it became apparent that there was going to be no quick confession from Jeremy Thomas he began to lose interest. He was always the same. He needed to be on the move, dealing with fresh information. Parsons understood his sergeant's strengths and weaknesses. That was why they were such a good team. Parsons pulled him off after the first hour-long interview. Todd Mallett carried on, along with a hard-case DS up from Plymouth, a man who specialised in losing his temper, or at least appearing to.

Mallett was right for the job, Fielding had conceded reluctantly. He didn't like Mallett, never had done, thought he was too slow and ponderous. A real plod. In many ways Fielding couldn't understand why Mallett didn't still have a pointy hat on. But the man was meticulous, no doubt about that. And he had a way of wearing witnesses down. Fielding liked to joke that people talked to Mallett in order to get him to go away. Actually, he was only half joking.

Nonetheless, Mallett's attention to detail was well known — it was what was said to have secured his promotion — and it was often detail that caught people out. Fielding believed that if Jeremy Thomas was the man they were looking for, Todd Mallett and his bad-tempered partner would break him sooner or later — after all, Thomas was no hardened villain, just a nineteen-year-old kid who might have lost it for a fatal few moments. Fielding had been happy enough to leave the interviewing team to get on with the job. He didn't like to get bogged down in any one area of a major investigation. He was better at the overview, the big picture.

While Charlie Parsons ran the show, directing the troops, controlling the policy, managing, Fielding would be his eyes and ears on the spot. That was the way they always worked.

And it suited Mike totally. He liked to be at the heart of a case. And the heart of this one was at Five Tors Farm. The press knew that, which is why they were staking out the place damn near twenty-four hours a day. Mike Fielding was one of the few policemen around who had a lot of time for newspapermen. They knew what they wanted and stuck at it till they got it. And most of them had an uncanny knack of being in the right place at the right time. They thought fast and knew how to follow their noses. Fielding only wished some of his fellow coppers were as quick on their feet.

He and Charlie Parsons, however, were very quick on their feet. They were already an acknowledged partnership and so far their results had been exceptional — so much so that Fielding reckoned he'd be an inspector even quicker than might be expected, certainly within weeks rather than months.

Eager as ever to get on with it, he had returned to Five Tors Farm immediately following his abandoned interview with Jeremy Thomas and from then on he shadowed the family. If the key wasn't with Thomas, then it would be with them. It almost always was. He was, as ever, confident that he had the knack of seeing through the cotton wool that always seemed to clog up a major investigation. So he stayed at Five Tors Farm, watching, waiting, prodding and probing.

He hadn't slept all that night. When there was a major investigation on the go and his adrenalin was flowing, he rarely seemed to need sleep. Indeed, the only person at Five Tors Farm who had actually been persuaded to go to bed had been Mary, weak and sick from her pregnancy on top of everything else.

Fielding had just sat at the big old table in the Phillipses' kitchen along, most of the time, with the rest of the family. He had been acutely aware of their pain as he drank copious amounts of coffee and went over and over the case in his mind. It wasn't that he really reckoned any of the Phillipses was responsible for Angela's disappearance, although you never knew for certain, even with an apparently close and decent family like them. It was more that if anybody knew anything which would give a clue to Angela's disappearance it was likely to be one of her immediate family, even if they didn't realise it. As for the boyfriend, he didn't really think so — the boy hadn't broken for a start and he had looked a pretty soft touch.

Mike felt in his gut that the case had a long way

55

to go. There were two possibilities: either that, dead or alive, Angela had been left in the immediate vicinity, or that she had been taken away from the vicinity, almost certainly in a vehicle.

But by mid-Monday morning the search team, including specially trained officers with dogs, had thoroughly combed a circle of more than a mile in diameter with the scene of the crime at its centre. There had been no further results. It became increasingly likely that Angela had been taken from the scene in a vehicle. But was it Jeremy Thomas's vehicle? Mike somehow thought it unlikely.

By two in the afternoon, lack of action had more or less brought his adrenalin flow to an end and he was starting to feel the effect of his sleepless night. Wearily, he was also beginning to wonder if he would, in fact, learn anything more from the family after all.

Then the telephone rang.

Lillian Phillips ran to answer it eagerly, as she had done each time it had rung since Angela's disappearance. Even though all the calls to date had either been from concerned friends and relatives or the press, it was quite apparent that she kept hoping to hear her missing daughter's voice on the other end of the phone.

This time, after putting the receiver to her ear, she seemed to freeze. 'Oh, my God,' she said. 'Yes, yes. How? Yes.'

Then, 'Wait, please don't go, is my daughter all right? Can I speak to her . . . '

Fielding's weariness left him at once. He launched himself across the kitchen where the entire family had been gathered round the old pine table and snatched the receiver from Lillian's hand. All he could hear was the dialling tone. He turned to Lillian Phillips, who looked absolutely stricken. 'Talk me through it,' he said. And he knew more or less what he was going to hear.

A muffled voice had told Angela's mother that if she wanted to see her daughter alive the family must pay a ransom of £50,000. 'And you can tell the filth they may as well call off the search. They'll never find her.'

The caller had said that he would ring back the following morning, when he expected confirmation that they had the money in cash to give him. He would then give instructions for its delivery.

Fielding cursed under his breath. A kidnap and a ransom demand were the last things he and the team had expected. If they had they would never have called for media involvement. Kidnaps were a staggeringly rare crime. From the kidnapper's point of view the success rate was minuscule. He knew that professional criminals would stage a kidnap only in exceptional circumstances and amateurs were highly unlikely to have the organisational skills required. They had had absolutely no reason to suspect that Angela's abduction would result in a ransom demand. Fielding felt the muscles in the back of his neck tighten into a knot of tension. The nature of her disappearance had led him, and Parsons and Mallett, to suspect, almost exclusively, a sex crime. Phone calls to Five Tors Farm had not been monitored. All the probabilities had been against a kidnap for ransom. Christ!

He made himself concentrate hard. Was that really what they had on their hands? They couldn't be sure yet, of course. There were all kinds of nutters out there who would get some sort of sick kick out of making a malicious phone call to the family of a missing girl. There was no proof so far that the call was genuine.

Lillian Phillips's stunned silence had turned into hysterical weeping. The sound cut through Fielding's thought process. 'There, there, love, don't carry on so,' he heard Bill Phillips soothe his wife. 'At least we know she's alive, think on that. She's alive, Lil, and we'll get her back, I promise.'

Abruptly Lillian stopped crying. 'Oh, Bill, you're right. Of course. She's alive. Thank God. She's alive.'

I wouldn't bank on it, thought Fielding. But he kept the thought to himself.

★ ★ ★

Within an hour Parsons arrived at the farm with Todd Mallett. Jeremy Thomas had already been released. The boy wasn't totally out of the frame yet. Particularly not while the ransom call could still be a hoax. But Jeremy continued to stick resolutely to his story and had, in any case, already been detained for almost twenty-four hours without any progress being made.

'Thought we could do with Todd's local knowledge,' said Parsons.

Fielding grunted unenthusiastically. But he had to admit that Todd was a hell of a lot better than him

58

at coping with the family. Better than Parsons, too. Everybody knew that Parsons's biggest strength was planning, not dealing with people. He was, however, an ace delegater, which was another of his great strengths.

There was, of course, something reassuringly solid about Mallett. Fielding hoped he himself was solid enough in his way, but uttering reassurance was not one of his finer qualities. Mallett had a calming effect on the family, whose first reaction had been to rush to their bank. 'First thing is to make sure this joker really does have your Angela,' he told them. 'The call may not be genuine, you know.'

They hadn't thought of that. It stopped them in their tracks.

Parsons, who had been largely silent till that point, allowing Todd to smooth the way for him, took over then, issuing instructions in his clipped, businesslike tones. 'Right, when this man calls again you ask him for proof that he's got your girl. OK? He'll be expecting that. Bound to be. If he can prove it, then you say yes, you'll pay up. But when he's given you your delivery instructions you play for time, say it'll take you a day or two to raise the cash, that kind of thing . . . '

'I don't want to stall,' interrupted Bill Phillips. 'I'm not playing games with my daughter's life. If the price of getting her back is £50,000 then I'm paying it. Right away.'

'I'm not asking you to play games, Mr Phillips.' Parsons was firm and authoritative, as sure of himself as ever. 'I'm asking you to accept that we have learned a bit about this sort of thing over the years. If we are dealing with a kidnapper, he won't expect you to move too fast; he might even be suspicious if you do. It's important for us to take the initiative, not to let him make all the running. We need to know where he wants you to make the drop and consider all the implications. We have to think of a way to make sure that he doesn't get the cash without your daughter being returned. If we move hastily and let him get the money without ensuring that he returns Angela — well, anything could happen . . . '

There was a silence while his words sank in. Lillian Phillips moaned. Her husband grasped her hand tightly. It was several seconds before he spoke. 'OK. Just tell us what we have to do,' he said eventually.

★　★　★

The call came as promised the next morning. This time fully monitored.

Bill Phillips had decided he would be the one to take it. His wife was more than happy to let him do so. Mike Fielding listened in on a specially installed extension.

At first Bill adhered strictly to his instructions. 'You have to give me proof that you've got my daughter,' he told the caller.

There was a brief silence, then a girl's voice, weak and frightened: 'Dad, Mum, it's me, Angela, please give him what he wants. Please. I want to come home. I can't stand . . . ' The voice ended abruptly.

The listening police noticed the click of a tape recorder.

Bill Phillips, predictably enough, did not. 'Ange, Ange,' he called plaintively. 'Are you all right, darling?' Then, getting only silence in response, 'Of course I'll give him what he wants, darling. I'll do anything to get you home. Anything.'

The muffled voice came on the line again: 'At midnight tonight you will put £50,000 in used ten-pound notes into a rucksack and leave it at the foot of a pine tree in Fernworthy Forest. I want your son to do it. On his own. No filth. Nobody else. You want to see your son again, don't you? Mess with me and he'll go missing too. Tell him to take the road around the reservoir. It comes to a dead end. Park there and walk approximately 150 yards due west into the forest. Ordnance survey map OL 28, reference 8390.6574. The tree will be marked with a red cross. The kid will be nearby. You'll find her.'

'I haven't got the cash, I can't get it till tomorrow morning.'

'Tell the filth to keep their snotty noses out. I know they're with you and I know their tricks. Tonight — or your precious Angela dies. Oh, and it won't be a pretty death . . . '

The caller hung up. So did Bill Phillips. His complexion seemed to be growing greyer by the minute.

His wife looked at him questioningly.

He shook his head numbly. 'So much about wanting to take control away from him,' he said. 'It's got to be tonight and I don't want any interference. I want it the way he's said. I'm not taking chances

61

with my children's lives.'

Parsons and Fielding exchanged glances. 'Can you raise the money that quickly, Mr Phillips?' asked Fielding.

The other man smiled weakly. 'One call to my bank manager,' he said. 'And I won't have to explain why.'

Fielding glanced around the big farmhouse kitchen. It reeked of affluent well-being. The house must have a minimum of eight bedrooms, he thought. He glanced out of the window over Dartmoor, taking in the five tors that gave the farm its name. He had learned that the Phillipses were mixed farmers, big on beef, some dairy, and several thousand sheep on their higher ground and moorland. Their more lush land, on which they raised their beef including one of the country's finest herds of pedigree Devon cattle, was to the rear of the farmhouse stretching back towards and beyond Okehampton. Fielding also knew the size of the farm, approaching 2000 acres, pretty big anywhere and huge in the West Country. He felt a bit silly having even asked the question that he did.

Parsons stepped in brusquely. 'You'd better do it in that case, Mr Phillips,' he said. 'And then we'll discuss the next step.'

Phillips turned away and picked up the phone again.

Fielding spoke in the DCI's ear. 'A word, boss,' he said.

Silently the older man turned on his heel and walked out of the room. Fielding followed him. 'Boss, we can't let Rob Phillips make the drop. Let me go in his place.'

Parsons looked thoughtful. 'I'm not sure, Matey obviously knows this family. Or all about them anyway. We don't know how well he might know Rob Phillips, do we? It's not at all unlikely that he's local, don't forget. At the very least he's done his homework. Almost certainly he knows what Rob looks like. That's the problem.'

'I'm about the same height and build. It'll be pitch-black out there. I'll keep my head down. The bastard'll never know the difference.'

Parsons considered for a moment. Then he nodded abruptly.

Rob Phillips, however, who had already been notified by his father of the kidnapper's instructions, needed a little more convincing. 'We mustn't take any chances,' he said, echoing his father's earlier remark. 'I don't want anyone standing in for me. I want to go get my sister. It's my fault she was taken in the first place.'

Fielding wondered if the young man was waiting for somebody to say that it wasn't his fault. But nobody did.

Parsons did have something to say, though. 'Mr Phillips, at the very least your sister is in very grave danger. I cannot allow you to put yourself in danger too.'

'What do you mean, you can't allow . . . ' Rob was bristling, quick to find a target for the anger inside him, which was really directed at himself.

His father interrupted. 'No, boy, the inspector's right. Your mother and I can't risk losing you too. Let the sergeant take the money. He knows what he's doing.'

Fielding just hoped Bill Phillips was right.

It took about half an hour to drive from Blackstone to Fernworthy Forest, mostly along dark deserted roads skirting the moor. Apart from Fielding himself, alone in Rob Phillips's Land Rover, there did not seem to be a soul about. There are few roads over Dartmoor and the heart of the moor remains remote and inaccessible, but the last couple of miles or so, from Chagford to the reservoir, cut right across the stretch of rugged moorland known as Chagford Common. At one point, as the Land Rover reached the brow of a hill, a pony loomed abruptly in its headlights and Fielding had to swerve violently to avoid it. As he swung the wheel, his nerves jangled far more than they would normally do.

The thing about surveillance was that it was so much easier in urban areas. People are the best camouflage. Want to lose yourself, go to a city. Policemen and villains both knew that.

The number one priority was to retrieve Angela Phillips safely — if that were even still possible, Fielding thought wryly. There were plenty of police officers waiting nearby for the call everyone hoped Fielding would be able to make, the call to say that he had Angela Phillips safe. But no attempt had been made to plant police officers at the delivery point. There was something about the kidnapper's approach, the use of precise map readings, which tagged him as a military man. Indeed, kidnappers often were. They were the kind who enjoyed plotting complex operations. Parsons had reckoned that close surveillance would not be possible. 'Not without Matey sussing it out pretty damned quickly,' he had said. And he hadn't been prepared to take that risk. So Fielding was pretty much on his own. His mouth felt dry, the palms of his hands were clammy.

On the car seat next to him was a freshly purchased Millet's rucksack containing £50,000 in used tenners. As instructed. It also contained a signalling device, concealed in the padding in the bottom. It might be discovered at once. Or Angela's kidnapper might just empty the cash into another container or straight into a vehicle. On the other hand it might just give out a signal for long enough for the police to close in on him. After Angela Phillips was freed, of course. Nothing was to happen until then. That was the priority.

It was all a matter of survival, really. And not just the survival of Angela Phillips, but also that of the senior police officers on the case. Fielding knew the way Parsons's mind worked. He was unlikely to catch much criticism, if any at all, over loss of the Phillipses' £50,000 as long as Angela was safely recovered. Indeed, he would be a hero again. So would Fielding himself, he considered with some satisfaction. As Todd Mallett had worked out long ago, he liked being a hero. But if Angela were lost, he and Parsons, already involved in an unorthodox operation, would both be deeply in the mire, whether or not the money was ever recovered. In fact, probably particularly if it were — if it looked as though any priority had been given to anything other than the safety of the missing girl.

He was also about to wander into a forest at the dead of night in the presence of an undoubtedly dangerous man who could well be a raving lunatic. Fielding licked his dry lips. He drove as instructed to the parking area at the end of the road, which ran round about half the circumference of Fernworthy reservoir. When he switched off the engine the silence was deafening. Fielding didn't think he had ever really appreciated that expression before. He switched off the Land Rover's lights too and was instantly swallowed up in pitch-blackness. Nowhere, but nowhere, is darker than a forest at dead of night, he thought.

A map-reading expert had pinpointed the appropriate reference for him. Fielding hoped his own skills were up to it. It should take only a few minutes to walk to the tree, but at night, making your way through a forest was far from simple, he could easily get lost and he would have to be careful not to trip over the undergrowth. He decided to try to find the appropriate tree straight away and then just wait.

With the help of a powerful torch, its beam cutting reassuringly through the darkness, Fielding, taking care to keep the light directed away from his face at all times, picked his way gingerly through brambles and nettles, weaving around the tree trunks. He found the tall conifer marked with the red cross more easily than he expected. It stood alone in a small clearing. He checked his watch. He was tempted to put the rucksack alongside it there and then, but decided against. The instructions were to make the drop at midnight. He would do it by the book. He switched off his torch, leaned against a nearby tree trunk and wondered if he were being watched. Almost certainly he was. He pulled the peak of his black baseball cap a little further down over his forehead. He was dying for a cigarette, but he didn't dare light up. As Parsons had pointed out, they had no idea how well the kidnapper knew Rob Phillips, whether personally or just by sight. Either way, it was far too great a risk to allow the flame from his lighter to illuminate his face.

He was standing quite still when he heard the crack of a twig nearby. His eyes were adjusted as well as possible to the darkness now and through the gloom he could just make out an approaching figure. Early, he thought. What should he do now? Should he have made the drop already after all? He was confused. The figure was coming closer. He hadn't expected the bastard to show himself like this. He passed Fielding within about three or four yards. He was wearing some kind of military-style camouflage jacket — but then, so did almost everybody nowadays, it seemed. The policeman could not see his face. He could see the shape of a gun clearly enough, though: a .22 rifle, by the look of it, fitted with some kind of night sight and a silencer.

The man moved almost soundlessly towards the tree with the red cross on it. Casually he propped his gun against the trunk. Then he undid his flies and had a pee.

Fielding could barely believe his eyes. What was going on? He tried desperately not to move a muscle. But something alerted the other man's attention. He could feel eyes boring into him across the clearing, peering through the darkness. Suddenly the man picked up his gun and took off at a run.

Instinctively Fielding called out, 'Hey, wait.'

The man kept running. Fielding was bewildered. He did not know what to do or think. He glanced at his watch. It was still only ten to twelve. Should he follow? He'd never catch the bastard anyway. The man obviously knew these woods. He'd taken off at a pace. Even with the help of his torch, if Fielding tried to chase him he would be sure to fall over or at the very least run into something.

For a few seconds he could make no sense at all of what he had seen. Then gradually his jumbled thoughts cleared. It only made no sense if the man who had run away was the kidnapper. But what if he wasn't the kidnapper at all? Of course! The most likely scenario was that sonny was a poacher out hunting, his appearance at the drop spot just a ridiculous coincidence. Poachers didn't like bright lights or big bangs drawing attention to their presence — hence the rifle with a night sight and silencer. Fernworthy's three square miles or so of dense forest land would be home to more than one herd of deer, Fielding reckoned. While Dartmoor hosted nothing like the herds of big red deer which roamed Exmoor, there were other breeds in its woodland areas, as there were throughout the West Country, come to that. And although the managed forest of Fernworthy was open to the public, unauthorised shooting was strictly forbidden. That had to be it: a poacher. But Fielding had no idea where that left him — or Angela Phillips, come to that.

He decided that the best he could do was to continue as if nothing had happened. It couldn't do any harm, surely. On the dot of midnight he strode across to the tree and dropped the rucksack at its base in a rather theatrical manner. Then he walked back to his original vantage point and waited. He waited and waited, heart thumping in his chest, for what felt like an endless period of time. Now and then he glanced at the luminous hands of his watch. Nobody came to pick up the cash and, if Angela Phillips was nearby, he could neither see nor hear any sign of her. After forty-five minutes he could stand it no longer. He had to try to find out what was going on. He turned and began to make his way back to the Land Rover.

When he got there he switched on the police radio, which had been hastily installed in the vehicle earlier that evening. Straight away a call came through from Parsons. 'It's off. Matey's called the farm already. Says there were armed police in the woods with rifles. Bill Phillips assured him there weren't. I even talked to him myself. He'd already made it clear he knew I was here. He's been watching our every move, no doubt about it.'

'Shit,' said Fielding. 'There was a man with a rifle. Night sights and silencer, too. I think he was a poacher. Matey must have seen him as well. I don't damn well believe it.'

He heard Parsons draw in a deep breath. 'Right, then, go get the money and come on back,'

69

instructed the DCI abruptly and only someone as close to him as Fielding would have detected the strain in his voice.

★ ★ ★

At 8 a.m. the next day, after another sleepless night of recriminations and distress at Five Tors Farm, the kidnapper made a further phone call: 'You've got a second chance. Same place, same time. But I'm fining you. The price has gone up to £70,000. This will be the last chance. Any hint of police presence this time and the girl dies.'

Fielding, mightily relieved, could see hope flickering over the faces of Angela's family. They too, he suspected, had begun to believe that Angela was probably already dead. Last night must have been unbearable for them. It had been bad enough for him.

'But you have to let me go this time, Inspector,' said Rob Phillips. 'Maybe he saw the sergeant's face. We can't take the risk.'

Parsons dodged the issue. 'Are you absolutely sure there is nobody you know who you think could be doing this?' the DCI asked for the umpteenth time.

The younger man shook his head. 'I can't believe it's anyone the family knows, I really can't.'

Ultimately it was agreed that Rob should make the second drop and secretly Fielding was glad not to have been given the task again. He couldn't quite stifle the nagging doubt that he might somehow have been responsible for the failure of the first exchange, although he did not really see how that could have been so.

However, Parsons had a plan to keep control. 'We tried to play it straight,' he told Fielding. 'You can't legislate for something like your damned poacher and that was probably our mistake. This time we take no chances. We get the armed-response boys in. Make 'em look like soldiers on exercise. There's enough of 'em up at Okehampton camp.'

'He'll know, he'll not fall for it,' intervened Todd Mallett. 'He's been spooked once by a man with a gun in the wood.'

'If we get 'em in position quickly enough he shouldn't even see 'em.'

The Phillips family, of course, were not told of the new plan. But at 10.30 p.m., half an hour or so before Rob Phillips was due to leave the farm to follow in Mike Fielding's footsteps of the night before, the kidnapper called again. 'Change of plan,' he said. 'Make the drop at Hay Tor. Leave the rucksack at the top of the tor itself. The very top.'

'Shit,' said Fielding. 'He's giving us the run-round. And Hay Tor, too — no cover for him, or the girl, come to that.'

'Or, indeed, us,' commented the DCI. Hay Tor was Dartmoor's highest point, bleak, exposed and at the other side of the moor from Blackstone.

'Maybe that's the point. I just don't know. I wonder what he's up to . . . '

He and Fielding were conferring in the main hallway of the farmhouse, out of hearing of the distraught family gathered, as usual, in the kitchen.

'I'm going to call off the armed-response boys

71

from Fernworthy and see if they've got any bright ideas on how they can give some sort of cover at Hay Tor without being seen,' Parsons said quietly.

Fielding listened uneasily as his boss got on the radio and began to issue fresh instructions. He had no sensible alternative suggestion, but was this really such a good move? he wondered. Within minutes it became clear that it wasn't.

Just as Rob was about to leave for the new assignation point, the kidnapper called once more. Bill Phillips answered the phone.

'Tell the pigs I didn't see the gun boys go into the forest, but I sure as hell saw 'em come out. Oh, and tell 'em — when your daughter dies I won't have killed her. That'll be down to them.'

He hung up at once, leaving a stunned Bill Phillips looking at a buzzing receiver. He turned to Fielding and Parsons. 'What on earth do you think you're doing,' he shouted at them. 'He's right. The bastard's right. If my daughter dies it will be down to you lot. All I ever wanted to do was to give him the money and get my girl back. But you couldn't settle for that, could you, not any of you.'

DCI Parsons looked him coolly in the eye, still the manager, still the chief executive. If he was as shaken by the turn of events as Fielding, he certainly didn't show it. 'Mr Phillips, I had to take responsibility for your son's safety as well as your daughter's. I'm afraid the kidnapper double-bluffed us on this one. We couldn't have guessed that.'

'Then you should have left well alone,' stormed Phillips. 'Let me do it my way. He's been scared off, now, and if we've lost him then we've lost Angela too. God knows what he'll do to her.'

If he hasn't done it already, thought Fielding. Aloud he said, with a confidence he did not feel, 'Try not to worry, Mr Phillips. He'll be in touch again very soon, I'm sure of it. He wants your money not your daughter.'

★   ★   ★

The kidnapper did not call again. Not that night. Not the next morning. Kidnaps were such a rare crime in the UK that there were few precedents. Those that did exist encouraged little optimism among the police team. And in the case of Angela Phillips some of the most important lessons learned in the past did not fully apply. The débâcle surrounding the abduction and murder of Lesley Whittle by the infamous Black Panther taught the importance of taking the press into police confidence and insuring a media clampdown over kidnaps for as long as there was a chance of safely retrieving the victim. Parsons and his team had not had the luxury of choosing that option, because following the discovery of Angela's shoe, they had promptly announced her missing and called for public help. Fielding suspected they would all be criticised for that sooner or later, but it was easy to be wise after the event.

By noon that day — it was already Thursday and five days after Angela had been taken — a kind of restrained panic was setting in. Still no further calls. Still no further clues. Parsons decided to throw caution to the wind and step up the hunt.

73

Territorial Army soldiers on their annual training at Okehampton camp were called in to continue the systematic searching of Dartmoor and the surrounding farmland. After the first ransom demand was received, Parsons had decided to keep the search fairly low-key, in order not to alarm the kidnapper. Now he changed tack and threw everything at it. Angela Phillips could have been taken miles away from where she had been abducted, of course, but nobody had come up with a better game plan than to stick to standard police procedure and to continue to search outwards from the crime scene, gradually taking in a wider and wider expanse of the moor and the surrounding farmland. The vast majority of victims of violent crimes were ultimately found in their own backyard.

But Dartmoor was notoriously difficult to search. Bodies, even after quite a short time, were unlikely to be discovered. Everyone remembered the nightmare faced by the parents of the children murdered by Brady and Hindley, and buried on the Yorkshire Moors. Without the help of the murderers, their graves could not be found. Even taking the optimistic view that Angela Phillips was still alive and hidden on the moor, the team knew she could be anywhere. There were cairns and old quarries, disused mines with a whole network of shafts, old sheds and storm drains. George Jarvis, who had policed the moor longer than anyone, was fond of saying that he reckoned the results of half the unsolved murders in England could be lying rotting somewhere on

74

Dartmoor and nobody would ever know.

By Thursday evening, a number of locals had joined the police and the Territorial soldiers and upwards of 150 people were involved in the search. They combed the moors, sifting through the bracken, checking out all the military lookout posts and hideaways, pouring over the remains of crofters' huts and old deserted tin mines, prising open boarded-up entrances, peering into long-abandoned shafts.

At ancient Knack Mine, in Steeperton Gorge, a remote granite-strewn classically rugged Dartmoor valley sandwiched between Okement Hill and Steeperton Tor, there were no visible shaft entrances left and the casual passer-by would probably be unaware that there had ever been a mine there at all. Little more than the foundations, covered with grass and fern, remained of the ruined buildings. But some years previously a group of Territorials from the camp had discovered a narrow overgrown entrance to a shaft, which they had used as a hideaway during exercises. They had contrived to roll a granite boulder in front of the shaft, which in any case had, at a glance, looked to be just a hole in the rocky hillside and had been already more or less concealed by an overhang. The searchers did not notice the old shaft entrance, nor could they have been expected to, so well was it hidden from view. And the part-time soldiers who had known it well were long gone and had never had call to return there. All except one, that was.

He lay in the bracken half a mile or so away on the brow of Okement Hill, home to the source of the River Okement, studying the scene below through powerful binoculars. He was wearing army-style camouflage fatigues and made sure he kept very still, hopefully hidden from sight. He shifted position slightly in order to get a better view. Suddenly one of the antlike figures down in the valley put a hand above his eyes and seemed to be peering directly at him. Then the figure began to raise a pair of binoculars.

The man in the bracken immediately slipped his own into the pocket of his jacket and started to wriggle backwards on his belly until he had manoeuvred himself over the brow of the hill and a little way down the other side where he knew he would be out of the view of the searchers. Then he rose to his feet and ran.

At Knack Mine the soldier who had raised his binoculars scanned the distant hillside. Something had caught his eye, a flash of reflected light. More than likely the glint of the evening sun reflected on binoculars, or perhaps even a gun. He studied the bracken-covered hill carefully. In the sky above, a buzzard drifted gracefully, soaring up and up on a current of warm air. There were some sheep near the spot where he thought he had seen the reflection and they continued to graze undisturbed. Nothing else moved. After a few minutes the soldier lowered his binoculars. But he was an experienced hand for a Territorial. He was quite sure he had seen something up there. He called out to the police sergeant in charge, and explained it to him.

'Let's take a look, then,' said the policeman and promptly led his team away from Knack Mine and off in the direction of the suspicious sighting.

Police dog handler Brad Davis tugged impatiently at the long leash of the young Alsation he was still training. Prince was going to be a credit to him one of these days, Brad was quite sure, but the young dog was still inclined to be wayward and had a yet to be controlled passion for chasing rabbits. He had been driving Brad mad all day.

Prince suddenly lurched away from his handler, nearly pulling Brad over, and began to bark in a frenzied fashion, the focus of his attention apparently a rather large granite boulder. Almost at once a pair of startled rabbits emerged from behind the boulder and took off in a frantic dash. Brad swore, pulled with all his might on Prince's leash and half dragged the dog away, breaking into a trot to catch up with his colleagues who had already moved on up the hill.

The old mine shaft that lay behind that boulder, the one-time Territorial hideaway so well concealed, remained undisturbed. But the man who had lain in the bracken up on the hill half a mile away had not stayed long enough to know that.

★　★　★

The days passed, then a week, two weeks, three. The Phillips family had made it quite clear by then that they no longer had any confidence in the police. Everyone seemed to be blaming everyone else. Todd Mallett reckoned they were in just the kind of mess fancy tricks always got you into. The word was that Parsons was about to be replaced as senior investigating officer. Fielding was keeping as low a profile as possible. Lillian Philips had indeed turned against her only son, as the young man had feared she would, and Rob didn't have much time for himself either.

Then, just two days short of a full month after Angela Phillips' disappearance, a body was discovered by a hunting spaniel dog, taking its owner for a walk in the area of Knack Mine.

It was still high summer, or what passed for it on Dartmoor. The spaniel began to howl and bark, and scratched furiously at a large granite boulder nestling beneath a rocky overhang, eventually managing to stick its nose into the small hole produced by its scratching. It began to whimper pitifully then, and neither threats nor gentle coaxing could persuade the creature to continue with its walk.

Eventually the spaniel's owner was obliged to investigate. He could not see anything amiss and had yet to be alerted by a sense of smell, which was, of course, far less acute than that of his dog, but when he leaned against the boulder as he tried to look behind it, he found to his surprise that it rocked very easily. And once he had discovered the correct leverage, the big hunk of granite rolled freely to one side. Behind the boulder was a foliage-framed hole in the earth, just big enough for a man to crawl through. The spaniel continued to whimper, but cowered back, leaving its owner to lean into the hole and peer within. The smell that had alerted his dog overwhelmed him then. The man gagged but carried on peering into the hole, as if compelled by a kind of morbid fascination. It took a moment or two for his eyes to become accustomed to the darkness. Then suddenly he threw himself backwards, almost as if he had been attacked, out of what was of course the opening to the old mine shaft the Territorials had used as a hideout, and was promptly sick on the grass.

Later he said he feared he would remember for the rest of his life the dreadful sight that had confronted him. Which was something he and Mike Fielding, the first police officer on the scene, had in common.

Mike was in his car on his way into Okehampton police station when Parsons radioed him with the news. The detective sergeant carried straight on to the call box on the edge of town where he was told the distraught dog owner was waiting, having used the phone to dial 999. He got there even before the team he knew Parsons was despatching. Fielding picked the man up and asked him to take him to the spot where he and his dog had found the body. The army-built loop road which cuts into the heart of the moor just above Okehampton leads almost to Knack Mine. Then a rough track runs most of the way down into Steeperton Gorge before finally disintegrating. Mike hurtled his car over the uneven ground, showing a complete disregard for its well-being, then, when finally forced to pull to a halt, he continued on foot, grabbing the torch he kept in the glove compartment, and half ran the remaining hundred yards to the old mine shaft the dog owner had pointed out to him.

The other man hung back. He said he had no

wish for a second look. A few minutes later Mike did not blame him at all.

The smell, as he peered in through the narrow opening, was horribly unmistakable. The bile rose in Mike's throat. For a moment he thought he also was going to be sick. But he had a job to do and he did not allow himself even to hesitate.

He lowered himself into the shaft, getting mud and grass stains all over his nearly new suit, for once neither caring nor even realising, and scratching his hands and face on brambles. He knew he should wait for the SOCOs, that he should not barge in. But he had to look at her properly. Mike had studied photographs of Angela Phillips so often he felt sure there was no question that he would recognise her, even allowing for the inevitable deterioration of her body. He could see quite enough from above to be as horrified as the dog walker had been. But he wanted more. He wanted to be sure this was Angela Phillips, lying like a dead animal in a hole. And he wanted to see for himself exactly the state she was in.

Mike Fielding was a hard cop, but the sight which greeted him when he shone his flashlight fully on the murdered girl really would haunt him always. And the stench, of course, even more overpowering once he was in the shaft alongside her.

It was her all right, he was quite certain — even though her face was discoloured and distorted. It was not just death and decay that had caused that. Her nose was badly swollen and he thought it had probably been broken. There was dried blood and bruising around her mouth. She had been viciously gagged with a nylon stocking or tights, which may well have been her own, but her lower jaw hung loose beneath the gag, displaying several smashed teeth. She was completely naked, lying in her own filth and blood. Her hands and feet were tied with electric flex so tightly that it had cut deeply into her flesh. It looked as if wild animals of some kind had begun to eat her. Probably rats. Foxes would have done more substantial damage by now, he thought, regarding her quite clinically for just a moment or two. There were small lumps of flesh missing from her body — and she had no nipples.

Fielding gagged again. But he forced himself to lean forward for a closer look. There didn't appear to be any teeth marks or signs of tearing around the breast area.

He didn't need a pathologist to tell him that Angela Phillips's nipples had almost certainly been sliced off with a knife.

4

It was Joanna, in the *Comet*, who originally dubbed Angela's killer the Beast of Dartmoor. It came to her as she filed her first piece after her recall to the West Country when Angela's body was found.

Joanna had trained on local papers in Plymouth and Torquay. As a cub reporter she had frequently worked on Beast of Dartmoor stories. There had also been a Beast of Bodmin and a Beast of Exmoor. Several of each, in fact, if truth be told. But previously these had always concerned sightings of big cats, possibly zoo runaways, or wild wolf-like dogs. This was something different. Very different. Yet the name could not have been more appropriate.

Like all really big stories, the Angela Phillips story damn near wrote itself. Her kidnap and killing had indeed turned out to be tragically reminiscent of the Black Panther and Lesley Whittle case. In common with Lesley, she had apparently been left to die horrifically in a dreadful hideout. Joanna knew that the general view was that this time the media side of things had probably been handled by the police as well as possible, in difficult circumstances. Although Angela's disappearance had been announced before it was known that a kidnapper was involved, Parsons had kept news of the ransom demands successfully under wraps and, when it became apparent that the case was not likely to be quickly resolved, he requested the Scotland Yard press office to contact relevant editors and news chiefs and ask for press silence on the kidnap angle. This was observed until after Angela's body was found. Even Fleet Street editors would not wish to be blamed for the death of a teenage girl.

However, when further details of their operation began to emerge, Joanna was not surprised that police action in several areas was called to account, and Parsons and his team accused of making a number of potentially catastrophic mistakes.

It was Joanna herself who found out about the armed-response unit fiasco through an old local paper contact and her story predictably made the front page yet again. The decision to call for the unit at all was widely condemned as a grave misjudgement. The leader writer in one newspaper went as far as to suggest that if more resources had been piled into stepping up the moorland search for Angela earlier, and less wasted on playing soldiers, the young woman might well have been found in time and her life saved.

Indeed, the post-mortem examination — the results of which would not be officially revealed until the inquest on Angela, but almost all hospitals leak information like sieves — showed that the girl had only died around two weeks before her body was discovered. Jo could hardly bear to think about that. It meant that Angela had lived for twelve days after her abduction, almost certainly imprisoned the whole time in the old mine shaft that became her tomb. She had been raped, beaten and abused, but had ultimately died of dehydration.

All the papers painted a suitably lurid picture of

this. The *Comet* carried a leader questioning the scale of the original search operation and criticised Charlie Parsons for concentrating on a maverick plan to do business with the kidnapper at the expense of fundamental police procedure.

One way and another the story broke with a vengeance. The Beast tag caught the imagination of the nation, with every other paper following Joanna's lead and using the name in all future reports.

Frank Manners, also on the case in Devon and smarting at Joanna's success, did his best to take the credit for it, apparently telling the pack he'd mentioned the Beast idea to his senior colleague and she'd promptly pinched it when she filed the first story. Shortly afterwards, though, Manners — who was a total pro, Joanna had to admit, even if she did consider him a thoroughly unpleasant human being — came back with a corker. He got the splash in every edition with his story of how Mike Fielding had impersonated Rob Phillips when the first ransom drop was attempted in Fernworthy Forest. This brought both Fielding and Parsons further criticism, of course. 'Family fears kidnapper knew he was being tricked by cop,' stormed the *Comet* alongside an unfortunate and no doubt hand-picked picture of Fielding looking inordinately smug and grinning broadly.

Joanna's first instinct was delight that her newspaper's coverage was so far ahead of the rest of the field — this was, after all, by far the biggest crime story there had been since her appointment to the top crime job and she was far too secure to worry about it being Manners's yarn. Her attitude was that whenever the *Comet* looked good on crime, as head of department at least some of the credit would always be hers. But she couldn't help feeling just a little sorry for both Fielding and Parsons. If their ploy had worked they would be heroes now instead of scapegoats. Particularly Fielding. She shrugged such thoughts aside. She had a job to do and, as ever, what she really cared about was doing it better than anyone else.

All the tabloids, as usual, were competing over who could supply the most gruesome details of the murder. And Joanna got a lucky break in that direction too. Out of the blue, Fielding called her in her Okehampton hotel room early one morning and asked her if she would like to have a quick drink with him. She wondered briefly if he was still playing sexist games, but he didn't seem to be in the mood. He sounded far more sombre and less cocksure than the man she had last seen almost four weeks earlier. Well, he had taken a bit of a hammering, she thought. And when he suggested they both drive separately to the Drewe Arms at Drewsteignton she knew that whatever he was up to it was something different. Any approaches he had made to her before had always involved giving himself maximum opportunity for showing off and he had only been interested in talking to her where he knew the other hacks would be gathered. So it seemed the policeman might genuinely want to have a quiet word with her.

She arrived in the pretty thatched village at the

85

agreed time and found a parking place in the square.

Fielding had got there before her and was already in the tap room nursing a pint of bitter, sitting on the wooden bench next to the hatch through which drinks were served. In the traditional style of old Devon pubs there was no actual bar at the Drewe Arms. 'What'll you have?' he asked.

'No, let me.' Joanna might not have been around as long as Manners and Co., but she knew the form right enough. If there was even the slightest chance that a cop was going to give you an exclusive lead you did the buying. She ordered herself a gin and tonic, a small one as she was driving, and raised an enquiring eyebrow at Fielding. ''Nother pint?'

Fielding shook his head. 'Large Scotch,' he said.

Joanna had heard he was a drinker, but it was only six o'clock and he had his car parked outside. He was as snappily dressed as ever, smartly casual in lightweight jacket and polo shirt, and he was not a man who gave a lot away. But she suddenly noticed how grim he looked. Perhaps he reckoned he needed a large Scotch.

He downed the whisky in one go, then turned to her. 'In case you're wondering, Frank Manners will never get another line out of me,' he said suddenly. 'He got me at a weak moment and I told him about making the drop. It was off the record, though, and he damned well knew it. I'd begun to think of him as a mate, I suppose, more fool me. The bastard's landed me right in it, but he may live to regret it yet. That's why you're here.'

She inclined her head in mock graciousness. It

was beginning to make sense now. Frank would have been so eager to get back at her after the success of her 'Beast' story that he would have broken the confidence of the Pope himself. And the old crime hack was an allegedly devout Catholic too.

'There's something I thought you'd like to know,' Fielding continued. He obviously had no wish to waste time or make small talk. 'This joker is some piece of work. He damn near tortured that girl to death. She may have died of dehydration ultimately, but my God she was a mess. Something specific. He sliced both her nipples off.'

'Good God, why?' Joanna could not imagine how even the most perverted killer could get a kick out of such a thing, but as she spoke she wondered if Fielding would think her naive to ask such a question.

If he did, he gave no sign. Instead, he smiled grimly. 'A knife fetish? Who knows what turns these sickos on?'

Joanna was astonished. Not only by the dreadful deed but by Fielding's eagerness to tell her about it. She wondered if his superiors knew he was planning to give her this line. Probably not, she thought. The detective might be a little chastened, but he was still a maverick. She glanced at him. Why was he telling her this? she wondered. What was his motive?

He carried on speaking, then, almost as if he had read her mind. 'I want him, Joanna, and I want him fast. The more public outcry we can whip up, the more help we are likely to get. Anyway, that's the way I see it.'

But not your bosses, more than likely, she

thought. 'Any more detail? How did he do it, and before or after she was dead?'

Fielding told her that a large sharp knife, possibly a carving knife or a hunting knife, was believed to have been used to mutilate Angela's breasts. 'And done while she was still alive, poor kid, definitely,' he continued bluntly. 'In fact, the SOCOs reckon Matey hadn't been near the place since soon after he took Angela there. Seems like he may have been scared off and just abandoned her.' He paused. 'Two theories: one that he raped her and sliced her breasts right at the very beginning, maybe after the first drop went wrong, and that when the second drop went pear-shaped he was totally scared off and just legged it and left her there. Two, that he went back to the mine and had a bit more fun with her and sliced her breasts after the second drop. Just for the hell of it, or for revenge or some such twisted thing. Don't know which scenario I like best, really. Do you?'

He made an attempt at his disarming grin but it didn't quite work. He picked up the remains of his pint and drained the glass. 'Oh, and she was buggered, of course, but that's no surprise.'

It wasn't, but Jo still hated to hear it. Rapists were very fond of buggery. It was all about degradation.

'Curious MO,' he went on. 'On the one hand Matey's a criminal out for gain. Organised. Done his homework. Knows the territory. He's hand-picked his victim, studied her family. On the other hand he's a psychopathic sex fiend. Those sorts usually perform opportunist crimes and gain doesn't come into it.' He stood up. 'But you know that as well as I do, don't you?' he said, looking down, his face serious.

Good God. He really was treating her like a grown-up suddenly, as if he had finally accepted that she was indeed chief crime correspondent of the *Comet* and not just a bit of a joke. But she had no illusions about him. He was an instinctive wheeler-dealer, you could sense that in Fielding. She didn't doubt he handled police politics very smoothly indeed. He seemed to have a pretty good grasp of the office politics of newspapers too. And Fielding was shrewd enough to know that if he wanted to stuff Manners, make him really mad, the best way to do it was not to feed a major exclusive to the opposition, but to tip off the woman who had been promoted over his head. That would hurt Frank Manners much more. In addition, Manners would be sure to guess that Fielding had fed her the line. He knew Fielding's style so well. And that would make him even madder, which was no doubt Fielding's intention.

As she left the pub, just minutes behind the detective sergeant, Joanna could not resist a chuckle. She didn't doubt, however, that Fielding believed what he said about stirring up a public outcry, nor for a second that he had been genuinely horrified by Angela's death and the manner of it. But there was this other side of him. He was a high-flyer, a man determined to reach the top in his career. While the bulk of the criticism of the police operation had so far been directed at the man in charge, DCI Parsons, Fielding was widely regarded as Parsons's right-hand man, so it reflected badly on him too.

The ransom drop which went wrong was especially damaging for him, of course.

Angela's family, the boyfriend she knew had been rigorously questioned after her disappearance, and all who had been close to the teenager, were now fully aware that if she had only been found earlier she could probably have been saved.

A shiver ran down Joanna's spine. She had been up to the remote spot on the moor where the body had been found, taken a look at Knack Mine. It was a stunningly beautiful place, actually, when you were out in the fresh air walking around, fit, well and free to leave when you wished. She could only imagine what it must have been like for a seventeen-year-old girl to be bound and trussed and held underground there. And raped. And buggered.

Word was that the girl had been a virgin, too. And on top of everything she'd been beaten and systematically tortured. Joanna found she had an all too clear picture in her mind, of Angela lying in that hole in the ground in her own blood and faeces, desperate for water, dying finally of dehydration. It was a wonder she didn't just die of fear. All that the bastard had done to her and in the end it was simply lack of water that had got her. The whole thing was almost too dreadful to think about.

But Joanna had not actually seen the poor girl's body. She had not had to look at those mutilated young breasts. Fielding had. Something else she could only imagine was the effect that would have on him. She knew he was a tough career cop. But she could not believe that he would not have been deeply affected. Certainly he seemed very different from the man she had first met.

She thought vaguely that maybe she could even get to like him.

* * *

Joanna's story caused quite a stir. It was just the sort of tale the tabloids loved. All the other news desks wanted to know why their crime teams didn't have the nipple-slicing line. She was pleased with herself. She was just as ambitious as Fielding in her way, and just as wrapped up in herself and her own world — aware as she was that it was a world many people considered to be more than a little distasteful.

Joanna was as disturbed by the horrors faced by Angela Phillips as any halfway decent person. But that didn't stop her giving the gruesome story, in the words of her first news editor, 'plenty of top spin'. Her report dwelt on every horrific detail. If she considered the effect of its being splashed luridly all over the *Comet* would have on those who were mourning Angela, it certainly didn't make her pull her punches in any way. She became even more popular with her editor than she had been before. Picking up sensational exclusives was beginning to become a habit with her.

Her popularity with her peers, however, sank correspondingly. The opposition were getting roastings from their news desks and Frank Manners, allegedly working alongside her down in Devon but as often as not quite clearly working against her, kept having his thunder stolen. And he didn't like it.

The pack picked up on her new connection with

Fielding, as, she supposed, had been inevitable. Their attitude to her became increasingly more offensive and her relationship with Manners in particular struck a whole new low.

'Good morning, Joanna,' he said, meeting her outside the incident room at Blackstone on the morning that her latest big story had appeared. Joanna, waiting with a small group of reporters for a promised briefing, was standing by her car, idly studying the modern, rather ugly village hall, which seemed to her to be quite out of place in picturesque Blackstone, and thinking how ironic it was that the building in which Angela Phillips spent the last evening of her life now housed the police team investigating her murder.

Reluctantly she turned her attention to Manners, greeting him without enthusiasm.

'You look quite radiant, darlin',' he told her. 'Had a good fuck last night, did you?'

Manners spoke loudly and with a big smirk on his face. Nick Hewitt and Kenny Dewar chuckled appreciatively. Joanna suppressed a desire to slap all their faces. Then she remembered that Hewitt and Dewar would both have received the old midnight phone call after that day's issue of the *Comet* had arrived at their night desks. She knew how pissed off that would have made them, particularly as it was her story, and immediately felt better.

'Which is more than you've ever managed, I should imagine, Frank,' she replied, and was rewarded with an appreciative chuckle from the *Daily Express* crime man. There were some good guys and Jo had a soft spot for Jimmy Nicholson, known as the Prince of Darkness because he invariably wore a Dracula-like black cape whatever the weather or occasion. He certainly liked women too. Jo had first encountered Jimmy Nic on the Spaghetti House siege, when Fleet Street's finest were staking out the Knightsbridge restaurant in which a number of hostages were being held. Jim had walked up to a group of young women chatting with some fellow hacks in a nearby pub, introduced himself by name and added 'I'm the big noise from the *Daily Express*.' The extraordinary thing was they seemed to fall for it, too. On that job Jo reckoned she'd encountered Fleet Street's first and only groupies.

She smiled to herself at the memory, then returned her full attention to the case in hand. 'Right, Frank, if you can tear yourself away from your chums I'd like a word in private,' she said. 'I have a game plan that should keep us as far ahead on this one as we are already,' she continued, smiling sweetly as she turned and headed towards the door.

Her remarks didn't shut the others up, of course. She overheard, as no doubt she was meant to, Hewitt asking pointedly, 'Anybody seen Fielding yet this morning?'

'Having a lie-in, I understand,' responded Dewar. 'Exhausted, poor chap. 'Course, everybody knows the woman's a raving nympho . . . '

This time Joanna held her tongue. Not only did women journalists only get their jobs through sleeping with the editor, they only got their stories through sleeping with their contacts. Wonderfully simplistic. Ability was never mentioned.

In a certain kind of mood Joanna even wished it could be like that. It would be a lot easier than working so bloody hard, she thought to herself wryly. Forcing herself to be businesslike and matter-of-fact, she started to discuss with Frank Manners how they could take the story forward.

The day turned out to be uneventful, however, and she was at her hotel early that evening when Fielding called her again and suggested a pint and a bite to eat, once more at the Drewe Arms. She agreed readily enough, but again there was something in his manner that left her unsure whether he wanted to give her a story or chat her up.

And as the evening progressed this was never really clarified.

'I like you, you're bright and I think you're straight as well,' he told her abruptly at one point.

'Thanks very much,' she said ironically. 'How about you, are you straight?'

'As a die,' he said, flashing her the disarming grin.

She smiled back. 'What am I doing here, Mike?' she asked.

He shrugged. 'This case has really got to me. You're someone I can talk to,' he said.

'Spare me the clichés. I do know your reputation, you know.'

'What reputation?'

'Don't be a prat. That reputation you have for being unable to stop yourself jumping on anything in skirts.'

'You flatter yourself.'

94

'Smug bastard!'

'Anyway,' he began, running an eye appraisingly over her trouser-suited figure, 'I've never seen you in a skirt.'

He grinned again. He was good company. And when by the end of the evening he had still not made a pass at her, she didn't really know whether she was disappointed or not. She'd had every intention of turning him down, of course. But that wasn't quite the point.

* * *

Joanna stayed in Devon for the best part of a week, returning to London only when it became obvious that there was no chance of an early arrest. She asked Manners to stay on for a little longer just to keep an eye on things. At least, then, she wouldn't have to look at the bloody man every day, she thought.

She left Dartmoor right after lunch, having filed an early story and manoeuvred herself into a situation where she would not be expected either at the office or the Yard. This meant that with a bit of luck she could be home in Chiswick soon after four o'clock. She wanted to get there early and make a special effort for her husband, something she knew she didn't do nearly often enough.

As she drove, Jo reflected on her marriage to her childhood sweetheart. She and Chris had been an item since, aged seventeen, she had surrendered her virginity to him in the back of a Mini Cooper. Now that had been a feat of some agility. The thought of it still made her smile in spite of everything. And, as so often happens with young people discovering sex together for the first time, Chris and Joanna fell head over heels in love. They married when she was nineteen and he was twenty-one. So they had already been married for eight years, and they were no longer a match made in heaven.

Joanna felt that she had moved on in life, that she had moved into worlds Chris had never got close to. She didn't believe that made her superior or even that her world was superior. In fact, on a bad day she would often concede that Chris's life and career were a damn sight more useful than her own. It was just that he seemed to have stood still. Chris taught at a primary school near their home in Chiswick. She had little doubt that he would remain a teacher throughout his working life. That was the kind of man he was: content with his lot; dedicated in his way, but unambitious. She had no illusions about him. She didn't even expect him to make deputy headmaster. Ever. And it might have been his chosen career, dealing with small children day in and day out, which gave him the kind of stick-in-the-mud naivety that was beginning to irritate her. He was always infuriatingly sure that his ideas, mostly formed in extreme youth, and his ways of going about things were the only right ones. Sometimes she felt that not only had he no concept of what her life was all about, but that he actually worked at keeping it so. Certainly he made it quite clear that he didn't like journalists. They distorted the truth, misled their readers, ruined people's lives. There was no talking about it with Chris. There was no middle ground.

She sighed. Since she had become a crime reporter he had increased his circle of most loathsome people to include policemen. She didn't think she'd ever even heard him voice an opinion on the police until working with them became a daily part of her job. Then he decided they were crooks and villains equal to the criminals they were supposed to be catching. His only problem was making up his mind which was the lower form of life, hacks or cops.

Her problem was that she still loved him. She couldn't help it. They went back a long way. And, in spite of everything, she was pretty sure he loved her too. After a week away she was determined at least that their first night together would be a good one.

The traffic was mercifully light. She was in Chiswick High Street at 4.15, parked the MG on a double yellow and nipped into Porsche's fish shop where she bought two large Dover sole, Chris's favourite. There would be potatoes and vegetables at home, Chris always kept the house well stocked with those, so all she needed to make the night special was a bottle of champagne, swiftly acquired from a nearby off-licence, and some flowers. One of the few things she bought regularly for their small but attractive cottage just off Turnham Green was flowers. Chris said it was because they hid her clutter. He was more than half right. She knew she was a lousy housekeeper. She left almost all of that sort of stuff to him, in fact, but she did like her flowers and she bought a big bunch of white roses, his favourite again, from a street seller.

She was at home soon after 4.30. Brilliant, she thought. Loads of time. She knew Chris was teaching games and wouldn't be home until six. She found vases and arranged the roses in the dining room, the living room and, feeling optimistic, the bedroom. Then she peeled potatoes. She was going to make a really creamy mash. Chris loved mashed potato. She inspected the vegetable cupboard and, deciding on a simple green salad, easy and good for them, selected a crisp-looking lettuce, some cucumber and a green pepper. When she had finished chopping she made a dressing, then want to have a bath and change her clothes.

She felt relaxed and refreshed when Chris arrived. 'Hi, darling, miss me?' she called as she heard his key in the lock.

His response was a barely audible grunt.

Joanna's smile of greeting faltered, but she carried on anyway. She walked towards him and wrapped her arms round his neck. 'Dover sole on the grill, mash with full cream ready to go, champagne in the fridge. Do you love me or what?' she challenged him.

He grasped her wrists with both his hands, flinging her arms away from him. 'You'd better invite one of your lovers round, then, hadn't you,' he told her.

'What?'

'Well, there's not much point in wasting champagne on me, is there? I can't get you a job or a story.'

'What the fuck are you going on about?' she

98

demanded, instantly regretting her use of the four-letter word. It just slipped out. But she knew how much it annoyed him.

'Keep that language for the scum you work with, will you? I've told you before it's got no place in my home.'

'Will you please stop being so dammed sanctimonious and tell me what has happened, because it's obvious something has.' Joanna's heart was pounding. What was going on?

He smiled. It was completely mirthless. 'Some of your chums have being filling me in on your extramarital activities — all in the name of duty, of course,' he told her, his voice heavy with sarcasm.

'In English, please,' she responded.

'Please don't try to be superior all the time, Joanna, it doesn't suit you, really it doesn't.'

She hated it when he talked to her as if she were one of his six-year-old pupils. But she made herself not respond. Instead, she waited.

'I've had some phone calls from someone explaining to me exactly how you get your stories,' he said eventually.

'Oh, for God's sake!' exploded Joanna. 'Come on. Tell me about it, please.'

She reached for his hand and this time he did not shy away from her touch, which at least was something. He allowed her to lead him to the kitchen table.

'There've been a series of calls while you've been away,' he said in a flat, expressionless voice. 'The theme's been the same each time. That you're a slut who'll do anything to get a story — particularly sleeping with policemen. Any policemen at all.'

She was staggered. 'Who made these calls to you?' she asked quietly.

He shrugged, not looking at her. 'I don't know, do I? The caller didn't leave his name, surprisingly enough!'

'Chris, for God's sake!' she said again. 'Have we come to this? You've let some nutter making anonymous phone calls get to you?'

'How would you like it?' he countered. 'Joanna, what am I supposed to believe? I don't see you for days on end, you're away on some story or other and then, when you are at home, you're out till all hours drinking with your alleged police contacts. How do I know what's going on?'

'It's my job, Chris,' she said mildly.

'Some job,' he responded. 'And who's making these calls? Some of your so-called colleagues, I suppose. You work with such charming people, Joanna, don't you?'

Now *that* she was inclined to agree with and she opened her mouth to tell him that she had a damned good idea who was making those calls. In fact, there was only one person she could think of who really hated her that much: Frank Manners. But she changed her mind. Things were getting to the stage where the less Chris knew about her work and the people she worked with the more chance she had of at least a tolerable home life. 'I don't have a clue who could be making these calls,' she lied. 'And I would sincerely hope it isn't someone I work with. Look, there's a guy I know at the Yard who specialises in sorting out moody phone calls.

I'll have a word with him. Maybe he can get a tap put on the line or something.'

'I don't want a tap on my bloody phone line, Joanna,' her husband shouted at her.

'Oh, stop being so damned unreasonable, Chris. What the hell do you want, then? You want this sorted, don't you? It's obviously upset you.'

'Yes it bloody well has upset me. What I want is for my wife to stop behaving like some kind of tart. Then I wouldn't have to put up with stuff like this, would I?'

All Joanna's good intentions disappeared in a wave of righteous indignation. 'You pious prig,' she shouted at him. 'Cook your own fucking supper. I should be in the office anyway.'

She was nearly through the front door when he called after her, 'There's one copper in particular, isn't there? A bit of a favourite of yours.'

'What the hell are you going on about now?' demanded Joanna.

'Detective Sergeant Mike Fielding. He's your latest, isn't he? I've seen him on the news. A real smooth operator. Just your sort. Going places, no doubt. Bit different from a poor bloody school-teacher.'

'Believe what you want to believe, you bloody fool.'

Joanna slammed the door behind her and headed for her car. If there was anything more infuriating than getting that kind of treatment from your husband when you really had done absolutely nothing to deserve it, she didn't know what it was. She had lapsed a couple of times since she and

Chris had been married, but considering how young they had both been when they had tied the knot she didn't think that was too bad. There had never been anything consequential with anyone else and she was pretty sure that Chris had lapsed once or twice, too. But she was also pretty sure that he had never had anything amounting to an affair either.

Funnily enough, she had believed for years that she and Chris had rather a good marriage. Better than a lot she saw, anyway. But recently they seemed barely able to be civil to each other and she really didn't think it was her fault most of the time. Sometimes she wondered if Chris was jealous of her success in her career, but she supposed that was a touch arrogant of her.

She left the house at 5.45 p.m. and pulled into the *Comet* car park around 6.20. She had actually been in the same room as her husband for little more than five minutes, she thought wryly. World War Three had broken out in about as many seconds. So she had left Chiswick early enough to beat the bulk of the theatre traffic and her journey was a reasonably easy one.

In the newsroom the day was just building towards its climax. Daily-paper offices in 1980 were noisy, smoky places where nobody cleared their desks and everyone tried to talk to each other at once, always at full volume, often while simultaneously conducting a phone call and frequently while also typing — still on clattering manual typewriters, of course.

So why was it she always felt as if she had been given an intravenous shot of adrenalin every time she entered the building — particularly in the evenings? It was her favourite time there. Indeed, it was every true newspaperman and -woman's favourite time because that was when the deadline was tightest, the fever pitch ran hottest and the presses were getting ready to roll. The news desk and the back bench were the hub of the paper at night. Passing the desk, she heard Andy McKane, the night news editor, on a call to a reporter apparently making a check call. Andy was one of the old-fashioned sort, a tough-talking Scotsman, convinced that any journalist who hadn't done a stint north of the border had not completed his apprenticeship and should always be treated with grave suspicion. As should most women journalists, of course, whatever their pedigree. 'When I want ye to know how I am, old boy, I'll tell ye, all right,' she heard him say in his thick Glasgow accent.

He must be talking to one of those new kids, she thought. Only a reporter who was very new and green would ever begin a check call to McKane with the social nicety of asking him how he was. She chuckled to herself. It was McKane who was famously responsible for a 1 a.m. call to a former showbusiness editor of the *Comet*, the only point of which appeared to be to slag off one of her staff. The woman had apparently listened more or less silently for some minutes, no doubt just hoping McKane would go away. Eventually she decided she should show some sort of support for her man and had told the night news editor, 'Oh, come on, Andy, Ron's done some bloody good stuff lately.'

McKane hadn't argued with that. Instead, he

103

replied in his guttural Glaswegian, 'Huh, only because you sit on his fucking lap and squeeze his fucking balls.'

The next day the showbusiness editor had approached McKane just as the editor was walking past. 'Andy, when you said that Ron had only done some good stuff lately because I sat on his fucking lap and squeezed his fucking balls, did you mean by way of punishment or encouragement?' she had asked in a loud, clear voice. Her timing had been impeccable. The newsroom had erupted in laughter. McKane had had the grace to flush slightly. The showbusiness editor's response had been spot on, of course.

The same woman, who was almost six feet tall, had once effectively dealt with a diminutive reporter who, upon returning from a heavy lunchtime session in the pub, had beerily informed her that he wouldn't half like to give her one, as he so charmingly put it. She had drawn herself up to her full height and replied, 'Well, if you ever do and I find out, I shall be very angry.'

Jo grinned at the memory. Let the bastards think they'd got to you and you were dead. Banter and lack of concern. Looking as if you couldn't care less — even when you did. Those were your only weapons. And they weren't much when you were one of a handful of women among several hundred men.

Paul Potter, a talented young feature writer, was still at his desk as Joanna had rather hoped he might be, working on a spread featuring unsolved murders of young women — the peg, of course, being the

Angela Phillips case. Joanna knew that he was looking into what had happened in the investigations into each case, some of them going back many years. He was talking to the families and the police officers involved, and sometimes to suspects. In the UK, no unsolved murder investigation was ever closed. The only exceptions were when the police were damn sure they had found the murderer but either could not gather enough evidence to go to court, or their prime suspect was acquitted. Then inquiries were often quietly folded.

There was plenty for Paul to work with. He was nice-looking in an unassuming sort of way, quiet, clever, thoughtful and a good listener. Sometimes she wondered what he was doing in Fleet Street. It didn't seem his sort of place. He was excellent at his job; it was just that he was so different from the others. It certainly never occurred to her, or indeed anyone else in those days, that he was particularly ambitious.

She paused to speak to him as she passed. 'How's it going?' she enquired.

He looked up in mild surprise. 'Hi, Jo, didn't expect to see you until tomorrow.'

'No, well, it was one of those times at home when I reckoned I'd actually rather be here. Anyway, maybe I can get a quiet hour or so to catch up with the backlog of stuff that is no doubt waiting on my desk.'

There was no one else in the Street of Shame to whom she would have confided even that much about her troubled home life. She knew all too well that another rule of survival in a newspaper office was not to bring your troubles to work with you. Not ever. The guys could do that occasionally, but never the women.

Paul accepted her small confidence without comment, as he almost always did. He never asked questions. 'Quiet hour or so? In this place? You have to be joking,' he told her with his familiar tight smile.

'Oh, well, quiet ten minutes, maybe?'

'No chance.' He smiled again. 'I'll have wrapped this up in the next hour, I reckon. It's been a tough one. Not very cheery material, either. Then I'm going to the Stab for a pint. Care to join me?'

The Stab in the Back was the name by which the *Comet* pub, the White Hart, was invariably known. 'Sure, that'd be good,' Jo replied casually. So much for working! But the truth was that the possibility of a quiet pint with Paul had been in the back of her mind since she had decided to go into the office. He was perfect company for her. Sometimes he seemed to be the only person in her life with whom she could spend time without some kind of stress. He did not indulge in the constant, often lewd, banter of so many of her colleagues. He made absolutely no demands on her. She could talk shop with him with more freedom than with anyone else and drown her sorrows without fear. Even if she later felt she had made a bit of a fool of herself, he had never let her down.

He was not only sensitive but also safe. To her those were his finest attributes. And it did not occur to her that he might regard her as anything more than a casual drinking mate.

5

Joanna was halfway along Knightsbridge on her way home from the *Comet* office just five days later when she was called on her car phone and told that a man had been arrested in connection with the abduction and murder of Angela Phillips. He had yet to be charged. 'I'm on my way back,' she said as, with a screech of tyre rubber, she instantly swung her car into an illegal U-turn just past the Beauchamp Place traffic lights.

The black cab behind her had to brake and swerve to avoid hitting her and the driver shouted a mouthful of abuse at her through his open window. Joanna barely heard him. She belted back along Knightsbridge, racing two red lights, and roared the MG around Hyde Park Corner without even attempting to wait for a gap in the traffic. The other vehicles could dodge her. And thankfully, unlike in America where they kept driving at you because they were so unused to motorists breaking rules, in London they almost always did dodge you — even if accompanied by much horn-blowing and colourfully vocal road rage.

On Constitution Hill, Jo switched her headlights on to full beam and drove down the middle of the road, hoping to God she didn't encounter a policeman. It was nearly nine on an early September evening, most workers had gone home or were ensconced in a central London pub or restaurant for the night, the theatre crowd were safely locked in for at least another hour. The roads were mercifully clear, for once. She belted past Buckingham Palace, sped down Birdcage Walk and turned left at Westminster along the Embankment. Big Ben was striking nine as she passed the Houses of Parliament.

There was only an hour to go until first-edition time, an hour in which to produce what would be regarded as an early story, to be expanded and updated for later editions. She knew Tom Mitchell himself was editing that night and was glad of it. Sometimes, when his deputy or one of the two assistant editors allowed to edit at night were on duty, they erred on the side of caution a little too much for her liking.

The night desk would already be on the case and almost every reporter on late duty would have been assigned a task which would form just a part of the night's coverage. When a big story like the arrest of the Beast of Dartmoor broke, every conceivable angle was covered as quickly as possible, somebody would be hammering out a recap of Angela's disappearance, a number of reporters would be trying to contact Angela's friends and family, and others would be trying to find out exactly who had been arrested. Frank Manners and Freddie Taylor would also have been alerted and put on the job. Manners had quite a track record of prising information out of police contacts. Joanna wanted to beat them to it.

She pulled off the Embankment by the Howard Hotel and hurtled up the tiny side street which led up to the Strand and the Aldwych, where she drove straight over the cobbles past St Clement's Church and turned right along Fleet Street. Jo swung a left into Fetter Lane, then a right into the office car park, manned twenty-four hours a day. She pulled noisily to a halt alongside the all-night attendant, jumped out of the car leaving the engine running, begged the man to park it for her and, within seconds, was belting up the back stairs to the newsroom. She was in far too much of a hurry to wait for the lift.

The newsroom was buzzing. You could feel it as soon as you stepped on to the murky brown carpet-tiled floor. Joanna felt the familiar rush of adrenalin. It was like getting a shot of something. On occasions it could be as good as sex. She had felt it many times before. The excitement rising inside her, the desire to get on with doing what she knew she could do so well. It was at times like this that she remembered why she had fallen in love with the job in the first place.

She went straight to the night news editor. McKane, shirtsleeves rolled up above brawny forearms, sat at the head of a clamorous news desk cluttered with piles of paper, grimy tea mugs and overflowing ashtrays. The phones didn't ring on the desk, that really would have been bedlam. Instead, lights flashed relentlessly on mini switchboards. There were only two desk men on duty, the normal night staffing, and each seemed to be taking at least three calls simultaneously. McKane, holding a phone to an ear with one hand, passed Joanna a narrow sheaf of Press Association copy with the other. 'Hold on a minute,' he commanded into the receiver, then turning to her, he said, 'This is about all we've got and it's bugger all, Jo. Where did this joker come from? We didn't even know they were close, did we?'

She shook her head. She had expected this approach. She knew exactly what McKane was getting at. The *Comet* was completely out in the cold on the arrest. She just hoped that none of the competition had been more on the ball. Had she let go her grip on the story a bit? She didn't think so. Either the suspect had come into the frame extremely suddenly or the boys in blue had really kept their drum tight for once.

'Any help you can give us, Jo. We badly need a line,' continued McKane before returning to his phone call while at the same time studying a piece of copy handed him by one of the regular night duty casuals. There was no sexist nonsense with him tonight nor would there be. He was doing what he did best. McKane was always at his most impressive when he was up against it, handling a major late-breaking story or chasing up a belter of an exclusive when the foreigns, the first editions of rival newspapers, dropped around midnight.

The only time he played games was when he was bored. And McKane got bored easily. So did most of them. It was one of things that made being married to a civilian difficult. The chaps seemed to manage it all right. Men had a way of moulding their women, or was it more that women had a way of turning themselves into the right kind of person for the man they married? Certainly women were

110

inclined to try harder, Jo was damned sure of that.

Frank Manners was at his desk. He had left the office long before her, but she guessed that he had probably been having a few pints in the Stab or Vagabonds around the corner. Frank was just finishing a phone call and, if he was under the influence at all, he didn't show any signs of it. But then, much as she disliked the man she knew him to be a professional, both as a reporter and a drinker.

He also was too busy to play sexist games.

He put the phone down with a flourish as she approached. 'James Martin O'Donnell,' he said and he was apparently too caught up in the story to sound as triumphalist as she might have expected. 'The Devon and Cornwall boys picked him up in London and took him straight back to Exeter. He's not been charged yet, but they must be confident to bowl into Met territory like that.'

Jo stared at Manners in amazement. 'Not *the* James Martin O'Donnell?' she asked.

'The same,' he responded, this time sounding just a little triumphant. And she didn't blame him.

Manners buzzed through to the news desk to give them the line, at the same time threading a sheet of copy paper into his typewriter and one-handedly typing a catchline in the top right hand corner — O'DONNELL.

Although she was standing a good four or five feet away and the veteran crime reporter was using a standard telephone held to his ear, Joanna could clearly hear McKane's roar. '*Fucking great, Frank me boy!* Right. I want every spit and fart. Got it?'

As Manners began to write, Jo took a moment to

consider the information he had obtained. There wasn't a crime correspondent in the country who didn't know who James Martin O'Donnell was — and not many members of the public, either, not if they ever read newspapers or watched TV. The O'Donnells were a criminal family of some stature. In the fifties and sixties the Krays had ruled the London underworld. By 1980 the O'Donnells were almost as big and had created around them the same kind of legendary personae. James Martin, known as Jimbo, was the eldest of old Sam O'Donnell's brood. He was the natural successor to Sam's dubious throne, although somewhere at the back of Joanna's mind lurked the vague impression that there had always been something suspect about him. She couldn't remember quite what.

Sam was one of the last of the old breed. You didn't more or less run the London crime scene for years on end unless you were quite an operator. And whatever you thought about Sam you had to have a grudging admiration for the man. He and his family were also the last people Joanna would have suspected of being involved in the Beast of Dartmoor case. The O'Donnells ran their rackets and pulled their strokes. They didn't harm civilians. Journalists, coppers, villains, they all talked about civilians. Poor Angela Phillips was a civilian. She'd been hurt. And how!

'Christ, Frank, raping and torturing an innocent kid, leaving her to die like that, that's not an O'Donnell sort of crime,' she said eventually.

The older man was already typing steadily. He did not stop as he glanced up at her. He had that smug look on his face, which he always got when he was going to show off. That was all right. She had no objection whatsoever to Frank Manners in show-off mood. The man had a memory to die for, and his knowledge of criminals and often long-forgotten crimes was encyclopaedic.

He was justifiably pleased with himself because he had got there first, but even though Jo would have liked, as ever, to be the one breaking the news, she was the head of department and preferred that any of her team should score, rather than the opposition.

'Jimbo's different,' Manners told her. 'He's always had a reputation for being nasty with women; word is he likes to knock 'em about. That's how he gets his kicks. Back in sixty-nine he was jailed for rape. Served eighteen months. It was a big story at the time.' He typed another sentence. Like almost all daily-paper journalists, Manners had perfected the art of performing several tasks at once.

That was it! A rape conviction. Joanna remembered it now, but not the details. She waited for Manners to continue as she was sure he would. He was invariably unable to resist displaying his superior knowledge of what he regarded as his patch. After just a minute or so he began to speak again. 'It was what they call date rape nowadays, or Jimbo would have got longer. He'd picked up this girl at a club somewhere and she'd invited him back to her place. She claimed he'd taken it for granted she would have sex with him and when she resisted he pulled a knife on her — that fits too, doesn't it, the bastard always liked knives — knocked her to the floor and forced himself on her. Big strong boy,

113

our Jimbo. But she didn't report it for almost a year after it allegedly happened. She claimed that when she realised who Jimbo was she didn't dare because she was too scared of the O'Donnells. He said she'd had sex willingly and there'd been no knife. But then, he would, wouldn't he?

'The jury convicted him on a majority verdict but it was never cut and dried. Hence the judge only gave him a fraction of the time he could have done. The girl was a right slag, too, and that influenced the judge as well, no doubt.'

No doubt, thought Joanna wryly. It drove her mad when judges pointed out that the victim of a sex crime had been dressed in a provocative way, or worse still, that she wasn't a virgin. The inference being that once a woman had surrendered her virginity that gave the rest of the male sex the right to do as they wished with her. The very idea made Joanna angry.

'The conviction alone was enough to get him drummed out of the Territorials,' Manners went on.

Joanna started involuntarily. 'Say again!'

'Thought you'd pick up on that. Yep, he was in the Territorials and yep, he did annual training up at Okehampton camp several times. Jimbo's always been a military freak. Crazy about the army. Wanted to join the regulars, apparently, only the old man wouldn't have it. From when he was kid James Martin was the apple of Sam's eye. And he never accepted that the boy had done a rape, of course. Never. You know Sam the Man. Like some fucking Mafia godfather. Built everything on respect, has Sam. Has his own strict moral code. Doesn't prevent him fitting the old concrete boots on his so-called chums every so often, but that's just business in his book.'

Joanna was silent for a few seconds, thinking. 'So it really looks like Jimbo's going to be charged, then, does it?' she asked.

'I reckon so. But what do I know? You're the one with the special police contacts now, aren't you?' Frank's voice turned into a sneer and he put heavily sarcastic emphasis on 'special', making his inference abundantly clear.

It had to come, of course. Manners could never behave like a reasonable human being towards her for more than five minutes or so on the trot. 'Fuck off, Frank,' she remarked conversationally, turned her back on him and headed for her office where she slammed the door behind her.

Soon after she had arrived in Fleet Street, young, eager, and terrified, Joanna had been introduced to the *Daily Mirror*'s legendary agony aunt Marje Proops, not a woman to be trifled with, who had given her advice on dealing with the chauvinists of Fleet Street, which she had never forgotten. 'Smile at them sweetly, dear, and if that fails just use the 'F' word.'

Jo found she was smiling at the memory as she tried to put a call in to Fielding. Predictably, he was not contactable. She spoke to a constable at the incident room who assured her he would pass on her message for the detective to call her as soon as possible. She did not, however, have high expectations. And she was genuinely surprised when he called back little more than half an hour later. 'Can

115

you tell me how sure you are?' she asked.

'We don't make a habit of arresting people without good reason, Joanna,' he replied rather prissily. He sounded cocksure again, more the way he had been when she first met him.

She knew all too well that getting a result did that to policemen. Even when they had a dead body on their hands. 'For God's sake, Mike . . . ' she began irritably.

'Fucking sure,' he interrupted her suddenly. 'Look, it fits like a glove. O'Donnell likes playing soldiers, always has done. Likes knives, too — we found a nice collection at his house. Also we know he's been a regular visitor up on the moor. Oh, and he was seen on the Phillipses' land the day Angela disappeared.'

'You've got more than that though, surely?'

'Fucking right.'

'Well?'

'Can't tell you.'

'OK, can you tell me what led you to him?'

'Seems the shock tactics paid off. We had a call from a minor Dartmoor villain. He'd seen Jimbo hanging around Five Tors Farm on the day Angela was taken and recognised him at once. Apparently he's done a bit of wheeling and dealing with the O'Donnells in the past, although he doesn't like admitting it. Jimbo was tucked in behind a hedge and looked as if he was watching the farmhouse through binoculars. It all made sense because, unless he was a local, whoever abducted Angela had definitely learned a bit about her and her family, almost certainly been watching them. Our man was

116

up to no good himself, as usual — sheep rustling is one of his favourite tricks and there's been quite an operation going on around Dartmoor lately — that's why he didn't speak out before. And he certainly didn't want to interfere with Jimbo O'Donnell. Said he backed off smartish when he spotted the bastard. Scared shitless of the O'Donnells, of course. All rogues are and with good reason. You don't shop an O'Donnell lightly and in any case when Angela disappeared he couldn't really see it as the kind of thing the O'Donnells would be involved in. Anyway, he was in two minds when the girl's body was found and the kidnapping angle broke. Then, when you printed the story about how her breasts had been mutilated, he finally came forward. Got a kid that age himself. Said he couldn't stomach it. Seems he told his missus then and she pushed him to speak out.

'So there you are. As I said. Fits like a glove.'

'It's an unusual profile, though, isn't it?' queried Joanna. 'An organised premeditated kidnapper who is also a vicious sex offender.'

Fielding grunted. 'O'Donnell's always been a sicko,' he said. 'Abuse is what turns him on. And young girls are his weakness. The Met say he's damned lucky to have only the one conviction for a sex offence. There was a particularly nasty rape of a teenage girl in his manor just last year, which they were sure was down to him. But neither the kid nor her family would point the finger, too damned scared of the O'Donnell mythology, they reckon.

'The kidnap of Angela Phillips was planned and premeditated all right. O'Donnell may even have convinced himself that it was no different from the kind of job the rest of his family might take on. Sam rules with a rod of iron, you know, and keeps a tight hold on the purse strings. Jimbo would have loved to have proved to his old man that he was a major league operator in his own right — and make a few bob, too. But no doubt the bastard always planned to have his fun with Angela as well. And once he'd got hold of her, his true nature ran away with itself.'

'Were you on the arrest team?'

'Yup. Bowled up to the Smoke at dawn this morning. In and out. No need to get the Met involved, the boss said. I enjoyed that. Enjoyed the swoop on Jimbo too. Thought he was on his heels, didn't he? He's always been a piece of work, Jo. You know that, I'm sure.'

'I do now, yeah,' said Joanna. 'You'll be charging him, then?'

'Fucking right.'

'When?' That was the million-dollar question. If O'Donnell was going to be charged that night the paper's whole coverage would become sub judice and be severely limited. If not, they could run at least some of Manners's juicy background. Although they would be unable to spell out the criminality of Jimbo's family, because that would be highly prejudicial, a little innuendo can go a long way in a well-written tabloid splash and most readers would in any case know at least something of the O'Donnells' dubious reputation, and be able to put two and two together. Even the *Comet*'s readers, thought Jo wryly. The paper would also be able to carry much of the additional information she had gleaned from Fielding.

Fielding knew all that. He was a media man. Jo was already beginning to think he knew as much about media coverage of crime as he did about catching criminals. 'You're all right, it'll be tomorrow morning,' he said.

'Thanks, Mike, you're a diamond.'

She could just hear his voice in the distance as she hung up. 'Aren't I, though?' he murmured.

★   ★   ★

O'Donnell was formally charged the following morning with the murder of Angela Phillips, as Fielding had told Joanna he would be. He appeared briefly at Okehampton Magistrates' Court and was remanded in custody. After that there was little coverage that the paper could give until the committal proceedings, which were expected to be a formality.

Nonetheless, Joanna drove down to Devon to be present at the committal six weeks later. She had been on the case from the start and she planned to see it through to the end, every step of the way.

Okehampton Magistrates' Court was an unlikely grubby white bungalow of a building tucked away on the northern edge of the town behind the Co-op supermarket just where the Rivers West and East Okement merged. O'Donnell was brought from the Devon County Prison at Exeter in a black van with barred windows. He climbed out by the entrance to the court, a big, rugged, broad-shouldered man in his early thirties, wearing combat trousers and a tight black T-shirt which emphasised the impressive muscle definition of his upper body. The sleeves were short enough to display upon the biceps of his left arm a large and particularly unpleasant tattoo of the upper torso of a buxom young woman one of whose obscenely oversized breasts bore the word 'love' and the other 'hate'. Yuck, thought Jo.

Apparently unbowed by what was happening to him, O'Donnell held his head high as the gathered crowd roared their loathing at him. His peroxide-blond crew-cut gleamed in the autumn sunshine. His eyes blazed beneath their heavy dark brows. There was no being covered up in blankets for this guy.

The car park outside the court, the road behind, and even the supermarket car park beyond that were teeming, and the mood of the crowd was not sweet. It was a fairly predictable reception for someone accused of a crime as horrific as this one. The crowd bayed for blood. The majority in government and, thank God, in Joanna's opinion, within the police force were against the reintroduction of capital punishment. This lot would no doubt rip O'Donnell apart limb from limb, were they able to get to him.

She thought there could be four or five hundred people gathered into the area around the court. A lot of them looked like farming folk, who would have been more at home on horseback or leaning on a farm gate somewhere. Instead, they were screaming blue murder at James Martin O'Donnell, who was securely handcuffed to two policemen and surrounded by half a dozen or so more as he began the brief journey into the courtroom.

If he'd lowered his head or kept his eyes downcast it might not have been quite so provocative, Joanna thought. But, as the Nikon choir formed by dozens of cameramen burst into flashing, whirring action, O'Donnell glared coolly around him, belligerent, arrogant, contemptuous.

There was a yell of outrage, which she somehow heard above the collective noise of the chanting throng. A figure managed to force his way through the police guards and hurl himself at O'Donnell. The accused man's big shoulders wrenched against the restraint of the cuffs round his wrists as he tried to defend himself. She could see the hands of the assailant raking O'Donnell's face, reaching for his eyes as if the intention was to gouge them out, and then it was all over. Standing on the courtroom steps with her back to the wall, Jo had a grandstand view as three hefty policemen pounced on the attacker and he was led away. She got a clear glimpse of his face, then, and was almost sure it was Jeremy Thomas, Angela Phillips' boyfriend. Silly boy, Jo thought to herself, but of course, not only had Jeremy had to deal with the loss of his girlfriend in such a terrible way, he had also had to put up with the anguish of having been suspected of the crime himself.

With the added excitement of the attack, the roar of the crowd reached a crescendo. O'Donnell tossed his head at them as he was finally hurried into the courtroom, almost as if he were a film star acknowledging the acclaim of his fans instead of a man standing accused of one of the most horrible murders Joanna had ever had knowledge of. She saw that there was a trickle of red running down his face. The attacker had drawn blood and the crowd loved it. Even execution would probably not satisfy this lot, the mood they were in, thought Jo. Certainly not if it was conducted humanely and in private. A public hanging might do, but better still, something like that lovely old Chinese way of doing things, death by slicing. Any government having trouble with its popularity should really consider that, she thought wryly.

With some difficulty she made her way into the court — there wasn't time to file the story of the attack on O'Donnell without missing the start of the proceedings and, in any case, there was no need to do so yet; her deadlines were still hours away. Once inside, she instantly spotted Mike Fielding. He was wearing a beige linen suit — he was fond of linen, obviously — a maroon silk shirt, a tie which carefully blended both colours in varying shades and a smug smile. She had never known a policeman who dressed like him. As for his smugness, she hoped he was not overconfident. This was no ordinary crime and Jimbo O'Donnell was no ordinary prisoner. Certainly he was no ordinary sex offender nutter. He was different. His back-up was different too. She already knew that he had a top legal team defending him.

The attack on O'Donnell provided an early diversion inside the court as well as outside. O'Donnell's lawyers made a big thing about their man getting first-aid attention. O'Donnell shrugged his big shoulders, asked for a handkerchief with which he wiped his face, said he'd be fine and grinned broadly at the magistrates. He was going to play to the gallery, no doubt about it.

After that the proceedings went according to plan. O'Donnell was committed for trial at Exeter Crown Court and was remanded in custody, of course. His lawyers knew better than to ask for bail; they'd never get it on a case like this.

As Jo left the court, Fielding was waiting in the foyer. For her? She didn't know, but certainly he stepped forward smartly to her side and put a hand on her arm. 'How's my favourite hackette, then?' he asked lightly.

His manner was flirtatious, as it almost invariably was with her, but again she was not really sure whether he was chatting her up or not. His body language and his words did not always match. On this occasion he stood much closer to her than necessary and he kept his hand on her arm in an almost proprietorial fashion as they walked together towards the door.

She decided to play it dead straight. 'I'm fine, how are you?' she asked him in a crisp businesslike way.

'All the better for seeing you, as ever, Joanna,' he said. And he grinned that grin, which would have been even more disarming if he were not so obviously aware of it. He was one of those men who appeared to think he was irresistible to women. There was a lot of that about, usually misguided. In Fielding's case probably not so misguided, she thought, but she was beginning to find that irritating too. Her brief period of getting to like him seemed to have come to an end. But she didn't want to antagonise him. He had already proved to be a most useful contact and it pleased her greatly to think that she appeared to have effectively stolen him from Frank Manners.

She was about to ask him if he would like a drink later when his radio pager bleeped. He studied it briefly. 'Have to leave you, darling,' he said. 'Much as it breaks my heart.'

God he was an annoying man. She could only follow him out into the street where mob rule still reigned. Anyway, Fielding wasn't the key to it today and she didn't really have time for buttering him up.

Pushing her way through the crowds, she hurried to her car, which she had sensibly parked in a car park on the other side of the town, just a few minutes' walk away, so that she was able to make a relatively quick departure from Okehampton and head out to Five Tors Farm. A load of hacks and snappers were already gathered at the end of the farm lane, as before, and although Joanna did not actually expect to get very far on this day of the committal with so many press around, she knew the importance of trying to get close to the Phillips family.

She planned to stay down in Devon for a couple of days to make yet another attempt to obtain proper talks with the family who had so far turned down all interview requests. The *Comet* was after what they called background, the bulk of which would not be usable until after the trial had concluded or else it would break the sub judice laws, and some of it would not be usable even then unless Jimbo was found guilty. She couldn't imagine that there was much doubt in this case, but regardless of the likely outcome, newspapers always spent a great deal of time and money on background. It was considered vital. The paper with the best background after a big case ended was always the envy of the rest of the Street.

Jo waited, chatting to the others, quite enjoying being out in the fresh air. It was a sunny day and unseasonably warm. Jo hated doorsteps, they all did, but at least it wasn't raining and you invariably gleaned a few nuggets of additional information when you were with the pack. She learned from the Press Association man that she had been right about the attack on O'Donnell. The police had announced that the assailant had been Jeremy Thomas and he had been arrested for assault which, harsh as it might seem, was only what she would have expected.

After about an hour, just as Joanna was wondering if she could be better employed and whether to ask the desk if Harry Fowler was free for the watching brief, a Land Rover came down the lane. Somewhat to the surprise of the pack, who had more or less given up on the family while still, of course, having to go through the motions, out stepped Bill and Rob Phillips. Neither had been in court that day. They both looked wan and drawn. Bill Phillips in particular seemed to have aged ten years since Jo had last seen him, a couple of days after his daughter had disappeared, making one of several public appeals for her safe return.

The old Nikon choir burst into action again. Cameras flashed. Motor drives whirred. The reporters also pressed forward, some clutching notebooks and pens, some brandishing tape recorders.

Rob Phillips barely seemed to notice the chaos going on around him as he spoke. 'We have nothing to say about today's court proceedings except that we hope justice will be done and that the dreadful death of m-my sister . . . ' He stumbled over the words and looked for a moment as if he was going to break down, then with what appeared to be a great effort of will he gathered himself together and continued. ' . . . the death of my sister A-Angela will be avenged.

'But nothing can bring our A-Ange back and we are horrified at what happened in Okehampton today. We know that . . . ' He glanced at his father as if confirming that he should go ahead with whatever they had agreed. ' . . . we know that there has been an arrest following an attack on the accused man. And, of course, we know who has been arrested. We don't want anybody else to suffer because of what has happened to Angela. Sh-she . . . ' He stumbled again. It seemed that whenever he said her name, no doubt thinking about her and what had happened to her, he faltered. 'She wouldn't want that either,' he continued. 'Thank you very much.'

Reporters and cameramen ran towards their cars in order to get to phones and wire points so that they could file their copy and wire their pictures. Joanna stood for just a few seconds, watching the two dejected men, father and son, climb into their vehicle, swing it round and return to their home. The home that would never be the same again.

There were good people around. Unless she had got things very wrong indeed she had just encountered two of them. It was almost impossible to grasp what that family were going through. And yet they were still trying to behave like civilised human beings, to do what they felt was right.

She found that she was quite moved. And that didn't happen very often.

★   ★   ★

During the long wait for the trial, which was scheduled to begin in April the following year, Harry Fowler took over the background down in Devon while Joanna and Manners concentrated on the London end.

The Phillips family continued to refuse to give interviews to anyone. Their brief statement at the end of their lane on the day of Jimbo O'Donnell's committal was just about the sum total of their relations with the press.

There was little to justify a chief crime correspondent spending her time in Devon on the story and Jo wasn't sure if she was sorry or glad about that. If there were to be any chance of saving her floundering marriage, then the longer she spent at home the better. Her trips away did not help anything, particularly since the anonymous phone calls, which seemed, mercifully, to have stopped.

Joanna was going through one of those torn-apart periods. She loved working for a daily newspaper and specifically covering crime. It was the sharp end all right — as tough as it got, but totally exhilarating. And, secretly, she revelled in being the first woman Scotland Yard hack. It was ground-breaking and she was damn proud of herself. But she was getting heartily sick of all the nonsense surrounding her job. Every time she saw Frank Manners she wanted to throw something at him.

She had not told a soul at the *Comet* about the moody phone calls. And neither, in the end, had she told any of her police contacts, in spite of suggesting to her husband that she would. This had been a deliberate policy. As ever, she was not going to give the bastards the satisfaction. She didn't want anyone, particularly Manners, to know that she had serious problems within her marriage. And in particular she didn't want to give Manners the satisfaction of thinking that he might be responsible for it. Nothing would please the toe-rag more, she was quite sure of that.

Instead, she concentrated on the job in hand, which involved getting alongside the O'Donnells. Joanna had met Sam the Man before, of course. So had any crime reporter worth tuppence. Like the Krays before him, Sam saw himself as a bit of a star, loved to make showbusiness friends and prided himself on having a good relationship with the press. He enjoyed appearing in newspapers. He sent journalists thank you notes for coverage, even when it had been far from complimentary, Christmas cards and, if he could find out when your birthday was you got cards for those too. Joanna had received a birthday card from him every year since, as a very young general news reporter, she had first written a story about the O'Donnells. Against her better judgement Joanna had never quite been able to stop herself liking Sam the Man — on a superficial level, at any rate. However, she had no illusions about how evil he could be.

Sam's right-hand man, Combo, a big burly minder whose build and blind loyalty to Sam made him a bit of a gangster cliché, took her call when she phoned Sam's Dulwich home. 'I'll get back to yer,' he said in his ponderous way. Not a man you wanted to quarrel with. Joanna had been told that he was given his rather peculiar name because in a fight he was famous for employing a devastating combination of fist, feet and head. In spite of this she was pleased to hear from him when he returned her call only ten minutes or so later to say that Sam would see her at the Duke the following day.

She knew where Combo meant, the Duke of Denmark, a big, noisy pub not far from Sam's home. They all knew the Duke. Sam held court there in a small back room behind the public bar. That's where he liked to do business. His home was for family and Sam was a great family man. Jo was not surprised by his ready agreement to see her and, again, neither was she under any illusions. Sam would no doubt have agreed to talk to all the nationals; that was his way.

Sam appeared to be his usual avuncular self when she arrived at the Duke at the appointed time — although she felt sure he must be shocked by the horrific charges levelled at his eldest son. If Jimbo had been arrested on a straightforward blagging or, more likely in his case, a hit job, Sam O'Donnell would have regarded it as part of the cut and thrust of business. His business. But the rape and murder of a civilian was totally against his personal code. She knew that Sam considered himself to be a good, honest villain. Nonetheless, if he was anxious or in any way distressed, he certainly wasn't showing it. Not to her, anyway. Arms outstretched in greeting, he rose from his big upright armchair to welcome her as the bartender showed her into the dark, wood-panelled room, its ceiling yellowed by decades of tobacco smoke. She noticed as he sat down again on the throne-like chair that a single spotlight on the wall behind cast the old gang boss slightly into silhouette, giving an edge of mystery and menace to his appearance. Always good at theatre, was Sam.

'A pleasure to see you, as ever, Joanna,' he told her. His voice was deep and throaty from smoking, his smile displayed expensive dentistry, his abundant figure was immaculately encased in a beautifully cut pale-grey suit, fingers and wrists dripped gold, his nails had obviously been professionally manicured. She knew he must be almost sixty, but he still had thick, wavy hair although the colour was too dark to be natural. However, the stylish cut flattered his big, jowly features. His eyes, small for his face and peering at her through folds of flesh, were astute and intelligent. Anyone who underestimated Sam did so at their peril. Combo stood at his right arm, just fractionally behind his boss. Combo's son, Little John, a teenaged clone of his father although already even taller and bigger, hence his ironic name, stood just a step or two back again. On the surface, at least, it was business as usual for Sam the Man.

Jo was untroubled by the beautifully presented

Godfather tableau. All she was after was good copy. She enjoyed the challenge, that was the truth of it. And although she had no desire to fall out with the O'Donnells, she wasn't scared of them. As a reporter she had no reason to be, she was the last kind of person the clan would want to harm.

Sam lit a large cigar and offered her coffee from a silver pot on the table by his side. He poured some for her into a dainty bone china teacup, the sort of cup which positively invited you to crook your little finger as you drank from it. It was well known that Sam didn't drink alcohol and neither did anyone else while they were in the back room. If you wanted a proper drink you were expected to go to the bar for it — but only when Sam told you that you could. Jo knew the rules.

'What I want is for you to put the record straight about my boy, Joanna,' Sam told her, puffing on his cigar and sending a cloud of dense smoke wafting towards the already discoloured ceiling.

'That's what I'm here for,' she replied, although they both knew it wasn't.

She would, however, appear to go along with anything Sam said. She needed him. She couldn't afford to let the *Comet* be out in the cold on this one as far as the O'Donnells were concerned. So she was quite prepared to appear to display a sympathy she did not feel for both the family and Jimbo's predicament.

'My boy's told me he's innocent and I believe him absolutely,' Sam went on. 'We O'Donnells don't harm innocent people and we never hurt women. None of us would hurt a young girl like that and the

131

filth should damn well know it. My boy's been fitted up. And we're going to damn well prove it.'

Joanna studied the tough old gangster appraisingly. He was dealing with his son's arrest in exactly the way Joanna would have expected. And he was giving nothing away. Down, but most definitely not out. Typical Sam the Man. She had already seen the names of the sharp legal team which had been hired for Jimbo. The O'Donnells had money, know-how, and influence — a lot more influence in all kinds of areas than they should have.

Jo just hoped the Devon and Cornwall Constabulary and the prosecution lawyers knew what they were up against. She didn't think they had villains quite like the O'Donnells in the West of England. Perhaps the family's biggest strength was the way they saw themselves. They had no real perception of themselves as crooks at all — rather as tough but fair businessmen working in a certain area and operating under a different set of rules from the rest of society. They dealt out their own rough justice and if ever challenged would insist that their integrity was as great as anyone else's.

Sam was still talking: 'Jimbo's never been able to keep his hands off the ladies, but that's not rape. He was just a boy when he let things get out of hand before and I never believed he raped anyone then either. He was led on. He doesn't need to force women against their will, he's too good for that, my boy. And this Angela Phillips thing. It doesn't make sense. Rape and torture of an innocent girl? No way, I'm telling you. And kidnap? Why in God's name would he stage a kidnap? It's the hardest scam of all.

Everybody knows that. And he's got no need, my boy, has he?'

Joanna didn't doubt that Sam had convinced himself he was telling the truth.

She also didn't doubt that he would move heaven and earth to get his son cleared of all the charges against him. And she knew he would be a formidable adversary.

6

The trial of Jimbo O'Donnell took place at Exeter Crown Court in April 1981, seven months after his arrest. Joanna returned once more to Devon to cover it.

She had not seen Fielding since the committal proceedings. Once the *Comet*'s background was in place there was little else that could be done until the trial began. Certainly very little that could be written. As far as Joanna was concerned there had been plenty of other stories to deal with. Plus Frank Manners. Plus all the other bastards. And plus, most important of all, her husband.

As she was driving down the M4 she considered again the grim reality concerning Chris. Their marriage was effectively over. They didn't have sex any more and could barely be civil to each other. She felt she had tried as hard as she could. For the first time she began seriously to wonder if there was someone else in Chris's life. He appeared to have come actively to dislike her, which she could hardly believe after all the time they had been together. Sometimes it seemed to her that he was almost inventing problems between the two of them and she couldn't help wondering if he was doing it deliberately.

Paul Potter was invariably around when she wanted a drink and a chat, but she continued to think of him only as a friendly face in the office and nothing more — someone who provided very welcome solace in an environment that in her eyes was becoming more and more hostile.

One way and another she found herself relieved by the prospect of being out of London for a bit.

As expected, O'Donnell, who continued to profess his innocence, pleaded not guilty. The historic Crown Court at Exeter lies within the great walls of Exeter Castle, which dates back to Roman times. A forbidding iron portcullis forms the only entrance and Joanna could never pass through it, into a courtyard where a gallows once stood and the old hanging judges ran riot, without a bit of a shiver running down her spine. James Martin O'Donnell, however, seemed totally undaunted. The grim ghosts of other crueller ages clearly did not trouble Jimbo. Imagination was probably not his strong suit, Jo suspected. And the influence of his legal dream team was apparent from the start. Jo was afraid yet again that Jimbo's lawyers, provided by his doting dad and led by a clever and already highly acclaimed young barrister called Brian Burns, might run rings round the police prosecutors.

Jimbo's appearance no longer bore any resemblance to the way he had looked at the committal proceeding and his behaviour was also completely different. The thuggish-looking peroxide-blond crew cut had gone. His hair, which was now mid-brown, presumably its natural colour, had been allowed to grow longer while he was on remand and had been neatly cut in conventional fashion with a parting to one side. The offensive tattoo on his arm was concealed. He wore dark suits, crisp white shirts and sober ties to court, and when he spoke he did so politely and with apparent respect for the proceedings. He no longer seemed to have an arrogant bone in his body. Jimbo had been given a complete make-over and had quite obviously been groomed in every way by people who knew exactly what they were doing.

Most of the evidence against O'Donnell was circumstantial, although some of it was quite strong, including that given by an ex-Territorial the police had called as a witness. He stated with absolute certainty that O'Donnell was among a group of them who had used Knack Mine as a hideout during military exercises. But the prosecution did not get off to a good start.

Jimbo admitted readily enough that he had been on the Phillipses' land on the day that Angela Phillips disappeared, but claimed this was just coincidence. He had been camping, not for the first time, on a part of Dartmoor not far from Five Tors Farm, and had unwittingly strayed on to Phillips land. When the prosecution claimed that O'Donnell had been keeping the farm under surveillance, checking on the movements of Angela and her family, Jimbo denied it hotly. 'I was birdwatching, that's why I had the bins, wasn't it,' he said ingenuously. 'I'm a twitcher, me!'

The very idea was so incongruous that Joanna had to fight against an almost irresistible urge to laugh out loud. However, when she glanced at the jury they seemed to be lapping it up. The concept of judgement by your peers, twelve good men and true and all that, left a great deal to be desired, she

136

thought, not for the first time.

The prosecution barrister, Malcolm Bowman, a slightly plump, earnest young man with a disconcerting squint, did not give up.

'You meticulously checked out the Phillips family,' he persisted. 'You appraised their property, you knew that they were a wealthy family well able to raise £50,000 in exchange for Angela's life. You have been obsessed with the military from an early age, have you not, Mr O'Donnell, and you used your Territorial training when you planned this terrible crime, didn't you?'

Jimbo stared straight ahead. 'I don't know what you mean, sir,' he said.

'You believed, because of your training, that you could deal with the logistical complexities of abducting and detaining a young woman against her will, did you not?' said Malcolm Bowman. 'And you had considerable local knowledge gained during your training at Okehampton camp.

'We have heard from a reliable witness, Mr O'Donnell, that you had personal knowledge of the mine shaft where Angela Phillips's body was found. You knew what an excellent hideout Knack Mine was, and I put it to you that when you abducted Angela Phillips it was already your intention to conceal her there.'

'No, that's not true, sir,' responded Jimbo mildly but firmly. 'In any case, if I ever did go to that mine when I was up at the camp, I just don't remember it at all.' He was so well briefed it hurt. Obviously acting under instructions, he just kept on calmly denying everything.

'You tortured, raped and mutilated Angela there to satisfy your own perverted desires,' continued Bowman doggedly. 'And then, when your attempts to obtain a ransom for her failed, you callously left her in the mine shaft to die.'

'No, that's not true, sir,' said Jimbo again, equally mildly.

Joanna knew that he had not left fingerprints on the little that had been found in Angela's dreadful tomb and the best forensic had been able to come up with, in the days before DNA, was that the semen found in Angela's body was from someone with the same blood group as O'Donnell. It was O Positive — the most common of the lot.

Malcolm Bowman was beginning to look frustrated and became even more so when he brought up the collection of knives found in O'Donnell's apartment, none of which, Joanna already knew, forensic had been able to prove had been the weapon used to maim Angela.

'They're military memorabilia, sir,' said Jimbo.

Bowman looked incredulous. 'Memorabilia, Mr O'Donnell? You are talking about a selection of potentially lethal weapons, including one almost new army knife of a particularly vicious design.'

'Well, they're all memorabilia to me, sir. I'm very interested in the military, you see.'

'And what exactly do you claim that you have used these knives for, Mr O'Donnell, if not to maim and kill?'

'I've never used them for anything, sir. I just like looking at them.'

It was ludicrous, but once again the jury did not seem to think so.

There did appear, however, to be one irrefutable piece of evidence — and Joanna realised it was this to which Fielding must have been referring when he had refused to give her the details during their conversation after Jimbo's arrest.

The prosecution claimed that a gold locket Angela Phillips was wearing when she disappeared had been found in O'Donnell's London flat. This was not circumstantial. This was hard evidence. This could swing it. Joanna felt her hopes rise. She was aware of a kind of collective gasp from the public gallery behind her, where she knew Angela's family were sitting, and even the jury looked impressed.

However, Jo's hopes were quickly dashed again. The defence had an answer — and Mike Fielding was at the crux of it. The locket bore O'Donnell's fingerprints clearly enough, and that was not in dispute, but it seemed that after claiming to have found it in a drawer in O'Donnell's bedroom, Fielding had triumphantly brandished his trophy at the accused man and allowed him to take it from him. Jo could see Fielding almost visibly squirming when, having been asked to take the stand, he was confronted with this.

He tried unsuccessfully to fudge the issue. 'Well, we found the locket, sir, no doubt about that, and whether or not Mr O'Donnell actually handled it . . .'

'DS Fielding, you know perfectly well that Mr O'Donnell did handle the locket,' persisted Brian

Burns. He was tall, slim, handsome and authoritative, in brutal contrast to the unprepossessing Malcolm Bowman. 'I suggest you tell the truth, Detective Sergeant,' Burns continued. 'There were other officers with you, were there not, who may not be as evasive as you are trying to be.'

Ultimately Fielding had no choice but to admit that he had allowed O'Donnell to handle the key piece of evidence. 'I was excited by the discovery,' he said.

'You were excited, DS Fielding? So you allowed a suspect to handle a key piece of evidence and put his fingerprints all over it? Do you really expect this court to believe that?'

There was no answer. Burns did not push the point any further but continued by asking: 'And what did my client say to you when you handed him the locket, Detective Sergeant?'

'I didn't hand it to him, he took it.'

Joanna felt almost sorry for Fielding. Didn't he realise that everything he said seemed to be making the whole thing appear worse?

'I see,' responded Burns casually. 'So, what did my client say when you allowed him to take the locket from you?'

Fielding looked defeated. 'He said he'd never seen it before in his life.'

Joanna groaned to herself. This was going seriously pear-shaped. She, too, found it hard to believe that Fielding would have made such a silly mistake. The alternative was that he had planted the locket. He had been the first officer at the scene of the crime. If the locket had been with Angela in the shaft at Knack Mine, Fielding would have had ample opportunity to secrete it away — to have the locket up his sleeve, as it were, just in case a little extra evidence was needed later on. She had known it happen before.

And that was just what Burns went on to suggest. Indeed, he finished his cross-examination by going way beyond suggestion: 'I put it to you, DS Fielding, that you did not find this locket in my client's home but that you calculatedly planted it on him. You needed a conviction, didn't you? You're a high flyer aren't you? You don't like unsolved crimes, do you?'

Burns was a slick operator and this was devastating stuff. There seemed to be holes in the prosecution case you could drive a bus through — or anyway there did when the dream team were at work.

★   ★   ★

The trial lasted six and a half working days including the day and a half it took for the jury to agree its verdict. They found James Martin O'Donnell not guilty — which, after the way the proceedings had gone, came as no great surprise to anybody. But it was a dreadful disappointment — to police, prosecution, the family and friends of Angela Phillips, and indeed to Joanna, whom Fielding had quite convinced of O'Donnell's guilt. She had not realised, in fact, just how much she had wanted to see him brought to justice for his appalling crime until he was cleared.

The jury could not be told, of course, of O'Donnell's previous conviction for rape, nor of his and his family's criminal reputations, although most of them must surely at least have heard of the O'Donnells, Jo thought. It was a majority decision, so maybe if the law were different and that kind of information had been made available to them — as many people thought, certainly in the case of sex crimes, it should be — the balance could have been tipped. As it stood, a majority of ten to two was all that was necessary for Jimbo O'Donnell to walk from the court a free man. And walk he did.

Joanna wondered if the clenched-fist salute Jimbo gave when their foreman read out the verdict made any of the jurors question their judgement. Certainly, once he realised the case was won he cast aside his demeanour of quiet respectfulness with alacrity.

She joined the crush to follow him outside the court. His father had been at the trial every day and now Sam the Man stood alongside Jimbo in the middle of the ancient courtyard, smiling for a cacophony of flashing snappers. 'Justice has been done — for once,' Sam announced with a big grin. 'My boy could never have done what they said he did. He's an O'Donnell. We don't hurt women or children. I never doubted him for a minute. Never. He's straight down the middle, my boy, look at him I ask you, look at him . . . ' Sam the Man reached up and ruffled his son's new haircut.

The younger O'Donnell did his best to look innocent, endearing and wronged — but he succeeded only in looking smug and pleased with himself. However, inside the court during the trial his performance had been convincing, certainly good enough to convince the jury, and that was all that mattered.

In stark contrast, the Phillips family, accompanied by Jeremy Thomas and escorted by a grim-faced Todd Mallett, tried to slip away quietly into a waiting car. They had no chance at all. The press swarmed on them. Joanna joined in, calling out 'Mr Phillips, Rob, Jeremy, just tell us how you feel' — to no avail. They all looked devastated. Reporters needed words to make copy, but snappers always insisted a picture could be worth several thousand of them. Certainly in this instance they were probably right, Joanna thought. Nothing any of the family might say would ever convey their feelings as effectively as their shattered appearance. Bill Phillips glanced towards her at one point, but all she could see in his eyes was the emptiness of a broken man confronting yet another tormentor.

Fielding and DCI Parsons were right behind the family and hurried them through the throng. They also refused to comment to the horde of press who surrounded them, making their passage difficult. Both men looked grave, but Joanna was riveted by Fielding. The normally suave, cocksure detective seemed stricken. His face was ashen.

She supposed he would bounce back eventually, he was that sort. But his career had suffered a potentially fatal blow. Apart from any other consideration it must be a policeman's nightmare to be accused in open court of having planted evidence. She felt almost sorry for him. His rosy future did not look quite so rosy any more, that was for certain.

She filed an early story and, with Manners under instructions to look after the police angle although nobody was expected to put their head up over the bunker for a bit, set out across Dartmoor and spent most of the rest of the afternoon and evening doorstepping the Phillipses. They continued to refuse to speak to the press, but nonetheless she had to wait until the desk sent Harry Fowler down to take over her watching brief outside the farm before she was allowed to leave at about 10 p.m. She was thoroughly exhausted and there appeared to be little more she could do. All she really wanted was to go back to her Exeter hotel room, order herself a large malt whisky and maybe some sandwiches, and take to her bed.

But on a whim she found herself making a detour to Heavitree Road police station. She swung the car into the car park, fairly empty at that time of night. There were still a couple of reporters and one photographer outside. Manners had been there earlier, she knew, but he was no longer about. Jo wasn't surprised. Not one to hang around on a doorstep, that man, but he never seemed to get caught out. He did have a way of covering his back, she had to admit that.

She walked straight past the reporters, both of whom she knew only by sight, and into the front office where she asked the clerk if she could speak to DS Fielding. She was never quite sure what made her do it. Did she really think he would give her an exclusive on a night like this or even talk to her about the case? Or did she, in the depths of her subconscious, have another reason even then for trying to contact the detective sergeant?

The clerk studied her without enthusiasm. 'He's not talking to the press and neither's anybody else. You may as well join your friends out the front.'

'Look, will you just ask him?' She treated the man to what she hoped was her winning smile.

He looked uncertain.

'Please. Just ask him. That's all.' Jo smiled again. She might draw the line at sleeping with guys for stories, in spite of what her husband thought, but would resort to feminine wiles at the drop of a hat. And she had the honesty to admit to herself that while Manners and the rest of the heavy mob wouldn't have a hope of getting anywhere with Fielding, she at least was in with a chance.

Quite deliberately, she bit her bottom lip and did her best to look as if she might be about to burst into tears. That did it. The clerk picked up the phone on his desk. Strange how she had somehow not doubted that Fielding would still be in his office at almost 11 p.m.

' . . . Joanna Bartlett, the *Comet*, yes, Mike, I told her you wouldn't . . . '

There was a pause while the man listened. He looked mildly surprised. Then he turned away from Joanna and lowered his voice. She could still hear him clearly enough, though: ' . . . Look, are you sure, mate? You don't need any more bother, do you . . . OK, OK, whatever you say.' With a sigh he replaced the receiver. 'You can go up,' he told her. 'Second floor. He'll meet you at the stairs.'

Fielding was waiting for her by the time she had climbed the two flights. If anything, he looked even worse than he had outside the court. He did not smile, just gave her a quick hello and escorted her to his office. She thought he had probably been drinking and it turned out she wasn't wrong. There was a three-parts empty bottle of whisky on his desk. He offered her a drink, which she accepted. He found a paper cup and poured her a large measure, waved her into a chair, sat down himself behind the desk, put his feet up on it, and took a deep swig straight from the bottle. Then he leaned back in his seat and closed his eyes. She could feel the blackness of his mood. She felt pretty down herself. She had believed in O'Donnell's guilt and had wanted to see him go down. And she had lost the bulk of her background. All that hard work for nothing. A huge chunk of it could not be printed now that he'd been acquitted, legally far too dodgy.

'I'm sorry it went so wrong for you,' she said eventually.

Mike opened his eyes, which she noticed then were bloodshot, and regarded her steadily. His skin still looked ashen. There was certainly none of his usual God's-gift-to-women smugness about him. His wits hadn't completely deserted him, though. 'Are we off the record?' he asked.

'Of course,' she replied quickly. It was probably unprofessional not to have attempted, at least, to get something from him on the record, but her response had been quite automatic. The man must have got to her in some way for her to behave in such an out of character way. Joanna was usually just as hard-nosed in her approach to work as the normally tough policeman she was talking to.

He took her at her word, as she expected him to. And she sensed him relax a little.

He tipped the whisky to his lips once more. 'What a fuck-up,' he said. 'What a bloody fuck-up.'

'Yours wasn't the only mistake,' she told him, sensing that he was blaming himself. 'You were a bit overeager, that's all.'

'Story of my life. The locket was the only really hard evidence. And I gave Jimbo a lifeline on it. Did that bloody jury really believe I planted it?'

She shrugged. They did, of course. They had to have believed that in order to acquit O'Donnell. She too had some doubts. Not about O'Donnell. Not really. But about Fielding, definitely. And so, presumably, did his superiors. Fielding was deeply in the mire and he knew it. She changed tack. 'You still don't have any doubts about O'Donnell, do you?'

'For Christ's sake, none at all. Bastard's as guilty as sin. Just that the might of the Devon and Cornwall Constabulary combined with the Crown Prosecution Service didn't have the wit to get him convicted, that's all. A major fuck-up to which I contributed . . . ' He paused as if seeking a word. 'Majestically,' he concluded with a bit of dramatic flourish.

'What'll happen to you?' she asked.

'Probably fuck all. Which is what I deserve. I won't make DI for years, now, that's for certain. Maybe not ever. There'll be an inquiry, of course. If it goes against me I could get chucked out. I doubt it, though. Whatever they believe privately, the bastards will prefer to sweep it under the carpet. At best I behaved like a bloody fool, at worst I tried to plant evidence. Sod's choice, isn't it?'

She didn't say anything. She could think of nothing to say.

He took another slug of whisky, got up from his chair and walked over to the window. He continued to talk as he stood with his back to her, looking down on the street below. 'I wake up at night and I see Angela, you know, lying there, mutilated, in all that filth.' There was a catch in his voice.

She was momentarily surprised. All she had really expected from him was self-pity. He was a professional detective. As hard-nosed as any of the villains he pursued. It took one to catch one. That's what they always said about the CID, wasn't it?

'I can't get it out of my head,' he went on. 'I've never been on a case that's got to me like this one. I thought, if we can send the bastard down, then that would finish it. But we've failed. And there's no second chances in this game.' She saw his elbow rise as he took yet another drink from the bottle. 'So that's it. I've let myself down and I've let Angela down.'

There was no doubt about it. There was definitely a catch in his voice now. Perhaps, after all, there really was more to this man than just another ambitious cop, she thought. She got up from her chair and walked over to join him at the window, gazing in silence for a moment at a lone car travelling along the road outside, its headlights picking up for a moment the two reporters still standing together, chatting, on the pavement. It was a beautiful night, the sky clear and star-studded. That didn't seem right, somehow. It should have been raining or, better still, there should have been a storm raging, something dark and moody to mark what had happened that day. 'You are not single-handedly responsible for it all, you know,' she told him. 'You did your best.'

He turned towards her then. She saw to her amazement that his cheeks were wet. 'Don't they say that's actually the worst epitaph you can give anybody?' he asked, attempting a smile, which didn't really work. It stretched his lips but failed to reach his eyes.

'No epitaph — you're not dead yet, Mike Fielding,' she said quietly and surprised herself somewhat by reaching out a hand to touch a tear-stained cheek. She knew it was probably the whisky as much as anything that was doing this to him. Nonetheless . . .

He took her hand and kissed it gently. Suddenly, awkwardly, she was in his arms and their lips had met. He tasted of whisky and tobacco but the sensation was wonderful from the beginning. He felt so good. Rough round the edges. Soft in the centre. Afterwards she was never quite sure how it happened, the two of them in the middle of a police station embroiled in a clinch. His tongue pushed her lips apart. She gave him hers. His grip tightened round her. She felt him hard against her. He pushed her back against the wall, his hands sought her breasts and she heard his little gasp when he touched a hard nipple. His hands pushed her legs open and simultaneously somehow pulled her skirt up round her waist. The fingers of one of his hands sought for her. She knew that she had become ready, couldn't believe it. She also knew that with his other hand he was starting to unzip his flies.

Then a moment of sanity gripped her. She managed to prise his mouth from hers and, pushing his hand away from her, said, 'For Christ's sake, Mike. No.'

He stopped at once, pulling back from her, breathing heavily. 'God, I'm sorry, Joanna,' he said. 'I don't know what came over me. I'm really sorry. It was just that . . . ' He paused, as if not knowing quite how to go on.

She shook her head. 'It's all right, I know what you're trying to say, I feel exactly the same.'

He had one hand on his trousers. He was trying to cover the bulge in his crotch, she realised suddenly with some amusement. He glanced at her in surprise. 'You do?' he enquired.

'Yes. I must be barking, but I want you like crazy. Only not here, you daft bugger. This is your office, remember. It's in Heavitree Road police station and the place is crawling with cops. Didn't you know?'

He grinned the disarming grin and started to laugh. His face was still tear-stained and his hand was still covering the bulge in his trousers.

In spite of the absurdity of it she wanted him more than ever. She reached out, pulled his hand away and replaced it with her own. She felt his whole body tense. He was very hard. She realised she could hardly wait. It was madness but she felt as if she had no choice. 'I do have a hotel room,' she began.

'So what are we waiting for?' he asked in a very low, husky voice.

On the way out Jo noticed a photograph on his desk of a pretty, red-haired young woman holding a baby in her arms. She assumed that was Mike Fielding's wife with one of their children. She didn't really want to think about his wife, any more than she wanted to think about her husband.

★   ★   ★

She left the station first, having arranged that he would follow her a few minutes later and make his way separately to her hotel. There was, after all, no need to advertise their intentions. Once they were in her room it was as if suddenly they had both made time to do the thing properly.

Without any of the desperate urgency he had displayed earlier Fielding sat beside her on the edge of the bed and kissed her face, her eyes, her cheeks, her neck before their lips met again. And that too was more gentle, more lingering. 'Will you undress for me?' he asked.

She nodded, stood up and took her clothes off. Just like that. She had no sense of embarrassment, she didn't play around, turn it into a striptease, simply took off her clothes and stood before him naked.

'You have a beautiful body,' he said in that same low voice.

'It's a miracle,' she said. And it was, too, the way she lived.

'My miracle,' he told her.

She hadn't expected him to be soppy at all about sex.

'Lie down, now,' he instructed.

Again she did as she was told, the excitement rising in her.

She lay down beside him and immediately he pushed her legs apart and buried his face in her. He didn't touch her with his hands at all. It was immensely exciting. And he carried on and on, until she began desperately to want him inside her and told him so. She needed that in order to reach a climax. She nearly always did the first time.

After what seemed like for ever he pulled his face away from her. She braced herself for what she expected to come next. Instead he wriggled up the bed and lay beside her. His lips brushed hers lightly. She could smell and taste her own sex.

She reached for him. He pulled slightly away.

'I'm afraid I've lost it,' he said. He was still wearing his trousers, which was fairly ridiculous. She realised there was no hardness there at all now.

'Do I put you off that much?' she asked lightly.

'The opposite,' he said. 'Maybe it was the whisky. I can't understand it. I'm like a fucking machine usually.'

She giggled.

So did he. 'That's not what I meant,' he said.

'I know.'

'Can I stay with you? In the morning it will be different, I promise.'

'Shouldn't you go home? What about your wife?'

He shook his head. 'She's used to me,' he said.

I'll bet she is, poor cow, thought Joanna. But she wasn't really in a position to be moralistic. And she certainly didn't want him to leave.

He undressed and she saw that he had a good body too, long and rangy, and covered with a down of sandy hair just a little darker than the hair on his head. He kept his underpants on, which made her smile, crawled into the bed beside her and wrapped his arms round her. Within minutes she could hear his breathing slow and become more shallow and even. He was asleep. It took her longer. She was too excited to fall asleep easily. She needed sexual release quite badly, but it appeared that she was going to have to be patient.

Ultimately, though, she did not have to wait until morning after all. Having fallen eventually into a fitful sleep lying on her back, some time during the night she was woken by the weight of him on top of her. She opened her eyes. His face was inches away from hers and he was smiling at her. They had left the curtains open and there was a full moon. She could see him quite clearly.

He looked very happy, suddenly, and very intent on what he was doing. 'God, you're wet down there,' he muttered appreciatively. In the next second he was inside her.

She came almost at once and he muttered encouragement to her. She managed another orgasm before he reached his own climax and she had never felt quite so fulfilled. He did things to her that were entirely new to her. He had no inhibitions and neither did she. Not with him. In the past there had always been something holding her back from complete sexual abandon. Not with him, there wasn't. With him she just felt so at ease. They lay together afterwards, limbs entangled, at peace. They barely spoke. They did not need to.

It was the best sex she'd ever had. By far. It was in fact so superior to anything she had experienced before that it was almost like the first sex she'd had in her life. At the age of twenty-eight for God's sake. She really could not explain why — but the fact remained that it was so wonderfully, stunningly, amazingly good that it frightened the living daylights out of her.

★ ★ ★

Fielding felt much the same way. He left her shortly after dawn. And he didn't want to. He wanted to fuck her all day. And then all night. And then all the next day. Actually, he didn't think he was capable of even one more time. But, he liked the idea of trying.

He felt elated and bewildered. How many women had he had? He'd long ago lost count. All shapes and sizes and ages. Even a couple of professionals. Most of them willing and eager to play any kind of sex game he fancied. Getting laid had, after all, always been just about his number one aim in life. That and the job, of course. Work as hard at seduction as he did and you were bound to get your share of success. So how was it that he had never felt like this before? How come sex had never been as good as this before? Come to that, he thought, smiling to himself, how come he had never been as good as that before?

He couldn't understand it. He shook his head to clear his brain. He really had to be sensible about this. Best not to see her again, probably. He had enough problems, after all. The last thing he needed was an affair with a Fleet Street journalist. He'd cool it, that was the only thing to do, he reckoned.

★   ★   ★

Meanwhile Joanna lay in bed reliving the night she had just enjoyed. She was not in the mood to be sensible at all. Her whole body glowed and she wanted more of it. She wondered how long she could string out her trip to Devon, and began to torture herself thinking of the kind of sex she and Fielding might have the next time — which she sincerely hoped would be very soon.

Then the phone rang. It was the news editor, Reg Foley, calling from his home at just after 7 a.m. to tell her that the editor wanted to buy up James Martin O'Donnell.

Joanna was not enthusiastic. She still thought Jimbo was a guilty man, didn't like the idea of her paper throwing money at him.

'He's been acquitted, Jo,' said Foley. 'That makes him innocent, OK? Anyway, it's what the editor wants, so let's give him what he wants, shall we?'

Taylor was already on the case but naturally Tom Mitchell wanted his chief crime correspondent to mastermind the buy-up attempt — which meant Jo was needed back in London pretty damn smartish.

155

So that was one question answered. Her trip to Devon was over already. She would certainly not be seeing Fielding again that day and she had no idea how long it might be before she did.

Obediently she packed her small bag. Before leaving the room she called Fielding at Heavitree Road. He hadn't arrived yet. Well, it was still not quite eight o'clock. She left a message, in what she hoped was a businesslike manner, saying that she had been called back to her office in London and would he please phone her there later that day.

★　★　★

He didn't phone. Not that day. Not the next day. Not all week.

Joanna was offended. She left a second message at Heavitree Road. Then she phoned twice more without leaving a message at all. She supposed she would have to accept that for him she had just been another quick lay. After all, she knew his reputation well enough. She had even told him that. Why should she think for a moment that their one night in the sack would have been any different for him than all the other times. She had thought so, though. And that was the problem. For her, certainly.

Apart from any other considerations, his silence made her feel cheap. Fortunately she had little time to dwell on it. The Jimbo O'Donnell buy-up took all her time and energies. First she was involved in the negotiations and then, when the *Comet* succeeded

156

in outbidding its rivals, Mitchell assigned her to do the interviews.

In spite of her feelings about O'Donnell it was always exciting to be at the sharp end of a big story and Jimbo was the sharp end all right. They took him to a remote hotel on the outskirts of Epping Forest in order to keep him away from the opposition until the series the *Comet* planned to run had been published. Joanna was booked into the room next to Jimbo and found that she was quite grateful that a *Comet* photographer was also booked into the hotel, plus another reporter whose job was primarily to act as a kind of extra minder.

There was something about the way the man looked at her which she found deeply disturbing. His attitude to her as a woman bordered on contempt. He had reverted to what seemed to be a penchant for wearing tight T-shirts to show off a torso which seemed to have become even more muscular during his stay in prison. Not to mention his horrible tattoo. He also wore overly tight black jeans and had an unpleasant habit of periodically and quite blatantly adjusting his crotch while staring at her challengingly. More than ever Joanna was convinced that he was guilty as hell, a sex monster who had got away with a truly dreadful crime — but in order to do her job she tried not to think about that.

Jimbo treated her to a predictable diatribe about his innocence and the police persecution that continually dogged him and his family. But among it there was some very good stuff, some pearls, in fact.I AM NOT THE BEAST OF DARTMOOR, MY

157

WRONGFUL ARREST NIGHTMARE, screamed banner headlines in the *Comet* when the paper ran the first instalment of a three-part serialisation of the Jimbo O'Donnell story just six days after his acquittal. 'I'd never hurt an innocent girl. I'm no sex monster. Just because some of my family have records, we're always persecuted. They said I raped before but she led me on. If it was rape it was only date rape. And I was just a kid. I could never kill etc., etc.' It was the story everybody wanted and Joanna was a good interviewer. She had coaxed Jimbo into talking about the earlier rape conviction, thus allowing the paper to print material it might otherwise have considered legally unwise.

She returned to the office on the day that the third and final instalment ran. Her job was over, the story written and published. The *Comet* no longer needed to mind Jimbo. The paper had successfully completed its scoop. Tom Mitchell was well pleased. Public demand had been such that the print run had been substantially increased. In the evening she went to the Stab to celebrate. It was always immensely satisfying to have a few drinks in Fleet Street pubs when you knew you had pulled off the big one — even if it was a buy-up, which invariably lessened the thrill a little for Jo.

It was nine days, now, since she had spent that one night with Fielding. Still no word. She didn't let herself think about it. She was on a roll, after all.

Paul Potter was in the bar and he bought a bottle of champagne, which they shared. But Jo left alone, the only way ever for a slightly drunk woman reporter to leave a Fleet Street pub, if she had any sense.

There was a car parked on the double yellow right outside and as she stepped on to the pavement its passenger door swung open, blocking her way. An arm reached out and a hand fastened round her wrist.

Alarmed, she almost cried out, then she realised who was in the car. It was Fielding. 'Christ,' she said. 'Are you stalking me or something?'

'You should be so lucky, darling, get in the car.'

He sounded angry. She hesitated. He half pulled her into the vehicle. 'I've been reading that shit of yours, I just wanted to tell you to your face what I think of you.'

She stiffened. This was the man she had been aching to see for over a week, but she had never imagined meeting him in this mood. Suddenly she felt very sober indeed. She made herself respond in an even voice, as if she were not at all concerned. 'And you've driven all the way to London specially, have you?' she asked casually.

'Don't flatter yourself. I wouldn't drive across fuckin' Exeter to see you.'

'I see.' She struggled to keep calm.

'You're just scum like all the rest of the hacks,' he hissed at her. 'How could you pay money to that perverted bastard? How could you give him a platform for his twisted bloody lies? How could you?'

She felt as if he had hit her. 'It's my job,' she said.

'Yes, and your job stinks.'

'Really,' she said. 'Unlike yours, then. At least I

don't go around planting evidence on people.' She got out of the car as she spoke and started to walk swiftly away from him.

He was too quick for her. He was alongside before she had even thought about breaking into a run. He grabbed her by one shoulder and pushed her against the pub wall. He looked absolutely furious. His eyes were blazing. He half shook her. 'You bitch,' he hissed at her through clenched teeth.

For a moment she really thought he was going to hit her.

Then the expression in his eyes softened, and the change in him was so fast that she was completely taken by surprise. He leaned forward and began to kiss her.

She responded at once, kissing him back with all her might, her body out of control. His hands found their way inside her jacket, she felt his fingers tighten round her breasts, his hardness shoving into her just as it had done the first time.

Almost as abruptly as he had begun, he stopped, pulling away from her. They stood on the pavement both breathing hard, looking at each other.

'I really didn't intend to let this happen again,' he said quietly.

She didn't reply, but reached for him, putting one arm round his neck, and drew his face to hers.

All too soon he pulled away again. 'We're standing outside your office pub, that's even worse than Heavitree Road police station, isn't it?' he enquired, his voice lighter now, his tone mischievous.

'You're dead right it is,' she replied. It was too. The extraordinary thing was she would probably have let him fuck her right there against the wall before she had even considered the implications.

'This time I'm the one with the hotel room,' he said, very serious again.

She just nodded and followed him to his car.

★　★　★

Unlike Fielding, she did make some effort to remember she was still married. She left his hotel at 4 a.m. and got a taxi home, creeping into the spare room where she spent most of her nights now anyway.

Alone in the small single bed, she put her hand between her legs and remembered the pleasure she had so recently experienced. God, why was it so good? She really had no idea, but it had been even better than the first time. And it wasn't over. Fielding had told her that he had to spend two more weeks in London. He had been sent to town to work on the London end of a long-running fraud case. It mostly involved endless boring days poring over records in Company House and he assumed he had been assigned to the operation so quickly after the O'Donnell trial principally in order to get him out of the firing line back in Exeter. He had also told her that he was already the subject of an internal inquiry following the allegations made against him in court.

The hotel wasn't much, just about the cheapest available, but she supposed they were lucky he wasn't in a section house. Apparently there had been no room. The sex had not been affected by the insalubrious surroundings. It had been, if anything,

161

even better than before. Fielding had asked Joanna if she could join him for the rest of his time there.

She didn't hesitate. In the morning she told her husband that she would be out of town for two weeks on a story. He didn't even bother to ask any questions. She knew he didn't really care what she did any more and wondered why she had gone through the motions of returning home the previous night. Habit, she supposed. She packed a small bag and at the end of the working day high-tailed it to Fielding's hotel room as soon as she could.

They had planned to go out for a meal. They didn't make it. Just went to bed instantly and stayed there. She marvelled at his sexual energy and invention, and, indeed, at her own. She couldn't believe how excited he made her. Fortunately it seemed to be the same for him.

'I can't get enough of you,' he told her. He admitted then that he had planned to walk away from her, that from the start his feelings for her had been so strong that he had considered it too dangerous to continue seeing her.

'That's why I didn't phone you, I never intended to contact you again after that first night,' he explained. 'Really I didn't. And when I confronted you outside that pub I had utterly convinced myself that I was just there to give you a piece of my mind about that fucking awful story.'

He smiled, softening his next words. 'I still think the O'Donnell buy-up was a fucking disgrace, by the way.'

She had not bothered to reply. They both knew that everything in their lives, even including, for

once, their respective careers, paled into insignifi-
cance compared with the desperate urgency of their
love affair.

'Then, when I saw you, legs up to your armpits,
hair down to your waist, knowing how sexy you are,
knowing what you're like there . . . ' He placed his
hand over her crotch. Quite lightly. But just the heat
of his touch was enough to send her wild again. 'I
just couldn't keep my hands off you,' he continued,
moving his fingers as if to prove the point.

'Thank God,' she breathed huskily, reaching out
for him.

Each time the sex seemed to get better and better.
Joanna wondered how long that could go on for.
She had never experienced orgasms like this before
and yet somehow the more she had of Fielding the
more she wanted him. She never seemed to be
satisfied. And even when neither of them was
capable of any more sexual activity she needed to be
close to him, to be touching him all the time, almost
as if continually to make sure he was still there.

Her feelings for him grew day by day during that
stolen fortnight. But she was confused by them. In
many ways he was just the sort of man she didn't
like, yet her desire for him knew no bounds. And, in
any case, there were so many different sides to him.

One night he confounded her. After making love
to her he rolled off her on to his back, then reached
out again with one hand and touched her mouth
lightly. 'I think I've fallen in love with you,' he told
her quietly.

Stupidly, perhaps, she thought at first he was just
teasing her. Fielding did not fall in love with the

women in his life. He bedded them and, when he tired of them, left them and went home to his wife. She knew that well enough and she had always believed that it was madness to get involved with him. She felt vulnerable with him and she didn't like that.

She decided to play him at his own game. 'That's what you say to all the girls, I know your reputation, after all,' she said lightly.

He wrapped his arms around her. 'Sleeping around and being with you are two different things, you silly cow,' he told her affectionately and kissed her on the end of her nose. God, he was a patronising, arrogant, sexist sod, she thought. Why did he have this extraordinary hold over her? 'That was then. This is now. I want to be with you all the time,' he continued.

'You have a wife and children, Mike. I know your kind. I write about them every day. You always go back to your families.' She didn't like to be taken for a fool and she still had a suspicion that was what he was doing.

His voice hardened. 'What do you mean, you know my kind? You quite obviously don't know anything about me. Do you really think I'm just fooling around with you? Do you think what we have is commonplace? Do you honestly think it could be like this between us if that were true. Do you?'

She shook her head lamely. She supposed he was right. How could it?

'Of course it couldn't be,' he continued more gently, not waiting for her to think of anything to say. 'I've never known anything like this before, never. Look, I've been thinking — I'm going to try for a transfer to the Met.'

'What?' She had really never expected anything like this from him.

'I mean it, Jo. I can't stay with Ruth any more. I'd be living a lie now I've found this with you. I'm going to tell her when I get home. And that'll be the end of it.'

7

He didn't leave his wife, of course. Although for a time Joanna really believed that he meant to. Their affair very quickly came to mean everything to her. And she had no reason to doubt that it was the same for him. The frequency with which he managed to manoeuvre time to be with her in London astonished her.

'When all you think about in life is one thing and how you can achieve it, it's surprising how much you succeed,' he told her, grinning. And she knew he was speaking the truth, because that was how it was for her, too.

It was as if every minute that she was not with him was a waste of time. She knew her mind was not on her job in the way that it had always been before, and wondered just how much that was being noticed in the office and at the Yard. She and Chris were living more or less separate lives and had discussed divorce. But for almost three months after the trial and the start of her affair with Fielding they continued to share a home, at least most of the time, and she still went through the motions of giving plausible work-related reasons for her prolonged absences. Habit again. But also she was trying to keep it as civilised as possible. And she successfully kept the affair from her husband — until the anonymous caller decided to start a new campaign.

It was towards the end of July when Chris

received a call, telling him, in graphic detail, all about it. Joanna was allegedly away on a story. Again. Actually she was with Fielding. The timing of the phone call was impeccable. The detailed knowledge impressive. But then it would be. You can never keep anything secret from a load of hacks. She had no doubt it was one of her colleagues who was being so malicious and still believed it to be almost certainly Manners.

'They're with each other right now, did you know that? They can't keep their hands off each other. He's even fucked her in his office . . .'

Not true but near enough.

Chris repeated the entire conversation to her on her return home. He appeared to be more upset than she would have expected. After all their marriage had deteriorated to the point of being virtually non-existent.

'Just tell me the truth, Joanna,' he said. At first he didn't show his anger, really. He didn't yell at her and he just looked sad.

She had no intention of lying to him. Not any more. Chris deserved better, she thought, and in any case her affair with Fielding was too important to lie about. 'It's all true, more or less,' she told him quietly. 'Not some of the details, thank God, but we are having an affair. I'm in love with him and he with me.'

Once she had made the admission her husband's attitude changed completely. Maybe it was just wounded pride, maybe he really was deeply hurt. She didn't know. But he totally lost his temper. 'Please, spare me the sentimental self-delusion,' he shouted at her. 'For God's sake, the man treats you like a slag. He's fucked you in his office, in the middle of a police station. Did the other pigs join in, or did they just watch? Over his desk was it, or on the floor doggie fashion? Give him blow jobs in taxi cabs do you . . . '

'Don't do this, please, Chris,' she interrupted him, resisting the urge to tell him that sex in the office was one of the details the bastard caller had got wrong — even if only just.

She reached a hand out to him. He knocked it away. It hadn't really occurred to her that her husband would be this angry, or, indeed, as wounded as he patently was. Not any more. She thought they had gone beyond that. And she cursed herself for not telling him about the affair before he had to learn of it in the dreadful way that he had. She had meant to. It was just that she'd always had a way of putting off unpleasantness and she had hoped eventually to extricate herself from her marriage in as dignified a manner as possible before Chris needed to know.

The next day she moved into a hotel and by the end of the week she had found herself a flat to rent in the Barbican. She'd always thought that the sixties development on the edge of the City was a bit of a concrete jungle, but the one-bedroomed flat had a beautifully spacious open-plan living area with a splendid wood-block floor and looked out over an ornamental lake to the old Roman wall and the church beyond. It was also very central, of course.

'Good,' said Fielding when she phoned him in Exeter to tell him the news. 'I've just got the job to sort out, then I'll tell Ruth. I'll be moving in with you before you know it.'

However, the months passed and nothing changed. They talked constantly on the phone. Most weeks Fielding seemed to manage to get to London for at least one night, sometimes more. Joanna had no idea how he managed it, but he did. It was nowhere near enough, though. The physical attraction between them did not diminish. The sexual chemistry seemed to grow more intense rather than less. Joanna was quite sure they were both deeply in love. But still Fielding did not leave his wife.

Christmas came and went, and Joanna found out just how hard it was at holiday times to be embroiled in an affair with a married man. He spent the festive season with his family, of course, and she volunteered to work on Christmas Day. The demands of a daily paper did have certain uses.

Early in the new year Mike claimed that he had finally told Ruth and his children that he was leaving them for Joanna. Later, Joanna was not even sure of that.

'I'm not going to be able to rush it, Jo,' he had said. 'It's my daughter who's the problem. She's ten now. I don't think I realised how much they take in at that age. She just cries all the time and begs me not to leave her. Every time I go out of the house she makes me promise I'll be coming back. I just have to give it some time, Jo.'

She agreed with him, sympathised with him even. Eventually he said he thought his daughter was getting used to the idea, that maybe she was beginning to understand at last that it wasn't her he was leaving. That he would never leave her. Maybe he would bring her to meet Jo.

He didn't, of course, but Jo was hopeful. For a while she thought he really was going to do the deed now. But no. Instead, he told her that his wife's mother was dying. She had cancer. 'She's been more of a mother to me than my own, Jo. We don't expect her to live more than a few weeks. I really feel I have to stay with Ruth to see her through this.'

She went along with that too. What choice did she have? She felt guilty enough about breaking up his family — though God knew why she should with her knowledge of his track record. If she had not become a threat to his marriage, then it would surely eventually have been something or someone else.

Then, when he told her that his mother-in-law had died, Jo's hopes were renewed again. 'It won't be long now,' he said. 'But Ruth is in a right state, so I may not be able to get away quite so much for a bit while I settle her down. I owe her that much, don't I? But it'll be over soon and we'll be together for good. In a month or two max — I promise.'

It never seemed to be over, though, and they were not together. Not in a month, or two months, or even three. And she was indeed seeing less of him than ever.

He explained one day that he thought Ruth was having a breakdown. She needed treatment. She was behaving in a totally neurotic fashion and that wasn't like her. 'She's threatening to take me to the cleaners if I do leave her, Jo,' he told her on the

170

phone, which seemed fast to be becoming their greatest point of contact. 'I've always said I'd provide for her and the kids, but she wants to wipe me out. I've got to sort it, somehow. She doesn't just want the house, she's after my pension, the lot. I can't let her have everything, can I? I mean, we have to be practical as well, don't we?'

Joanna agreed, in a distant kind of way, that yes, of course they must be practical.

When she hung up she made herself think clearly about the situation. Fielding had come up with every possible story in the family package — distraught child, neurotic wife, dying elderly parent, financial problems. It was beginning to dawn on her that she had probably been right in the first place. Mike Fielding was not going to leave home, for her, or for anyone else.

Somehow she didn't doubt that he had genuinely intended to. She believed that he had fallen head over heels in love with her. Indeed, she believed that he remained head over heels in love with her. But in the end that didn't seem to help much. He was tearing her apart. As far as her own feelings were concerned, sometimes she was no longer sure whether she hated him or loved him. What she was sure of was that she could not let it go on this way. She was drinking too much and smoking too much. She had lost weight, and she felt tired and listless all the time. She lived for her meetings with Mike, yet she knew she was being destroyed by a relationship she had started to realise was going nowhere.

Displaying a strength she did not know she still had, she eventually issued Fielding with an ultimatum. It was the oldest one in the book. 'Leave your wife or stay away from me,' she told him. 'And I'm not going to let you touch me again unless you do leave home.'

He had just arrived for yet another stolen night. He had caught the train from Exeter that evening and had to leave again early in the morning. 'Oh, come on, Jo, I'm doing my best,' he told her. 'It won't be like this for ever.' He didn't sound too shocked or upset.

She realised he probably didn't believe her. This was what women usually said to married men, wasn't it? And they almost never meant it, just kept on putting up with the three-card trick. But Joanna had never said this to him before. He had brought it on himself with more than a year of broken promises. And she meant every word of it.

'Well you're not chucking me out right now, surely,' he said, trying to sound jokey. 'I've just come on a two-and-a-half-hour train journey.'

'You can sleep on the sofa,' she told him and she meant that, too. But he cheated, something at which he excelled, she considered wryly. He got up in the night and slid into her bed and damn near into her before she awakened. The excitement rose in her as it always did. They made love, and all the while he told her how much he loved her and promised they would be together. They really would.

In the morning she felt angry again, with him and herself. And as he left she said, 'I still mean what I said, Mike. This really will be the last time unless you keep your promises, unless you do leave home. I've never pushed you, the decision has always been yours and that's still the case. But you can't have it both ways any more.'

He smiled in that rather patronising way he had and left.

He didn't leave home and Jo kept her word to him and to herself. She told him it was over. Then she refused even to talk to him on the phone. Once he turned up at the office and another time at her flat. She didn't open the door, but for several minutes she heard him outside in the corridor, ringing the bell and calling through the letter box. 'I know you're in there, Jo. Please open the door. You don't understand . . . '

But I do, she thought. Oh, but I do understand so very well. And so, I imagine, does your wife. With a great effort of will she sat quietly in her living room until he finally left. And so, in August 1982, just over a year after she had left her husband, Joanna brought the most exciting, most mesmerising relationship of her life to an end. It nearly broke her heart. But ultimately she preferred losing him to sharing him.

★ ★ ★

Paul Potter remained a good friend to Joanna throughout the whole thing. Although her affair with Fielding had, with the usual alacrity, become common knowledge in the office, Paul was the only person she ever confided anything in.

After she left her husband, on the countless evenings when Fielding was not around, the end-of-day drinks in the Stab had frequently stretched into supper at Jo Allen's or the Bleeding Awful. It was called the Bleeding Heart, really, and was actually rather a good restaurant and wine bar, and certainly not awful at all. But juggling with names was a permanent fixture of Fleet Street life.

During that period she began to tell Paul more and more, even about the anonymous phone calls, and how the last one had brought things to a head with her husband and led to her finally leaving him, and also about how unsure she was of Fielding and what he really intended, in spite of his promises.

'Well, at least now your own marriage is over you'll find out soon enough what he's prepared to do about his,' Paul had said sensibly. 'And I don't have to tell you how rarely men with families leave them for somebody else, do I?'

She had shaken her head. Potter was just what she needed in a friend. His feet were so firmly on the ground it might help her keep hers there. Paul was such easy company, clever, funny, unthreatening. She began to enjoy her times with him more and more, and to seek him out with greater frequency. It didn't ever occur to her to wonder at how readily he always made himself available for her. She knew he was single and lived alone, but she had no idea what commitments or relationships there were in his life. Certainly he always made time for her and she was grateful for it. But she continued to think of him as just a friend.

'The pillocks in the office probably think we're having an affair too,' she told him after several drinks one night and laughed as if at the absurdity of it.

'More than likely,' Paul had said, with a shrug and a brief smile.

Looking back later, she wondered whether she would have had the strength to finish with Mike in the way that she had without Paul's support. Somehow she rather doubted it. Paul had played an important part just by being there and being someone to talk to. Someone trustworthy, someone who never seemed to tire of listening.

It was not until a month or so after she split with Mike that he made any kind of move on her.

He suggested they go to dinner at the Ivy to celebrate his recent appointment to assistant editor. She had agreed readily enough. She loved the Ivy and she had been very pleased for Paul about his promotion. It had become apparent to her that the career of this quiet yet very talented man was beginning to take off, and Joanna found that she was delighted. The more senior a position he managed to achieve the better, she thought. She reckoned it would make a pleasant change from the old-fashioned bulldozer sort to have a man who was cleverly thoughtful and imaginative at the helm.

They had an excellent dinner and yet again she thought how much she enjoyed his company and how entertaining he was. Indeed, she barely remembered Fielding all evening.

Outside the Ivy he asked her if she could manage one more drink.

She was beginning to get the taste and said she was sure she could.

He hailed a taxi and gave an address in Kennington, which she assumed was his home. 'I have a rather good bottle in the fridge,' he said.

He lived in a beautifully restored four-storey house in one of those lovely Kennington squares. Not all the houses were renovated to the standard of Paul's home, though.

'It was falling down when I bought it and I got it for a song,' he told her. 'I think it's quite nice now, don't you?'

She told him that was an understatement. The house was drop-dead gorgeous. Paul's taste was impeccable. It was simply decorated and furnished, and some very striking abstract originals by Clive Gunnell, one of the few artists whose work she recognised immediately, hung on the plain cream walls.

The more you got to know this man the better he seemed, she thought. But he was something of a dark horse.

He produced a bottle of vintage Bollinger and only when they had almost finished it did he make a very gentle pass at her, kissing her lightly on the lips. It was in stark contrast to the impassioned first clinch with Mike, Joanna thought, but perhaps this was just what she needed in life. Certainly she could do with a sexual encounter again, that was for sure. Even a month seemed like a long period of abstinence, coming after the intense eroticism of her relationship with Mike.

As she had expected, sex with Paul Potter did not live up to that. Not straight away, at any rate. But Paul was a man who worked at what he did, whatever it was. The more she was with him, the better the sex became as he grew more aware of what she wanted, what she needed.

After that first night together their relationship moved very fast. Perhaps because she was unused to living alone and to being single, before she realised quite what was going on they were spending just about every night together either in his house or her apartment.

And suddenly, and she had little idea how that happened either, they began to talk about marriage. She found herself agreeing that it would be a rather nice idea. One evening he turned up at the Barbican with a beautiful diamond ring, which she allowed him to slide on to the third finger of her left hand. He helped her rush through her divorce and arranged for them to be married in the City with just a handful of friends present.

It was only later that she realised how much work he'd put into all the plans and all the arrangements, for the divorce, the forthcoming wedding and a honeymoon in New York. There was little doubt that for Joanna her marriage was something that happened on the rebound.

But Paul made absolutely no secret of the fact that it was something he had longed for and always hoped might happen one day if he were patient.

She had yet to learn how determined and focused her husband-to-be was, beneath his quiet and unassuming exterior. But as their wedding day loomed — December 1982, two weeks before Christmas and just three months after they first slept together, Paul said there was no point in hanging around at their age, after all he was quite sure of his own mind and she hoped she was of hers too now — she began to realise that she felt happy and content for the first time in almost as long as she could remember. There were no longer these huge tensions and uncertainties hanging over her. She didn't have to sit around waiting for the phone to ring, wondering if the man she loved could get away to be with her and how long he could stay. Her life was suddenly completely stress-free. Paul made absolutely sure of that and it was a very pleasant change to be looked after in this way.

However, the knives remained out for her in the office. The small but powerful coterie of male journalists who disliked and resented her so much, led as ever by Manners, were apparently out to get her with a vengeance still, their resentment no doubt fuelled by her projected marriage to a man now fairly obviously destined for big things in the newspaper world. Their continual comments in the office, to each other but clearly meant to be overheard by her, were getting extremely tedious. Particularly as they were using that familiar old trick. She could not really defend herself because she could never be absolutely sure that the snatches of barbed comment, more often than not obscene, were indeed directed at her. She was pretty damned sure, though. And it infuriated her.

'He's hung like a donkey of course, that's what she likes . . . '

' . . . lets him give it her up the arse . . . '

'No wonder there's a fucking queue for her.'

Jo had no choice except to pretend she did not hear. But boy, did it make her mad. She did not repeat any of this to Paul. There was no point. She did not want to stir things up any more and she feared any intervention by him would just make matters worse. She just tried not to think about it.

But three days before their wedding she returned to the Kennington house they now shared, unusually a couple of hours later than her fiancé, to find Paul oddly angry. 'I've just had a phone call from your old friend,' he told her at once.

'What do you mean?' she asked, taken completely unaware.

'The same perverted creep who plagued you and Chris, I assume,' he said. Paul's lips curled in distaste. 'You can guess the sort of thing, 'Do you know how your girlfriend gets her stories? She just takes her knickers off.' More and worse. I don't even intend to repeat it. It's just sick.'

She was horrified. 'Oh, my God, now the bastard's starting on you,' she blurted out. 'I am so sorry. I promise you, Paul, I've not even seen Mike since you and I have been together.'

'Don't worry, I know that, darling,' said Paul. He glanced at her with concern. 'Jo, you didn't think I was angry at *you*, did you? Absolutely not, I can assure you. If you think for one moment that I would let some twisted creep harm our relationship then you don't know me very well.'

Jo thought he might still be right about that, but the more she did get to know him the more she was coming to like and respect him. And love, too, she supposed. He was some man, that was for certain. Paul was treating the kind of incident that could rock long-term marriages with cool disdain. He was angry. Yes. But he was also calm and thoughtful. She studied him with open admiration.

'I have the advantage over poor Chris,' he said. 'In the first place I believe in you and trust you absolutely. In the second place I know that bastard Manners and, in spite of his somewhat pathetic attempts to muffle his voice, talking into a handkerchief or whatever, I am absolutely sure it was him on the phone. In the third place, I am in a unique position to deal with him.' He smiled his enigmatic smile. 'Now come here and have a cuddle,' he commanded. Gratefully she went into his arms. Paul's strength was such a comfort. His certainty such a relief. With him there seemed to be no problems that couldn't be overcome with extraordinary ease. She felt the worries that had been beginning to settle on her shoulders again lift once more. With Paul she never seemed to have anything to worry about. To her annoyance she started to cry into his shoulder. But her tears came from relief and happiness.

'That's it, my darling. Cry as much as you want. You're safe now. I'll sort it out.'

* * *

Joanna was in the press room at the Yard the next day when a call came through on the *Comet* phone — a direct link with the news desk — summoning Manners back to the office for a sudden meeting with the editor. Later Tom Mitchell phoned Jo personally, as head of the crime department, to tell her that the older man had been offered, and had accepted, a redundancy package. He had been asked to clear his desk at once. Joanna knew perfectly well that early retirement would never have entered Manners's head. He was the kind of old hack who would try to hang on by his fingertips long after his sell-by date because — one of the reasons Joanna's appointment as chief crime correspondent had so incensed him — his job had always been his life. Actually, she wouldn't knock him for that. It was true of some of the best. 'What happened?'

'I'm afraid that's between me and Frank,' said the editor.

'There must have been a reason . . . ' her voice tailed off.

'Private reasons, isn't that what they say?' said Tom and she realised she was getting nowhere.

For once the office gossip network got nothing either. She confronted Paul, of course, but as usual, he gave little away. 'Now what could I possibly have had to do with it?' he remarked. But the wide smile he treated her to was not as enigmatic as usual. In fact, it was decidedly self-satisfied. And the next time he made love to her he held her very tightly and told her that there was something she must always remember. 'For as long as you and I are together nobody will ever harm you, Jo,' he said. 'I will always make sure of that, I promise you.'

She was beginning to realise that she was marrying a quite exceptional man.

* * *

Fielding only found out that Joanna had married again when he rang her office, for the umpteenth time, in yet another fruitless attempt to speak to her. Until that fateful moment he had been quite unable to believe that he would not be able to persuade her to see him again eventually. The secretary who answered the phone told him casually that she was on her honeymoon. Very carefully he replaced the telephone receiver. He was in love with Joanna Bartlett. He had really meant to leave his wife for her and still did not quite know why he had been unable to.

Joanna had been right about him. His feelings for her had been, still were, entirely genuine. And he had always intended to fulfil his promises to her. It was simply that somehow, when push came to shove, he just couldn't. Joanna had been right in another way too. He had indeed never even told his wife about her. He didn't know why he had not managed to do that either. He had meant to. And, more important, he did not know why he had lied to Joanna continually. The excuses — the distraught daughter, the dying mother-in-law — had been the easy way, of course, a method of smoothing his path, keeping Jo sweet. He had been unable to bring himself to face the upheaval required in order to commit himself properly to her and he had been terrified of losing her. So he had lied. Maybe if he had been honest with her he might have been able to keep her.

She had known he had lied, he was sure of it, known he had continually deceived her. And in the end she wouldn't stand for it. He had respected her for that — more than he respected himself, that was for sure.

His life was becoming a complete mess. The internal investigation into Jimbo O'Donnell's evidence-planting allegation against him had petered out, as Fielding had predicted it would and he'd never even been suspended from duty. But he was quite sure that his high-flying career had been dealt an almost fatal blow. The word was always going to be that at best he was flawed and couldn't be trusted, at worst he was bent. Certainly there had been no sign of his previously expected promotion coming through. Nor, he felt, was there likely to be for a very long time.

Now, with Joanna irrevocably out of his life, he could not imagine that he'd ever again be half the man he had once been. Not in any way.

Jo was married again. He was so stunned he had not even asked to whom. It was extraordinary. They had only been apart for four months and she was married already, and he didn't even know who her new husband was.

All he knew was that he'd lost her. Really lost her. For ever.

Fielding did what he usually did. He reached for the whisky bottle.

Part Two

8

Twenty years after the murder of Angela Phillips, the whole chain of events still seemed so vivid to Joanna at her desk in Canary Wharf. It had been the most important time of her life, really, in many different ways. And yet it was a part of her past she was not sure she wanted to delve into again.

Hearing Mike Fielding's voice had somehow not been the surprise it should have been after so long. Maybe it was just that she had always half expected that one day their paths would cross once more.

He hadn't said his name. He would have known he didn't need to. Not to her. Not even after almost two decades.

'Hello, Mike.'

It seemed a long time before he spoke again. Perhaps he was hoping she would continue. But he had phoned her. He could take the lead.

'How are you?' he asked eventually.

'Fine. How are you?'

'Oh. I'm fine too.'

Awkwardly polite, what a way for them to be after all that had happened between them, she thought. But then, eighteen years or so was a big chunk out of your life.

'Something's happened, though, something I thought you might want to know about, maybe help with . . .'

'So you phone after all this time because you want

187

my help, do you? Bloody typical!' She wasn't sure if she was angry or amused, or maybe just exasperated. He didn't seem to have changed much, that was for certain.

He didn't respond to her remark, but continued as if she had not spoken. 'The Beast of Dartmoor — we've got a DNA match,' he told her flatly. 'And it's O'Donnell.'

'Ah!' Again she wasn't surprised. Like Mike she'd always believed in O'Donnell's guilt and had never been able quite to forget the case, however much she pretended to herself that she had. She had been almost as involved in it as Mike had, perhaps always believed it would one day come back into her life again.

He told her all he knew, about the drink-driving arrest, the routine DNA swab, the computer picking it up.

'Bang to rights, but I can do bugger all about it,' he finished. 'I don't need to tell you about double jeopardy. The bastard can't be tried again.'

'No, but why don't you guys do what you usually do in these situations?'

'What do you mean?' he asked sharply, instinctively on the defensive, even with her, perhaps particularly with her.

She gave a small tut of irritation. 'Get him for something else, of course. He can't stand trial for murder again, but what about rape and kidnap? If O'Donnell's guilty of murder he's certainly guilty of both of those, and he's never actually been charged with either.'

'Doesn't work, Jo,' he said. 'We tried. Put just that

to the CPS and they threw it out. Still part of the original circumstances. Abuse of process. Not in the public interest after twenty years. Prospect of a conviction unlikely. Usual crap.

'You've no idea how tough it is to get the Crown Prosecution Service to accept that kind of sidestepping nowadays. And the mess the law's in over DNA doesn't help. If they don't have a precedent to look up in some dusty old book, lawyers don't have a clue.

'Apart from double jeopardy the biggest snag with O'Donnell is that you can't use DNA obtained during one case, a drink-driving offence or anything else, come to that, as evidence in any other unrelated investigation. Section 64 of PACE. Bloody daft, if you ask me and high time it was changed — but there it is.'

Joanna leaned back in her chair. PACE. The Police and Criminal Evidence Act. Of course. She'd kind of known that part of what he had told her. But he was right. It was complex. 'Presumably you haven't still got the blood and urine samples taken when he was originally arrested for murder?' she asked.

'Destroyed on his lawyers' instructions right after the case. Acquitted man's right, as you know. And, God knows, he had the kind of legal team who weren't going to miss that.'

'You've checked, I suppose? It's not unknown for those forensic boys to keep samples they should have destroyed, is it?'

'No, it's not. It's a lottery, though. In fact it's always a lottery whether or not samples from a twenty-year-old case are still in store. But if they had been we would have had a match come up before the drink-driving thing, because we went through every outstanding murder and rape on our books about three years ago and did DNA checks on all the suspects whenever there were samples still available — I think every force in the country has done it now. That's why O'Donnell's DNA, taken from Angela Phillips's body, was already logged.'

'And you can't make him give a new DNA sample because the CPS won't let you charge him with anything?' She was beginning to remember now. PACE again. The police had the power to take non intimate-samples — like head hair or a buccul swab — without a suspect's permission only under quite precise conditions, basically if he is charged with a recordable offence or is being held in police custody on the authority of a court.

'Exactly.'

'Of course, you could pop round and ask the wanker if he'd like to give a voluntary sample, to clear the matter up once and for all, as it were,' continued Joanna.

Fielding's laugh was mirthless.

'You mean you don't think there's much chance of him co-operating?' she queried ironically.

'I've been round, actually . . . well, I just happened to be in his neighbourhood.' Fielding paused. 'Only it was unofficial, if you see what I mean . . .'

She saw. And she wasn't surprised. He'd been told it was over, that there would be no further police action, but he couldn't resist jumping straight in. 'Brilliant,' she said. 'And how far did it get you?'

'Not very. I just wanted him to know that I knew. That's all.'

She could imagine it all too well. 'Did he say anything?'

'Smug as ever. Even if we could prove he'd had sex with the dead girl, so what, he said. Maybe she'd been a willing partner, maybe she'd begged him for it. Didn't mean he'd killed her. I tell you, Jo, I nearly smashed his face in.'

'You didn't, though, I hope.'

'Let's just say it was a very close thing.' He chuckled.

'Mike, not even a jury would swallow that 'willing partner' crap, surely. Not with what happened to that poor kid?'

'I don't think so either, but it's irrelevant, like I've told you, certainly as far as police action is concerned.' His voice suddenly became very earnest. 'Look, Jo, I've gone over and over in my mind what we could do to get the bastard. I reckon there's only one thing left. A private prosecution.'

'But double jeopardy still applies. And the burden of proof is the same.'

'Yes. I reckon he could be done for rape and kidnap in a private action, though. The CPS wouldn't have to be involved and I believe a really good barrister could swing it. I really do. Particularly if we made sure that the committal proceedings were after October.'

'What happens in October?'

'The Human Rights Act finally comes into force in the UK,' he said.

Of course. She should have remembered that. 'But it won't change double jeopardy, will it?' she asked. 'It's supposed to be about protecting people's rights, after all.'

'Yes. But the rights of victims as well as suspected criminals, Jo. I've just been on a course. It's mandatory for coppers now, it's got to be, or the whole damned lot of us will end up being locked up instead of the fucking villains. You can start forgetting Westminster and the Law Lords. Think Strasbourg and Brussels. Mostly it's a nightmare, but hard to believe as it may be, Europe's actually come up with one thing that might help those of us who are at least supposed to be on the side of the good guys. Look it up. The Seventh Protocol of the European Convention on Human Rights, Article Four. Oh — and then go to Section Six of the Human Rights Act.'

'OK,' she said casually. 'I'll look it up. I don't quite get where this conversation is leading, though. Why are you telling me all this?'

'Because I want you to go to that poor kid's family and persuade them to take out a private prosecution,' he said.

'Oh, is that all?'

'Christ, Jo, you're a bit heavy on the sarcasm today, aren't you,' he countered, the irritation clear in his voice.

'You really don't change, Mike,' she murmured softly.

'I was thinking just the same thing about you,' he said.

'OK, why do you want me to go to her family?

Why don't you go to them yourself? Do they know about the DNA match, has anybody told them?'

'No, they don't know and the brass have decided they shouldn't be told. No point, too painful, some such bollocks. I don't agree with it, but I don't dare go against them. I've only got two and a half years to do for my thirty and I have enough blots on my record as it is.'

'Maybe you have changed after all,' she said, her tone lightly bantering.

'Maybe,' he said. 'Or maybe I've just settled for what I've got. I've risked enough already. There comes a time. The Phillipses wouldn't want to hear from me anyway, they blamed me, you know, left me in no doubt that they considered me responsible for the whole damn cock-up. I'm the last person to persuade them to get involved in another major court case, to drag it all up again.'

'I don't think they were exactly mad about me in the end either,' she remarked wryly. 'Not after the buy-up.'

'Perhaps, but you didn't have the same personal involvement — and you've still got clout.'

'What's that supposed to mean?'

'Well, I'm damn sure they'd still like to see their daughter's murderer get what's coming to him, but whether or not they'll be prepared to take on a case against him by themselves I very much doubt. Apart from the anguish of it, there's the financial side too. A case like this could cost hundreds of thousands if it went wrong. I know they were wealthy people then, but I'm told their fortunes have changed considerably. I don't think they'd dare take the risk.

Not after all this time. I was hoping you might be able to get the *Comet* behind this one. Get the paper to finance it.'

'Mike, for God's sake. What planet are you on? Papers don't throw money around like that any more.'

'C'mon, Jo. They do if a story's big enough. We both know that. You do a deal with this family and you get everything first. Think about it. It'll be a huge ground-breaking court case and the *Comet* will be on the inside. All you have to do is pay the costs and it's yours.'

'Just like that,' she responded.

'Just like that,' he repeated expressionlessly.

'Well, it's not just like that, Mike, not any more, not if it ever was. What if it all goes pear-shaped again? The CPS have turned you guys down. The risk factor of a private prosecution would be huge. Apart from anything else, there's a big argument that, right or wrong, this case was buried a long time ago.'

'I don't think it ever will be, not for you and me,' he said quietly.

He was right, of course, and perhaps it was that which made her so angry. 'Oh, grow up, Mike,' she snapped. 'The case, you, me, everything — it was two decades ago, for Christ's sake. It's over. Anyway, even if I wanted to get involved again I honestly don't think I would have a hope in hell of getting the *Comet* to back it, not in the present climate.'

She knew she must sound patronising. She knew how much he hated being patronised, particularly by her. But she still didn't expect him to come back to her quite the way he did.

'I wouldn't have thought you'd have any problem there, Joanna,' he shot back at her. 'After all, you are sleeping with the editor.'

The anger overwhelmed her then. 'Fuck off, Mike,' she told him.

★   ★   ★

Joanna put one hand to her head and glared at the telephone, which she had promptly slammed down on him. Just who did Mike Fielding think he was? How could he be so damned arrogant? How could he think he could just bowl back into her life with all his baggage? The whole O'Donnell business was his problem, not hers. She had just been a young crime reporter covering the case — not the detective who blew it wide open because, as usual, he was in too much of a hurry. For her it was history. She had a new life. She had the column she had always wanted, 'Sword of Justice', a weekly eulogy championing the rights of the individual against the restrictions of a government and a legal system which purported to be liberal but actually, in her opinion, encroached upon freedom more than any other in her lifetime. She was proud of 'Sword of Justice', even though she knew well enough it was little more than the *Comet*'s sap to great campaigning days long past.

She also had a family she was proud of, an eleven-year-old daughter who was the apple of her eye — and a husband. A husband who happened to be the editor. Anybody but Mike would have said,

'After all, you are married to the editor.' Not Fielding. He had always had a way with words. He could always out-snide the best. He could never resist going just that bit further than other people would.

Her eyes were drawn to the photograph on her desk. She and Paul, taken at their wedding reception. Both beaming at the camera. She was wearing a tailored cream silk suit. It still seemed very beautiful to her, as indeed it should have been. It was Paul Costelloe and had cost nearly £1000 even then. Her bridegroom had wanted the best for her. For them both.

She studied him closely. Even features. Average height. Mousy brown hair, thick and springy, slightly longer then than would be fashionable now. Horn-rimmed glasses. He was never a typical Englishman in any way. She always thought he had looked more like a Harvard preppie in those days, a real American WASP. He was glancing at her sideways, smiling proudly, shyly almost. He did not have the appearance of a remarkable man at all. He had never looked like one or, in his younger days at any rate, appeared to behave like one.

She switched her attention back to her own image in the photograph. The long mid-blond hair framing a thin person's narrow face, her smile easy and wide, displaying even white teeth. She'd had them professionally scraped and cleaned four times a year then, in order to keep the nicotine stains at bay. That had been her big vanity. She hadn't been able to stand the thought of yellow teeth, but she never even considered giving up smoking, not until years later.

All too often it had felt as if only the cigarettes got her through the day. She looked happy in the picture and she supposed she had been happy, though what she actually remembered more than anything else was her sense of bewilderment.

She looked into her husband's eyes in the photograph, masked by those thick-lensed glasses. She had often thought they must be very convenient to hide behind and once she had asked him if he really needed such thick lenses. He had laughed lightly and changed the subject. She had never asked again.

Absently she stretched out her right hand and placed the tip of her forefinger very precisely over his smile so that the lower part of his face was covered and you could only see his eyes. Masked by those heavy lenses they were, as ever, merely cool and fathomless.

She sighed. As well as being a bloody great editor he was an attentive, caring husband and a brilliant father who managed to find time for both his wife and daughter in spite of holding down one of the most demanding jobs in the modern world.

Their daughter, Emily, was bright, well adjusted, healthy and self-possessed. Perhaps a little too self-possessed, but certainly she had so far given neither of her parents much anxiety about anything. Of course, Joanna realised that might all change when Emily reached the dreaded teens. However, perversely she knew, she sometimes found herself rather looking forward to having a petulant adolescent to deal with. Occasionally it felt as if life were just too well ordered.

The family lived in a dream home on Richmond Hill. Joanna spent three days a week in the office of the *Comet* and the rest of her time enjoying herself. House and daughter were undemanding. Both were impeccably organised, almost all according to her husband's direction, and with the help of a four-times-a-week cleaner and an au pair who picked Emily up from school every day and supervised her until whichever parent returned first.

Joanna had never had reason for one moment to doubt the love of the man she had married, nor his commitment to her. Her friends thought she was immensely lucky and she knew she was. She supposed that she loved him too, but it was not something to which she gave much thought.

She ran her hands through her hair, still more or less the same shade of blonde it had always been although helped along occasionally by streaked highlights, but now cropped short in a fashionable up-to-date style. She had put on some weight but her body was still in good shape — muscles firmish, no dreaded cellulite yet, thank God — maintained these days by regular workouts at the gym. People said she had changed little over the years. She had suddenly reached the grand old age of forty-seven, with another birthday approaching fast, although she really didn't know how the hell it had happened, but a well-defined bone structure had kept her face from falling — so far, anyway. Her complexion remained clear, her skin lined a little around the eyes and mouth but still relatively smooth and unblemished. She supposed that one of the advantages of never having been a great beauty or even particularly pretty was that you didn't change so much with the years. She certainly felt much the same as she had always done, but then, that was always the problem of ageing. You did feel the same, inside. She realised that she was tapping the heel of her left foot rhythmically on the ground. She felt disturbed, unsure of herself, for the first time in years. In fact, truth be told, she couldn't remember the last time she'd felt anything much for some years.

She had probably been too close to the Beast of Dartmoor case, too aware of the way Fielding and the rest of the team had handled it.

Now, twenty years later, she couldn't resist being intrigued by what Mike had told her, but one half of her didn't even want to think about it, really didn't want to get involved again. For many years she hadn't allowed herself to think about the case or anything else that it represented to her. She had definitely not allowed herself to think about Mike Fielding — which had made for a considerably easier state of mind.

She had half convinced herself that she really had forgotten him, that both he and the case were completely over for her. She had been wrong on both counts and that had come as something of a shock.

Suddenly it seemed like yesterday. The bloody man could still get under her skin like nobody else. And the case that had brought them together had always been much more than just another story. The poor murdered teenager had got under her skin, too. As had James Martin O'Donnell. The thought of playing a part in at least achieving some kind of justice, after all those years, appealed greatly, albeit against her better judgement. The problem was that all of it was tangled up inside her head with her memories of Fielding and what he had meant to her.

She wasn't sure that she wanted to risk becoming involved in anything which might affect the life she and Paul had built for themselves. They were, after all, the golden couple of the media world: attractive, rich and privileged. In demand at all the right dinner parties. Rumour had it Paul was up for a knighthood. That would make Jo Lady Potter. Potter. Not the sort of name that went all that well with a title, really, she pondered. But Paul wouldn't mind. He had worked towards it in the way that he worked towards everything in his life. Quietly. Assiduously. He had been editor for twelve years now, by far the longest of any of the other tabloid editors and something of a miracle in the modern world. The knighthood would not be so much a reward for longevity, however, as for the *Comet*'s so far more or less unwavering support for the present prime minister — for whom bestowing a knighthood was a small price to pay to ensure the continuing brainwashing of the paper's ten million or so readers. Paul was also one of the few of the current crop of tabloid editors who had always managed to keep his nose clean.

He had to be the cleverest man she had ever met. There was little doubt about that. He remained deceptive in his manner, which was still quiet and relatively unassuming. Look him in those unfathomable brown eyes, though, and you got a glimpse of how exceptional he was. Theirs had never been a relationship born of great passion — not for her at any rate. They just fitted together, somehow. She always felt that she had found the right man. Certainly all her friends and family thought she had. She and Paul were generally regarded as having the ideal Fleet Street marriage. And she supposed they did. More or less.

She sighed and gazed out of the window. The *Comet* offices were on the twenty-first floor of the giant shining tower block known as 1 Canada Square. From her desk she could see right along the River Thames to Greenwich. It had been almost as good a day in London as in Devon. The sun had already set behind the distinctive dome of the Royal Observatory and had left a stunning afterglow. Streaks of crimson blazed across a darkening sky. The view was sensational. She looked around her. Her desk was at the far end of a huge open-plan room, as far away as possible from the editor's office. After all, he was her husband. She preferred her own space.

The whole working area was clean and efficient-looking. There was very little clutter, the furniture new and streamlined, silent computers sitting on pristine desks. The atmosphere was calm and quiet. A bit like the editor, really. Rows of subs and reporters sat staring at flickering screens, barely moving. Certainly not talking. There was no chatter, no noise at all. Just still heads and busy fingers. Even the litter was sanitised. Empty plastic salad boxes had replaced greasy fish and chip papers.

God, she could even remember the smell of the

grubby old offices at the top of Fetter Lane. There had been an airconditioning system, of sorts, which never seemed to work properly. It was always either too hot or too cold, and by about this time in the evening the air would be acrid, the odour of fish and chips and bits of decaying burger mixed with stale cigarette smoke, beery breath and the odd blast of whisky fumes. Why was it that she and all the other dinosaurs yearned for the old days? More than anything, she knew, it was the atmosphere of excitement which had hovered over them continually, like a great big cloud waiting to burst, and which somehow seemed to be lacking from modern newspaper offices. The sheer hubbub of the place had been so much a part of that. The way the whole building shook when the presses started up. The clattering typewriters, journalists who talked to each other, often shouting across the room, instead of sending e-mails. Internal e-mails really irritated her. She had once suggested to Paul that he ban the practice.

His response had been heavily sarcastic. 'Ban in-house e-mails. A really good progressive idea that. What age are you living in, Joanna?'

Interesting, really, Paul accusing her of living in the past when here she was confronted with it and finding it not welcome at all. Far too disturbing.

Absent-mindedly Jo nibbled at a thumbnail. She had weekly manicures now, of course, but she still couldn't seem to stop herself biting her nails occasionally. She successfully chewed off a small piece of nail that had been irritating her and it dropped on to the sleeve of her jacket. She brushed it away. She was expensively dressed, as usual, in a sleek grey silk trouser suit, which would take her on to the chattering classes dinner party she and Paul were heading for later. There was no doubt she was in pretty good order for her age and she was probably fitter than she had been twenty years ago thanks to those gym sessions.

She had stopped smoking, of course. Hadn't everybody? But she still drank just as much, maybe more. The media world might have entered a new puritanical age but she wasn't giving up the booze even if she did seem to be surrounded by bright young things who thought a bottle of Mexican beer with a bit of lime shoved incongruously into its neck was the height of decadence and sophistication.

She wondered what they would have made of an era when a trolley laden with wine, beer and spirits used to be trundled weekly around the offices of the *Comet*, and senior executives were invited to choose supplies for their fridges and drinks cabinets. Free of charge, too. Even she, as chief crime correspondent, had had a couch and a fridge in her office. She didn't qualify for the free booze, but it was common practice for those who did to order a few extra bottles in order to help out those who didn't. Editorial meetings, particularly on Friday evenings, were inclined to turn into parties. On hot days in the summer the editor and his top men sometimes used to decamp for the afternoon to a swanky Thames-side hotel up near Maidenhead, from which, in the days even before faxes, they would edit the paper long-distance with the aid of a few extra telephone lines and a squad of swarthy despatch riders, laden with page proofs and bundles of subbed copy, running a motorbike shuttle service between the hotel and Fleet Street.

Nowadays, of course, alcohol was banned from the offices of the *Comet*. Even the editor had a fridge containing only soft drinks with which to entertain visitors.

She smiled nostalgically before reminding herself of the dangers of looking back at the past through rose-coloured spectacles. She made herself remember the appalling antics of Frank Manners and his cohorts. But even most of that merely widened her nostalgic smile. If you told the kids today, of either sex, the way the guys back then had behaved they wouldn't believe it. After all, if a chap in an office nowadays made the most polite of personally admiring remarks to a woman colleague he was likely to get done for sexual harassment. 'You're looking good, Joanna. I bet you had a really great fuck last night,' as a form of casual greeting would be quite beyond their comprehension.

Strange thing was that while she loathed sexism and certainly sex discrimination as much as the next woman, she did not remember being too discomfited by the things that had happened — until Frank Manners became completely out of control. But at least those guys were human beings, albeit often pathetic ones, and not pre-programmed robots. Joanna was not entirely in favour of political correctness. Apart from anything else, it was so damned dull.

She glanced at her watch. She still had the best part of an hour to kill before Paul would be ready to leave for the dinner party — if he didn't decide to cancel at the last moment, which was not at all unknown, particularly if there was a big story on the go — and they didn't get much bigger than the cracking of the DNA code, the day's huge revelation that would be all over the paper the next morning.

She got up and walked to the coffee machine over by the elevator and helped herself to a decaff. She no longer drank real coffee after lunchtime. She reckoned decaff was probably every bit as harmful, but at least it didn't keep her awake all night, tossing and turning.

Sipping from her polystyrene cup, she wondered why she bothered with the stuff at all. It tasted pretty much as if all the flavour had been removed along with the caffeine. She tried to clear her mind. Did she really want to get involved with the Beast of Dartmoor case again? Just hearing Fielding's voice had bothered her much more than she would ever have expected it to. 'Damn the bloody man,' she muttered to herself, apparently louder than she had realised. A sea of silent heads turned towards her, then away again. Christ, she could remember a time when you'd hear screaming in the office and wouldn't bother to look up. Nothing short of an actual physical punch-up caused any kind of stir in those days — and she'd seen a few of those too.

Upon reflection she decided it would be not only unwise but also dangerous to start delving into the case again. It really would be best to leave well alone. Absolutely no doubt about it.

She drained the last of her ghastly decaff, crushed the polystyrene cup in her fist and threw it at the nearest wastepaper bin. She missed and the cup slid untidily across the highly polished floor. A passing twelve-year-old, wearing an overly crisp white shirt, stopped, picked it up and put it neatly in a bin, glancing smilingly towards her as if he expected thanks or something. He didn't get any. Joanna merely observed him without enthusiasm, her eyes only half focused, her mind twenty years away.

Of course she feared she wasn't going to leave well alone. There was no real chance of that and had not been since she had taken Fielding's call. She was going to get embroiled in the case all over again even though she honestly didn't want to. She knew she was not going to be able to stop herself, so she might just as well get on with it.

Across the newsroom she could see young Tim Jones, upright in his chair, engrossed as usual in his computer screen. Tim, a bright diligent chap for whom Jo had considerable regard, was the *Comet's* chief crime correspondent, the job Joanna had just landed when she first met Fielding. Jo's title was now Assistant Editor, Crime. It didn't mean a great deal in that she was not one of the three assistant editors allowed, along with the deputy editor, to run the paper at night and in Paul's absence, which rankled a bit. Paul had apologised and said he didn't feel able to give his wife that authority. However, she couldn't grumble as she was primarily only a part-time columnist now.

She hoisted herself upright and walked over to Tim's corner of the room. When she told him what she wanted he gave her a cheery smile — he always seemed to be cheery, bless him, but then he was still so young and new — and swiftly fished both a copy of the European Convention on Human Rights and Britain's Human Rights Act out of his desk drawer. Trust Tim to be up to date.

'Anything else I can help you with?' he asked, as she turned away from him. Tim had a boyishly open face, very dark curly hair and even darker eyes, and was definitely far too handsome to be let loose in a newspaper office.

Jo thought of all manner of glib answers, muttered a 'no thank you' over her shoulder and made herself refrain from turning into the ageing female equivalent of all those tired old male hacks she'd had to deal with when she had been his age.

Back at her desk, she first opened the small purple Human Rights Convention booklet with its four white European stars on the front and turned to Article Four of the Seventh Protocol.

Paragraph One reaffirmed the right of all never to be tried again for an offence of which they had been acquitted.

Paragraph Two gave a proviso hitherto unknown in British law. There could be a retrial 'if there is evidence of new or newly discovered facts, or if there has been a fundamental defect in the previous proceedings, which could affect the outcome of the case'.

As it happened Joanna thought there had been a number of fundamental defects in O'Donnell's prosecution for the murder of Angela Phillips. But that was not what was at issue, nor was it ever likely to be. There was, however, certainly new evidence.

She studied the booklet carefully. Tim Jones had helpfully scribbled HRA alongside the articles which had been adopted into Britain's Human Rights Act due, as Fielding had reminded her, to become law on 2 October 2000. Article Four of Protocol Seven was not among them. She was not surprised. She might not have been on a Human Rights course, and now that she was no longer actually an on-the-road crime reporter she might not be quite as on the ball in certain areas as she would once have been, but she was sure that had such a major change in the law been imminent she would not have missed it.

Nonetheless she turned obediently to the Human Rights Act itself and leafed through until she came to Section Six. 'It is unlawful for a public authority to act in a way which is incompatible with a Convention Right.'

Courts were public authorities all right. The law was invariably open to interpretation — but put those two clauses together and you had possibly the biggest fundamental change to the whole basis of British law since Magna Carta.

Joanna felt the familiar tingling in her spine that she invariably experienced when she was confronted by something special like this. Something which could be a really great story — which was inclined to overshadow all other considerations with her. She couldn't help it. Never had been able to. She had been born a natural newspaperwoman.

9

She made herself pull back then. Sleep on it. At least not do anything more, including talking to Paul who, apart from anything else, was not exactly likely to be delighted that she was back in contact with Mike, until she had had time to think things through properly. Fielding still seemed to know how to pull her strings in more ways than one. She wasn't entirely pleased about that. But although she had been angry with him initially she realised suddenly that she was just as angry with herself. Predictably enough Paul had indeed dropped out of the dinner party at the last moment, leaving her to make excuses for both of them. She didn't blame him, she knew well enough the pressures a daily paper editor was constantly under, and she certainly hadn't wanted to go without him. She was grateful, actually, for time alone.

In her car on the way to Richmond — a state-of-the-art BMW now, the much-loved MG was long gone — she went over it all in her mind. If she took this any further there would be risks involved, both personally and professionally.

Risks for the Phillipses too. Was it fair for her to dig up the past for them all over again? Would they thank her, even if they did succeed in getting O'Donnell into court again. Would they think it worth it? She sighed. She rather suspected they would, but she also knew they would never be able to think about any of it objectively. That was what she must try to do. And it wasn't easy for her, not with Fielding involved and not with the old journalistic adrenalin rush, which she hadn't experienced in a long time, threatening to take over every other consideration.

Yes, there were all kinds of dangers. But on balance she was pretty sure Fielding could well have been right when he'd said a good barrister could swing it. You never knew what could happen once you ventured into a court of law, but the ammunition was all there. There had to be a way to get an admissible DNA sample out of O'Donnell and it really did seem that the Human Rights Act might be that way. Certainly Mike was right that a private prosecution of this nature would be staggering, ground-breaking stuff. The *Comet* could clean up. The *Comet* could also end up with egg all over its front pages. But by God, the whole thing was an exciting prospect.

By the following morning she had reached a decision. Perhaps the inevitable one. She would at least contact the Phillipses and sound them out, see if they would consider a private prosecution.

Over breakfast with Emily — well, cereal for her daughter but only tea for Jo, she never could face eating when she had just got out of bed — she planned how she would go about it. Fortuitously it was one of her days at home. Paul had already left in his chauffeur-driven car for a breakfast meeting. She didn't know how he managed to work the hours he did. Vaguely she was aware that Emily was talking to her.

'So can I, Mum?'

Oh, God, thought Jo, realising she hadn't heard a word her daughter had said for some minutes. 'Can you what?'

'Oh, Mum! Can I sleep over at Alice's tonight?'

Jo agreed that she could. Having paid her daughter such scant attention, she had little choice. She reached across the table and took Emily's hand, trying to make amends. 'And on Saturday we'll go shopping, just you and me, maybe look for that new computer game you've been going on about.'

Emily beamed at her. Like most kids she was potty about computers. But Jo felt guilty. Why did she always seem to be buying her daughter's affections? Emily was so bright, so precocious, sometimes it seemed that she didn't need her parents for much else. That was ridiculous, of course. She was only eleven. And if she was overly self-possessed it was probably that the lifestyles of her high-flying parents had made her so. Which was maybe the main reason for Jo's lurking feelings of guilt. She loved Emily to bits, but she just wasn't the naturally maternal type. To make further amends Jo decided to drive Emily to school, instead of leaving it to the au pair as she usually did.

On return to the house she went to the little garden room she used as an office when she was working from home, sat down at her desk, reached into the bottom drawer, rummaged about there for a bit and finally retrieved a battered black-covered book held together with a rubber band so that its many loosened pages would not fall out. It was her old contacts book, 1980 vintage, painstakingly compiled long before the days of palmtop computers and electronic organisers, indeed, long before the days of computers at all in the newspaper world.

She leafed through the smudged, untidy pages until she came to P. P for Phillips. She had to play around with the code, which had changed over the years, but the number was still good as she had somehow expected it would be.

Bill Phillips answered the phone. He sounded like an old man, tired and slow. She realised he must be well into his seventies now, but she also knew how dramatically he'd aged after the loss of his daughter.

They'd all suffered, of course, the whole family and Jeremy Thomas. He'd been in trouble with the police on and off for years after his girlfriend's murder. His attack on Jimbo O'Donnell outside Okehampton Magistrates' Court had been merely the first of many outbursts of violence and vandalism, often enhanced by drink. Eventually he had crashed another car one night when he was drunk and that time he had not walked away. Jo knew that Jeremy's parents had always blamed Angela's murder, and their son having been at first suspected of it, for the dramatic deterioration in his behaviour and ultimately his death.

Bill Phillips remembered Joanna's name as she had guessed he would. She thought he would probably remember the names of all the journalists and all the police officers who had been involved in his daughter's case. The Phillipses had kept the press at arm's length, but she had phoned often enough and written in the hope of getting close to them.

Not surprisingly, he did not seem pleased to hear from her. She knew he would also remember that she had been the reporter who had written the big series with Jimbo O'Donnell after he had been acquitted. Nonetheless she persevered. She asked Bill if she could drive down to see him.

He was unenthusiastic, to say the least. 'What for?' he asked in his dull, tired voice.

'There's some new evidence . . . ' she began. She didn't have to tell him what the evidence was in connection with. There was only one thing it could be.

'Then why haven't the police contacted us?'

'They don't think you should be told. I do.'

She could hear him sigh. She knew what he was thinking. Much the same as she had thought earlier, only for him the pain would be so much more acute. Would he want to drag it all up again, relive the horror of it?

She knew that he didn't have a real choice, though. Maybe, in a way, none of them did. The memories were too powerful.

$$\star \quad \star \quad \star$$

She arrived at Five Tors Farm just after 1 p.m. The place was very different from the way she remembered it. Then the farm had been beautifully kept, hedgerows immaculate, gardens manicured, the farmhouse itself gleaming with fresh paint, sparkling windows, geraniums in tubs by the front door and all the other signs of tender loving care bestowed on a cherished home. The entrance had been impressive too, with that big white gate hanging from granite pillars, and an access lane which was more of a smart driveway with a smooth tarmac surface.

Now the gate, no longer white, had fallen from rusting hinges and the surface of the lane had broken up and was deeply pitted. It was all for the best that Joanna drove a BMW instead of the precious old MG, because she doubted if she could have manoeuvred the low-slung roadster safely along the lane and into the unkempt farmyard. The adjacent lawns were only roughly mown, the flower and vegetable gardens overgrown and in need of weeding, the farmhouse crying out for a coat of paint. She parked to one side of the yard by the stables, glancing towards them as she climbed out of her car. She thought they looked as if they were empty. Even the top doors to most of the boxes were closed. She could see no horses' heads at the doors of those remaining open and neither were there any traces of the usual signs of horsy occupation. No hay or straw, no pile of drying dung.

She had heard that the Phillipses had got rid of all their horses after Angela's death, finding the animals too painful a reminder of the young woman who had been perhaps the most enthusiastic horse lover in the entire family. It surprised her, though, that it seemed they still had not replaced them.

Mind you, she remembered what Fielding had told her, the air of neglect and abandonment which hung over the farm might not all be merely a legacy of their great tragedy. The Phillipses' financial situation was not what it was, Mike had said. The family had no doubt been badly hit by the slump currently enveloping virtually the whole of Britain's farming industry.

A young man wearing jeans and a T-shirt, cropped blond hair, fresh-faced, came striding out of the house, presumably having heard her car arrive. For a split second she took him to be Rob Phillips, but realised her mistake at once. Rob would be over forty now, like her. Funny how time stands still in your head sometimes. This must be his son, born prematurely a couple of months or so after Angela's body was found.

He said 'Hi' in a non-committal fashion, adding, 'I'm Les.'

Now it came back to her. The boy had been named after his dead aunt, Angela Lesley Phillips. A bitter-sweet reminder always for the entire family. Joanna felt sorry for him. Poor lad. What a burden he must have had to carry throughout his young life. He did not smile as he turned and led the way into the big farmhouse kitchen.

The entire family were sitting around the table. Bill Phillips had shrunk into a little old man. His wife Lillian had a lost look in her eyes. Rob stood up and shook her hand. He too had changed beyond recognition. You would expect a farmer approaching middle age to have leathery skin and a lined face, but you would also perhaps expect a certain glow of health brought about by the outdoor life. Instead, Rob looked tired and wan, almost ill. The strain sat heavily on him. He could easily have been a man in

215

his mid-fifties rather than early forties. His wife, Mary, whom Jo remembered as being strikingly pretty, if just a little on the plump side, had ballooned. She wasn't very tall and Jo guessed that she probably weighed sixteen or seventeen stone. Her once pretty features had disappeared into folds of fat round her neck.

Jo tried not to show her shock as, although none of the family bade her do so, she sat down and joined them. In a murder case the one who died was never the only victim. Far from it. She remembered having been told that by one of her early police contacts. It remained the grim truth.

Bill Phillips had no time for pleasantries any more, it seemed. 'Right, you'd best tell us what you've come to say and get it over with. I don't want the missus upset again without a damned good reason.' He put an arm on Lillian's shoulder. She barely seemed to notice, just carried on staring straight ahead in that lost and slightly bewildered way.

So Joanna told them straight. About the chance arrest of O'Donnell and about the DNA match. She gave them the probability count. Several million to one, maybe as much as ten million to one. 'Beyond any reasonable doubt it has to have been O'Donnell,' she said flatly. 'A guilty man walked out of that courtroom, which I guess you have all always suspected.'

There was silence when she had finished speaking.

Rob glanced nervously at his mother who did not seem to be reacting at all. It was almost as if she had not heard a word Joanna had said. His father was fiddling with a teaspoon on the table before him, turning it round and round, staring down, intent, as if what he was doing was of vital import.

Mary Phillips spoke first. 'I don't see what difference it makes,' she said, holding out her hands palm upwards, which made the fleshy parts of the tops of her arms wobble alarmingly. 'It was more than suspecting. We've always known that bastard killed Angela.'

'The difference is that now it can be proved. Beyond reasonable doubt.'

Bill Phillips looked up. 'Is there going to be another trial, then? Is that it? So why haven't the police told us?'

Joanna shook her head. 'O'Donnell can't be tried again, not for murder. Not an acquitted man.' She explained about double jeopardy. 'The police decided not to tell you because they didn't want to upset you all over again when they are not in a position to do anything constructive about it.'

She could feel Bill Phillips's tired old eyes boring into her. Red-rimmed. Just as they had so often been all those years ago. 'That wouldn't worry you, of course, upsetting people, would it?' he snapped at her. 'Your lot don't care who you hurt, do you, as long as you get a story. So what are you after this time, that's what I want to know? Last time you paid O'Donnell to talk to you, tell you his lies, make money out of what he did to our poor dead Angela. This time you've come to us. What can we possibly tell you that will make a headline in that dreadful rag you work for?' His voice grew louder and angrier

217

as he spoke. 'What do you want with us?' he shouted at her finally. Then he slumped back in his seat, breathing heavily. The exertion of his outburst took it out of him. Joanna saw Rob glance at his father with the same weary concern he had earlier displayed towards his mother.

This poor bloody family, she thought. All their lives in tatters because of this awful thing.

She took Bill Phillips's comments on the chin. It was what she had expected and what she had tried to warn Fielding about. Bill Phillips had indeed remembered the O'Donnell buy-up and her byline. She doubted he had ever been able to forget anything concerning his daughter's disappearance and death. Joanna could find little to quarrel with in any of the charges Bill had levelled at her. She had always been quite deeply affected by the family's plight and by what had happened to Angela, but she could hardly expect the Phillipses to believe that. 'I want justice,' she said quietly. 'That's why I'm here. That's why I've come to see you. I want justice for Angela, as I know you do. And only through you, through this family, can that be achieved.' She knew she had attracted their attention. Each set of eyes was riveted on her.

She carried on then, explaining everything. Telling them how the CPS had turned down the police application to try O'Donnell for kidnap and rape and on what grounds. 'But the CPS is a public service using public money. They rarely knowingly take chances, however slight. Not in the public interest is a euphemism for saying that there are other prosecutions pending with virtually no risk factor at all. I believe the CPS is being overly cautious on this one. I believe this is a situation crying out for a private prosecution. You see, the law is starting to change. Timing could be every-thing . . .'

She told them about the Human Rights Act and how it would become law in October, and the implications it would have on cases like O'Donnell's; how even though the double-jeopardy exemption article in the European Convention was not being adopted, British courts would still be required to take it into consideration. 'The right barrister could make hay with that,' she said, unsure whether she had used the farming analogy deliberately or not.

She could see she had excited the family's interest, won them round a little. She was good at winning people round. That was, after all, what she had done for a living almost all her adult life.

'Would it really be possible, after all this time?' asked Rob.

She nodded and was about to speak when Bill Phillips effectively killed the moment.

'No it won't be possible, Rob,' he said, his previously quavering voice quite firm. 'Have you any idea how much a court case like that would cost? If we lost, the costs would cripple us. You know better than anyone the financial losses we have suffered over the last few years. All this family has left is this farm — and the boy, of course.' He glanced fondly towards his grandson. 'I want him to have Five Tors and a chance to build it up again. The rest is history.'

Again Joanna was about to speak, to explain what it might be possible for the *Comet* to do for them, when she was prevented from doing so by Les Phillips.

'No grandad, it's not history,' he cried out suddenly. 'All my life I've been haunted by what happened to Angela. I never even knew her and it's as if she's by my side day in and day out. Sometimes I don't even want the farm. The memories it carries haunt me. Let's take this bastard to court and maybe we can finally bury Angela at the same time as we bury O'Donnell.'

The rest of the family stared at him in shocked silence.

Les flushed and spoke again at once, suddenly realising, it seemed, what he had said and the way it must have sounded. 'Uh, I'm sorry, I didn't mean it like that . . . ' he began.

His grandfather touched his hand with his. 'We know, boy, we know,' he said gently.

Joanna spoke then. Very quietly, very deliberately. 'The *Comet* may be able to help,' she said. 'I may be able to persuade the editor to pay for the case. It won't be easy . . . I'll have to deliver. You'll have to help me . . . '

'Yes, and I can imagine only too well the kind of help you want.' Bill Phillips still didn't sound very friendly, although Joanna thought he was perhaps more resigned to the way things were than anything else.

Rob shifted in his chair as if he was in physical discomfort and yet again glanced at his father anxiously. Joanna knew that after the trial and the

Comet's publication of O'Donnell's side of the story the older man had never talked to the press again. And he had always been outraged when money had been offered, making it quite clear that the very thought of making money out of his daughter's torment was repugnant to him. That was the way the whole family had always seen it.

Would that be the way they would see it now, too, she wondered. It was different. There was something concrete on offer. Something perhaps that could be done in the name of justice. Or was that as much of a joke to him as it all too often was for her? She waited, as did the rest of the family, for Bill to speak. He might be old before his time and frail, but he was still the acknowledged head of this family, there was no doubt about that. They were a traditional lot the Phillipses.

'I'll think about it,' Bill told her eventually. 'The family needs to talk. Alone,' he added pointedly.

She took the hint and left.

★   ★   ★

Two days later Rob Phillips called her on her mobile. 'OK, we'll give it a go,' he said. 'But I tell you now, if this goes wrong it'll kill my father.'

'It won't go wrong, Rob, not again, I won't let it,' she responded instantly.

She began to put the plan into operation then. First she had to convince Paul, who needed quite a lot of persuading to allow the paper to become involved. He had no doubts about the newsworthiness of a reincarnation of the Phillips case, but he

221

needed to be certain that the case would be won. No newspaper ever wanted to back a losing cause. He also wanted to be sure of the family's commitment and of Joanna's control over them. 'If we go ahead with this I don't want it known that we are funding the prosecution,' he said. 'That would put a question mark over the integrity of our coverage of the case and also, if I know your average jury, probably prejudice the likelihood of a successful prosecution. They all love to hate the tabloid press, which you're every bit as aware of as I am.'

Jo gave him more assurances than she had any right to, as journalists almost always do when trying to sell a dangerous idea to their editors. As a rule the fact that she was his wife made no difference at all to any editorial decisions he might make concerning her. But she did wonder later if he had been influenced by his relationship with her on this one occasion. He knew how much it had always affected her.

'OK,' he said eventually. 'I'll go for it, but I want a proper legal assessment first. Get yourself an appointment with Nigel Nuffield.'

Joanna's heart soared. She had never met Nuffield but she knew his reputation, based on a near hundred per cent success record. He was a top bleeding-hearts barrister. He saw himself as a leading human rights campaigner — at least that was the image he liked to cultivate. Joanna doubted his sincerity, as she did that of virtually all the barristers she had ever encountered, but Nuffield was high profile, a great performer and clever. He was also publicity-mad. Defence was his usual game, justice for the wrongly convicted. Attempting to get justice for a victim in such unusual circumstances would be a new departure for him. But then, it was all going to be new. That was the whole point.

Jo didn't think the man would be able to resist.

★　★　★

Nuffield saw her the very next day. Joanna wasn't surprised. Any case a paper like the *Comet* was behind was likely to excite his interest and this one more than most.

It was with considerable satisfaction that she watched his reaction to her story, as she sat in an armchair — several inches lower than Nuffield's own chair, which she did not doubt for one moment was a deliberate arrangement — in the famous barrister's Lincoln's Inn chambers. Gilt-framed English landscapes — Jo was almost sure one was an original Constable — hung from oak-panelled walls lined with unmistakably expensive antique furniture. Whether or not his concern for human rights was genuine, Nigel Nuffield certainly always made sure he got his pound of flesh.

He was tall, handsome and elegant with abundant white hair — the recipient of regular silver rinses, Jo suspected — swept back from a learned forehead and gold-rimmed spectacles perched on an imposing nose. He oozed Old Etonian charm and self-assurance. His personal vanity was legend. Nuffield was special and he knew it. Jo didn't think she liked him much, but she didn't care. There surely could not be a better man for the job. Approaching sixty now, Nigel Nuffield had been at the summit of his profession for more than twenty years.

'It would certainly be a ground-breaking case,' he remarked languidly, unknowingly echoing Fielding's earlier comment. 'Of course, the rights of victims also deserve to be fought for. And I quite agree, if we make sure we go for committal after 2 October there will be a whole new slant to the proceedings. I think we could win. I really do. Tell Paul that's my considered opinion.'

★ ★ ★

So Joanna high-tailed it straight back to Canary Wharf, secured the final nod from Paul, and produced a powerful story focusing on the Phillipses' intention to take out a private kidnap and rape prosecution against the man they believed had killed their Angela. Whatever her husband's reasons for allowing her to go ahead, he could not be anything but pleased by the result, in the first instance at any rate. Joanna's story was highly emotive stuff. And it was of course the *Comet*'s splash the next day.

When Paul Potter made a decision he knew how to follow through, how to have the courage of his convictions. That was one of the many qualities which made him such an impressive editor. A leader article, written by Paul himself, called for Britain's ancient double-jeopardy laws to be changed, and for

Article Four of the Seventh Protocol of the European Convention on Human Rights to be adopted into the forthcoming UK Human Rights Act. That was not feasible, of course, the process of Parliament being far too lengthy and involved for such swift action, but it was a nice attention-grabbing ploy. The leader also demanded a realistic, specific and up-to-date review of the laws concerning the use of DNA in Britain's courtrooms.

Inside was the heart-string-pulling interview with Angela's mother, which Jo had already persuaded Lillian to give and had put together while still waiting for the final go-ahead. NEVER A MINUTE PASSES WHEN I DO NOT THINK OF MY ANGEL was the headline on the kind of centre spread calculated to leave not a dry eye at any breakfast table in the land. *May her killer rot in hell* screamed the strapline. 'All we want is justice,' was another line.

Potter and the paper's lawyers had pored over the copy all the previous evening. O'Donnell was an acquitted man and they could lay themselves open to a crippling lawsuit from him. But Joanna knew that her husband had seen his paper to bed very happily — satisfied that the *Comet* had gone as far as it could in convincing the nation that O'Donnell was guilty as sin without ever actually saying so.

Next day there was uproar. Every other news outlet in the country, print, TV, radio and Internet, picked up the *Comet*'s story.

Fielding phoned Joanna some time around mid-morning. 'I knew you'd do it,' he said, to her immense irritation. Followed by, 'Fucking great. You're a genius. This time the bastard's going down. I can feel it in my water.'

He would never get to be politically correct, would Mike.

10

The next four months flew by in a kind of mad whirl for Joanna. Having made the case happen, she was determined to be at the heart of it. She felt that the Phillipses needed her constant support, there were meetings with Nuffield in London and there was her column to write — in which she mercilessly flagged the forthcoming prosecution as much as she could without too blatantly flouting the law. And then there was Emma, seemingly so self-possessed and independent, but whose very lack of reproach made Jo feel all the more neglectful as she spent far more time away from home than usual in the office or in Devon, and half the time when she was at home on the phone or tapping into her computer.

However, this was the kind of campaigning journalism she had always wanted to be involved in. And although it was draining, everything went remarkably smoothly. Until the committal proceedings at any rate, for which a date was eventually set, more or less according to plan, at the end of October at Okehampton Magistrates' Court. The Phillips family, once they had made their decision, displayed determination and tenacity in bringing about their private prosecution and even began to show signs of looking forward to this first step in the legal proceedings which could ultimately bring O'Donnell to justice. Joanna was with them all the way.

So was Nigel Nuffield, it seemed, who was confident that the case was strong enough, and the new legal gobbledegook such that he would be able to convince the Okehampton magistrates without too much difficulty to commit Jimbo O'Donnell for trial at Exeter Crown Court. 'Once he's committed, we've got him,' Nuffield told her. 'Either on remand or in custody, he'll be on a charge for rape and kidnap. That means the police will be legally entitled to get a DNA test from him whether he likes it or not. Finally we get PACE on our side.' The barrister was also confident that once the private prosecution had secured a committal the CPS would step in and take over the case.

'Between you and me I've been tipped the wink, Jo,' he confided. 'It is what happens ninety-nine times out of a hundred with a private prosecution after all. Once the likes of us have taken all the risks, done the spadework and demonstrated that there is a case to answer, then the Crown Prosecution boys are more than happy to step in. Doesn't make sense for them not to.'

It was looking good, Jo thought. The CPS might not have been prepared to take on the case themselves, but to have made this commitment, albeit off the record, indicated that they must have confidence in the prosecution.

Nuffield then duly laid the indictment. He rang to tell her that it had not been necessary to take out a summons against O'Donnell, whose lawyers, almost exactly the same dream team as before, informed the court that their client would be appearing voluntarily.

The barrister seemed delighted that it was all going so well, but Joanna wasn't entirely sure she liked the sound of it. She had somehow expected Jimbo and his lawyers to try every trick in the book and out of it in order to prevent him even having to defend a prosecution at all.

Nuffield was his usual totally confident, benign, pompously public-school self. 'When their bowlers give us something to worry about we'll do so, Jo,' he said. 'Meanwhile we'll just make sure our innings is unassailable. A daunting opening stand, that's the thing!'

Jo didn't understand cricket. The most she knew about the game was that when you were in you went out, and when you were out you came in. Nothing about that reassured her at all.

* * *

Unlike the Phillips family, who seemed to become increasingly buoyant as the date of the committal proceedings approached, just glad, perhaps, to be doing something to gain justice for their daughter after so many years, Jo became more anxious. Every instinct said something wasn't right. She desperately wanted to know what the O'Donnells were up to. After a deal of thought she came to the conclusion that she had nothing to lose by at least attempting to see Sam O'Donnell. Her aim was to try to find out what he thought now about his elder son. Sam was still the Man. If he had turned against Jimbo that would have great influence on the outcome of the case, Jo reckoned. Apart from anything else, she would hazard a large bet that the O'Donnell money remained firmly in Sam's control. She knew that was the way he ran his firm. She also knew that although he was knocking eighty, Sam was still very much in charge.

She called unannounced at Sam's Dulwich home, aware that she wouldn't be a welcome visitor. She was sure that if she had phoned first there would have been no invitation forthcoming. Not like the previous time. Information travels fast among police and villains. She had little doubt that the O'Donnells would have a fair idea of the part she was playing in the pending private prosecution. Officially the *Comet* remained in the closet and the Phillipses had kept their promised silence. But the O'Donnells were streetwise. In common with the *Comet*'s rival newspapers, they would have little doubt about the true situation as they saw exclusive after exclusive written by Jo for her paper.

The O'Donnell operation was now run almost entirely from Sam's home, the big Victorian villa in a leafy Dulwich street. Sam had grown older. And he no longer had Combo, who had died five years earlier, to drive him around and pander to his every need. He spent little time at the Duke nowadays. Jo had heard that they'd even put a pool table in the famous back room. Sam's house was currently a mix of home, office and shrine, where the faithful came to pay homage. Sam O'Donnell really was the nearest thing London had to a godfather. Jo was not surprised when Tommy O'Donnell opened the front door. Tommy had his own home nearby with his family, of course, but he was acknowledged now as

Sam's right-hand man rather than his older brother Jimbo.

Tommy, still in his early forties, was ten years younger than Jimbo. He was a tall, broad-shouldered man, like all the O'Donnells, but he looked lean and spare, his light-brown hair, yet to show even a hint of grey, flopped over a protruding forehead, another family trademark. Unlike his elder brother, however, there was nothing remotely thuggish about his appearance. Jo knew his reputation as the brains of the family. An intellectual O'Donnell was actually quite a worrying prospect. Tommy had won a place to grammar school, passed A levels. He was keen on education. Perhaps too keen. Tommy's fourteen-year-old-daughter, Caroline, had taken an overdose of her mother's sleeping pills and killed herself six months or so earlier, allegedly in a panic over her end-of-term exams. Jo always found it hard to believe that young people would commit suicide over their school work. But she knew they did. Tommy and his wife had, of course, been devastated by the loss of their daughter in such a way. Like all the O'Donnells, Tommy was a devoted family man, although Jo knew he also had a tough side. He was his father's son.

Tommy's eyes narrowed when he saw her standing on the doorstep. There was no visible security around the house. Jo assumed the O'Donnells didn't think they needed it. Fear was one hell of a deterrent. It was hard to imagine who would take this lot on. Even the police hesitated — which had always been one of the problems.

'You're not welcome here,' Tommy greeted her challengingly.

'Look, I just wanted to talk. I know how you and Sam stand on crimes like this. Jimbo's a black sheep, isn't he? I want to see Sam. I'd like to know how he is dealing with this.'

Tommy stood with a hand on each hip, elbows akimbo, blocking the doorway. As if Joanna would be daft enough to try to barge her way in. That was never what reporters did, as it happened. They wheedled themselves into people's homes. They were sensitive in their approach, personable, well-dressed, easy of manner, full of wonderful self-deprecating stories. They used charm, not brute force. Their victims thought they were lovely and felt no pain at all — until the next morning's newspapers plopped through the letter box. The old foot-in-the-door myth was exactly that. And in any case, to try it on an O'Donnell she, or any other hack, whatever their gender or size, would have to be totally and absolutely barking mad. Come to that she was probably pretty damned barking to try any kind of approach on an O'Donnell.

'You've got no chance,' Tommy told her laconically. 'You ain't seeing Sam and as for Jimbo, he's been acquitted once and you lot have found a way of doing him again for the same crime. Now that can't be right, can it?'

'Last time your brother stood trial for murder. This time it's kidnap and rape. Different crimes. Different evidence. One way and another Jimbo will be brought to justice. The law may have tied itself

232

up in knots, but you can't argue with DNA, Tommy, and you know that.'

'Do I? What if, and I'm only saying what if, mind, Jimbo did have sex with that Angela Phillips. Who's to say he didn't pick her up on her way home, they get in the back of his truck and she's as eager as he is, what about that, then?'

'She was a seventeen-year-old virgin, Tommy.'

'She'd had a row with her boyfriend. She wanted to get back at him. She went with Jimbo, then he dropped her off. Nobody can prove different.'

'I know that story, Tommy, that's what your brother told DS Fielding when he went round after the DNA match was discovered.'

Tommy raised both eyebrows. 'You two still close then, are you?' he asked with a knowing leer.

God, she thought, was nothing private in her world? She ignored the inference. 'It'll never stand up in court,' she told him.

'It won't have to,' he said confidently and he winked at her again as he closed the door in her face.

*　*　*

Jo was highly disconcerted. She couldn't take in that the family still believed Jimbo was innocent, she really couldn't, but they were continuing to stand by him. Maybe it was just that they felt they couldn't be seen to turn on one of their own. Certainly appearances would be a big part of it. And what did Tommy mean when he said with such confidence: 'It won't have to'?

Jimbo O'Donnell continued to protest his innocence in spite of what everyone concerned considered to be overwhelming evidence. Predictably he was pleading not guilty. Yet he had not waited to be summonsed before agreeing to appear in his own defence against the private prosecution. What was going on?

Jo had not seen Mike Fielding during the four months preceding the committal, although she had spoken to him frequently on the phone. She couldn't help wondering what the detective would be like twenty years on, but the opportunity to find out did not seem to present itself and her involvement with the case, coupled with her normal work-load and family obligations, such as they were, meant that she had little free time. Once or twice, belting up and down the motorway between London and Dartmoor, she did consider arranging to meet up with him. But she never quite got around to it.

Later she also thought that maybe she had been putting off deliberately what was bound to be a strange and disturbing meeting. However, she reckoned Mike was probably keeping his distance from her for other reasons. He had already stepped out of line in the case. He probably felt he could not risk any further direct involvement.

Also, of course, she was totally preoccupied by all that was happening. At night she would lie awake sometimes, her stomach muscles clenched, wondering what the O'Donnells were up to, whether she had done the right thing. There was so much at stake. She knew the case that had been put together was a strong one and that Nigel Nuffield wouldn't have taken it on were that not so. She also knew it wasn't watertight. It explored a completely new avenue of law, for a start. There was bound to be an element of a gamble and a lot depended on Nuffield's apparent invincibility. But what choice had any of them had? There would never be another opportunity to bring O'Donnell to justice for a crime that was already twenty years old, that was for certain.

On the day the committal proceedings began, Jo sat with the Phillips family at the back of Okehampton Magistrates' Court waiting for O'Donnell to arrive. The place had not changed much, still little more than an extended white bungalow on the north bank of the River Okement, tucked away on the outskirts of town behind the same supermarket, which had now metamorphosed into a Waitrose, the proceedings still held in the unassuming room that also housed the meetings of West Devon District Council. Still the rows of ordinary office chairs giving a vaguely inappropriate air of informality.

Outside there had predictably been a considerable gathering of press photographers and TV news cameramen, but few members of the public. It was certainly a very different scene from the near riot of twenty years ago. In spite of the *Comet*'s fanfare, in spite of the ground-breaking nature of this hearing, as far as the people of Devon went it seemed that the teenager's murder was indeed history.

Except for Angela's family, of course. Jo could feel the tension in each and every one of them. Bill Phillips sat staring straight ahead, his face giving little away except for a periodic nervous twitch of his right eyebrow. Lillian looked likely to burst into tears again at any moment. Rob Phillips kept licking his lips, as if he was thirsty. His wife Mary repeatedly turned her handbag round and round in her lap. Their son Les looked excited, expectant, eager even. But then, he hadn't been through it all before.

Jo kept glancing towards the door. She had to admit to herself that she was waiting for Fielding's arrival as much as for that of O'Donnell. Although the detective was officially not actively involved in the new case she knew he wouldn't miss being there. He turned up just seconds before O'Donnell.

She was expecting to see him. And yet her first sight of him in twenty years made her catch her breath. Some things you never forget, that's the trouble, she thought. He looked older, of course, his hair greyer and thinning, but he had retained his slim build. He was wearing a very ordinary grey suit, well worn and not particularly well fitting. That was different. He would never have been seen dead in a suit like that when she had first known him. By and large, though, he didn't seem to have aged badly. He hurried in, checking his watch, and walked right past her, heading for a couple of empty chairs towards the front. That was familiar. Fielding had always been in a hurry, had always arrived everywhere at the last possible moment.

Then he turned to look at her — directly at her, straight away. Maybe he had felt her gaze on him. Certainly he seemed to focus on her immediately and when their eyes met she saw, and it made her feel so sad, just how much disappointment and weariness there was in him. His physical frame might have worn well, but the man himself had changed a great deal. There was somehow no doubt about that. He smiled and raised a hand slightly in greeting as he sat down.

She was still studying the back of his head when a suppressed murmuring in the court indicated that O'Donnell was being ushered in. Lillian Phillips gave a low moaning sound. Out of the corner of her eye Jo noticed Bill Phillips take his wife's hand in his and squeeze.

Jo had not seen O'Donnell for twenty years either. He too looked older and greyer. Fatter as well. She was struck by the way he had developed facial similarities to his now elderly father. Sam the Man, loyal as ever, keeping up appearances as ever, walked, leaning heavily on a stick, into the courtroom just behind his elder son. It would be important to Sam, to be seen giving family support, showing solidarity. He looked weary, though, every step obviously an effort. Well, the gang boss was eighty and his granddaughter's death would have taken its toll, as well as the new charges brought against Jimbo. Both father and son had the same folds of skin around the eyes, now, the same jowly features. Jimbo was much less the tough guy, that was for sure. But he'd clearly been groomed for the part again. He wore a dark business suit very similar to the ones he had sported twenty years previously. Just cut a little more generously.

The three magistrates came into the court almost immediately. Two men and a woman chairman. All three looked the part, sombre in manner, soberly dressed, their body language oozing superiority. If they weren't pillars of the community they certainly believed they were. Jo frowned as she studied the woman chairman. There was something familiar about her but for a while she could not place it.

O'Donnell was represented by more or less the same legal team as all those years ago. Brian Burns was the lead counsel again. At the previous trial Burns had been something of a young blood, the golden boy of the legal profession. Now he was an elder statesman, his brilliance if anything even greater than it had been then. Some things don't change, she thought wryly.

What became quickly apparent was that O'Donnell's lawyers had briefed their client on a policy of total denial. It seemed ridiculous that knowing he was faced with such irrefutable forensic evidence the man could just continue to deny everything. But he did. Of course, he would know that the DNA evidence could not be used, not yet anyway.

O'Donnell's admission to Fielding that he had had sex with Angela was not even on the agenda. It couldn't be. The detective had been acting unofficially. There was no proper record of the interview. O'Donnell had at no stage made a formal statement. Jo didn't even know if the confrontation would come out in court. It was certainly not part of the prosecution case and she assumed Fielding was hoping that it did not feature. She knew Nuffield was.

Brian Burns, of course, although a leading top

defence lawyer, didn't really believe in defence at all. He believed in attack. 'Your Worships, I submit that my client has no case to answer,' he began. 'I intend to prove abuse of process. A private prosecution has been brought against Mr O'Donnell only because the Crown Prosecution Service has, quite correctly, turned down a police application to bring charges of kidnap and rape against him. As is a matter of public record, Mr O'Donnell has already, many years ago, been properly tried and acquitted of the murder of the unfortunate young woman in question and therefore by inference of any related offences. I further submit that to proceed at all with this case would be in breach of double jeopardy, hence unlawful.'

The chairman of the magistrates puckered her brows. Suddenly it came to Jo. She was Lady Davinia Slater, a well-known figure in the West of England whom Jo had first encountered in her local paper days when Lady Slater had tirelessly led a long-time campaign to prevent a reservoir being constructed on her beloved Dartmoor. Now a thin, bright-eyed, leathery-skinned woman in her mid-sixties, Lady Slater looked as fit and tireless as ever. She had always been fiercely independent, with her own strongly held beliefs and ways of doing things. Jo knew that Lady Slater could rarely be swayed by others and just hoped she would make up her mind against O'Donnell, because once this particular chairman of magistrates did make up her mind there would be no changing it.

Lady Slater shot a puzzled glance in the direction of the clerk to the court who promptly approached the bench. Magistrates rarely have much more than a lay knowledge of the law and are inclined to rely heavily on their clerks who, Jo reckoned, could become disproportionately important. It seemed this trio were much the same as most of their kind.

The clerk leaned close to all three magistrates and spoke in a low voice but in the relatively small and low-ceilinged courtroom Joanna quite clearly heard him use the dreaded phrase 'part of the circumstance'. She groaned inwardly.

Nigel Nuffield, however, was swift to respond. 'I must draw Your Worships' attention to Article Four of the Seventh Protocol of the European Convention on Human Rights which allows for 'the reopening of a case in accordance with law and penal procedure of the State concerned, if there is evidence of new or newly discovered facts, or if there has been a fundamental defect in the previous proceedings, which could affect the outcome of the case'. This clearly allows for exceptions to be made to the laws of double jeopardy in circumstances which I submit are applicable in this prosecution. And, in view of Britain's Human Rights Act which, as I am sure Your Worships are aware, came into force on 2 October . . . '

Lady Slater might not have been familiar with all aspects of the law but she was certainly familiar with the antics of lawyers. She picked up immediately on Nigel Nuffield's convoluted phraseology. 'Are you saying that this article is now law in the United Kingdom?' she interrupted sharply.

'No, Your Worship. It has yet to be adopted here. But I would also draw Your Worships' attention to

Section Six of the British Human Rights Act. 'It is unlawful for a public authority to act in a way which is incompatible with a Convention Right.''

All three magistrates looked more bewildered than impressed, Jo feared.

Nuffield, determined, it seemed, to dazzle them both with legalise and his grasp of it, hardly paused. 'I must also alert Your Worships to Section Two of the Act. 'A court or tribunal debating a question which has arisen in connection with a Convention Right must take into account any judgement, decision, declaration, or advisory opinion of the European Court of Human Rights . . . ''

Lady Slater interrupted again, leaning forward, thin lips pursed in disapproval. 'Did you say European, Mr Nuffield?' she enquired.

'Well, yes, Your Worship, but . . . '

'And I think you just told us, did you not, that this Article Four of the Human Rights Convention, to which you referred, is not in fact the law of the United Kingdom?'

'Well, not exactly Your Worship, but the Act makes it quite clear that the rights laid down in the European Convention should be deferred to whether or not they are actually United Kingdom law . . . '

'Not in my court, Mr Nuffield. I am presiding over an English Magistrates' Court and until I am actually bound by European law I can assure you I have no intention of deferring to it.'

Christ, she's a died-in-the-wool Euro-sceptic, thought Joanna. That was all they needed. She had to be, of course. A woman who wouldn't allow her territory to be invaded by what had actually been a very necessary reservoir was highly unlikely to be impressed by the demands of Strasbourg.

Nigel Nuffield had his back to Jo, but she could tell that he was dumbfounded. You didn't encounter the likes of Davinia Slater at the Old Bailey or the Law Courts on the Strand. The officialdom of London bowed more and more towards Europe, as indeed it had to do. But it wasn't like that in Okehampton yet. This was factor X. Any idea originating in Europe had to be a bad one. Jo had not given that a thought and neither, she suspected, had Nigel Nuffield. Davinia Slater was a dinosaur in every respect and Jo hadn't realised that magistrates like her still existed. They did in Okehampton, apparently.

The clerk saved the day, albeit only momentarily. He approached the bench again. Once more Jo was able to catch odd phrases: 'Should be seen perhaps to take into account'. 'Must be careful not to be unlawful'.

The furrow in Lady Slater's brow deepened. However, she seemed to have been persuaded that at least her court should listen. Even if grudgingly.

'Very well, Mr Nuffield. You may continue. I assume you are going to tell the court that you have new evidence sufficient to warrant the extraordinary measures you are suggesting?'

In reply, Nuffield asked the defence if O'Donnell would come to the stand.

'Of course,' responded Brian Burns smoothly. 'We are all here today in the interest of justice.' Nuffield ignored him as Jimbo made his way to the dock.

'Mr O'Donnell, do you know what DNA evidence is?' he asked.

'Not really, sir, I just know I never did anything to that girl.'

'DNA is a genetic blueprint. For example, were your DNA found in relevant samples taken from Angela Phillips, that would give absolute proof that at the very least you must have had sexual contact with her.'

Jo wasn't quite sure what Nuffield was doing. He was skating on thin ice, that was for certain. She reminded herself that all the barrister had to do was persuade the magistrates to allow the case to go forward for jury trial.

Predictably Brian Burns rose to his feet at once to object. 'I would remind the court that no attempt at any such DNA match would be either lawful or indeed possible in this case, as there are no admissible DNA samples available,' he said. 'Only DNA extracted specifically in regard to the particular charge my client faces could, of course, be admissible.'

Lady Slater's frown deepened even more. The clerk approached the bench again and there was another conflab, this time in voices so low that Joanna could not catch a word.

'This is surely not the alleged new evidence to which you earlier referred, is it, Mr Nuffield?' the chairman of the magistrates asked eventually.

'Partly, Your Worship,' admitted Nuffield.

'But I am advised that all such evidence is indeed inadmissible.'

Nuffield threw back his shoulders and projected

243

his voice in his most theatrical and what he presumably thought his most impressive manner. 'At this stage and in this court, yes, Your Worship. However, if Your Worship were to commit the defendant for trial this would allow admissible DNA samples to be taken from him. I have reason to believe that such samples would link him inexorably with Angela Phillips. That is the new evidence to which I have referred.'

'But Mr Nuffield, you know very well that we can only pass judgement based on evidence which is admissible in this court.'

Of course he knew. But Nigel Nuffield also knew exactly where he was leading. 'Indeed, Your Worship,' he boomed. 'I would therefore like formally to ask the defendant if he will voluntarily submit to a new DNA test, a blood test, perhaps, the results of which would of course then be admissible in any court. Surely, if he and my learned friend are to be believed then Mr O'Donnell would be anxious to clear up this matter without question.'

Jo thought that was a highly convincing ploy and Nuffield's confident authoritative manner was awesome. This was a man with virtually no concept of failure.

However, before she could begin to share his apparent confidence a little more, Brian Burns was quickly on his feet. 'Your Worships, my client would be more than happy to submit to a blood test, but unfortunately he has a phobia against needles. This is, as I am sure Your Worships knows, a medical condition, from which my client has suffered since he was a child.'

Joanna could barely believe her ears. This was farcical. Yet everyone in the courtroom seemed to be taking the protestation perfectly seriously. She remembered with foreboding the case of a famous Fleet Street columnist who had claimed needle phobia as a defence against a charge of refusing to take a blood test after being arrested on a drink-driving offence. He was acquitted.

Looking at big, burly O'Donnell in the dock, the thing was too absurd for words.

But Lady Slater, bless her, was at least not rolling over. 'There are other methods of obtaining admissible DNA evidence, are there not, Mr Burns, and would your client not submit to those either?' she enquired frostily.

Thank Christ, thought Jo. She mightn't like Europe, but she's no fool. Maybe Nuffield could still pull it off.

'Your Worship, we both feel that my client has suffered enough indignities,' replied Brian Burns. 'This case has been trumped up against him by people who will not accept the proper verdict of a court of law twenty years ago. My client is an innocent man and as a matter of principle should not be submitted to further tests.'

All three magistrates looked unconvinced. For a fleeting moment Jo began to feel almost optimistic. She should have known better.

It was almost as if Brian Burns were playing a game with the court. Being a barrister, he quite probably was, Jo thought later. He played his trump card then. And it was an ace. 'In any event, Your Worships, I would submit that even if a new DNA

245

sample were on offer, and whether or not this were volunteered by my client or taken with or without his permission after his committal to trial, such a sample would still be inadmissible.

'I must draw the court's attention to the case of Michael Weir whose conviction for murder was overturned by the Court of Appeal in May this year on the grounds that although the prosecution had offered as evidence DNA obtained from a second sample taken when Weir was arrested for murder, without a first ineligible sample from an unrelated crime he would never have been linked to the murder scene.'

The magistrates looked a bit bewildered. The clerk approached the bench yet again. There followed two or three minutes of *sotto voce* mutterings and head noddings, once more quite inaudible.

The PACE ruling that DNA samples could not be used in any investigation other than the one for which they were acquired was bad enough — when you took it a stage further like this it made a nonsense of science as well as justice, Jo thought. But she had not known about the Michael Weir case and neither, she feared, had Nuffield. She reckoned the barrister had not done his homework as well as he might have. She suspected that Nuffield had long ago reached that stage in his glittering career where he no longer believed he could lose, and it suddenly looked to Jo as if this might be the case where this would finally work against him and all those who had risked so much to put O'Donnell in the dock again. Her heart sank.

The defence wasted no time in pressing home its advantage. 'My client has waived his rights, appeared here today of his own free will ... ' droned Brian Burns, spending several minutes repetitively pushing his point. Then he turned to O'Donnell, who somehow contrived yet again to create the impression of dignified injured innocence which had so irritated Jo all those years before, and asked him to explain to the court why he had pleaded not guilty.

'Because I never touched that Angela Phillips, let alone harmed her,' said Jimbo, who had patently expected the question. 'I'm an innocent man. I've been acquitted once. I should never stand trial again, that's my right. But they bring these Mickey Mouse charges against me, no disrespect, Your Worship, and if they weren't Mickey Mouse there wouldn't have to be a private prosecution cos the Crown would have done me, wouldn't they? Stands to reason, doesn't it?'

How such a monstrous man could ever come across as endearing was beyond Jo. But he did, no doubt about it.

There followed a brief exchange with Lady Slater about how O'Donnell shouldn't think for one moment that anything that happened in her court was Mickey Mouse and that he might yet find there was nothing Mickey Mouse about the powers it possessed either. O'Donnell grovelled a bit, but Jo suspected from the expressions on the faces of Lady Slater's two fellow magistrates that his words had already had the desired effect, on them at least.

She didn't like the way things were going one

little bit. O'Donnell was good, no doubt about it. She dreaded to think about what might be coming next.

And she was right to dread it. Very skilfully Mr Burns led his client into continually stressing what was being presented as unfairness as well as the alleged illegality of the private prosecution.

Suddenly O'Donnell went off on a tack which Joanna had most certainly not been expecting. 'It's that DI Fielding, he's always had it in for me,' he blurted out. 'Came to see me, didn't he, accused me of murder. Twenty years later, mind. And he had no right. No right at all. I'm innocent. I've been properly tried and proven innocent. I didn't murder that Angela Phillips, I didn't. And I didn't kidnap her or rape her either. How many times have I got to prove myself against this Mickey Mouse stuff? Begging your pardons again, Your Worships . . . '

Joanna looked across the court at Fielding, saw him slump in his seat. She didn't have long, however, to consider his discomfort before she too was targeted by O'Donnell. 'It's him and that woman Joanna Bartlett from the *Comet*,' O'Donnell continued, actually pointing across the court at her. 'They set this up. They set me up. It's bleeding harassment, that's what it is. The Phillips family didn't take this case out against me. Not really. They did. She did, anyway. The *Comet* agreed to pick up the costs and more. It's nothing to do with new evidence. They're getting paid for it, that's why they're having another punt at me after all this time. For money. That's why!'

There was, of course, pandemonium. Bill Phillips

looked as if he'd been punched. His son lowered his face into his hands. Young Les looked stunned.

Joanna was horrified and shocked rigid. She really hadn't expected this. Neither had Fielding. Paul had seen the dangers, but she had reassured him. She had been so certain of herself, or at least pretended to be. As for Nuffield — she'd got the impression that the bloody man thought he was invincible. Indeed, he had always seemed to be so. Jo couldn't bear it. Was the inevitable blow to his invincibility going to come now? She feared it was.

The O'Donnells might have guessed about the *Comet*'s involvement, but how had they known it was Fielding who had put her up to it, she wondered. Perhaps they guessed that too. But there were many ways — not least that Fielding, so delighted that the case was going to happen, had boasted about his part in it to his colleagues. Particularly if he'd been drinking. Joanna assumed that he still drank. Probably more than ever.

Anyway the damage had been done now. These were bold tactics on behalf of the defence. They were also probably very clever ones. You could never underestimate the sanctimonious hatred the British public profess to have for the tabloid newspapers they read so avidly. And their sanctimony invariably knew no bounds if they found themselves in a position, as magistrates, or sitting on juries, where they felt they had these scurrilous rags and those who produced them at their mercy.

Unwelcome examples flashed through her head. Jo didn't see how anyone in their right mind could have believed Jeffrey Archer's ridiculous story that he had arranged for an intermediary to hand a bundle of cash to call girl Monica Coghlin on King's Cross Station, not in return for her silence but out of the goodness of his heart.

But as far as the jury had been concerned the alternative was that the *Daily Star*, the most downmarket of all the British tabloids, had been telling the truth. Jeffrey Archer, bold and streetwise as ever, had correctly gambled that no jury would willingly allow that possibility.

By focusing on a tabloid newspaper's involvement in his prosecution, O'Donnell was in effect playing the role of an innocent man being persecuted by the press — with a little bit of help from a maverick policeman. And the magistrates, Jo feared, were lapping it up. She was still numb with shock and could hardly bear to think about the possible consequences.

It was all over that same day. The magistrates withdrew for just a few minutes shortly before four o'clock. Then Lady Slater delivered the verdict of the bench. In doing so, she predictably strongly criticised the *Comet* for its role in the débâcle. Mike Fielding also got a roasting for irresponsible behaviour, which Lady Slater decreed could indeed be regarded as harassment. She threw in all the relevant legal jargon — 'part of the circumstances' and so on — and concluded: 'The laws of double jeopardy still stand in this country. In spite of the arguments of prosecuting counsel, it seems to this court unconstitutional that unadopted clauses of the European Convention on Human Rights should have any bearing on our proceedings and it is the magistrates' inclination to adhere only to what is actually the law of the land until and unless a much higher court than ours rules otherwise.

'However, in any event, the only new evidence offered by the prosecution is indeed, and will remain, inadmissible. There are no properly obtained DNA samples available in this case, nor can there be, in any circumstances, because of the manner in which the defendant was linked to the crime in question. We have no alternative, therefore, but to uphold the defence's submission of abuse of process. We find that there is no case to answer and I duly dismiss the case.'

O'Donnell had got away with it. Again.

He and his mob had run rings around the law once more, and she and her newspaper had been made to look foolish. Jo supposed she had been naive to think that the paper's involvement could be kept quiet. She certainly hadn't expected anything like this, though. She was furious, but not nearly as furious as she knew her husband would be.

She sat for just a few seconds in a kind of stunned daze, only vaguely aware of Bill Phillips, his face like thunder, pushing past her and rushing out of the courtroom. The rest of his family followed at once. They did not try to speak to her, which was all for the best, because for just a few seconds she was not sure that she was able to speak. Slowly she stood up and began to make her way outside.

It was quite a cool, breezy late October day, but Joanna was sweating. She was wearing a woollen trouser suit and beneath the jacket her cotton shirt was sticking to her. Her face felt as if it were burning. She had previously not really given much thought to the consequences of this case collapsing. She had not allowed herself to think about it.

On the steps of the court she was confronted with the nauseating sight of O'Donnell giving one of his impromptu press conferences. His father was by his side as ever. Frail in body Sam might be, but his toughness and strength of character had not left him — as much of his earlier weariness seemed now to have done. Still leaning heavily on his walking stick, he used his free arm to clap his son on his back, beaming, openly triumphant. Extraordinary. Joanna continued to find it hard to accept that he could really believe in his elder son's innocence, because she genuinely thought that Sam the Man would find this kind of crime as repugnant as would almost everyone else. Surely the only explanation could be that Jimbo really was the old man's blind spot and that when it came to his favourite son he truly couldn't see what everyone else could so clearly. She knew that was what Fielding thought. Fielding. All she wanted to do was get away as quickly as possible, but the crush of bodies on the steps impeded her progress. She looked around for the detective. He was right behind her, as desperate to escape as she was, she suspected. Their eyes met briefly again. There was a blankness in his. His mouth was set in a firm, hard line. Come to think of it, he looked pretty much the way she felt.

Apart from anything else, O'Donnell had made certain that the link between them was public knowledge. And under privilege in open court too — which meant that the papers could print what they liked free from the restriction of the laws of libel.

With half an ear she was aware of O'Donnell's slightly whining voice. She could catch only snatched phrases above the hubbub of the crowd but it was enough to know he was repeating yet again the now familiar story: ' . . . I'm an innocent man. I've been persecuted . . . harassed . . . set up . . . '

Suddenly the pitch of his voice changed. 'There they are, there they are now,' he shouted, and this time neither she nor anyone else within a half-mile radius could have any difficulty in hearing him. 'There they are!'

To her horror, she realised Jimbo was pointing at her and Fielding, his face screwed up in hatred as he spat out the words.

The gathered hacks and snappers turned as one and surged forward towards them. Jo was about to learn the hard way what it felt like to be on the receiving end of this level of press attention. Suddenly a flash exploded in her face and she was dazzled, momentarily blinded. At almost the same moment someone lurched into her side. She stumbled, almost fell. A strong hand grasped her elbow, supporting her. She looked round. It was Fielding. He was half smiling, a wry, resigned sort of smile. She smiled her gratitude back. More cameras flashed.

Joanna Bartlett and Mike Fielding were no longer just a journalist and a policeman who had worked on the case. They had become an important ingredient in the whole Beast of Dartmoor saga.

11

All Joanna wanted to do was go home and hide. And for perhaps the first time in her marriage she quite desperately wished that she did not share her home with her editor. The large, impeccably furnished and decorated house on Richmond Hill was going to be no hiding place at all.

She had no idea where Nigel Nuffield had disappeared to so swiftly after the devastating verdict or, indeed, exactly how, but in any event she did not really want to see him. Not yet. She was too angry. Too defeated.

On autopilot she filed what story she could. The *Comet*'s news editor was a woman now, virtually unheard of twenty years earlier. And Pam Smythe's measured approach was a far cry from that of the bombastic McKane and Foley, who had been traditional Fleet Street newsmen of a very different mould, but Pam was razor sharp and could be quite cutting enough when it was called for. On this occasion she actually sounded embarrassed. Banter was not what it was any more, but even the old guys would probably have held back in this situation. Joanna had screwed up big time and back in Canary Wharf they damn well knew it.

When she had finished her call to the office there was something else she felt she had to do before she could head home to the dubious reception which inevitably awaited her. She set off across the moor to

Blackstone to visit the Phillips family. They too had managed to make a quick getaway, somehow getting past the press pack and presumably driving off back to Five Tors. Jo didn't really want to see them but she felt she could not just walk away from them on this dreadful day. The pack were gathered, just as they had so long ago, at the end of the farm lane, having no doubt already knocked several times on the farmhouse door and been sent away.

Joanna drove straight past them, swung her BMW into the yard and parked right outside the kitchen door, which was opened almost immediately when she knocked on it. They would have heard her arriving, of course, and recognised her car.

Rob Phillips beckoned her into the big kitchen where the entire family were, yet again, gathered round the kitchen table. Without being asked she pulled back a chair and sat down. Just as before. Nobody spoke to her. But at least they had allowed her in.

She glanced around her. Bill Phillips sat head down with his hands clasped round a mug of tea as if drawing comfort from the warmth of it. She could see that his fingers were shaking. He did not look up and for that she was quite grateful. She did not want to see how much more pain there was in his eyes.

Lillian Phillips was sobbing quietly. Joanna thought she had probably been in tears ever since the verdict was announced. Her daughter-in-law had her arm round her but had obviously given up trying to comfort her. What comfort could anyone give this woman, Joanna wondered. Lillian stared at her through her tears, a stare which was a mix of accusation and pleading.

Mary was tight-lipped. Eyes bright in their folds of flesh. She was deceptive. The fat made her look like a West Country version of jolly Ma Larkin. Her voice was a gentle Devonshire burr, but it had a hard edge when she broke the silence. She was, of course, as damaged as the rest of the family by the legacy of the terrible twenty-year-old murder and in reality her personality could not have been further removed from that of the carefree Ma Larkin.

But how could it have been any other way? How could anybody in this family ever be carefree again? As his mother began to speak she glanced at Les, the youngest of them, Angela's nephew. The lad looked as if he was carrying the cares of the world on his shoulders. Unlike the others, he had not gone through anything like this before. This was his first taste of it. She thought the look of panic in his eyes came from the grim realisation that this had been the family's one chance to put an end to it all, finally to bury Angela, as he had put it. Now he must know that there would be no end, that Angela's ghost would probably haunt him for the rest of his life. Joanna couldn't imagine the bleakness he must be feeling.

Mary Phillips's words washed over her: harsh, deserved, expected. 'What was the point of it all? What was the point of dragging it all up again? There is no justice in this country. We should not have listened to you, Joanna Bartlett. Look at the state mother is in, look at her. You did this to her, you and your precious policeman boyfriend. We trusted him before and he let us down. Now we've been let down again. By you. By everyone.'

Joanna did not reply. What was there to say? She wondered a little at even Mary referring to Fielding in this way.

Young Les spoke up then. 'I don't understand it,' he said. 'You promised us we'd get him this time. You promised us it would be all right . . . ' There was a catch in his voice.

Joanna sighed. 'Les, I'm not the chairman of the bench. I'm as sorry as you are, as sorry as any of you.' Even as she said the words she knew they were a mistake.

From Bill Phillips there came a kind of strangled sound; it was actually a sort of dry, mirthless laugh. He looked up for the first time. She tried to avoid his eyes but could not. If there had been pain before, now there was agony in them. 'No you're not,' he told her in a quiet, even voice without much expression. 'No you're not and please don't ever again say that you are. You don't know what sorrow is. You have to lose what we have lost to know. We've lost our daughter and our own lives too. Look at that boy there . . . ' He gestured at Les. 'What's he known in his life but our misery?'

She didn't dare speak.

'Why have you come here tonight?' he asked sharply.

Her reply was honest. 'I don't know,' she said.

'After another story for that so-called newspaper of yours, are you?' he persisted.

'No, this is off the record, I promise. I just wanted to see you . . . ' Her voice tailed off.

'We've had enough of your promises,' he told her.

There was another silence before he spoke again, his voice even sharper, his look challenging. 'You are going to honour our contract, you are going to pay up, I assume. Or will that be another broken promise?'

'You won't be out of pocket, Bill, I suppose that was the only promise I could make and have some control over. Of course the *Comet* will pay you, as agreed.'

She spoke with a confidence she did not feel. So far the paper had only paid a nominal £5000 to the family for interviews given once it had been decided to put a private prosecution into motion and before the court case. As ever, and apart from any other considerations, what further material they could publish, if any, would be severely limited by the man's acquittal.

Costs had been awarded against the Phillipses. That meant they had to pay O'Donnell's legal fees as well as their own and he, as ever, had fielded the dream team. The total bill, even though the case had not got beyond the committal proceedings, could well end up approaching £100,000 or so. Brian Burns was famous for quite extortionate fees, which had become a part of his mystique and which his clients always seemed to pay without a murmur because of his extraordinary record of success. And Nigel Nuffield did not come cheap, in spite of his bleeding-hearts pretensions.

Joanna's heart sank to her boots as she made herself consider it all. She dreaded Paul's reaction. He had agreed to the deal being struck. She was not just a senior columnist on his paper but also his wife. This was the kind of mess that could bring editors down.

She had a feeling he might refuse to pay. And sitting at that kitchen table looking around at those sad, broken people, she wished the quarry-tiled floor would split in two and swallow her up.

* * *

They didn't hate her, really. They just wanted someone to blame. After a bit Mary offered her a cup of tea. Jo didn't actually want it, but gratefully accepted the olive branch. In the end she stayed for just over half an hour and when she left to begin her drive back to London Lillian was still weeping. Her sobs grew drier and drier as if she had no tears left, but she carried on going through the motions.

Jo had at one point quietly asked Mary if she thought maybe she should call a doctor for her mother-in-law.

'No,' the other woman had replied with forceful certainty. 'She'll be better just left alone.' Then, pointedly she had added, making Jo feel smaller than ever: 'We'll all be better left alone now . . .'

That seemed to be her cue to go. And once she was safely in the cocoon of the BMW, Joanna found she had to take deep breaths in order to prevent herself breaking down. She rattled the powerful motor down the lane, not bothering even to attempt to avoid the potholes, and, much faster than she knew she should have done, hurtled past the assembled pack who were shouting out at her, desperate for a few crumbs from her table. As she pressed her foot a little further down on the accelerator, she wondered why on earth they should think she had any crumbs left after what she had been put through in the courtroom that day.

A photographer she knew vaguely and had never liked stepped out into the road in front of her, brandishing his camera. She accelerated even more and was mildly gratified by the surprised and frightened expression on his face as he was forced to leap into the hedge in order to avoid being run over.

She did remind herself, as she carried on in the direction of the A30, that there was nothing worse than poacher turned gamekeeper, and she lifted her foot, just slightly, off the accelerator slowing to an almost sensible speed. Her hands were shaking on the wheel. Her bottom lip was trembling and she had to fight like mad to prevent herself from bursting into tears. Apart from anything else, she was afraid that if she started, like poor Lillian Phillips, she would not be able to stop.

The A30 blended with the M5 just before Exeter and within half an hour or so of leaving Five Tors Farm the Exeter Services loomed ahead of her and she pulled off the road, telling herself that she might as well fill up with petrol straight away. There was, of course, another reason.

This time she intended to give in to her impulse. She didn't have anything much more to lose anyway. She really did want to see Fielding. She used her mobile to call him. She guessed he would be in his office at Heavitree Road just as he had been on that other occasion all those years ago. For all sorts of reasons she did not dare turn up unannounced as she had then. Their relationship, whatever it was, and God knew she had no idea what it was, particularly as they had yet even to talk in person this time round, was now too public. They had somehow become almost as much a part of the story as O'Donnell and poor Angela Phillips.

But there was something else, too. Suddenly the memory of what had happened between them after that other trial, that long-ago acquittal of O'Donnell in Exeter Crown Court, had become overwhelmingly vivid. Once more, and after so long, she felt very strongly that only she and Fielding could help each other.

He answered his direct line at once. 'I was hoping it might be you,' he said quietly.

She was very slightly taken aback. Was he too thinking of that night twenty years ago? 'Can you get out?' she asked. 'I thought we might have a drink.'

'I've got a report to write. I'm in the shit over this, deeply in the shit.'

She interrupted him. 'Me too.'

'Yep,' he murmured. 'Story of my life, though, isn't it?'

There was a slightly awkward pause.

'Look, if I don't have this report in the chief constable's office by tomorrow morning I'm dead.'

'It's OK, you're right, it was probably a lousy idea anyway.'

'To hell with it,' he interrupted suddenly. 'Where are you?'

She told him.

'Right. Not any of the pubs here.'

She understood his reasons well enough as he gave her directions to a pub she had never heard of. 'See you there in twenty.'

She phoned Emily on the way, trying not to give any indication of how upset she was, but telling her daughter and the au pair that she would be late home and Emily shouldn't even think about waiting up as she had school the next day.

Fielding was at the pub before her, sitting at a corner table nursing a pint. He'd taken his tie off and his jacket looked rumpled. She was reminded again of what a snappy dresser he had once been, always particularly noticeable in a member of a profession not known for sartorial elegance. He looked worn out and fed up. She was aware again of the disappointment and weariness in his eyes.

He got up and kissed her lightly on the cheek. Strange how natural that seemed. She accepted his offer of a drink and ordered a Diet Coke. She had a long drive ahead of her.

He bought the drink for her and sat down opposite. Neither of them spoke for what seemed a long time but was probably just a few seconds.

'You look tired,' she said eventually.

'Thanks a bunch,' he responded. 'I've seen you look better too.'

'I've just come from the Phillipses,' she said.

'Oh, fuck.'

'Exactly.'

'And now you're off home. Something else to look forward to.'

'Yup.'

'I keep trying to figure out what went wrong.'

'Yup,' she said again.

'I was sure the bastard would go down. Instead it's all the rest of us who are down, right down the pan in my case.'

He looked so miserable. A completely different man from the one she had first encountered all those years ago. Like a small boy, really, but a very old small boy. She felt a sudden urge to give him a cuddle. But those days were long gone and this was certainly not the moment to rekindle anything. 'We did the right thing,' she said, as much to reassure herself as him.

'Did we? And since when did the likes of you and me even try to do the right thing?'

She sighed. 'We do sometimes.'

'And sometimes not.' He looked down at his hands, holding his pint glass on the table in front of him. 'I was remembering when we met after O'Donnell walked the last time . . . '

He didn't need to explain further. She had known that would be as much in his mind as it was in hers. It had to be. 'So was I,' she said softy.

He looked up at her. Suddenly there was just a spark of the old Mike Fielding. 'God, we were good,' he said. And his eyes twinkled.

'We damn well were, weren't we?' she responded, and for what seemed the first time in for ever she managed a big broad grin.

But that was the only reference they made to their old relationship. One thing was obvious — and that was how much they both remembered it, how easy it was for them to relive their time together. Nonetheless, although they continued to talk about

263

the old days they spoke more about other people than themselves.

'You used to drive that old bastard Frank Manners crazy, you know,' he said.

'Didn't I, though,' she replied with some satisfaction. And they had almost managed a bit of a giggle at that. It was as if by silent consent they did not want to talk about anything that might be contentious in any way. They stayed in the pub together for more than an hour and also, perhaps surprisingly, talked very little about that day's courtroom disaster. There was, after all, little point. Neither of them could see any way of taking the matter forward. Or their relationship, come to that. This stolen hour had been a great comfort to her somehow and also, she suspected, to him. But it could not be more than that.

'I've really got to get back to that report,' he said eventually. 'If I want to keep the small chance I have of hanging on to my pension.'

She found it sad to hear him talk in that fashion. The Mike Fielding she had known before had been convinced that he was going straight to the top. That Mike Fielding would not have believed that twenty years down the line he would have progressed just one rung up the promotional ladder and be grimly hanging on to the remains of his career, desperate not to lose his bloody pension.

Was that really all his lifetime's work amounted to? She was lucky in that respect, she reflected. She already had total financial security, albeit thanks largely to her marriage to Paul.

Paul. Seeing him that night promised to be a

perfect end to a perfect day. 'I have to go too,' she said. 'I've got a long drive ahead of me.'

'Good luck,' he murmured. He still seemed to know what she was thinking. Did he also know that thanks to him, and for reasons she could not quite explain to herself, she now felt more able to deal with what lay ahead? Certainly both stronger and calmer than she had done when she arrived at the pub.

Outside the pub they kissed goodbye on the cheek, like the old friends she told herself they could only ever be again, particularly after this latest débâcle. How come they always seemed to cause each other trouble? How come she had not been able to stop herself feeling some of the old longing for him? And how come she was so convinced that he still felt it too?

He looked different. He was different. He was weary and disappointed, a failure, more or less, hanging on in there. And yet as she watched him walk away from her to his own car she did not see that at all. No. She saw the same bold, high-flying young maverick, with his to-die-for grin and winning ways, that she had fallen in love with twenty years earlier.

★ ★ ★

Whatever succour she had gained from her meeting with Fielding rapidly disappeared on the way back to London when she finally made herself call Nigel Nuffield on his mobile phone.

The barrister answered at once. She wanted,

265

irrationally or not, to scream abuse at him, but there was no point. 'I just need to know if you think there is anything else we can do, Nigel?' she asked. 'Is there any kind of appeal procedure at this stage? And if so, is there still any reasonable chance of success?'

'My dear Joanna, I only wish there were,' he told her, sounding as languid as ever. 'We could appeal to the Queen's Bench on a point of law over the Human Rights Convention issue, and we would be in with a chance on that. Somebody will have to get a ruling on it sooner or later. But I'm afraid we've been bowled a googly on the DNA admissibility issue and that is our only new evidence, as that infuriating woman magistrate pointed out.'

Bloody cricket again. She wished he wouldn't do that. Her irritation got the better of her. 'Nigel, you quite obviously didn't know about the ruling on the Weir case . . . '

The barrister interrupted her. 'Jo, you know as well as I do the confusion over interpretation of the law regarding DNA,' he asserted. 'If we'd had a different umpire we might have won the day regardless, worried about the next step then. As it is I played all the shots but the decision went against us. Badly, I'm afraid.'

A different umpire? Played all the shots? The man was infuriating. She really wasn't going to let him get away with it. 'Nigel, I'm sorry, I think our case was ill-prepared and I'm going to tell Paul so, and if I have my way the *Comet* will damn well sue you.' She very nearly shouted the last few words into the phone.

Nuffield replied in a slow, slightly amused drawl, his public-school vowels even more extended than usual, 'Joanna, Joanna, calm down. This is litigation not life.'

She completely lost it then. 'That may be how it is for you, prancing about in your damned silly wig, but for real people it is their lives, you overpaid, over-hyped patronising fucking bastard,' she yelled at him. Then she switched her phone off.

Unprofessional. Unhelpful. Yes. But oh, it was also the only fleetingly satisfying moment in a truly nightmare day. A day which had yet to end.

★   ★   ★

Paul was sitting on the big black leather sofa in their spacious living room surrounded by the next day's papers when she finally arrived home just after midnight. The walls and the floor were cream. The only colour came from Paul's collection of vibrant abstract paintings. The scattered newspapers were the only clutter in the room. Probably in the house. Paul was like that. So too was their daughter, hopefully sound asleep upstairs by now. Emily took after her father in personality. She was self-contained, capable, organised, meticulously tidy. Unnaturally so, Joanna sometimes thought. All Emily's contemporaries seemed to be congenitally lazy and specialised in leaving a trail of debris behind them. They were, well, sort of normal really. Jo shrugged away her vague disloyalty and forced herself to concentrate on the unwelcome confrontation she knew was about to begin.

She sat in the armchair opposite her husband. Dinah Washington was playing loudly on the music system. Paul liked to listen to classical music quietly in the background when he was working in the office and loud jazz when he was relaxing at home. He didn't look very relaxed. Dinah was singing 'What a Difference a Day Makes', which, Joanna thought, was certainly appropriate.

She felt drained. She kicked off her shoes and closed her eyes. After a moment or two the music stopped abruptly and she guessed that Paul had turned it off with the remote control.

'You took your time getting back,' he remarked eventually.

She opened her eyes just a little. 'I went to see the Phillipses.' She carefully omitted mentioning her meeting with Fielding.

He didn't reply.

'They're devastated by what's happened.'

He regarded her coolly. 'So am I,' he said.

'Look, I reckon Nuffield really let us down . . . '

'Don't search for scapegoats, Jo. It was you who convinced me this case could be won and I gave you the absolute top man in the country.'

That was true.

'He does say we could take it to the Queen's Bench . . . '

He interrupted her again. 'Don't even think about it, Joanna. There is no 'we'. As far as you and the *Comet* are concerned it's over.'

She didn't have the energy to argue. And in any event, even Nuffield, never one to pass up the opportunity of a further fee, had warned against

268

attempting to take the case any further. There was one subject she could not stop herself broaching. 'Look, Paul, you know costs were awarded against the Phillipses . . . ' She regretted the words as soon as she said them.

'My heart bleeds for them.'

'You are going to honour the contract . . . ' She regretted those words too. She knew she should have waited until at least the next working day, picked her moment. But she had been worrying about the financial side of it all the way home.

'There is no contract, Jo.'

Her heart sank. It was all too true. There had not been any contract because she had convinced the family it would be prejudicial for the *Comet* to be seen to be financing the case. She had been right enough about that at any rate. She had also convinced them that her word was as good as a contract. 'National newspapers don't renege on deals,' she had told them. 'We don't dare. We need our contacts and the people we do business with to trust us. If we make a deal we keep it.' Once upon a time that really had been the truth. Nowadays, by and large, it was bullshit. But this time she had really willed it to be true. 'Paul, if the Phillipses go public on this it will be even worse,' she said. 'They'll deny it to the wall as long as we pay up.'

'Joanna, think about it.' He spoke with exaggerated patience as if to a small child. Obliquely she wondered why all the men in her life seemed to do this to her. It had been understandable, perhaps, with her primary schoolteacher first husband. From Paul it was especially infuriating.

'It's already public,' Paul continued. 'We have been accused in court of masterminding this whole farcical trial, of leading a campaign of persecution against an already acquitted man — which is more or less the truth, isn't it.' He picked up a couple of newspapers at random and threw them at her. 'Look at this lot, for Christ's sake. We're being crucified.'

She had already seen the headlines as the papers were all lying around him on the sofa, open at the appropriate spot. CRETINOUS COMET LEADS MURDER VICTIM FAMILY IN SUICIDE COURT CASE was an average offering. The strap on that one was good too: *And they're paying for it.*

She knew what Paul was going to say before he said it. 'We can't pay the Phillipses, Jo, and you may as well accept it now. I should never have given you the go-ahead on this one. I should have known better.'

She suspected that he *had* known better. She suspected that, maybe for the first time during their marriage and his editorship, he had let the fact that she was his wife sway his judgement. He had known how important this story was to her. She was grateful to him for that but now she could feel the chill of his anger. He obviously felt she had let him down and maybe she had.

She could only continue with what she had begun. 'Paul, if we don't pay the Phillipses I think they could even lose their home,' she said. She didn't know if that was true but they had told her they had already been forced by the farming recession to remortgage their property to the hilt.

He was unimpressed. It wasn't that he was an

unfeeling man but, apart from any other considerations, it was a very long time since he had been on
the road. She had noticed from her first days in
Fleet Street the differences between front-line
troops and the back-room boys, as she still in her
mind divided up the staffs of newspapers. To the
back-room boys a story was simply that — words on
paper to be manipulated in whatever fashion would
give greatest effect. The people behind the stories
only existed to the front-line troops who, all too
often, were out there on their own.

She tried again, a different approach. 'Look,
together with the Phillipses we tried to get a
monster locked up where he belongs. That's in the
glorious old campaigning style of the *Comet* and I
think we should do more of it.'

'Some glorious campaign,' he snapped at her and
threw another newspaper across the room, front
page towards her. I'VE BEEN PERSECUTED, CLAIMS
INNOCENT O'DONNELL screamed a banner headline.

'Innocent O'Donnell,' she muttered irritably.
'That's a contradiction in terms. What about the
poor bloody innocent Phillips family, that's what I
want to know.'

'Do you, Joanna?' He was as angry now as she
could ever remember seeing him. 'I'm not entirely
convinced of that. I'm beginning to wonder if the
reason for your blind obsession with this case isn't
exactly the same as it was twenty years ago. One
Mike Fielding.'

She was startled. She had tried to mention
Fielding's involvement with the case as little as
possible.

'Take a look at page five of the *Mail*. It's inside most of the others too.'

With growing apprehension she did as she was bid. There, staring her in the face, was the photograph which, if she had allowed herself to think about it, had been bound to appear. She and Mike were standing close together on the courtroom steps, smiling slightly at each other, his arm protectively round her shoulders. 'Damn,' she thought. 'Damn and blast.'

Sometimes she forgot just how astute her husband was. He missed nothing. She suddenly felt sure he had guessed that she had been with Fielding that evening.

His next words convinced her that she was probably right. 'Don't take me for a fool, Joanna,' he told her icily.

Part Three

12

Two months later James Martin O'Donnell disappeared.

The *Daily Mail* broke the story, to Joanna's intense irritation and her husband's fury.

'Where's my boy?' asked Sam O'Donnell in a lengthy centre-spread feature, which focused on what he claimed was a campaign of persecution against his eldest son. 'The police and a major national newspaper have colluded in hounding my Jimbo. And now he's disappeared. I fear I'll never see my boy again.'

It was nauseating stuff, once more making O'Donnell sound like some innocent caught up in a whirlwind of events none of which were of his own making. Sam O'Donnell had apparently gone to the *Mail* in preference to reporting his son missing to the police. That made a kind of twisted sense. It was hard to imagine the O'Donnells calling on police help for anything. This way they brought the case into the public domain and ensured that police inquiries would be made without actually directly calling on plod for help.

No doubt the O'Donnells had already scoured their own dubious contacts nationwide before taking this step. They must have drawn a blank. That in itself was intriguing. In fact, the whole thing was fascinating. However, Joanna could not sit back and enjoy any kind of objective assessment. She was too involved. And the *Daily Mail* story was yet another kick in the teeth for the *Comet*.

At one point Sam O'Donnell damn near accused the police of having played a part in Jimbo's disappearance. Fielding got a specific mention:

> That detective down in Exeter is obsessed with getting my boy. It's more than harassment. He's stalked my Jimbo. That's what 'e's done. Stalked 'im. I know for a fact he was behind this so-called private prosecution. Him and that dammed woman from the *Comet*.

Joanna groaned. Here we go again, she thought.

> Twice now, my boy's been cleared of having anything to do with Angela Phillips's death. Twice he's had to stand trial. And that's not supposed to be the law in this country.

The *Mail* had tried to get to Fielding, of course, doorstepping him, no doubt. The paper reported that he had refused to speak to them and the only other police comment was from a Met spokesman pledging that of course inquiries would be made in the normal way into Mr O'Donnell's disappearance, but pointing out that he had not even been officially reported missing yet. There was a small picture of Fielding hurrying out of Heavitree Road police station looking extremely fed up and harassed.

On its leader page the *Mail* made it clear that it was not in any way supporting Sam the Man, many of whose business activities had frequently been the subject of police investigations, but the events leading up to O'Donnell's disappearance must undoubtedly have some significance. If he were guilty of any involvement in the abduction, rape, or murder of Angela Phillips then police mishandling must surely be evident. If he were not guilty, and he had after all now been found innocent of all three charges in courts of law, then his father was probably quite correct in alleging harassment. Certainly Jimbo O'Donnell's disappearance and the varied events leading up to it should be thoroughly investigated by independent officers.

It was all good stuff. But not for the *Comet*.

'This whole story is turning into a fiasco, Joanna,' Paul stormed at the end of morning conference, giving her a roasting in front of the entire senior editorial team, which she was quite sure they all thoroughly enjoyed witnessing. The days when female staff were fair game for any kind of nonsense and sexual harassment in a newspaper office might be over — but an assistant editor and high-profile columnist who was also the editor's wife fell into a unique category, and to see her lampooned in this way was bound to be regarded as excellent sport.

'First we get publicly humiliated. Now the opposition is running rings round us. Again. I let you have a free hand with this one, Jo, because I believed you were on top of it. Let's see if we can't retrieve something out of this mess, shall we?'

It was fair comment. Joanna could not argue with him and did not.

Instead, she went to work. She had already called the O'Donnell house, in fact, had done so when the first edition of the *Mail* had dropped the previous night. A *Daily Mail* reporter had answered the phone. She had not been surprised. The *Mail* had obviously done a deal. And in the circumstances the O'Donnells would hardly have come to her and the *Comet*.

She phoned Fielding. She had called him before, leaving messages at Heavitree Road and on his mobile message service that morning. He had not replied. This time she got lucky.

He answered his mobile at once.

'Another fine mess,' she began.

'I don't know what you're worried about, the rubber heel boys are over me like flies again,' he said. He meant Complaints and Discipline investigators.

And she wasn't surprised to hear it. Or all that interested. She had her own troubles. 'Christ, Mike, you could have called me yesterday when the *Mail* got on to you.'

'For God's sake, Joanna. Don't you think maybe I had something else to think about?'

There was none of the unspoken warmth between them that there had been that evening at the Exeter pub. They were both under too much stress. The mess was getting worse rather than better. In normal circumstances Jo could imagine nothing she would like better than to think that O'Donnell might have come to a sticky end at the hands of some of his particularly venomous cohorts. But these were not normal circumstances.

It seemed that she and Fielding were getting blame thrown at them at every step.

'I'm sorry,' she said quietly.

He mellowed a little. 'Look, if I hear anything and if I possibly can, I'll call you,' he told her before saying an abrupt goodbye.

She pondered for a moment. She dared not call the Phillipses. That relationship was over for good. Paul was still refusing to pay the family and she had to realise that by his own standards he had good reason not to.

She had even been forbidden by Paul from explaining the situation to them. 'Joanna, there was no contract between this newspaper and the Phillipses,' he had reminded her repeatedly. 'That is the legal truth and we're sticking to it. Classic denial. It worked for Jimbo O'Donnell and it'll work for us.'

That had made her feel even more of a rat, of course, but what could she do?

'It would be madness for you even to try to contact them, Jo,' he had continued. 'You must see that. If they've got any sense they'll have a lawyer in on the act now. They've probably been told to tape any conversations they have with you or anybody representing this newspaper. You really mustn't even discuss it with them.'

She had known he was right, which made it harder.

He'd put a hand on her arm, continuing more gently, 'Look, Jo, I know you feel bad about this and so do I.'

She hadn't been convinced of that, but she let it pass.

'There's just no alternative. At least we tried to

279

help them, tried to bring O'Donnell to justice. Nobody could have predicted that it would all go pear-shaped again.'

She hadn't been convinced of that either. Her own and Fielding's judgements had so far proved to be faulty in every aspect of this case. And Nuffield had turned out to be a huge disappointment.

For once she did as she was told. She dodged all phone calls from the Phillips family and never called them back. Eventually they got the message.

Both she and Paul had since received letters from a firm of Exeter solicitors saying that they represented Bill and Rob Phillips who were planning to take them to the Press Complaints Commission and sue them for breach of contract if they did not pay the costs of the court case as agreed.

Paul said they didn't have a cat in hell's chance of winning such a case and, anyway, he'd have a large bet that when it came to it they wouldn't take the risk. 'Let's face it, they can't afford to, can they?' he remarked.

Joanna squirmed inside.

As for the Press Complaints Commission, Paul went on to say that he would be more afraid of them if he paid the Phillipses than if he didn't. Inasmuch as any editor was afraid of the commission, he concluded.

Again she had been forced to agree with him, even though she didn't like it. Everything about this whole case continued to leave a nasty taste in her mouth.

Paul was proved right. There had so far been no

follow-up to the letter from the Exeter solicitors. It seemed likely that the Phillipses were indeed not going to proceed with their threat to sue the *Comet*. But Joanna had got one prediction right. When they finally realised they were not going to get any more money out of the *Comet* without one hell of a fight, the family decided to go as public as possible, giving an interview to a local news agency, which put out their story to all the nationals.

Unfortunately, the family's bad fortune continued and their timing was atrocious. They had embarked on this course of action only yesterday, thus having to do battle for space with the story of O'Donnell's disappearance. The *Mail*, glorying in its exclusive, did not even give the Phillipses' allegations a line. The other papers ran stories in their first editions — although not as big as might have been hoped because more or less the same claims had already been made in open court — but the 'O'Donnell missing' revelation virtually wiped them out of later editions altogether. Rather guiltily, Joanna had to acknowledge that while unlucky for the Phillipses, it was quite fortunate for her that the two stories had broken on the same day. Jimbo's disappearance had so overshadowed the Phillipses' story that Paul seemed barely to have even noticed it.

Joanna tried to put out of her mind everything about which she could do nothing, and concentrated on attempting to find a really sensational follow-up to the *Mail* exclusive. She did not succeed but, fortunately for her, neither did anyone else.

The *Mail*, predictably, remained ahead. After all, they had the O'Donnells tied up and they were famously good at this kind of story. The *Comet*'s involvement with the private prosecution, however misguided it now seemed to have been, had until this latest development at least meant that the paper had been continuously ahead of the game. The *Mail* did not like to be beaten. Ever. Now it was firmly in front. The day after its initial exclusive the *Mail* carried a picture story of an old and frail-looking Sam O'Donnell, his walking stick to the forefront, outside the police station at which he had finally officially reported his son missing.

It was a brilliant image. However, the word was, in spite of official police protestation to the contrary, that Sam had been greeted with no great enthusiasm and there were few signs of any major police activity in looking for his son.

Joanna called Fielding again.

He had calmed down somewhat and seemed to be taking some pleasure at last from the prospect, however remote, that Jimbo O'Donnell might have come to harm. 'You're right, nobody's rushing around on this one up at the Met,' he told Jo. 'But why should they? It's not just that we all know the bugger's a villain and of a particularly nasty kind, too. He's also a grown man and, unfortunately, a free one. He's not considered vulnerable — that would be a laugh. He could have gone anywhere off his own bat. There's no evidence to show that he may have been taken against his will or harmed in any way — not like poor Angela.' She had heard him sigh at the other end of the phone. 'There's no reason why there should be a major search on for him. He'll go on the missing persons register, now that it's been reported that he's disappeared, and that will be about it. For a while, at any rate. Nobody could expect otherwise,' he paused. 'Except Sam the Man, of course,' he reflected wryly.

★　★　★

Joanna's discomfiture continued. Three days later *Private Eye* dropped with an uncannily accurate summary of Paul Potter's public rollicking of his wife. In the notorious 'Street of Shame' section they referred to Potter as Smile in the Back and predictably dubbed Joanna his 'pouting hackette spouse'.

> Cracks are showing at last in the tabloid world's dream marriage [pronounced the magazine with obvious satisfaction]. And Old Smile in the Back will be straight-faced indeed if any kind of scandal rocks his long-coveted desire for a knighthood — widely expected to be announced in the new year's honours list.
>
> However, Potter needn't worry. The *Eye* is assured that rumours of recent Ugandan discussions between the gorgeous pouting Lady Potter-to-be and DI Mike Fielding, her old flame now in deep water over the part he played in the revival of the O'Donnell case, are completely unfounded.

Joanna groaned inside when she, alone at her desk thankfully, encountered the barbed item in her early copy of the magazine. There was no telling how Paul would react. He too, of course, received the earliest possible edition of *Private Eye*, as did virtually everyone in newspapers. It was a bit like a house magazine, really. Paul would have scanned the rag already and read the piece. If he hadn't, some kind soul would be sure to point it out to him.

She saw her husband several times during the day, including at morning and afternoon conference, but he made no mention of the *Private Eye* piece. She didn't either, in spite of being well aware of occasional little giggling groups of staff falling into unnatural silence as soon as she approached. But she kept her own counsel, pretended not to notice, said nothing. Give nobody the satisfaction of seeing that you were hurt or in any way affected. That was one thing that had remained the same throughout all the changes she had witnessed within newspapers. If there was one thing worse than being the subject of a typically snide *Private Eye* piece, it would be to let the buggers know they had got to you — in particular the buggers who had been responsible for supplying the relevant information.

Though Paul did not mention the item to her that day, or even give any indication that he had read it, she knew him well enough to be quite sure that he had, and that this was the reason for him looking unusually tight-lipped. She dreaded the confrontation that was surely coming.

At home that evening, over a nowadays increasingly rare late supper together, Paul at last brought up the subject. 'I'm absolutely fucking furious about that *Private Eye* piece, Jo,' he told her, and she knew he really must be, because he so rarely swore.

'I know. It is bollocks, though, I hope you realise that.'

'What?' He glanced at her with his eyebrows raised as if not quite following her train of thought. 'Oh, you mean the Fielding stuff?' Paul's tone was very reasonable. 'I don't enjoy reading that sort of thing about my wife, but I suppose it was bound to happen sooner or later after the court case. That damned picture everybody carried didn't help. And you do insist on still remaining in contact with the man.'

'He's the best contact we've got on this, in fact, he's about the only one left, Paul,' she said.

'Yes, I know,' he countered. 'You still have a fixation for him, though, I'm aware of that even if you're not yourself. But I don't really think there's anything between you any more. And anyway, it's not that which has made me so mad. It's all that stuff from morning conference. If I knew which one of our guys had sold us down the river like that I'd sack whoever it was at once. Jesus!'

She couldn't help a small smile. Paul's reactions were rarely predictable. He never failed to surprise her and often to impress her.

★   ★   ★

The following day the law lords ruled that the appeal court which had overturned the murder conviction of Michael Weir had been wrong. This was the case which had been used as a precedent by

285

the defence in the ill-fated private prosecution of Jimbo O'Donnell.

The appeal court's judgement that DNA samples obtained during the investigation of one offence could not be used in an unrelated case had been crucial to the failure of the committal proceedings.

The law lords, however, were damning. 'The austere interpretation which the court of appeal adopted is not only in conflict with the plain words of the statute but also produces results which are contrary to good sense,' they said.

Too late, thought Joanna glumly. If only O'Donnell was in court now, that ruling could have made all the difference. But Jimbo had now faced every possible charge concerning the abduction and death of Angela Phillips. Double jeopardy was still the law. He couldn't be tried again.

Four days later it all became academic. James Martin O'Donnell's body was discovered on Dartmoor, not far from the disused tin mine which had become the tomb of the raped and murdered Angela Phillips twenty-one years earlier. He had been found early one morning by a group of ramblers and it was as if his killer had planned for him to be discovered. Jimbo had been buried in the shallowest of graves which, although in a remote part of the moor, had been only roughly filled in and was almost on the edge of the kind of track that was bound to be popular with walkers. The grave was so shallow that the heavy rains of the previous evening had washed away enough of the loose soil covering Jimbo for the fingers of his right hand to be left actually sticking out of the ground. It was this grisly sight that had alerted the ramblers.

O'Donnell was naked, his body caked with his own blood. And his cut-off penis had been stuffed into his mouth. Medical examination was later to prove both that his penis had been removed with a none too sharp knife shortly before his death and also that he had been buried alive.

13

Joanna learned of the discovery of O'Donnell's body from Fielding. He might be out of favour with his bosses but Dartmoor remained his patch. The seasoned detective didn't miss much.

She was stunned. It was something else she hadn't expected. Was this story never going to roll over? In her mind she had half dismissed the whole business of Jimbo's disappearance as yet another O'Donnell stunt. But he had been murdered, and in such a dramatic and significant way. Buried alive. His cock in his mouth. Found near where Angela Phillips had died. The first constructive thought that crossed her mind was that it had to be a revenge killing.

'It's going to be announced at a press conference later today, after he's been formally identified,' Fielding told her in a telephone call just after morning conference. He was at Heavitree Road police station. He spoke very quietly. She could understand that he did not want to be overheard. It was good of him to call her. She supposed it was for old times' sake. Mind you, she had stuck her neck out on his instigation and, thanks to him, her head was almost as much on the block in a different sort of way as his. She deserved his help. That did not mean he would necessarily always give it. On this occasion, though, Fielding had come up trumps. 'Tommy O'Donnell's on his way to the mortuary in

Exeter as we speak,' he went on. 'It's a formality, though. We all know what O'Donnell looks like well enough. He hasn't decomposed that much yet, and there's that tattoo on his arm. I thought you'd like a lead on it.'

'Thanks, Mike, I appreciate it,' she told him. She did too. The *Mail* would already be working on it for certain. They would be keeping their grip tight on the O'Donnells. If Tommy O'Donnell was on his way to Exeter the chances were that a *Mail* team was hard on his heels — maybe even with him. She didn't have the O'Donnells and she sure as hell didn't have the Phillipses any more. All she had was one Mike Fielding.

She pumped him for any extra information he could give her. 'Have you seen the body yourself?' she asked.

'Nope. C'mon, Jo, I'm off the case, aren't I? If I survive this lot at all I'm not likely to be doing much more than shuffling papers till I can pick up my pension and get out.'

Not that again, she thought. But she passed no comment. After all, she did realise that her own financial situation was a very fortunate one.

There appeared to be little more that he could or would tell her. When she ended the call she realised that neither of them had expressed their feelings on O'Donnell's death or the manner of it. Nor the significance of it. That was perhaps strange. For herself, she had been too shocked. She leaned back in her chair, stretching out her legs, and allowed herself the luxury of a minute or two to think over what she had just learned. She could not avoid a

289

sense of satisfaction that Jimbo O'Donnell had met both an early and undoubtedly agonising death, but not nearly as much satisfaction as she would have obtained from seeing him found guilty of the murder or at least the kidnap of Angela Phillips and properly revealed as the monster he had undoubtedly been. As far as the law was concerned he had died an innocent man and she was almost surprised to find that still mattered to her.

However, she had no time for further philosophising if she wanted to make the most of the advantage she and the *Comet* had been given by Fielding. She reached for her phone and called through to Paul's office.

'Come in now, get news and pix and Tim Jones,' he instructed. He meant bring in the news and picture editors along with Jones as chief crime man. Together they worked on the story all day, Pam Smythe directing her news team, Tim and his number two working through the Yard and their own contacts on either side of the law, and Joanna mercilessly exploiting whatever contacts she had left who might be able to help her on the story.

She spoke to Mike again a few hours later, to check on developments, homing in on every possible angle he might be able to give her that could put her and her newspaper ahead of the pack. 'So it is a revenge killing, then?' she asked. 'For Angela? Is that what your lads think?'

''Course they do. Where he was found, the way he died, his cock in his mouth. Unless we're just being made to think that.'

'You're getting complicated.'

290

'Yeah. Well. I try to think round things, don't I? Which is maybe why I was never going to make it big in the job . . . '

His bitterness and disappointment were never far from the surface, she thought. She stayed silent.

He continued after a brief pause 'No. You're right, Jo. Revenge for Angela is the number one theory. The Phillipses will be questioned, of course.'

'You don't think any of them would be capable of what was done to Jimbo, do you?'

'As it happens, no, I don't. And Jimbo O'Donnell was never short of enemies. But they're obviously going to be on the list, aren't they?'

Jo supposed so. She felt a sharp stab of pity for the family, together with a pang of guilt. If she and Fielding hadn't opened the whole can of worms again the Phillipses would not be in this situation.

She had no time to dwell on it, though. She had work to do. And fast. The material was dynamite and she knew they had put together a really good package by early evening conference at 5.15 p.m. The official Yard announcement did not come until about half an hour before that. Fielding's tip had given them a lead of the best part of a day. The *Comet* had been handed a huge advantage over its rivals, with the exception, she had little doubt, of the *Mail*. For about the first time since the whole thing had started again she allowed herself to feel a little bit pleased with herself. Just a little. And O'Donnell was dead, brutally murdered, which really was beginning to give her a nice warm feeling. Whoever had done the deed.

After the conference Paul gestured for her to stay

behind. She knew he would consider the story the *Comet* would be putting to bed that night to be at least something of a recovery. And, indeed, he seemed to be in the best mood he had been in for some time. 'I had lunch with Cromer-Wrong today,' he told her cheerily. Ronald Cromer-Wright was the *Comet*'s senior lawyer. Naturally he was invariably known as Cromer-Wrong. Nicknames like that were traditionally every bit as much a part of Fleet Street life as of the gangland world. It was instantly reassuring to Jo that Paul had referred to the lawyer in the familiar vernacular. Had he not been quite so cheery she might have wondered a little uneasily, in view of her recent exploits, where this opening remark was leading.

'Apparently Cromer-Wrong bumped into a rather well-oiled Nigel Nuffield at some chambers do who informed him that he would never be doing business with him or anybody else at the *Comet* for as long as you remained employed here, but refused to elaborate,' Paul continued, sounding highly amused now. 'Actually, I'm beginning to come round to your way of thinking, that maybe that's no great loss. But Nuffield's been paid by the Phillipses, apparently, so that's not his problem. I just want to know what you did to him, Jo.' Paul was grinning as if in anticipation.

This was almost like the old days, thought Joanna. 'I told him he was an overpaid, over-hyped, patronising fucking bastard,' she explained casually. 'Oh, and I think I may have mentioned something about prancing about in a damned silly wig . . . '

'I've told you before, Jo, about being afraid to say

292

what you mean,' remarked her husband solemnly. Then he started to chuckle. She could still hear him chuckling as she left his office, closing the door behind her.

Paul had always had a wicked sense of humour, buried as it all too often was beneath that cool, rather distant exterior, and it pained her that she, at least, seemed to be seeing less and less of it nowadays. He also had a liking for journalists who stood their corner and showed spirit. Even the one who was his wife, it seemed. By the time she reached her desk she was remembering all the reasons why she had married him in the first place.

Then, just before first edition time, he phoned down and asked her to come along to his office. She was still feeling buoyant — until he told her he was taking her byline off the main story.

'Sorry, Jo, you're too much at the heart of it all. The Phillipses might still sue. I can't take unnecessary risks. And God only knows what the O'Donnells might yet come up with. I want to distance you from it all. Having your name all over the splash every time something new breaks on this one just won't do.'

'Fine, whatever you say,' she told him crisply. She made no further comment, but she did slam the door to his office on the way out.

As she walked back to her desk she couldn't help but think back to the days when in an unhappy situation like this the first person she would have chosen to drown her sorrows with would have been one Paul Potter.

She told herself not to be so dammed stupid. If

she hadn't been his wife she doubted Paul would even have bothered to tell her about the byline, and she would have known nothing about it until the first edition dropped. It was utterly ridiculous that a byline should matter so much to her at her age and after all she had been through in newspapers, after all she had achieved. But it did matter, of course. Particularly when she was the one who had got the lead on the story. It was actually even more than that. This was her story, through and through, and had been from the very germ of the beginning of it to whatever decaying bones of it there were now. She had taken the flak when it had gone so badly wrong. She should also get any credit that was going. Even after all these years it was still important to her to be seen to be achieving, to be seen to be at the top of her particular game.

It mattered all right. And the day that it didn't would be the day when she might as well not bother to continue even pretending to be a journalist.

* * *

The red-top Sundays had a field day. The *News of the World* homed in on Rob Phillips who gave a near-hysterical interview in which he said that O'Donnell had finally got what he deserved and that he only wished he had had the nerve to do the job himself. 'What happened to O'Donnell is poetic justice,' he said. 'I just hope he died in agony and in terror, like my poor sister did. But no end, however dreadful, could ever be quite bad enough for that evil bastard.'

It was hard-hitting stuff. The fact that O'Donnell was officially an innocent man twice acquitted for crimes against Angela, including her rape and murder, in two different courts of law, received little attention. Because O'Donnell was dead, the *Screws* had a clear run at the story. You can't libel the dead.

The *People* featured an almost equally hysterical outburst from Tommy O'Donnell. He more or less accused the entire Phillips family, Rob Phillips in particular, of involvement in the murder and even suggested that Mike Fielding probably had a part in it too. Joanna was only surprised that she didn't merit a mention somewhere along the line.

She thought the *People* was on by far the most dodgy legal ground, but who was going to sue? Certainly not Mike Fielding who in any case appeared just to want the whole thing to go away so that he could ensure the safety of his pension. And certainly not the Phillipses. They would not have the bottle for yet another court case, she was sure of it, nor the cash, come to that. And in any event, with Rob Phillips's rantings coincidentally appearing in the *Screws* on the same day as the Tommy O'Donnell stuff was in the *People*, what sort of case would they have? If, indeed, it was a coincidence. She thought it probably more likely that they had known over at the *People* what the *Screws* was running. After all, from about Friday morning onwards every week half the aim of the news teams of the two big red tops was to find out what the other was splashing on. And if they'd had early knowledge at the *People* of the *Screw*'s exclusive, that would have greatly influenced the advice of the paper's lawyers and the decision of its editor.

She called Fielding the next day. 'Just wanted to see how you were doing.'

'I'm not quite sure,' he said. 'O'Donnell's death has taken the heat off a bit.'

'What do you mean?'

'Somewhat takes the attention away from all those claims about me pushing you guys and the Phillipses to get the private prosecution case against O'Donnell set up, doesn't it?' he said.

Typical, she thought. He always saw everything in terms of how it affected him and his career, always had done. Jimbo O'Donnell being found dead with his cock in his mouth was no exception.

And what did he mean 'claims'? That was the trouble with Fielding, sometimes he seemed to bend the truth so much inside his head that he got to believe his own fabrication. Which was, of course, exactly what journalists were so frequently accused of. 'Did you see all the stuff in the Sundays?'

'Yup. Predictable, I suppose.'

'I wondered if you knew how the investigation is going. Any progress?'

'Don't believe so. Not that I'm allowed to get a look-in, of course. One thing's for sure, there's a longish list of folk who wouldn't have minded topping Jimbo.'

'Yeah. And you are on it according to his brother Tommy.'

He chuckled drily. 'The O'Donnells think everybody's idea of justice is the same as theirs,' he said mildly.

'Well, I must admit I'm glad the twisted bastard's

dead,' she replied. 'I'm beginning to get quite a warm feeling about it, in fact.'

'Yeah.' There was a silence.

Surely he had more to say than that? She waited.

'Yeah,' he said again, a little more life in his voice at last. 'Come to think of it, so am I.'

★ ★ ★

Fielding told himself that for him it was good news not to be involved in the case any more. Things seemed to be straightening out quite nicely. With Jimbo dead the Complaints and Discipline guys did indeed seem to be losing interest in him and the part he had played in the private prosecution. He knew he would be sure to be interviewed by the team investigating O'Donnell's murder, and he determined that he would be respectful and to the point, and not let any of his personal feelings get in the way.

Unfortunately he was called in by the senior investigating officer on an afternoon when he was least expecting it. He had spent far longer than he ought to have done that lunchtime in the pub and had also drunk far more than he should. Confident of spending the rest of the day doing nothing more challenging than the 'paper shuffling' of which he was so scornful, he had downed four or five pints of bitter, he couldn't quite remember which, each after the first one accompanied by a large whisky chaser.

To make matters worse, the senior investigating officer was Todd Mallett. Detective Superintendent

Todd Mallett. Mike had known that, of course, but he had tried not to think about it. Apart from anything else, it really rankled that the other man, whom Fielding had always considered to be thoroughly inferior to himself as a police officer, had ultimately achieved a rank far senior to his own.

Fielding had never doubted that he had both greater ability and greater intelligence, not only than Todd Mallett but than most of the officers he had worked with over the years. That made his failure to progress beyond the rank of DI all the more infuriating. Particularly as even he had to accept that the stagnation of his career was at least partly down to his own behaviour.

Mallett interviewed Fielding himself, rather than delegating the task to one of the lower-rank officers on his team and Fielding knew that was a gesture of respect. But he still couldn't help the way he felt. Particularly after that ill-fated lunchtime session. From the moment he opened the door to the second-floor office which Mallett, who was actually based at HQ at Middlemoor, had been allocated, Mike seemed unable to stop himself appearing uncooperative and belligerent.

Mallett greeted him in his usual courteous, affable fashion.

Fielding, in the sort of mood which ensured that even the other man's affability irritated him, responded abruptly; 'Right, what do you want with me, then?'

He was aware of Mallett studying him appraisingly. Apart from anything else he supposed it would be highly optimistic to think that the detective superintendent would not notice that he had been drinking.

Certainly when Mallett spoke again he was no longer affable. He had greeted Fielding pleasantly and informally, and addressed him as Mike. The interview suddenly turned very formal and not a little hostile. His own fault again, Mike knew.

'I suggest, Detective Inspector, that you watch your attitude. There is no doubt at all in my mind that you have already gone against the instructions of your senior officers in passing on certain information, albeit through a third party, to the Phillips family, and that by then encouraging them in every way you could to take out that ill-fated civil prosecution you opened the whole can of worms which has led to James Martin O'Donnell's death . . .'

'Look,' interrupted Fielding, 'I've been through all that with the rubber heel squad. None of you can prove a thing.'

'Really,' said Mallett, leaning towards Fielding across the small table which separated them. 'Well, that's down to Complaints and Discipline, although I wouldn't be quite so sure of yourself if I were you, Inspector. As it happens, all I am interested in is any leads you may have acquired during your extremely dubious and meddlesome 'enquiries' which could help us find Jimbo O'Donnell's killer.'

The drink really got the better of Fielding then. Or maybe it was not just that. Whatever the reason, one of those flashes of the old devil-may-care stick-it-up-your-jumper Fielding, which he tried so hard to suppress nowadays, came roaring to the forefront. 'For fuck's sake!' he yelled, jumping to his feet.

Todd involuntarily swung away from him as if half expecting to be punched in the face. Fielding wanted to punch him, too, and only just held back. Pompous, patronising, sanctimonious bugger, he fumed. But fortunately he had just enough restraint and sense of preservation left not to say so. He couldn't stop himself launching into the rest of his diatribe, though. 'Jimbo O'Donnell was one of the most twisted, evil, perverted bastards ever to walk free from a courtroom. Now he's got his. And you think I'm supposed to give a fuck who topped him? Well, I fucking don't! The world is a better place this week because somebody somewhere had the balls to do to the fucker what the whole of the justice system of this country couldn't do — put him somewhere where he can never harm some other poor bloody kid. There is such a thing as natural justice, you know, Detective Superintendent.' He did his best to make Todd's rank sound like an insult and succeeded fairly well.

The other man eyed him impassively. 'I think we'd better continue this interview when you're not so emotional, Mike, don't you?' he enquired eventually, informal again, but very cool. He returned to studying the papers spread out on his desk in a gesture which clearly dismissed Fielding who made gratefully for the door without another word.

Outside in the corridor, Mike closed the door quite gently behind him and leaned against it for a moment or two. He had been surprised at how articulate he had been in the circumstances and was actually, on one level, quite pleased with himself.

But then the full implications of his outburst struck him. 'Oh, God,' he murmured to himself. 'If that fucker reports me on top of everything else that really will be the end of my fucking pension.' And, weaving very slightly from side to side, he set off down the corridor, heading for the back door out of the station. The only further decision he intended to make that afternoon was which pub he was going to go to. He certainly had no intention of returning to his desk. He might as well compound his own felony, he thought.

Anyway, he was just beginning to feel no pain, which more and more often was the only state he really liked to be in nowadays.

★ ★ ★

A week later a professional London heavy called Shifter Brown was arrested on suspicion of the murder of Jimbo O'Donnell. There was no formal announcement because ultimately Shifter was released without any charges being brought against him. But the news leaked around the Yard like flood water seeping through a wall of sandbags. Only quicker.

Joanna knew of Shifter Brown, although she had never met him. He was the kind of thug others hired to do their dirty work for them. Shifter would give a man a good going over for a hundred quid or so and throw in a broken leg or two for not much more. That was well known. Shifter looked the part. He

301

was a big, muscle-bound guy in his early forties with thinning red hair and a broken nose. As a kid he had been a budding professional heavyweight boxer until a particularly vicious blow to the head dislodged the retina of his right eye and he had been banned on medical grounds from ever fighting again. After that it was back to the streets for Shifter. Officially he was a nightclub bouncer, standing patiently, trussed up in a dinner jacket outside some of London's hottest nightspots, his thick neck threatening to burst open the collars of his shirts, which invariably seemed to be a size too small. But the word had always been that Shifter was up for extras. He had twice served time for GBH over the years. Nobody had ever been able to pin a murder rap on him, although he had been the primary suspect in at least two gangland killings, but there seemed little doubt that killing, too, was just a job for Shifter. All part of his business. The only difference was probably the price.

After all, that was more or less how he had got his name. He had been christened Arthur Richard Brown. They called him Shifter because he shifted people.

Reminiscent of the original prosecution of O'Donnell for murder, it seemed that just about all the police had against Shifter was circumstantial evidence. He had been seen at night by a witness bundling an obviously unwilling passenger, hands bound, the witness had thought, into the back of his white Ford Transit. The same van had been seen in Devon, parked, apparently empty, just off the army's Dartmoor loop road by a range warden from Okehampton camp in charge of clearing the area for a night-fighting exercise. As a matter of record he had obligingly jotted down the van's number before going on a quick reccy of the area to ensure that the vehicle's driver had not strayed into danger territory. On a further check visit to the spot where the Transit had been parked, the warden found that the vehicle had been removed and thought no more about it until after O'Donnell's body was discovered, when he passed his invaluable information on to the police.

If Shifter Brown really had bundled O'Donnell into the back of a van that way, then the vehicle could well hold forensic evidence which would convict him. However, when he was arrested Shifter simply claimed that his van had been stolen. And certainly nobody could find it.

Intensive police interrogation failed to make much impression on Shifter. He was a pro. He said nothing. Even if he had believed that the police had enough to charge him and that fingering whoever might have hired him could help his case, Shifter was firmly of the 'I don't grass, governor' breed. Ultimately the arresting officers had to admit they had insufficient evidence with which to charge Shifter and he was released after the maximum thirty-six hours in custody.

A couple of weeks after that the inquest into James Martin O'Donnell's death was held in Okehampton — once again in the familiar room in the grubby white extended bungalow which was the moorland town's unprepossessing Magistrates'

Court. The verdict, of course, was death by unlawful killing.

Joanna travelled down to Devon for the hearing, carefully avoiding telling Paul that she planned to be there. She somehow could not resist witnessing this final chapter in O'Donnell's life and she knew her husband would not approve. He appreciated her contributions to the story and the additional information she was sometimes able to provide, but he still seemed to want her to back off from any public involvement.

The Phillipses were not at the inquest. Joanna reckoned they'd had quite enough of courts — and of the police. She had not expected them to be there and would indeed have been horrified had she had to confront them.

Tommy O'Donnell was there. He glowered at her across the courtroom but made no attempt to speak to her. His father Sam didn't make an appearance and neither did Mike Fielding.

Joanna knew that Mike, too, was being forced to take a back seat and thought that maybe he had in any case reached the stage where that was all he wanted to do.

She called him on her mobile afterwards and they agreed to meet again at the same pub as before. She didn't like to think about what was continually drawing her to him, but she had to admit it was something more than just what he could give her professionally.

He looked even wearier and as if he had been drinking already, which was probably par for the course, she suspected. He arrived in a taxi. Gone were the days when policemen dared to take liberties others might not with drink-driving laws. In the present climate a drink-driving offence almost invariably meant instant dismissal. And the end of the pension, the prospect of which, as Mike had so frequently indicated to her, seemed to be about all he was looking forward to in life.

In response to her query about his welfare he told her the story of his interview with Todd Mallett.

She couldn't help smiling. 'How to win friends and influence people, the Fielding edition,' she said.

'Tell me about it,' he responded. 'Too much to bloody drink again, I suppose. Mind you, I always drink more when I'm bored and I'm bored rigid. It's not just this case the bastards won't let me near, you know. Its every damn thing. They're giving the impression they're doing me a favour just by letting me work out the next twelve months or so for my thirty years.'

Here we go again, she thought.

He drank deeply from his pint, his second since they had arrived there ten minutes earlier.

'So Mallett didn't take any official action against you, then, or you wouldn't have that to worry about maybe.'

'No maybe about it. I suppose Mallett did me a favour really.' He sounded very grudging, but then Jo knew enough about the relationship between the two men to understand how difficult Fielding must find it to accept their respective positions. 'He didn't report me. Just called me in the next day and suggested we do the interview all over again. Told me to consider that I was being given a final warning, though. Step out of line once more and he'd make sure I was out. And stuff my pension.' Mike smiled wryly. 'Anyway you don't want to hear all that; all you want from me is information, isn't it?'

Was it her imagination or did he sound bitter yet again? She played it straight and spoke lightly. 'If you say so.'

'It's OK, I know I owe you.'

He'd told her that before, too. But, rather stupidly perhaps, she hoped that wasn't the only reason he was helping her. And in any case, he might be a bit down and out by his standards, but Fielding was not at all beyond using her to pass on information he wanted to see in print. His reasons were invariably his own. He was the kind of man who had always had a private agenda, always found it hard to toe the official line. The difference was that when you were young and flying high, and cracking cases others couldn't get to grips with, it was all right to be a bit of a maverick. When you were pushing fifty and drinking too much and you had lost that early flair, albeit because it had been knocked out of you rotten, then it wasn't all right any more.

She knew that and was honest enough with herself to wonder how she would be faring in her world were it not for her marriage to her editor. All too many of her peers had been either unceremoniously cast on the scrap heap when they were in their forties or early fifties, or else so badly humiliated they had felt forced to resign in order to save their sanity. And, all too often nowadays, without the buffer of the huge pay-offs that had been pretty well standard right up to the early nineties.

She studied Fielding sympathetically. She had to pity him, although she knew how much he would hate to know that. 'You don't owe me anything,' she said flatly. If it was a lie, what did it matter?

He grinned at her. In spite of everything the grin had barely changed. Extraordinary. Still to die for, still cheeky and challenging and warm and inviting all at the same time. It was just that she reckoned it was a pretty rare sight nowadays.

'Whatever you say,' he told her, and there was even that old hint of laughter in his voice. But he continued in matter-of-fact more serious tones, 'Mallett's convinced Brown did it, Jo. Don't waste your energies on any other theories. I haven't got a lot of time for Todd Mallett, but there's little doubt he's right.'

She studied his face and his voice as he spoke. He had always been different when he talked about policing in this way. It was what he did, what he had once done so well. He sounded almost authoritative and sure of himself, the way he used to, even though this was not his case any more and any further unofficial involvement in it could only damage, if not destroy, the remains of his career.

But it appeared that he had been keeping his ear to the ground as much as he invariably did. She wondered fleetingly why she had thought he would ever really change.

'They'll get him eventually, Jo, no doubt about it. But the big question will remain, won't it? Who paid him to do it? Guys like Brown only do it for dough.'

Back in London, Joanna got Tim Jones to sort out a phone number for Shifter Brown. Then she called him and asked if he would like to meet her for lunch. And, unlike perhaps most members of the public who had never had dealings with a villain like Brown or his kind, plus perhaps the bulk of the current crop of rookie reporters, she was not at all surprised when he accepted.

Her predecessors in crime reporting had all been on the Christmas lists of the Kray bothers, and Reggie Kray continued to write and send cards from Parkhurst jail to his 'friends in the press' right up to his death. Jo herself had got used to the same kind of treatment from Sam O'Donnell. Although she would never get another card from Sam, that was for certain.

She knew that Brown had always seen himself as a kind of folk hero, a modern-day gunslinger who would maim and maybe even kill, but, in common with Sam the Man O'Donnell, whatever he did was strictly according to his own moral code. Like the good-guy gunfighters of the Old Wild West who would only kill in a fair duel and never shoot a man in the back, or so legend had it anyway, Brown would only administer what he saw as rough justice within the criminal world in which he moved. It was all business to him. He considered himself to be one of the last of a dying breed, the sort who looked after his own and harmed no one outside his own circle. And like the Krays and the O'Donnells, certainly Sam the Man, he saw himself as a kind of celebrity and could rarely resist an opportunity to talk to the press. He was certainly not afraid of media people. But Shifter Brown was the sort who would not admit to being afraid of anything.

Jo arranged to meet him at a good but unfashionable Soho restaurant. She did not particularly want to be seen in his presence. He arrived looking immaculate in an expensive dark suit, snowy white shirt and flamboyant multicoloured silk tie. Gold and diamonds flashed on his fingers and at his wrists. Shifter doubtless reckoned that he looked the business and in a way he did, even though there was more than a touch of the Del Boys about his appearance. He did not notice the way the other diners paused in their conversations as he passed them by, but then he wouldn't.

It wasn't just his great size, the broken nose, the weathered features, and the overly flash clothes and jewellery which marked Shifter as one apart. It was everything about him from the set of his jaw to the way he squared his broad shoulders and how his big, beefy hands hung at his sides almost like a shotgun carried loosely but cocked ready for use.

He beamed a greeting at her when he was ushered to her table and proceeded to be charm itself. 'I'm delighted to meet you, darling,' he told her. 'I've always had you down for one of the good 'uns.'

Joanna smiled back as if flattered, but she wasn't. She had met his sort before often enough. She knew perfectly well that he was another evil bastard, albeit with, like Sam O'Donnell, his own twisted morality.

He did have rough charm, though. And, by God, he was funny. Particularly if you were into seriously black humour. Which of course, as an old crime hack, Joanna was. He told her some wicked gangland stories, playing to the gallery. First there was the tale of legendary London gang boss, Charlie Richardson, hard as they come but famous for his devotion to his mum and love of animals, who had an adored but wayward pet monkey which his newly acquired mistress insisted he get rid of after it effectively destroyed her collection of Capo di Monte porcelain. ''It's that creature or me,' she said. Now Charlie wasn't too sure which to choose at first but eventually he gets on to Mad Frankie — Frankie would always do anything for him, loved Charlie, did Frankie — and asks him if he'll look after this bleeding monkey for a bit, and Frankie says OK boss and takes it home with him. Well, the monkey's shaking and shivering all the time, and it's just the way its nervous system is, but Mad Frankie doesn't know that. He thinks, poor little bleeder, come all the way from Africa, it's cold, innit? So he wraps it up in an electric blanket. Then the monkey goes and pees itself in fright and gets electrocuted.'

Shifter paused for effect. Jo began to giggle helplessly.

'Well, Frankie gets together with the rest of the boys and they think up some yarn to tell Charlie about the sad demise of this blessed monkey, cos God knows what Charlie would've done if he'd thought Mad Frankie was to blame. Anyway, somehow or other they get Charlie to accept that it died of natural causes, but he's gutted. Right gutted. He goes and fetches this monkey home to his house in Peckham and then he arranges a burial service for it in his back garden.

'Well, he's a man who commanded a lot of respect, Charlie. So you end up with about two dozen of the hardest nuts in the business all done up in their best whistles, black ties, the lot, standing in Charlie's backyard doffing their hats at a funeral for a bleeding monkey.' Shifter threw back his big head and roared with laughter. Jo laughed with him. Everybody in the restaurant stopped eating and drinking, turned and stared.

He really was a showman. And it was annoyingly difficult not to find him likeable. Joanna hated it when she liked villains. She had gone to Brazil once to interview Great Train Robber Ronnie Biggs and she had felt much the same about him. The man had been a serial thief, widely believed to have been the unfeeling bastard who had casually smashed the innocent train driver viciously on the head, ruining and cruelly shortening his life. She had arrived in Rio de Janeiro determined to dislike Biggs intensely. But Ronnie had played the role of lovable rogue so well that she hadn't been able to stop herself falling for it, at least up to a point, even though she knew only too well that a large part of it was just a carefully cultivated act. And it was much the same with Shifter Brown.

''Ere, I've got another funeral story,' Shifter continued. 'Well, it's a wedding story, really, about Charlie and Mad Frankie again. When Charlie's

311

daughter got married they had this posh do down in Kent and the invitations said 'Morning dress'. Well, poor old Frankie, he didn't know any different, he thought it meant mourning dress, so he gets this undertaker suit, everything black, black tie, shiny black shoes, and when he turns up Charlie says: 'Fuck me, Frankie, I thought you were a bleeding gangster kissogram.'

Shifter grinned broadly, then his expression turned suddenly serious. 'Whoops, sorry, Joey doll, I didn't mean to use that language to you, girl, honest,' he said.

Joey doll? That was a new one. Joanna wondered what Shifter would have made of the vernacular of an old-fashioned newspaper office. Not a lot, she didn't think. He might be a gangland hit man but he still considered himself a gentleman.

Indeed. She made herself concentrate on what he did for a living. How he got his name. He shifted people. And, most particularly, what he might have done to Jimbo O'Donnell. Joanna was glad O'Donnell was dead. She was even glad that he had suffered such an appalling death. But it was bizarre to think that she was sitting in a smart restaurant with an engaging, immaculately dressed companion who had probably removed another man's sexual organs and buried him while he was still alive.

'You did him, didn't you, Shifter?' she asked eventually. 'The cops know. It was a pro job. It had your mark all over it.'

Arthur Richard Brown held both his hands out towards her, palms upwards in a gesture of supplication. 'Now would I? Would I do a horrible thing like that?' He grinned. Gold fillings gleamed among large yellowing teeth. 'I'm innocent, darling, upon my baby's life, I am,' he told her.

And then, just like Mike Fielding the very first time she ever met him, he winked broadly.

14

A month later Shifter Brown was rearrested. It was simple. The police found his Transit van which, although it had been washed and vacuumed and even given a new coat of paint of sorts, contained enough forensic evidence to prove that Jimbo O'Donnell had been transported in its rear compartment. Almost certainly under duress. The amateurish coat of paint had, in fact, contributed to Shifter's downfall.

Tim Jones got the full story from the Yard. It seemed that a sharp-eyed young constable had spotted the signs of a cheap, hasty respray on the now red Transit. A thin film of red paint had strayed on to both rear and front bumpers, along the bottom of one of the side windows and even into a corner of the windscreen. The constable had fed the registration number into the PNC and found that it did not match the vehicle he had spotted. At the time there was a major car theft scam operating in the capital and the young officer had been told to watch out for vehicles that might have been stolen and, if he had the slightest suspicion, to do a check. With the diligence of a newcomer to the job, he had done so even though the battered Transit, which had obviously seen better days, was not the kind of vehicle professional car thieves would normally target. And certainly he had no idea whatsoever that he might have stumbled across something far more serious.

The van's driver had been taken in for questioning. It turned out that he was a minor villain called Colin Ferris who ran a scrapyard in the aptly named Gravesend and had been suspected in the past of dealing with hot vehicles.

Meanwhile further checks were run on the Transit. It turned out to have been registered to Shifter Brown. Under intense pressure, including threats to have his business closed down straight away, Ferris admitted that Shifter had brought him the vehicle and had paid him to destroy it. He was supposed to have crushed it in his crusher. But he hadn't done so. 'It was a good set of wheels and I needed a van, you see,' he explained. 'Shifter'd put a nearly new engine in it, hadn't he? But it didn't look much and Transits like that one are all over this manor. So I figured if I changed the colour and the reg I'd get away with it.'

Ferris was not the brightest of characters, evidently. And if he had ever known or suspected what Shifter had used the van for and why he needed it destroyed he denied it hotly.

*　*　*

Shifter Brown was rearrested at once. This time there was hard evidence against him. By the time the van was discovered in the dubious care of Colin Ferris there had been very little forensic evidence left — but just enough in an age when the science has become so exact that DNA can be extracted from the moisture left behind by breath on glass. Small spots of dried blood found on the floor and sides of the vehicle's rear compartment matched O'Donnell's.

Shifter capitulated. He was an old-fashioned villain. He didn't think he stood a hope in hell of bucking that evidence. He didn't have a legal dream team behind him, either, as the man he had killed had always done. And he believed a court would go easier on him if he confessed and pleaded guilty. So Shifter was co-operative. He knew when he was beaten. Shifter was into damage limitation, only he didn't call it that.

Todd Mallett did the interrogation himself. The detective superintendent went back a long way on this case and still he didn't reckon the investigations had got anywhere near to the bottom of it. He wanted to be hands-on.

Although Shifter would not say who had hired him to kill Jimbo, he was quite happy to reveal that it was indeed someone who wanted revenge for the death and degradation of Angela Phillips. Shifter always liked to appear justified in his actions. However, there were a number of points which continued to puzzle Mallett. 'Why did you use your own van, Shifter?' the detective asked.

'Well, you never know quite what's best to do in a situation like this, you see, Mr Mallett,' Shifter began to explain, frowning in concentration. He sounded as if he were giving the policeman a lesson in criminology. 'I had to take Jimbo right back to Dartmoor where Angela Phillips was found, that was part of the deal. And I had to take him alive and do him there. On the spot like, buried, more or less the same way the girl was. Now — if I'd nicked a motor I could easily have got stopped on the way, couldn't I? So I figured that it would be safer to use my own wheels. The Transit had seen better days anyway. I reckoned if I wrecked it I was being paid well enough to buy myself something better. That toe-rag Ferris, though, he landed me right in it, didn't he? He gets paid to make a motor disappear and then he gets greedy. Thinks he'll take his bung and keep the van. I'd like five minutes with him, I'll tell you that for nothing, Mr Mallett . . . '

'I'm sure you would, Shifter, but I think you may have a long wait,' said Todd wryly.

'I know that, Mr Mallett,' replied Shifter.

Todd had one final try at extracting the information he really wanted. 'And you also know how much it would help if you told us who hired you, don't you, Shifter? You could get a lot less time.'

Shifter nodded. He knew all right. But he wasn't budging. And frankly, neither had the detective superintendent expected him to. 'I don't grass, Mr Mallett,' said Shifter flatly.

★   ★   ★

Joanna phoned Fielding on his mobile to talk again about who might have been behind the contract. That was her excuse, anyway. She didn't like admitting to herself how much she liked to hear his voice. Even when he sounded old and tired, and whined about his pension, it was as if someone else were speaking. Every time she saw him, every time she spoke to him, she could only remember the way he had been before. That was how she thought of him and that was how she still saw him.

He told her he would be in London for a couple of days later that week. 'Fancy a spot of lunch?' he asked.

Joanna took a moment or two to answer. She did fancy lunching with him. There was no doubt about that. However, it was against her better judgement that she finally heard herself agreeing to meet him in the same Italian restaurant, tucked away just off the Strand, where they had eaten together many times twenty years previously.

She was surprised he even knew it was still there. She did, of course, and invariably felt a twinge of nostalgia every time she walked past it.

'Well, we both know where it is, don't we,' he remarked casually.

And she agreed with that too, as if she believed it really was his only reason for choosing the place.

He was already there, sitting at a table for two in the far corner, when she arrived. She noticed that he no longer looked crumpled as he had done on the occasions she had seen him in Devon. Obliquely, she wondered if he kept his best clothes for London nowadays. Or maybe for her. No, she was flattering herself. But certainly he was every bit as smart as she remembered him from the old days, dressed in a fashionable dark-beige linen jacket, cream shirt and a brown and cream striped silk tie. His eyes still held that disappointed look she had become so aware of, but he no longer seemed tired and world-weary. He stood up to greet her. He was a funny mix. He could be so well mannered and charming, and he could be such a pig.

There was a bottle of white wine on the table before him and she saw that he had already drunk about a third of it.

Without asking first, he poured a glass for her as soon as she sat down.

The mineral water culture would never be for Mike Fielding. She hardly knew anybody any more who bought wine by the bottle at lunchtime, she realised.

They made small talk for a few minutes.

'How's it going with the rubber heel brigade?' she asked.

'Looks like I'll be exonerated. They can't prove a thing and they know it,' he said. 'The muck's stuck, of course, like it always does.'

She nodded and took a deep draught of the wine. She must have become as brainwashed as all the others by the new puritanical age, she realised suddenly. She had almost forgotten how good a chilled glass of wine tasted in the middle of the day. And this was very nice wine indeed, at the perfect temperature. She didn't know much about Italian wine, but she did know that Mike always had bought better wine than he could afford. Mind you, the rate at which he was drinking it you wondered if it made much difference, she thought, noticing that he had drained his glass again already.

'They've put me out to grass, Jo,' he told her abruptly. 'I've been appointed the Devon and Cornwall Constabulary's Best Value Manager.'

'What the hell's that?'

'Well may you ask! Officially I'm in charge of ensuring all our resources are managed properly; it's a legal requirement now for every force in the country. Unofficially I'm being kept out of trouble, aren't I? No more proper policing for me. Instead, the backwater of admin. I'm not even allowed to remain in a proper police station. I've been transferred to HQ at Middlemoor. My life is to be a merry round of seminars, working parties, and God knows what else. I'm in town for meetings at the Yard of the Met National Committee and, to tell the truth, I don't even really understand what we're supposed to be doing. I told you I'd be a paper shuffler from now on, didn't I?'

'I'm sorry, Mike,' she said. He had been a hands-on detective all his life. She knew how unhappy he must be about his new job.

He grunted, refilled both their glasses to the brim and ordered another bottle.

What the hell, she thought, taking another good long swig. She couldn't remember when she had last had a real boozy lunch. And to think that she had been brought up in the days when a Fleet Street lunch wasn't really considered lunch unless it ended after dark. In the summer. Any amateur can make lunch go on until after dark in the winter, the lads used to say.

'So what about Shifter, then?' she asked, eventually focusing on the subject she most wanted to talk about. 'Are there any theories about who hired him?'

'Oh, yeah. Theories by the hundredweight. But

the same old suspects, none of which really hang together. Any one of the Phillipses, Jeremy Thomas's family, they always reckoned Angela's murder did for their boy. Even Sam the Man himself, secretly disgusted by Jimbo and afraid of what he still might do. I don't reckon that myself, though, family's family to Sam regardless. Anyway, he always was blind about Jimbo.'

'So what do you think?'

'I don't have a clue, Jo, to be honest. Even if I thought it was, say, Rob Phillips, he's a Dartmoor farmer, for Christ's sake, who's never been in trouble with the police in his life. How would he know how to set about hiring Shifter Brown or his like? Of course, Shifter's done jobs before for the O'Donnells, but topping one of their own, however nasty a piece of work he is — I just don't see it. There's another possibility. Jimbo's made enough enemies in his time. It could still be somebody completely unconnected with the Angela Phillips case.'

'But even Shifter believes he was hired for a revenge killing; he's admitted that much, hasn't he? Why else would he have taken Jimbo to Dartmoor and killed him the way he did? Shifter was told what to do, presumably. For Christ's sake, he cut Jimbo's dick off — the inference is obvious. If it wasn't revenge for Angela, then it's one hell of a coincidence.'

'Unless all that was a smokescreen designed to deflect attention away from those really responsible. But as there's nobody remotely in the frame apart from people involved in the old Beast of Dartmoor case, what would be the point of that? The more you think about it the more you keep going round in circles.'

'Maybe Shifter will come clean eventually. He must know it'll go easier for him.'

Mike shrugged his shoulders. 'Of course. But you know his sort. Do their bird and keep stumm. It's a way of life.'

They ate grilled sardines and fresh pasta, and began to reminisce about old times again.

'Do you remember the day we came here and left before the main course?' he asked her mischievously. She did, of course. They had eaten a starter of some sort and had suddenly become so desperate to be in bed together that they couldn't spare the time for the rest of the meal.

She didn't know whether she wished he hadn't mentioned it or not. They were on the third bottle of wine now. He had drunk considerably more of it than she had. She was, however, mellow enough to accept that the attraction was still there. For both of them. But she was admitting nothing. Not to him. 'Vaguely,' she said, as if in any case it were not very important.

Suddenly he became very serious. He leaned across and touched her hand. 'I still regret that I didn't leave home for you,' he told her abruptly.

She studied him carefully, his eyes a little bloodshot now, his voice just very slightly blurred around the edges. The truth was, she suddenly realised, that she knew she still regretted it too, but she was dammed if she was going to admit it.

She did not respond to his comment. Instead,

after a few seconds she said in an even voice, 'I think we could both do with some coffee, don't you?'

'Nope,' he said. 'The only thing I could do with is you. Nothing's changed there.' He closed the fingers of his hand around hers.

She wasn't sure she wanted to hear that kind of comment from him, not after all this time, it was a little too glib. She tried to withdraw her hand.

He tightened his grip.

'Let go, Mike, please,' she said, her voice calm.

If anything, his grip tightened even more. He leaned forward so that his face was very close to hers. She could smell the alcohol on his breath and the old attraction did not seem quite so strong after all.

'How about we skip the coffee, for old times' sake. My hotel's ten minutes from here in a cab . . . '

Underneath the table she felt his other hand grasp her knee.

Suddenly she became very angry. It was as if she was overwhelmed by all the unhappiness he had caused her. She could not believe that he could be quite so crass as to grab her and make a comment like that in the middle of a restaurant, particularly this restaurant. It really was the clumsiest pass she had ever been on the receiving end of and his excessive alcohol consumption was no excuse. A few minutes ago Joanna had felt warm and mellow, even a little elated, in his company. Now she was angry and humiliated. And she wondered if his choice of restaurant had been more than nostalgia, a deliberate ploy in some plan he had hatched to seduce her. Part of her fury, of course, stemmed from the knowledge deep inside that, had he handled it better, he might have succeeded. 'Take your hands off me, you bastard,' she told him very quietly. Her voice was very cold and so were her eyes.

He obeyed at once, holding the offending hands out towards her, palms up in a gesture of supplication, but still grinning the grin that she had so often found disarming and now, perhaps because he was half drunk and perhaps just because of her anger, simply thought made him look really stupid.

'All I ever was to you was a cheap lay, wasn't it?' she enquired conversationally.

He began to protest.

She stopped him at once. 'Save it and fuck off,' she said. 'I really don't know why I had anything to do with you again.' Then she stood up and walked out of the restaurant, leaving him sitting there, aware of his eyes boring into her back.

He didn't try to stop her. Perhaps he knew that he really had gone too far. It gave her some small satisfaction to think that she had left him to pay a bill he could doubtless ill afford and that, taking into account the amount and quality of wine that had been consumed, it would undoubtedly be quite substantial.

★ ★ ★

Fielding had one more day to spend in London before returning to his Exeter base. He knew what an idiot he had been in the restaurant. He'd downed a swift pint and a couple of large Scotches before even going there to meet Jo, and then he'd probably drunk the equivalent of two of the three bottles of wine he had ordered. It was getting to be disconcerting just how much he could drink nowadays without feeling much different from the way he felt when he hadn't had a drink at all. But that kind of quantity was excessive even for him. He'd been deeply distressed by his dreary new appointment, which he'd been well aware he had absolutely no choice but to accept if he wished to survive at all, but that was no excuse.

At his desk on his first day back at HQ in Exeter he found it difficult to concentrate on anything much. Par for the course nowadays. There was always so much on his mind. His thoughts kept turning to Joanna. He made himself work through the morning at the various dull routine tasks which were now his lot, reminding himself that the way things had been going he was lucky still to have a desk. Even if it was at Middlemoor, and even if that was about all he had.

With a great effort of will he kept himself out of the pub at lunchtime, reasoning that it was time he kept his head clear for a while. Several times during the day he very nearly picked up the phone to call Joanna in London. Each time he stopped at the last moment. He didn't think she'd want to hear from him. He bet she was going into the office every day. He knew that she was supposed only to work a three-day week, but he also knew that Jo was desperate to come out on top in the Shifter Brown case. He had been intrigued to realise over the past few months that she was just as ambitious as she had ever been. She hadn't changed a bit. She had so much in life, wealth, a family, an impressive professional track record, a column, which he suspected most of the other hacks envied, and day-to-day crime coverage was no longer her responsibility, officially at any rate. Yet she couldn't bear to be beaten by the rest of the pack. She had to be number one. That was Jo. And she'd be pulling out all the stops right now to make sure she stayed number one. Mike managed a wry chuckle. He bet she was working seven days a week on this one, whether or not she was actually in the office. She wouldn't stop trying. Not Jo. He knew her.

And he had surprised himself by the growing realisation that he would like to get to know her much better again. But he was afraid he had effectively scuttled his own chances. He hadn't planned to make a move on Jo. Certainly not in the way he had. He couldn't believe he had made such a damn stupid, clumsy pass at her. Throughout his life he had almost always got those things right. He had invariably been able to sense the moment. Know when to do and say what. And Joanna had been right up to a point — most of those women had never been anything other than cheap lays to him. But not her. Not Jo. She was wrong about that. Joanna remained the one woman ever really to have got under his skin. It was only now he had seen her again that he realised how little that had changed.

He had been speaking the absolute truth when he told her he wished he had left home for her. But he'd had the opportunity and he'd baulked at it.

He'd messed up Jo's life then, he knew that, and it seemed pretty reasonable that she wouldn't want to give him the opportunity to do so again. In any case, she was the woman with everything. Jesus, it was amazing she had any time for him at all any more. What was he, after all? Just a broken-down middle-aged cop working out his time for his pension.

And then he'd made that dumb pass at her.

Around five in the afternoon he decided to send her an e-mail apologising. He couldn't bring himself to phone and doubted she'd take his call. But he was desperate to have some contact with her. He had never quite got used to the way e-mails disappeared into cyberspace — but it was better than nothing.

He really did want to see her again. Even if it could never be anything more than just lunch or a drink.

★ ★ ★

Joanna was at her desk trying to write her column, which should have been completed at least two hours earlier. This wasn't like her, or she would never have lasted as long as she had at the top, even with a husband as editor.

Her mind, too, had been wandering that day and even though she was over her deadline she found it hard to concentrate on her writing. She was, as Fielding had thought she would be, preoccupied with landing a really big exclusive on the Shifter Brown case, but she was also thinking about him.

When her anger had subsided she had found herself dreadfully disappointed that the lunch had ended so badly. It had been his fault but, even though she knew it was silly, she was nevertheless upset by his crass behaviour. Trouble was, Fielding could still get to her. No doubt about that.

And when an e-mail arrived from him she couldn't help being pleased.

Hi, Jo. This is just a note apologising for my stupid behaviour in the restaurant. I must have been drunker than I thought. I can't believe what I did and I hope you'll forgive me.

I'd love the chance to make it up to you. Would another meeting be totally out of the question? Have lunch with me just one more time and I promise to keep my hands strictly to myself and not to do or say anything daft.

She had to smile. There was something schoolboyish about the message. She sat at her desk thinking for a moment or two when Tim Jones came over to tell her he had a call for her from someone who wouldn't give his name saying he had information on the Shifter Brown case. 'Deep throat will only speak to the 'Sword of Justice' lady, he insists, and I'm afraid to transfer because I've lost two calls that way already today — I think the system's playing up again,' Tim went on.

She agreed to take the call on his line, got up from her chair and hurried across the editorial floor to Tim's desk, with the young crime reporter ambling along just behind her. 'More than likely a nutter but you never know,' she muttered.

★ ★ ★

Shortly after Jo left her desk Paul came looking for her.

It had not taken her long to deal with the call. Within four or five minutes she was quite certain that the caller was indeed a nutter with nothing constructive to tell her or anyone else. The majority of such calls were. But she'd learned early on that a journalist with any sense always took time to listen. The one you ignored was certain to be the big one. News desk assistants spent half their day listening to calls from readers, ninety-nine per cent of which were a complete waste of time. But a result once in a hundred times made it imperative that they all got heard.

When she returned to her desk Paul was standing behind her computer screen, staring at it, his face grim.

The Fielding e-mail was still on the screen.

This, she thought, is all I need. She opened her mouth to explain. A mistake in more ways than one.

Paul raised a hand to silence her. He would never have any kind of personal conversation with her in the public arena of the newsroom. 'I need to talk to you about this week's column. Would you come into my office when you have a minute, please, Jo?' he requested mildly enough.

She nodded silently and, as he walked away, sat down at her desk, read the offending e-mail one more time and deleted it — as she should, of course, have done in the first place. Then, resigned to a difficult exchange, she made her way to Paul's office at the other end of the newsroom.

By the time she got there Paul was already sitting in the big antique leather armchair behind his desk and he did not get up when she walked in. Neither did he ask her to sit down. She did so anyway. She was damned if she was going to stand before him like a schoolgirl being given a telling-off by the headmaster.

'I want you to explain to me exactly what that e-mail meant, Joanna,' Paul demanded. His tone was chilly and precise.

She was suddenly very irritated by him. She decided to go on the attack. 'And I want to know what you were doing reading my bloody private e-mail?' she countered.

He sighed. 'I came to see you to ask you where your column was; it is, as you know, very late and I looked at your screen in the vain hope that you might be working on it.' He spoke with exaggerated patience. 'Silly of me,' he finished.

She relented a little. She didn't feel guilty about Fielding, but old habits died hard and she always felt guilty when she was late for a deadline. Deadlines were sacrosanct. On a daily newspaper it didn't matter how brilliant your copy was if it was too damned late. 'Look, Paul, it was nothing,' she began. 'We had lunch, he had too much to drink, he made a silly pass. Mike was apologising. For God's sake, you read the dammed thing.'

Paul stared at her steadily. 'You didn't tell me you

330

were having lunch with him,' he said flatly.

'Do I usually tell you everyone I'm having lunch with?' she responded, trying not to react.

'Mike Fielding is not everyone, not as far as you are concerned, Joanna,' he said.

'Paul, you're making something out of nothing . . . '

'Am I?' he interrupted her. 'When *Private Eye* ran their piece I gave you the benefit of the doubt. Absolutely. You know I did. Embarrassing though it was, I dismissed it out of hand. But now we have this . . . '

She interrupted him then. 'You gave me the benefit of the doubt? Honestly, Paul, I sometimes wonder who the hell you think you are.'

'I think I am your husband, Joanna,' he said. His voice was louder than normal and he didn't sound quite as cool and controlled as usual. 'And I think you've been forgetting that lately . . . '

'I turned him down, Paul. I said no. No! OK?' She spat the words at him. They had never indulged in anything remotely resembling a personal row anywhere in the *Comet* building before. She wondered vaguely if his secretary or anybody else could hear what was going on.

'Yes, and why did you have to turn him down? That's what I want to know,' he stormed at her. 'How exactly did you find yourself in that situation?'

'For God's sake, Paul,' she said. 'If we have to continue this can we at least do so at home and not in the bloody office?'

He muttered something indecipherable. She'd had enough. She got up and left.

If she had been angry with Fielding in the restaurant it was nothing compared with the anger she felt against Paul now. She had never been unfaithful to her husband. Not once during their eighteen-year marriage. In fact, there had never been anybody else since the first time she had slept with Paul. She had turned Fielding down, for God's sake, and she told herself that she had never had any intention of doing anything else.

Until now. She wasn't sure quite what she intended now. Not after the ridiculous interrogation Paul had submitted her to.

Several heads turned towards her as she walked back to her desk. She realised she was doing what they told her she always did when she was angry — the Bartlett Stomp, positively thumping her way across the newsroom. She slowed down and eased up — just a little. But her anger did not subside.

To hell with it, she thought. She sat down at her desk, picked up her phone and dialled Fielding's mobile number.

* * *

He was in his car on his way home when he took the call, unusually having stuck to his plan to have a sober day. He was delighted to hear from her and told her so.

'It's OK about the restaurant,' she said. 'We'd both had too much to drink. You must have done to behave the way you did. No style at all, Mike, I have to tell you. Not like you!'

Alone in his car, he smiled. 'I know,' he said.

'Perhaps I'm losing my touch.'

'What a relief for the women of the West of England.'

'You flatter me.'

'Indeed I do. Anyway, you're on. Lunch next time you're in town. How could I deny you the chance to make amends.'

He took his left hand off the wheel and punched the air. 'Yes,' he shouted to himself silently.

Aloud he said, 'Great. I've got to come up again next week. Any chance?'

They agreed on the following Tuesday and when their call was over he promptly called the inexpensive hotel he had so disastrously attempted to take her to after their previous lunch and booked it for that day.

He had lied to Joanna. He had no call to be in London the following week. But he could take a day off and go up by train. Even though the hotel was reasonable by London standards it would be a pricey trip without any expenses to claim back. He didn't care. There was no way he was not going to have a room booked. If the opportunity arose he wanted to be prepared. Maybe he was pushing his luck, but he had a gut feeling that might not be so. He couldn't stop smiling as he continued his journey. Perhaps his pass had not been so clumsy after all.

15

Yet again they met in the same Italian restaurant. This time she was there before him and she wondered if that was significant. When he arrived the first thing she was somehow instantly aware of was that he had not been drinking. He had maybe decided that had been a mistake previously. He moved quickly and deftly across the restaurant towards her. He had always moved well for such a tall, rangy man. The second thing she noticed was his clothes. He was wearing a mid-blue jacket and darker-blue trousers. So was she. His face broke into a crooked smile the moment he saw her and he was still smiling when he sat down opposite her.

'We match,' she remarked in greeting, smiling back.

'So we do,' he responded lightly, looking as if he had almost said something else in answer to that.

Like we always have matched, Jo thought to herself.

Afterwards she could not remember the details of their conversation through the meal. They talked about O'Donnell, of course, and Shifter Brown, because that was always there between them, but they both knew that was not what their meeting was about. Not this time.

Joanna had no plan, she had made no decisions before the lunch. What happened at the end took

334

her half by surprise even though she was the instigator.

They both turned down dessert. Then he asked her if she would like more wine or coffee. They had drunk much less this time, just one bottle between them. Still enough at lunchtime to shock the new puritans rigid, she thought obliquely.

She suddenly heard herself say: 'No, thank you. Life's too short, don't you think, and for all too many people turns out to be a lot shorter than they might reasonably expect.'

She sensed the change in him at once.

He became very still, his gaze steady and serious. She knew he would be determined not to make a fool of himself again. Not twice. Not Mike Fielding. He was a picture of restraint. 'That's true enough,' he murmured eventually in a noncommittal way. But she knew he was already on her wavelength.

'Well, you said it yourself last time, we never used to waste too much time over lunch.'

His eyes widened. He had been fiddling with his wineglass, turning it round and round on the white linen tablecloth. He took his hand away and sat back in his chair. 'Are you suggesting what I think you may be suggesting or are you playing games with me?' he asked. This time he sounded almost stern.

Typical Fielding, she thought, he would never let someone else be in charge for long. 'Now would I play games with you?' she enquired, in a bantering sort of way.

His eyes narrowed.

She'd make him angry if she carried on like this. Maybe neither of them was quite as good as they thought they were. Not any more, anyway. 'No games,' she said, absolutely serious now. 'Have you got a hotel or do we need to find one?'

His eyes softened at once. For a second or two she thought she could see tears welling in them. She had seen that before, in the days when most people would have said Fielding did not have an emotional cell in his body. God, the man was a curious mix all right.

But that moment was over almost as it began. He said nothing. Just stood up, reached into his pocket, half threw a handful of notes on to the table, gestured for her to rise too, put a hand on her arm and steered her quite firmly out of the restaurant, almost as if he feared she might change her mind.

She had intended to pay the bill this time. But it somehow did not seem an appropriate moment to start fishing out her credit cards. Instead, she let him be masterful.

★ ★ ★

It was not the best of hotels. One of those slightly sleazy ones in Southampton Row. Joanna could have afforded something much better, but he would have hated that. She had no idea, however, that he had paid for the room himself, just assuming that it was on expenses, as in the past. Fielding had always been good at fixing things to fit in with his personal life. If you were married and had also been embroiled in as many affairs as she knew he had, then it wasn't surprising. But she really did not want to think about that. Not now.

They had taken a black cab to the hotel, even though it was really quite close, each sitting at opposite ends of the bench seat, as if they were afraid their bodies might touch by accident. They barely spoke. The room had only a single bed, she noticed, which was a nuisance, but at least it indicated that he had not been taking her for granted. She was unaware, of course, that he had quite deliberately decided to book a single, not to save money — although God knew he could not afford to pay out for too many London hotel rooms — but to create exactly the impression she had indeed gained.

She felt awkward in that bare, impersonal room with its cheap furniture and nasty net curtains. It was hardly romantic. But then, afternoon sex in downmarket hotel rooms was not about romance and she'd known that well enough before re-embarking on it after so many years, she told herself.

He seemed awkward, too. He took off his jacket and tie, and stood looking at her. She had not even removed her jacket. The only furniture in the room apart from the narrow bed and a small fitted wardrobe was a single hard wooden chair. She too was standing, over by the window, half pretending to be looking out at the street below through its grubby metal-framed panes.

He crossed the room to her, turned her towards him, wrapped his arms round her and kissed her. A proper kiss. Full on the lips. She felt their bodies melt together, just as they had always done — without either of them appearing to move, really.

He was a good kisser. One of the few men she had known who actually enjoyed kissing and for protracted periods of time. The years seemed to disappear. The magic had not gone. It was as if it were only yesterday that they had last been together like this.

He drew away from her. 'Undress for me,' he said, smiling.

The same words he had used the very first time so long ago, the same command. The same husky voice. She knew he had done it quite deliberately, but she was moved nonetheless. At least he had remembered. But then, would either of them ever forget? She supposed that was what this was all about.

So she did what she was told, just as before. Slipping her clothes off, no game playing, no stripper antics, just slowly removing her jacket, her trousers, her silk T-shirt and her underwear, until she stood naked before him. She wasn't self-conscious any more. Strange, that. But from the moment he had come to her and kissed her it had all felt so natural again.

He gazed at her appreciatively. 'God, but you're still beautiful,' he whispered.

She knew that her body looked good, thanks to those workouts at the gym, but she loved hearing the words from him.

He took her hand in his and drew her to the bed, made her sit down and kneeled before her. Still fully clothed, he buried his head in her. Something else she began to remember was how good this had been with him, just how good it had all been. And how much it had always made her want more, and more.

Eventually he stood up and began to take off his shirt and trousers. Standing right above her looking down at her, there was great longing in his eyes.

'I'm not sure how able I am going to be,' he began. She liked to think of him being just a little uncertain. He had always been so sure of himself before.

As he was climbing out of his trousers she reached out and touched him. 'I don't think we'll have any problems,' she said.

And they didn't. He wasn't the super stud he had been twenty years earlier. However, she hadn't expected him to be. They were both slower and more lingering in their approach to their lovemaking. She had wondered, even as they rode in the taxi from the restaurant, whether it might be a let-down after so many years. Perhaps even half wished that it would be — after all, that would probably at least ensure that their renewed relationship would not become a problem. But it wasn't a let-down at all.

They soon found the narrow bed too confining. They half rolled on to the floor using the duvet cover as a kind of mattress and the pillows to help them find more imaginative positions. She was a bit surprised they still had the athleticism, but they also spent quite a lot of time just lying very still in each other's arms. And that was sweet too. She felt the sense of belonging she had always felt with him and tried very hard to dismiss it, because it really could not be. She could never belong to Fielding. Not now. Maybe the truth was that she never could have done.

Because of the growing strain between her and Paul it was weeks since she'd had sex at all, let alone sex as good as this. It was just so mind-bogglingly good still — which was disconcerting as well as wonderful.

Perhaps it was because they were older, perhaps because they had both wanted it so much, perhaps because of the almost subconscious desires we all get from time to time to slip back into our own pasts — whatever the reason, to her it seemed better than ever.

★   ★   ★

She left the room first. He hadn't told her that he was going home to Exeter that night. That would have given the game away, made her realise that he had booked the hotel specifically for the purpose for which they had used it.

He had wanted her so much, yet, like her, had thought that maybe he wouldn't mind too much if the sex hadn't been that good. He really didn't need any further complications in his life right now and Joanna Bartlett had always been a complication for him. But the sex had been sensational. Like it always used to be. The best he had enjoyed in years. The best since the last time with her, if he were honest. It had always been what had drawn them together. He might have considered himself a bit of a stud in the old days and certainly his enthusiasm had been limitless, but with her it always seemed that sex reached a unique level of excitement and fulfilment. It was them, together, that did it. Something special.

Something indefinable. Something undeniable. And it hadn't changed. It was still there.

He liked the look of her, the feel of her and, by God, he adored the taste of her. He wondered if he were still in love with her — indeed, if he had ever stopped being in love with her. He knew that he wanted to see her again, but just like the first time he was afraid of seeing too much of her.

He comforted himself that geography and both their other commitments, particularly hers, would probably look after that for them. It was unlikely that they would be able to meet very often, even if they both wanted to. He knew that this time it would not be like before. That at best it would be no more than occasional snatched meetings. Never again would they dream of being properly together. That, at least, was over.

★ ★ ★

In July 2001 Shifter Brown stood trial at Exeter Crown Court. He didn't stand a chance of leniency. Not under the most intense police pressure, nor in court, would he say who paid him to kill Jimbo O'Donnell. He was sentenced the mandatory life for murder and the judge recommended that he serve a minimum of twenty-two years. It was even worse than Shifter had expected, perhaps, but he had resolutely refused the one piece of information that could have helped. There was no jury, because Shifter pleaded guilty, and the hearing lasted only two days. Joanna went to Exeter to cover it, arriving the day before the proceedings began and leaving the day after.

Until then, she and Fielding had been together just three times during the four months which had passed since their afternoon in the Southampton Row hotel room. Geography had indeed taken care of it. That and fear.

Joanna had a very practical side to her. She did not want to wreck her marriage or her life. In her mind she had tried to think of Fielding as a failed policeman, a bit of a sad case. But there was nothing failed or sad about Mike when they were making love. She had been forced to admit that regardless of his failings and what she knew he regarded as the failure he had made of almost everything except, most perversely, perhaps his marriage, he remained the love of her life. That frightened her. Perhaps it had been partly curiosity that had led her to that Southampton Row hotel room. She wasn't sure. Partly anger at her husband, of course, no doubt about that. But she hadn't really expected the old feelings to be quite as intact and it had been something of a shock.

She couldn't stop herself sleeping with Fielding whenever the opportunity presented itself, although she was not prepared to take any silly risks. It seemed he felt the same. So they had to settle for very occasional torrid afternoons.

The trial, however, gave them, albeit for such a short time, almost unlimited opportunity.

God knows, she thought, what Fielding told his wife, but he more or less took up residence in her Exeter hotel room for the three nights she was there, slipping in and out via the fire escape, which she opened for him at agreed times, so that he would hopefully not be seen by anyone who might recognise him.

She couldn't believe the sexual energy they managed to maintain.

'Not bad for two middle-aged folk,' she said one night after their lovemaking had been particularly extravagant.

'I forget what a tired, worn-out old bugger I am when I'm with you,' he told her. And his eyes went all crinkly as he smiled and reached out for her yet again.

When the trial ended she had not wanted to return to London, even though she did feel guilty whenever she thought about Paul and Emily. Particularly Emily, whom she had found herself phoning much more often from Devon this time than she usually did when she was away.

She realised she was going to miss her lover dreadfully. And yet she knew that something else had not changed with the years: she and Mike Fielding were not going anywhere. Not ever.

★   ★   ★

Two weeks after his sentencing, Shifter Brown phoned Joanna from jail and asked her if she would visit him. He had something to tell her, he said, something he was sure she would want to know. And he was planning to tell her exclusively. 'I'll get a visiting order sent to you, personal, like. You can be my cousin. I wouldn't want them to know who you really were.'

It would take a bit of getting used to, being Shifter Brown's cousin, but Joanna was consumed with curiosity.

'I've got a story for you, Joey,' he said. As ever, it made her want to giggle when he called her that. 'It's a corker,' he went on. But he would give her no clue as to the subject matter.

She could not resist, of course. She accepted his offer with alacrity. Shifter was in the Devon county prison at Exeter, where he had been held on remand before his sentencing and then returned for assessment. It would be another couple of months before he would be despatched to serve out the rest of his term at a maximum-security jail like Parkhurst or Longlartin.

On the appointed day, less than a fortnight later, Jo set off down the M4 heading west. She was so focused on what she was doing that she did not even arrange to see Fielding, although she was going into his patch. 'Maybe I'll call him after I've seen Shifter,' she had thought to herself as she swung off the M5 at the Exeter exit. But her mind was intent on the task at hand. Maybe this was the big exclusive she had been chasing. Certainly any sort of interview with Shifter inside jail had to be a story, whatever he eventually told her. She was hoping, naturally, that he was going to tell her who had hired him, although she couldn't think what would have changed his mind about that. Shifter didn't grass, after all.

He was convicted now, though, so sub judice no longer came into it. Shifter would be well aware of that. He was a pro. She wondered about his motive, as well as his intentions.

She was quite preoccupied with the prospect of talking to him, but had decided not to tell anybody else about it. Not even her husband and editor. In fact, particularly not him. She had made sure that her visit to Exeter prison had been arranged on one of the days when she was not expected in the office, and had deliberately delayed leaving home until her husband had already departed for Canary Wharf and Emily was safely despatched to school.

At the grim old county jail on the hill opposite Exeter Castle she was searched and her VO pass inspected before being led to the visiting room. She had been seated first at one of the small wooden tables and then Shifter was led out to her. He was wearing prison denims, which stretched over his huge shoulders. The clothes did not seem quite big enough for him. She thought that would probably offend a man who wore the kind of beautifully tailored suits she had last seen him in. He walked just as he had in the restaurant, however. As he always did, she suspected, with his huge hands hanging like weapons waiting to be loaded and put into action. He did not show the great strain he must surely be under. She had to remember that to the Shifter Browns of this world doing a stretch in prison was just a part of life, he was of the breed who prided themselves on being able to survive it. But twenty-two years! That was some sentence and surely must have shaken even him. If he served the full time recommended by the judge Shifter would be well into his sixties before he got out, even with full remission. She studied him closely as he walked towards her. She had noticed in court that he looked even fitter than when she had lunched with him. His waist was slightly narrower, stomach flatter, jaw a little more squared. He would be spending his days working out she supposed, that was what the old lags did. They believed that if you kept the body in top condition, the mind would stay that way too. The one thing they all feared was losing their minds. Stir crazy, they had called it once.

Shifter loped across the room towards her and beamed a greeting as he sat down. 'All right, Joey doll?'

'I'm fine, Shifter. How about you?'

'Been better, doll, but I can handle it.' There was something about his expression which made her realise then what an effort he was making, not just with her for this visit, but probably every day of his life inside, determined not to go under, not to let himself be beaten.

'You copped the big one, didn't you?'

He nodded sagely. There was not a hint of self-pity in him. 'Yeah, well, it wasn't any more than I expected.'

'You could have done yourself a favour, told them who put out the contract on Jimbo.'

'But I don't grass, do I?' He smiled again.

'So what have you brought me here today for, then? What is this corker you have for me exactly?'

'I want to tell you the truth behind Jimbo's murder, of course. All of it. The works, Joey. It's yours, doll.' He paused. 'At a price, naturally.'

'Ah,' she said. So that was it. He was after money.

She made no further comment.

He continued almost at once. 'I'll give you the lot, everything I know. If the price is right.'

She shook her head. 'You know papers can't pay convicted criminals any more, Shifter. You know the way things are as well as I do.'

'All I want is for you to look after my family,' he said then.

'Well, that's pretty much the same thing.'

'Leave it out,' he responded. 'There's always ways. You can do it if you want to. You know you can.'

Joanna wasn't too sure of that, not after the Phillips deal fiasco. She would never forgive herself for that. It had made her wary of deals. But at least the courts had already done their worst with this one. Everybody knew where they stood before she and the *Comet* had been invited to get involved. 'Is that why you didn't speak out before?' she asked. 'Because you wanted to do a deal?'

He nodded. 'Yeah. I knew I was done up like a kipper the moment the police got their hands on my van, that whatever I did I was going down for a long, long time. I figured I couldn't do a whole lot about that whatever I told them. But then I thought that if I gave the story to a paper, exclusive like, maybe at least I could do something for my family. And I knew it was no good to anybody before the trial because you couldn't have printed it, could you? So I reckoned the only way was to keep stumm till after I got sent down and then do a deal.' He paused. 'It was always going to be you, Joey doll, cos I like you, girl, trust you too.' He smiled his strangely ingenuous smile.

God, not again, she thought, wishing for the first time in her life that she were not quite so good at getting people to trust her. All except her husband, it seemed. And with justification now, she reminded herself. 'I'll do my best, Shifter, but it truly won't be easy,' she said.

He reached in his shirt pocket and produced a photograph, frayed around the edges from much handling, of two angelic-looking little blonde-haired girls. 'That's Melanie, she's ten, and that's Abigail, she's nine, they're my little princesses,' he said, his voice full of pride.

She looked at the picture and then at him. Shifter, a professional much-feared hit man and heavy, was smiling softly down at his daughters, his eyes misty, his whole face suddenly gentle. What was it with these East End villains that they so often had this other side to them, particularly with their children? 'I have a little girl, too, Shifter,' she said. 'Well, not so little, she's almost twelve now.' She'd told him that not because she had any desire to share any part of her family life with him, but because it was a knee-jerk reaction for her to seek out common ground with an informant or an interviewee. It was what journalists did. It was automatic.

'You know what it's like then, Joey, don't you, doll? You'll do anything for them, won't you, anything at all.'

Joanna nodded. She didn't think she'd ever been a particularly good mother and her daughter was absolutely the most self-possessed eleven-year-old she had ever encountered, but Shifter was right, of course. She would do anything for Emily. Whatever it took. Then an unwelcome little niggle, stemming from guilt no doubt, flitted into her mind. Even give up Mike Fielding? She pushed the thought away for the time being and focused all her attention firmly on Shifter, who had started to speak again.

'It's them I want looked after. I've had it, doll, haven't I? I just want to do what I can for my little princesses now.'

And if you hadn't gone around topping people for a living you could be doing the one thing they need most, being with them and being a proper father to them, Jo thought. She didn't say it, of course. She wanted this story dreadfully. And in any case she wasn't sure she was in a position to make moral judgements, not even on a professional hit man. 'Look, Shifter, you'll have to come up with someone you trust, someone unrelated to you we can pay. We'll set up a trust fund for your kids, how's that? But we need a third party — and preferably not some villain with a record even longer than yours.'

Shifter grinned ingenuously. 'I can do that. No problem. I still got some diamond mates. But how much, that's what I want to know? It's got to be worth having, Joey doll, worth something to the kids, you know . . .'

She knew. There was no point in offering a derisory amount, or he just wouldn't talk. She thought fast. It was that tricky moment. You got nothing unless you offered money, but you didn't really know what you were going to get until after you had. This one had to be good, though, it just had to be. 'Ten grand,' she said.

He shook his head. 'No way. I want thirty minimum.'

'You won't get it, Shifter, not from me, not from anyone. Not any more.'

'Well, you'll have to do better than ten.'

She checked her watch. 'Shifter, there's less than half an hour left of this visit. I'm not going to waste it playing games. I'll double my offer. Let's call it twenty grand. You'll not do better.'

He studied her closely. He wasn't a fool. He was streetwise and surprisingly bright. Certainly his grasp of how newspapers worked and how he might best at least get something out of his predicament was quite impressive. As so often with villains, she thought what a shame it was that Arthur Richard Brown hadn't used what brains and ability he had for something more worthwhile. And in his case, she had to remind herself, something less horrible and violent. Shifter, she knew, justified what he did as a kind of rough justice in the weird underworld in which he moved. It was true that you couldn't imagine him mugging old ladies. He'd be much more likely to help them across the road or pay their bus fare. Similarly he had the abhorrence of most professional villains for sex crimes and child offences. He'd probably been quite pleased to get the contract on Jimbo, come to think of it. But he was still a thug — albeit a curiously gentlemanly one. And what he had done to Jimbo, much as she thought the bastard had deserved it, was too awful to contemplate and demonstrated all too well what Shifter was capable of.

'Do you have the authority to offer me twenty

grand, girl, just like that?' he asked astutely.

'Shifter, I'm married to the editor. You know that. We're a team. Of course I have the authority. You said you trusted me, didn't you?'

She was lying through her teeth. But if the story was good enough she reckoned she'd get away with this one. She certainly didn't want another broken deal. The Phillips fiasco had stretched her credibility to its limit. Shifter might be a villain, but if she made a deal with him she had to ensure it was adhered to or she would have no credibility left at all.

He stared at her for a moment or two. 'Right, then, it's a deal,' he said and he stretched one of his big, ham-fisted hands across the table. She reached out her own, which was promptly enclosed within his impressive grip. She felt her fingers scrunch together and heard one of her knuckles crack. It occurred to her fleetingly that there could be reasons other than her journalistic reputation why she really had to ensure that this deal was not broken.

16

Shifter did not let her down. His story was every bit as much of a corker as he had promised it would be. It was quite sensational. 'I don't know who paid me to do O'Donnell,' he told her. 'I got an e-mail, didn't I?'

Joanna stared at him. 'You got a what?' She'd heard him all right. It was a pretty banal response. But she was absolutely staggered.

'I got an e-mail,' Shifter repeated very precisely, as if she were a bit on the slow side. 'I got the contract by e-mail.'

'And you don't know who from?'

'Not a clue. I tried to e-mail back after I was lifted the first time, do a bit of digging, like, but I never got any more answers.'

'So you got an e-mail from an unknown source asking you to top Jimbo O'Donnell and you just did it?'

'Only after I'd been paid half the readies.' He spoke indignantly, as if she were taking him for a fool.

Oh, that's all right then, thought Joanna. 'So you're really into the Net, then, are you?'

'Gotta be nowadays, you know that, Joey doll. I'm a businessman, see? Same as anybody else trying to make a crust. I just move in a different kind of world, that's all. The Net's the future, isn't it?'

And you've not got one any more thanks to it,

then, she thought. 'So how often have you been hired to do a job on the Net then?'

'Oh, now and then, doll. I had my own website you see.' Shifter spoke with considerable pride.

'Did you, indeed? And what form did this take?'

'Oh, you know, just offering my services, like.'

'Like what, Shifter?'

' 'Got problems, get Shifter, he'll shift them.' That sort of thing.'

She couldn't help smiling. This was extraordinary. 'And so anonymous people just got in touch and asked you to . . . ' she paused ' . . . shift their problems?'

'Yeah. That was the idea, see. They didn't necessarily have to let me know who they were, like. People seemed to find that' — he stopped as if thinking of the right word — 'sort of reassuring.'

'So how did these anonymous folk pay you, then?'

Shifter grinned conspiratorially. 'Ways and means, girl, ways and means.' He tapped the side of his nose.

'All right, how about the O'Donnell job? How'd you get paid for that?'

Shifter grinned even more broadly. 'That got put into a Swiss bank account for me,' he said. And the pride in his voice was even more evident. Never mind that he was a convicted murderer doing twenty-two years, Shifter patently thought of himself as a thoroughly modern businessman.

Joanna was momentarily speechless. An East End heavy who got hired to kill someone by e-mail and was then paid into a Swiss bank account. Well, it was certainly original, she thought.

'Didn't the police check out your computer?' she asked.

'Always killed my e-mails straight after I read them. And I never kept any files to do with the business. Kept it all in my head, see.'

'Unless you're a lot cleverer than me, Shifter, it would all still be there somewhere on your hard drive.'

Shifter shrugged. 'Yeah, well, depends how hard you look, I suppose. Anyway, I don't reckon the filth even realised I had a computer. I'm just a dumb villain to them, aren't I?'

'Isn't it in your home? The police would have searched the place when they arrested you the first time. That's standard procedure.'

'Oh, yeah, all over my gaff like a rash, they were. And it was there all right. Looking depends on what you think you're going to find sometimes, though, doesn't it? The only computer in my house was in my kids' room.' He chuckled. 'Kids have all got computers, haven't they? Switch my girls' rig on and all you'll see is a stack of Disney games, a load of girlie stuff and their homework.'

Jo felt her jaw drop. What Shifter was saying was crazily simple. It made total sense. She could see quite clearly how that computer in his children's bedroom would have been overlooked.

The big man began to talk again. 'The Simms, that's my two's favourite, you know, it's the game about this family; you get them jobs and houses and stuff, even marry them off. What's your girl's favourite game, Joey? I bet she's a bright one, your kid.'

Jo nodded. Emily was bright all right. Jo also realised that she did not have a clue what computer games her daughter liked best. Paul would know. He often surfed the Net with Emily and said that playing computer games with her relaxed him. But somehow Joanna never seemed to get involved. She was ashamed of herself and experienced another sharp stab of guilt. Could Shifter Brown really be a better father than she was a mother? Surely not. He had got himself banged up for twenty-two years, hadn't he? But she really did not want to explore that area of her life with him. 'E-mails can be traced back, Shifter. We could still do that.'

'Nope,' said Shifter. 'Excite address, wasn't it? I had a Hotmail one. And all the real hooky stuff I just went down the cyber caff for. You pay cash, get on-line, make up a user name, put any old rubbish on the sign-on. I can't swear to it, doll, but I'd have a fair old bet that whoever hired me to do Jimbo would have used a cyber caff too. He'd be a mug not to have done.'

'Look, Shifter, I could get an expert to check out your computer. Maybe your punter wasn't that careful. Remember the love-bug hackers? Even they didn't know that Microsoft software has a hidden flag. It's all traceable.'

'Not if you buy second hand at a street fair, doll,' said Shifter, proudly displaying his knowledge again. 'That's what I did. You get your rig from a dodgy market and pay cash. The trail ends with the last authorised user.' He grinned. 'Anyway, after I was arrested the first time I trashed the lot. Put a hammer through the hard drive and took it down the tip. Then I went down the market again and bought another one.'

Amazingly simple and almost certainly foolproof, thought Jo, reflecting yet again what a pity it was that Shifter hadn't used his brain for better purposes over the years. She set about prising all the information she could out of him. 'OK, so how much did you get paid?' she asked.

'Fifteen grand. Ten before and five after.'

A fair amount of money for what Shifter would regard as little more than a day's work, Jo supposed. But a cheap price for a life. Even the life of Jimbo O'Donnell. 'And where's that money now, still in your Swiss bank account?' Even as she mentioned that Swiss bank account Jo had to fight an urge to laugh aloud.

''Course not, doll,' said Shifter predictably. 'Spent it already, haven't I?'

Well, he wasn't going to admit that he still had his ill-gotten gains, was he — even though Jo couldn't imagine there would ever, in any circumstances, be much chance of British authorities retrieving it from the gnomes of Zurich. 'How was the money paid into your account?' she asked.

'It was transferred from another Swiss account.'

All clever stuff. 'And I don't suppose you'll be revealing the number of your account, or the other account, or authorising anybody to look into it, will you, Shifter?'

'C'mon, doll. I don't grass. Do I?'

There was something else that Jo was intrigued to know. But she wondered if Shifter, still operating under his own peculiar moral code, would refuse to tell her. 'What e-mail address did your . . . ' she hesitated and continued with a small smile ' . . . client use, Shifter?'

'Contractor@excite.com.'

Well, that was straightforward enough. Shifter was obviously quite confident that his 'client' could not be traced. 'And your address?'

Shifter grinned. 'Enforcer@hotmail.com.'

Dear God, thought Joanna. There was nothing like being blatant. Shifter had used the most modern technology but his e-mail address was the stuff of gangster legend. Enforcers were traditionally the heavies who did the dirty work for the big gang bosses. Everybody knew that Shifter had always been an enforcer of some kind and she had already experienced his sense of humour. Even now, his amusement at his own wit and daring in labelling himself in such a way was abundantly apparent. 'And your password?'

Shifter's grin faded. He looked suddenly sheepish. Perhaps he was not prepared to reveal his password, even now, in spite of his apparent confidence that all tracks were effectively covered. But no, that was not what was causing his hesitation it seemed. 'It's Sinatra,' he said eventually, adding with solemn reverence, 'well, Frank was the guv'nor, wasn't he, doll?'

★   ★   ★

The drive back to London seemed endless, particularly the last bit across the city. Jo didn't call Fielding. For once didn't even think about him for

357

some hours. Not after what she had just learned. She decided to drive straight to Canary Wharf. Only 'straight', of course, was hardly the way to describe the journey.

It took her three hours to drive the 200 miles or so from Exeter prison to the Hogarth roundabout at Chiswick, then another hour and a half to crawl across town to the heart of dockland, just fifteen or sixteen miles further. She didn't have a parking space, like most of the journalistic staff, and Paul was certainly not inclined to arrange anything special for his wife. So she had to find a meter.

It was almost 7 p.m. before she stepped into the lift which would carry her to the twenty-first floor and she was exhausted. She half wished she had simply driven home to Richmond, waited for Paul to return that night and told him all about it then. But it wouldn't have been a good time to try to discuss something new and controversial with him. And she certainly couldn't wait until the next day.

She checked her watch and decided to give her husband an hour or so before she went along to his office. She wanted to catch him during that usually quiet period right after the first edition had gone to bed.

Meanwhile there were things she wanted to try to do, although she suspected she would probably be wasting her time. She switched on her computer, logged on to the Net and called up Shifter's website. It was blank — except for a message telling her the page was no longer available on that site. Shifter had told her he'd killed his web page. Nonetheless she thought she'd check. It might not in any case have taken her much further, but she would have liked to have seen it.

Next came the big one. She called up Hotmail and tapped in Shifter's user name and his password: 'enforcer', 'Sinatra'. It really was hilarious stuff.

Both user name and password still worked. But as Jo had suspected when Shifter had so freely supplied her with them, all his e-mails, in and out, had been deleted. The only place they could possibly be retained would be on the computer he had used to keep in contact with 'contractor'. The one in his home had been trashed and Shifter refused to tell her which cyber café he had used for what he referred to as 'the really hooky stuff'. There weren't that many cyber cafés around, it would be most likely that Shifter had used one in his own manor, certainly in London, but that sort of detective work was almost certainly one for the pros — a police matter. In any case Jo reckoned she already had all she needed for a major ground-breaking crime scoop, which would be the envy of all the *Comet*'s rivals.

When she finally decided the moment was right to approach her husband and editor she found him, as she had expected to, alone in his office, leaning back in his chair with his feet on the desk. The door was always open. There was no culture for anyone to knock — which didn't mean that everybody, including her, wasn't inclined to be cautious about entering. Only the angle-light on Paul's desk was switched on, its narrow beam palely illuminating just a part of the room. Mozart played softly on his CD player. Paul's eyes were closed. She knew he wouldn't be asleep, but he had a knack of relaxing completely for just a few minutes whenever the opportunity arose. It helped him greatly in getting through the extraordinarily long hours Fleet Street editors worked.

'Hi, Jo,' he murmured. His eyes were still closed and she had not seen him open them. It didn't surprise her, though, that he knew she was there. Maybe he'd peeped, or possibly he really did have that sixth sense his staff sometimes attributed to him.

She sat down opposite him, rehearsing her approach in her head, waiting for him to appear ready to talk.

'What are you doing here tonight anyway?' he asked eventually. It wasn't one of her days in, after all.

'I've got this extraordinary story,' she began. And she told him all of it.

★　★　★

Paul listened very carefully. He had always been a good listener. By the time Joanna had finished speaking he was almost as excited as she was.

Paul Potter was a newspaperman, through and through. His reaction to news was involuntary, instinctive and overwhelming, just like his wife's. When something big and special broke he experienced the same burst of adrenalin rushing through his system as she did. As did all the best ones. But he didn't show it, of course, it wasn't his style. And in any case it was his job to think the

360

thing through, to be clear on the legal aspects and to work out how to make the most of what they had.

'Just e-mail a killer.' It was wonderful. 'Enforcer@ hotmail.com.' — magic. Pure magic. And so was the idea of a hit man being paid through a Swiss bank account. But the source was a convicted murderer and Joanna had agreed to pay him for the story, albeit indirectly. Jo had jumped the gun and had, of course, had absolutely no authority to pledge the *Comet* for that sort of money. But this time Paul didn't blame her. He would have done the same himself. Make the promises. Get the story. Sort the rest out later.

It was a dangerous game, paying money to villains. He had done it before, of course, and so had most editors, even if they wouldn't admit it. He still didn't like it. Nobody did. But apart from any other considerations there was always the element of if you didn't do it, somebody else would. And this time it was just such a big story. But they would have to be very, very careful about paying Shifter in some indirect way. Paul didn't think he could renege on another of Joanna's deals. Even though she was his wife, he wasn't really concerned about her reputation and all that old-fashioned stuff about allowing her to maintain the trust of her sources and contacts upon which specialists traditionally had relied. He was both a pragmatist and a realist as far as newspapers were concerned. And frankly, although he liked it no more than the next journalist, he thought those days were gone. But the *Comet*'s reputation, such as it was, had to be protected. One journalist was neither here nor there.

However, if it became widely believed that the *Comet* would casually break a deal whenever it thought it could get away with it, the paper could be badly damaged.

No, if they went with this one — and they had to, it was too good to miss — then Shifter would have to be paid. The sum of money Joanna had agreed to did not worry Paul. It was cheap, actually, for a story of this calibre. It was all the other factors that had to be so carefully considered.

'Shifter was right, it is a corker,' he said eventually. 'Well done, Jo. We'll go for it, of course. Two things. Tell nobody else. It's 'need to know' until we print, right? There's no question of squeezing it in tonight and you were right not to try to do this one long-distance. It's a major exclusive and I want it to have all the space and projection the *Comet* can give it. We'll run the main story as the splash the day after tomorrow, 'Murder on the Net, Jimbo killer hired by e-mail', something like that, and over four and five. Let it run, too, Jo, every word he said. I'd like the spread as well. 'Just e-mail a murder — Is this the future?' that kind of thing. Detailed analysis of how it can work, plenty of graphics and a break-out on just how secure Swiss banking is, all that sort of stuff. Big picture of an old-style villain carrying a bag of swag or something and an even bigger one of some sharp-suited bastard hacking into his laptop. Maybe a computer-enhanced job superimposing Shifter Brown's face . . . Yeah! Let's do that . . . ' Paul was motoring, warming to his theme. He was always at his best in this kind of situation. That's why he was so successful.

Joanna nodded enthusiastically.

'So get busy, Jo. You've got a lot of writing to do. I don't want anybody else involved, not until they have to be. I'll do the layout myself and we won't get your copy subbed until the last moment. We'll need to get pix on to it first thing in the morning but they can work blind — which won't make much difference. Some of the stuff they put up to me I can't help thinking that's what they normally do.' He grinned. 'OK?'

'OK, boss,' said Joanna and she beamed at him.

They had always worked well together. They might have lurking personal problems now, but that was still the case, he thought to himself.

She got up from her chair as if she were about to leave his office. Then she stopped and spoke in a more hesitant voice. 'And the deal with Shifter?'

'We'll honour it, of course,' he said and he saw the relief wash across her face. 'But I'll want Cromer-Wrong involved — we've got to make it watertight.'

She nodded and beamed at him again. 'I'll make a start, then.'

She was just like him in so many ways. He had seen when she had entered his office that she looked exhausted. But his response and the promise of all that space in the paper had re-energised her. She was buzzing when she left.

As he watched her go his heart ached for her. She had always been the only one for him, right from the start. She was his and he could not bear it when they were not close. He still loved Joanna so much. He did everything he could for her and yet sometimes it seemed that nothing was enough. He thought his feelings were probably stronger than mere love. She possessed him. She always had. And he just wished he could believe that she felt half as strongly about him.

He also wished he could show her how he felt. For more than eighteen years they'd been married, he and Jo, and he still couldn't do that. Neither could he explain to himself why not.

★ ★ ★

The *Comet* ran its splash, four, five and spread on the e-mail killer almost exactly as Paul had so quickly mapped it out in his office. 'This newspaper has made no payment to Arthur Brown,' read the disclaimer at the end of the story. There was no mention, of course, of the pledge to set up trust funds for Shifter's family.

The police response was instant.

On the morning the *Comet*'s exclusive dropped Detective Superintendent Todd Mallett called first thing and demanded an interview with Paul and Joanna. He was already on his way from Exeter to London, he told the news desk early man, and indeed he arrived at Canary Wharf shortly after morning conference. He came heavy-handed, accompanied by a detective sergeant and two uniformed boys. Todd was angry. He wanted to show muscle. Unlike Mike Fielding, he had no time at all for journalists.

Paul offered at once to share all the information the *Comet* had concerning Shifter Brown and his e-mail contract. After all, he had nothing to lose, not now that he had published. The *Comet*'s big exclusive was already in the bag.

Which was exactly the way the detective superintendent saw it. 'Don't you think that's a bit late, Mr Potter?' asked Mallett coldly. 'You should have informed us as soon as you received the information which led to your story this morning — not after it was printed. And you damned well know it.'

'I'm sorry, Detective Superintendent, but I think this newspaper behaved properly throughout. We don't work for the police, you know. This country still has a free press — just about.'

'That is one name for it, Mr Potter,' stormed Mallett. He looked as if he would like to arrest them both. Joanna knew that Mallett had a reputation for being unflappable. But on this occasion he certainly did not look it. She supposed that to see a major development in a case you had more or less failed finally to crack splashed all over the tabloid press when you knew nothing about it was, to say the least, a little annoying.

She also knew that Paul would have expected a strong reaction from the police and would not be fazed by it. Her husband certainly looked cool enough. After all, this was the kind of argument that was perpetual between the law and the Fourth Estate.

The policeman's biggest concern seemed to be that there were more major disclosures lurking in

Joanna's notebook. In particular, the identity of the mystery e-mailer who had hired Shifter. There weren't, of course, although she would have loved there to be. And she had no more idea who the e-mailer was than anyone else — and that included Shifter, she was able to inform Superintendent Mallett. Or so the jailed man continued to insist, at any rate.

The big burly policeman seemed to accept that. But you could see he was still only barely containing his fury. 'There's something else, Mr Potter, I know damn well you and your newspaper have paid Shifter Brown for this story, and you know that I know. We both also know that breaks every code in the book.'

'I can assure you no money has been paid to Mr Brown,' said Potter.

'I bet you can. Someone close, aye? Someone handling it for Shifter's family?'

Uncannily accurate, thought Joanna. But Mallett had been around a few years. It was no surprise that he was spot on.

Her husband obviously thought that too and remained as cool as ever. 'I can also assure you I am well aware of all the codes of practice that apply and that this newspaper always treats them with the utmost respect,' he said.

'Spare me,' muttered Mallett and he led his team away.

'I told you we had to be careful, Jo,' said Potter after the policemen had left. But he looked pretty pleased with himself.

Over the next couple of days there was pandemonium. All the other papers were fighting to catch up. There were questions asked in the House of Commons concerning regulating the Internet and the usual rumblings about the dogged single-mindedness of the gnomes of Zurich who took no notice of any law except their own.

The *Mail* got to both the O'Donnells and the Phillipses, but neither family seemed able to add anything to the story. Or if they could they certainly weren't doing so.

Joanna basked in the glory of her scoop. She was more excited than she'd been in years. And, as her husband had noted, with the excitement of her triumph came a great flood of extra energy.

She really wanted to see Fielding. She felt guilty because working on her big story with Paul had somehow brought her and her husband together in a kind of closeness that had been absent from their relationship for months. But that did not lessen her need for her lover — although it was not until four days after her interview with Shifter, when all the possible follow-ups had also been written that she eventually called Mike on his mobile.

He sounded distant, quite cool. Almost a bit like Paul when he was displeased about something.

And that sent a shiver down her spine. 'Anything wrong, Mike?'

'Nope.' Just the one word. She suspected that he was miffed with her because she'd obviously been in his territory and not contacted him. He had left a message on her mobile on the day after her trip down to Exeter, but she'd been so preoccupied with her big story that it was not until now that she'd even remembered it. 'I'm sorry I haven't been in touch before; it was just that everything seemed to happen at once,' she explained a little lamely.

'Don't worry about it.' He still sounded offhand.

She pretended not to notice. Hearing his voice, with an edge to it, heightened her need for him. As usual. She decided to go straight for it. 'I need to see you,' she said and she knew she had been unable to keep the desire out of her voice. Hadn't tried very hard, really.

When he replied, after a short pause, he sounded a little warmer. 'I can't get away at the moment, Jo. I've swung just about every trip I can to London recently.'

She had been ready for that. 'That's OK,' she told him. 'Can you steal a couple of hours if I come to Exeter?'

'You'd come all this way for a couple of hours?' Now that sounded much more like his normal self.

'Yep.'

'I'm flattered. But not Exeter. Look, do you mind cheap and cheerful?'

'Have we ever had anything else?'

'Feel free to book the Ritz any time you like.'

She didn't want to waste time on any more banter. 'Next time you can get to London,' she said. 'Meanwhile I don't give a damn as long as the place has a bed and a door with a lock on it.'

He laughed.

That was better, she thought.

'The Lodge at Taunton service station,' he said. 'Far enough away from here for me to be reasonably safe and just a ten-minute cab ride from the station for you.'

'T'riffic,' she said, striving to maintain the lightness. She hated it when he was off with her. 'The cabby'll love it. What on earth could a woman on her own be doing getting dropped off at a service station motel, I wonder?'

'Get him to drop you in the car park, you silly bitch. That should confuse him. Anyway, what does it matter? I know you're wildly famous, but not down here, you're not.'

'Not as a journalist, I'm damn sure of that. I fear I've still made more of a stir through my personal involvement in the Beast of Dartmoor saga than by anything I've actually written about it.'

'Yesterday's fish and chips,' he said.

She wasn't sure which he was referring to, her journalism or the other stuff. Anyway, she didn't really care. Suddenly she just so wanted to be with him again. Or, to be more precise, in bed with him again.

They arranged to meet the next day.

★ ★ ★

He was late. She had travelled all the way from London and he was late.

He didn't even apologise. Didn't speak. Just jumped on her.

She didn't mind it like that sometimes but she was taken by surprise. He was usually a man who

369

enjoyed taking his time, savouring every moment and, by and large, she preferred that. She had got to expect it with him. 'You were in a hurry,' she said afterwards.

He lay beside her, panting, his eyes tightly closed. He had been far too quick for her. She needed time these days to reach a climax. Time and much more attention.

'I needed you,' he muttered.

'I still need you,' she said bluntly.

'Patience,' he said.

He recovered surprisingly quickly. And the next time he did all the things that so excited her. She didn't quite know what it was he did with his tongue that nobody else she had ever slept with had seemed to manage. She just knew it drove her mad, made her desperate to have him inside her and that when she did start to orgasm it was more acute, more extreme, with him than it had ever been with anyone else. Just like always.

When she had finished he held her very close. Her body felt weightless. She was in a state of complete relaxation. It was probably only after really good sex that she ever relaxed like that. She closed her eyes and revelled in the moment. Then she must have fallen asleep because when she opened her eyes again he was no longer lying beside her but standing, still naked with his back towards her, over by the window. 'Are you all right?' she asked.

'Uh huh,' he said, but he didn't sound very happy.

She propped herself up on one elbow. 'Are you sure? I thought you were a bit off on the phone yesterday. Is there something wrong?'

'You don't even know what you do sometimes, do you?' he sounded quite tetchy now.

'Sorry?'

'This past year, ever since the O'Donnell thing began I've given you everything I've got. Story after story. Kept you informed. Thought I owed you that. Then you get the e-mail killer stuff and you didn't even bother to let me know. I read it in your newspaper like all the other cretins.'

So that was it. She had half suspected as much. 'It didn't even occur to me until afterwards . . . '

He interrupted her. 'And that, Joanna, is exactly my point.'

'But Mike, I'm a hack — you're a policeman. It's different. I didn't think you'd even want to know about the case any more. It's over for you, isn't it? You've told me that enough times.'

He turned abruptly towards her, punching the air with his right arm, fist tightly clenched. Involuntarily she flinched back into the pillows. He looked absolutely furious. 'For God's sake, Joanna, it will never be over for me, don't you understand that? I'm never going to be able to let go. I just can't.'

The vehemence of his outburst took her by surprise. He shouted the words, his features contorted in anger. But his nakedness gave the scene an edge of the ridiculous. Maybe he thought so too.

He turned away, walked across the room, picked up his underpants and trousers from the floor where he had thrown them in his haste such a short time ago, and quickly pulled them on. 'I'm supposed to be a tough cop. You don't let on,' he told her through clenched teeth. 'You just get on with the

371

next job. Trouble is, I was first on the scene when Angela Phillips was discovered. Everybody knows that. Nobody, but nobody, knows what it was like. I'll never forget it. Never. It was the worst thing that ever happened to me. The second-worst thing was knowing I had the bastard who did it and seeing him walk free out of court twice. I thought you understood that. Didn't you realise how much it took for me to call you up after all that time, ask you to help me? Didn't you realise how I felt when it all went pear-shaped yet again? O'Donnell didn't just get away with murder, he wrecked so many lives — including mine as near as damn it. And he's even fouled up the remains of my career yet again, twenty years on.

'Do you think there will ever be anything to do with that bastard that I don't want to know every spit and fart on? You talk to the man who topped O'Donnell, you get all this new stuff, and you don't even contact me because it didn't occur to you? What didn't occur to you, Jo? That I'd be interested, or that I would care?'

'Mike, I'm sorry . . . ' she began.

He had begun to button up his shirt by then. She could tell she was going to get nowhere with him this afternoon. She had known that happen before with him, and with her first husband, come to that — although never with Paul who was too controlled. After lovemaking, just when you hope for tenderness and peace, the truth was inclined to come out. Any lurking resentment or bitterness surfaced.

Fielding interrupted her again. Calm now, but icy

cold. 'Look, don't worry about it. Why should you understand? Nobody else does. I can't talk about it now, anyway. I've got to go, I've already stayed longer than I should have.'

She was hurt, but she realised she had been completely thoughtless. After all, she had always known how much the Angela Phillips case had got to him. He had been genuinely moved by the poor girl's fate and had wanted desperately to see her murderer brought to justice. But it was more than that. It had become personal for him, as it had for her. Certainly she had already been aware that Mike took O'Donnell's two acquittals, and all the baggage that had come with them, personally. But maybe she had not realised before just how emotionally affected he still was.

'Can't you just stay a few minutes more?' she asked. 'I don't like you leaving like this.'

'No, I can't, Jo,' he said. He was no longer shouting; in fact, his voice was now quite soft, but as he spoke he pulled on his jacket and began to walk backwards towards the door. 'It's all right, really,' he told her. 'I'll call you, OK?'

Joanna pulled the sheet up tight to her chin and watched him go. There was nothing else she could do. Maybe another time he would talk to her reasonably about it all. She hoped so. She found that she was feeling very anxious suddenly.

This was yet another side of Mike that, after all these years on and off, she had not really seen before. She knew he could be much softer than he seemed. She had learned that long ago. She knew so much about him. But she was deeply disturbed by the glimpse he had just given her of a level of obsession she had not suspected. She became very thoughtful and she did not like the path down which her thoughts were leading her.

How far would this man, who still had such a hold over her, go to get what he thought was justice, she wondered. He'd know how to fix it, that was for certain. He was computer-literate too. But then, so would she, up to a point. So would many people whose lives had been blighted by O'Donnell and his terrible crime. How far would she go? If it was important enough, if she thought she could get away with it. She made herself think about that too. It wasn't just Mike. Far from it.

Nonetheless, as she showered and dressed, and prepared to drive back to the husband and child to whom she had given no thought at all during the time she had spent with her lover, she found herself growing increasingly uneasy.

Mike had never liked to be beaten, had he? In order to get his man he had always been prepared to go that little bit further, push that bit harder . . .

17

Back in the office in Canary Wharf the next day and right through the following week, Joanna tried to concentrate her mind on her work. And particularly on any developments in the e-mail murder case. She hardly dared contact either the Devon and Cornwall Constabulary or Scotland Yard on this one — she had become a bit of a pariah in those areas, particularly as far as Detective Superintendent Todd Mallett was concerned — so Tim Jones was on the case. And all he could do was assure her that the police had made no further progress at all.

They had, of course, gone back to Shifter's house and searched it again. The only computer found had indeed been newly acquired and contained no hidden 'contractor' and 'enforcer' e-mail files and, in fact, nothing at all relating to Shifter's dubious business.

Shifter was extensively interviewed all over again by the police, but refused to reveal any more information about either the Swiss bank accounts or the e-mail correspondence. He also continued to refuse to reveal which cyber café he had used, but diligent foot-slogging inquiries by officers carrying photographs of the distinctive Shifter resulted in the staff of a cyber café not far from Brown's home admitting that they were almost sure Shifter had used their computers on several occasions to go on-line. However, they had unfortunately recently upgraded their stock.

'The police are not going to be able to trace the stuff beyond the dealer the caff traded with, not without a miracle,' Tim told her. 'Chances are it's already been sold on through one of those street markets like the one Shifter bought his rigs from. That's what usually happens.'

★ ★ ★

Meanwhile Jo forced herself not to phone Fielding. She knew she should allow him to contact her in his own time. But after eight days she began to wonder if she would ever hear from him again.

On the evening of the ninth day after their tryst in the Taunton motel Fielding finally called.

Joanna felt that familiar physical lurch inside. She was just so relieved to hear from him. The sound of his voice still brought her up in goose bumps.

'I'm sorry I was such a pig, sometimes everything seems to get on top of me,' he told her at once.

She reassured him. 'It's fine, Mike, honestly.'

'Look, I can swing a trip to town next week, that's if you still want to . . . ' His voice tailed off.

'Oh, yes, I want to,' she replied quietly. And she did, too. Deep, deep inside she could already feel the dull ache of anticipation.

★ ★ ★

Their lovemaking seemed to become more and more urgent every time they were together. It was Fielding who took the lead. Again this time, once more in the downmarket Southampton Row hotel, he had no time for any niceties. There was no finesse. There were no preliminaries. He barely spoke to her and there was no foreplay. He just pushed her down on the bed, not even giving her time to undress properly, and entered her roughly without even taking his trousers off, just undoing his flies and thrusting straight into her. His eyes were fixed on the wall behind the bed, his teeth gritted in concentration, his features distorted in effort. And his face was coated in sweat. He held each of her wrists down above her head. He didn't hurt her and yet there was a kind of cold brutality in his lovemaking. It couldn't really have been called that. He just pummelled into her, apparently quite uninterested in how she might be taking it. Again he didn't give her a chance, didn't even seem to care. He did not pause until it was over for him.

When he had finished he rolled off her straight away. 'I'm sorry, next time will be for you,' he muttered haltingly, his breath coming in great gasps still.

He had never been quite like that before. She didn't think she liked it very much. In fact, she was quite sure she didn't like it. And yet — and maybe it was because of his desperation — she was immensely excited by it. Her desire, her need, seemed to increase with his disregard for it. And as in the motel in Taunton her own satisfaction, when he finally concentrated his attentions on her, seemed greater than ever. When she climaxed she thought she had never experienced quite such acute pleasure. Not even with him.

This time it was a snatched early evening meeting. He had a police dinner to go to that night. And he dressed and left her in bed again, although she had to leave shortly afterwards. She was glowing, almost burning inside, and she just wanted a few more minutes luxuriating in the feeling.

He came to the bed and kissed her firmly on the mouth before he left, tantalising her with his tongue. Making her whole body remember what it had just enjoyed. 'It gets better every time,' he told her with a smile, and he ran one hand down the entire length of her body lingering for just a few seconds over one breast and between her legs, before stepping back, shaking his head sorrowfully, turning and heading for the door.

At least their parting was more pleasant than the last time, she thought, as he shut the door behind him. He had always been a moody bugger, and his mood the last time they had met had been very disconcerting. As had been the sex they had just had.

Gradually the uneasiness that had been lurking ever since that afternoon at the Taunton motel overwhelmed her, forcing out all those nice warm feelings that came from great sexual satisfaction. She lay there thinking about the way these sea changes came over him, how he had shown that disturbing side of himself to her, and then she noticed his laptop computer on the small table by the window.

She couldn't stop herself. She dragged the sheet off the bed, wrapping it around herself, grabbed the little machine, sat down on the room's only chair

378

and switched on. It was password-protected, of course, but she felt she had at least a chance of second-guessing him, given time, which she had a reasonable amount of. She checked her watch. It was just past 7.30. Fielding wouldn't be back until after midnight, she was sure, and as long as she was at home in Richmond before ten she would easily be there before Paul.

However, she had been trying to break into the machine for only a couple of minutes when the door burst open.

Fielding hurried into the room. 'I had to turn the taxi round, I forgot my damned phone . . . ' He saw then that she was working on his laptop and stopped dead. 'What the hell do you think you're doing?' he asked very quietly, his voice full of menace.

She felt a hot flush rise somewhere around the bottom of her neck, and spread across her throat and face until it reached her temples. She knew she must be bright red. She could think of nothing to say.

'I asked you what the hell you thought you were doing?' he enquired yet again, equally quietly.

'I was just . . . ' Her mind was suddenly blank. She could think of no excuse. 'Just looking for something . . . ' she finished lamely.

He strode across the room and snatched the laptop away from her. He glanced at it, taking in that she had failed to gain access, shut it down and closed the lid. He did it all very quickly. She remained sitting on the chair, still wrapped in the sheet.

He caught hold of her shoulder, his fingers

digging into the flesh. 'And what were you looking for?'

'I don't know . . . ' She stopped, shook her head.

'C'mon, Joanna, what did you think you were going to find?' The fingers dug harder into her shoulder. He made her eyes water for the second time that evening. 'C'mon, Joanna,' he repeated.

She had to tell him something. It might as well be the truth, she thought, in any case she didn't have the wit at that moment to come up with anything else. 'It's the way you are about Angela Phillips and O'Donnell,' she began. She saw his eyes narrow. His grip did not slacken. 'All that stuff you told me the other night. You were right. I hadn't understood. Not really. I hadn't realised quite how strongly you felt about him, your job, all of it. Not until now. And I wondered . . . I wondered . . . ' Her voice tailed off.

'You wondered what, Jo?' he whispered, his lips very close to her ear.

She shook her head again and said no more.

'You wondered perhaps if I felt strongly enough to do something about it all, is that it?' He still spoke very quietly.

His grip tightened yet more. His fingers were digging into her so hard it felt as if they were going to meet in the middle. That was something else she had not ever been so aware of before about him — his tremendous physical strength. She had found him physically threatening just once before, in the Exeter motel room, but that was nothing compared with this. She nodded. There was no point in pretending.

'You wondered if I had hired Shifter, didn't you? You wondered if I were the mystery e-mailer. And you thought you'd have a sneaky look around in my laptop to see what you could find . . . '

There was real menace in him, but she supposed she could hardly blame him. She nodded once more.

He snatched his hand from her shoulder. Involuntarily she glanced down and put her own hand there, as if to take the soreness away. She saw that his fingernails had drawn blood.

He backed away from her, sat down abruptly on the edge of the bed and lowered his face into his hands. She still couldn't think of anything more to say.

When he looked up he seemed more sad than angry. 'I can't believe you would think something like that of me,' he told her.

She removed her hand from her shoulder and rested it against her forehead, took a deep breath and went for it. 'I'm sorry,' she said. 'It's just that I started wondering about how far you would go to get O'Donnell. You've always been very determined, Mike, always been someone who wants to win. And this case, well, it's always been the one, hasn't it? Don't they say that we all have one great love in life and a policeman has one great case? Good or bad. One case that overshadows all others. This was always yours, wasn't it, Mike? And it's always been a can of worms, hasn't it? I just wondered how far you would go to close that can of worms, that's all, I just wanted to know . . . ' she finished lamely again.

'You could have asked me.'

'I didn't know how.'

He grunted derisively. 'So what about you, then?'

'What do you mean, what about me?'

He smiled humourlessly. 'What about you, Joanna?' he repeated. 'This case got to you too, didn't it, from the beginning, and in the end O'Donnell made a fool of you. He mocked you, didn't he, humiliated you and that apology for a newspaper you work for. God knows, you don't like being made a fool of. And in front of your peers . . . '

'You're being ridiculous Mike,' she began.

'Am I?' he interrupted. 'And you, I suppose, are not — ridiculous, offensive, insulting? I'm a police officer, for fuck's sake.'

'Yes, and a good one, always — but . . . ' The weak attempt at flattery proved to be a big mistake.

'Save it,' he said. 'I really don't want to know. If you can believe, even for an instant, that I'm evil enough to hire a fucking heavy to slice another man's dick off and bury him alive then there's not much point in anything any more, is there? Not between us, anyway.'

To her immense irritation she felt tears forming in her eyes. She was suddenly overcome with guilt and remorse. Now that he was talking to her like that, sitting in front of her, the whole thing seemed absurd. Fielding was impetuous, yes. Impatient. Sometimes too willing to cut corners. Over eager to get a conviction. All those things. But a cold, calculated killer, albeit at a distance? No, he couldn't be that. It was just not possible. 'I'm so sorry, Mike,' she stumbled. 'I don't know where I was coming from, I really don't.'

'Neither do I, Jo. Now you'd better get dressed and go. I'm certainly not leaving you alone in my room again. If you want to go through my pockets you'll just have to do it while I'm here.'

'Mike, please!'

'Just get dressed,' he told her, in such a way that there could be no more argument, no more discussion. Perhaps, she thought fearfully, not ever. Perhaps this time it really would be over.

★   ★   ★

She drove home feeling thoroughly ashamed of herself. She had been cheating on her husband without compunction, she had been neglecting her daughter, maybe even endangering Emily's secure future. She had been carried away by her affair with Fielding, it had taken over her life again just as it had done all those years ago. Hard as she fought against it, his fascination for her, which she had never been able to explain, had become all-consuming. And yet she was still able to believe that her lover could be guilty of arranging such a horrific crime. Able to suspect that of a man for whom she had been putting her marriage and her whole existence at risk.

Joanna's emotions were in turmoil. She found herself consumed with guilt over her behaviour towards both her family and her lover. She could not wait to get home to Richmond and sneak a look at her hopefully sleeping daughter, and maybe even prepare a late supper for her husband, who she knew loved her — although she wished he wouldn't always be so self-contained and controlled about it. At the same time she wished she could swing the car round, go back to Fielding, grovel her apologies and shag him rotten for the rest of the night.

She took one hand off the steering wheel and thumped the passenger seat in frustration. What *was* wrong with her? She had a dammed good life, a damned good husband, a lovely daughter, a lovely home, plenty of money. She was indeed the woman with everything. And yet again she had let this bloody case and that bloody man Fielding put it all under threat. The biggest threat, she knew, came from within her own head and heart. Fielding was under her skin again and half of her sincerely did not want him there.

Her thoughts strayed to what he had said to her when she had more or less accused him of hiring Shifter Brown: 'And what about you, Jo?'

Laughable, of course. But any more laughable than her accusing him? And Mike did have a point, she supposed.

There was nothing in the world she hated so much as being made a fool of. Even after all these years it irked her ever to be beaten, to be in any situation which she felt gave the opposition, particularly her rival crime journalists, reason to be able to gloat over her.

She made herself focus on the case. That at least was a safer preoccupation than Fielding. For the umpteenth time she went over in her mind the list of people who might have wanted to take terminal revenge against James Martin O'Donnell.

She knew that Todd Mallett and his team had questioned the Phillipses and the O'Donnells all over again since her e-mail killing story. Modern farming is a highly complex operation and, like so many farmers these days, the Phillipses virtually ran their whole business on computer. Apparently all the family were reasonably computer-literate. But were they streetwise enough to have found a killer on the Net and to know how to cover their footprints? It was also fairly laughable even to consider them coming up with a user name like 'contractor'. And, at the end of the day, devastated though they had been by all that had happened to them and their daughter, would they really take the law into their own hands in that way?

As for the O'Donnell family — would they hire a killer on the Net? Surely that wasn't their style? For a start, they still had their own enforcers, didn't they? Combo was dead, but his son, Little John, that chip off the old block, was, she knew, still in the employ of the O'Donnells. And indeed, would they have the know-how to do so? Tommy O'Donnell probably would, but he was the one trying to lead his family away from the old ways of hit men and the like. Joanna was pretty sure old Sam O'Donnell wouldn't have a clue about using the Internet, certainly not at the required level.

Nonetheless she wondered about Sam the Man. Just how ruthless was he capable of being with his own flesh and blood? She knew he would have hated the sex angle and the DNA evidence concerning his son must surely have given even him proof of what he had always chosen to deny. Had he finally accepted the inevitable and taken action he would previously not have countenanced? She could not believe Sam would ever put out a contract against his own son, but you did have to consider it.

She knew she would not be welcome, but she decided that the next day she would at least try to get to see Sam the Man.

★ ★ ★

Emily was indeed already asleep when Jo arrived home and the au pair was in her room watching TV. Very carefully, Joanna opened the door to her daughter's bedroom. The light from the landing was sufficient for her to be able to see Emily without waking her by switching on any more lights, but it took a moment for Jo's eyes to adjust. Emily was lying curled on her side, in deep sleep looking younger than her almost twelve years. Jo always reckoned that their daughter resembled Paul more than her; she certainly had his eyes, but she had inherited her mother's blond hair, straight and grown to well below shoulder-length, just like Jo's at Emily's age. At least — that was the way it had been when Jo had last seen her daughter at breakfast that morning. She took a step into the room for a closer look. Yes, she was right. Emily's hair was now cropped short and spiky with a purple streak running right through it Mohican style — although mercifully not shaven on either side. My God, thought Jo, she really is growing up.

She was smiling when she left the room, which a few minutes earlier she would not have thought possible. Some mothers might freak out at the sight of their young daughter with purple-streaked hair. Jo found it mildly amusing. Perhaps this was the start of the kind of idiosyncratic teenage shenanigans she was so perversely rather looking forward to.

She considered pouring herself a drink, but then realised she was very tired, although, in her own home with her family around her, Jo did not like to think about what had tired her so. She decided to go straight to bed, fell asleep immediately and was not even aware of her husband returning. He must have crept quietly into the bed beside her. He had certainly made no attempt to wake her. He rarely did nowadays. In the morning there was little chance to talk even if either of them had wanted to. They were woken by the phone just after 7.30 a.m. It was the news desk for Paul. Situation normal. Shortly afterwards came the sports editor and then somebody else with a problem only Paul could deal with. She and her husband breakfasted only on tea and orange juice, consumed on the run. Emily always ate a large bowl of muesli with fresh fruit which, in her usual grown-up way, she prepared herself.

It was one of Jo's days in the office, but she wanted to drive straight over to the O'Donnells so she declined Paul's offer of a ride in his chauffeur-driven car.

He had raised his eyebrows at his daughter's hair but said nothing about it at first. Well, he hated confrontation, but Jo knew he wouldn't approve. Paul was very conventional about appearance. Eventually he reached across the table and touched

Emily's hand. 'You used to have very beautiful hair,' he told her mildly. 'Until yesterday, in fact.'

Emily was not abashed. 'Oh Dad, it was *sooo* boring,' she said.

Paul smiled. 'Oh, well, we can't have that, can we?'

Emily shot him a quizzical look. Like her mother, she obviously found it difficult sometimes to work out what her father was actually thinking. She would have known he wouldn't make a scene, though, and she was right.

Paul passed no further comment. He left just before Jo and kissed her absently on the cheek. He was polite and distant. Same as ever. She couldn't help comparing him, so self-contained, so con-trolled, so successful, with the volatile, mixed-up, disappointed man she could not get out of her mind. Then she resolved that she *would* put Fielding out of her mind. She *really* would. This stupid affair was doing her no good. When it began again she had known she must regard it as just an occasional roll in the hay and in many ways it still wasn't much more than that — nor could it be. But with Fielding there was always more to it than that. And, in the cold light of dawn, it just didn't seem worth it. So maybe the previous day's confrontation had not been such a bad thing after all. It had jolted her out of a kind of trance. She would not sit waiting for Fielding to call again. And neither would she call him. She truly didn't want to go on like this, she told herself.

In any case, she had a tricky job to do today. And the guilt was really kicking in.

She offered to drive Emily to school, a duty normally undertaken by the au pair. She was aware of her daughter, still sitting at the kitchen table eating her muesli, glancing at her in mild surprise. Jo stood up and ruffled the remains of Emily's hair. 'Well, I quite like the new look,' she said. She wasn't at all sure that she did, even though she found it amusing, but she somehow desperately wanted to feel close to her daughter that morning. She might have realised, of course, that the vanity of adolescence, however misplaced, had arrived along with its new spiky purple hairdo.

Emily pushed her hand away. 'Oh, don't, Mum, don't,' she muttered with a frown.

However, later in the car, just as Jo pulled up outside her school, Emily surprised her mother by leaning across from the passenger seat to give her a big sloppy kiss on the cheek and ask, 'You are all right, Mum, aren't you? There's nothing wrong, is there?'

Jo was inclined to forget that Emily was every bit as perceptive as her father and it made her panic momentarily as she wondered if Paul had also picked up on anything amiss in her behaviour lately. 'I'm absolutely fine, darling,' she said, kissing her daughter back and then forcing a big bright smile. 'Go on. Off with you. And have a really good day.'

Damn, she thought, as she drove off in the direction of Dulwich. She really must stop putting her family at risk.

★　★　★

She arrived at Sam O'Donnell's house, unannounced again, just before 10.30 a.m.

Tommy answered the door, as before. He stared at her coldly for a moment or two and she quite expected him to slam it in her face. 'You gotta cheek, I'll give you that,' he said eventually.

'Look, Tommy, I just want to talk.'

'Yeah, your kind always do,' he told her coldly. But to her surprise he opened the door and beckoned her in.

She crossed the threshold and stood uncertainly in a chintzy hallway, thick-pile richly patterned carpet, a gilt mirror on the wall to the left of an ornate mahogany hatstand. To the right a gallery of framed family photographs, almost all including Sam and his wife, at their wedding, with their newborn children, their two sons and their only daughter, and at their children's weddings. It was her first time inside Sam's home. She had been told that the house was a shrine to Tommy's dead mother and that seemed about how it was. Apparently all the furnishings and decorations were kept the way Annie O'Donnell had had them. Sam allowed no change. On the wall opposite all the family photographs was a huge framed portrait, maybe four foot by three, of Annie.

'Right,' said Tommy. 'Everything you see and hear in this house is off the record. All right?'

She hesitated. It wasn't all right. She hated off the record. You never knew what you were going to get and all too often it was useless unless you could use it fully and attribute it.

'It's either that or out,' said Tommy.

Jo sighed.

'And when I say off the record I mean you can't print anything. There is just something I want you to know. To be aware of. Yes or no?'

She said yes, of course, unhappy though she was about it.

Wordlessly he showed her into the sitting room. More chintz, patterned wallpaper, deep-pile carpet and family photographs. She barely took in any of it, though, such was the shock of her first sight of Sam the Man.

Arguably the most feared and respected villain in London, he was sitting slumped in a wheelchair in the middle of the room. One rheumy eye seemed to half focus on her. She wasn't sure. The left side of his face was cruelly distorted and his left arm hung loosely over the arm of the chair. Sam was dribbling. He showed no reaction to her. He did not attempt to speak.

She gave a small involuntary gasp.

'He had a stroke soon after Jimbo's last trial,' said Tommy. 'Been like this ever since. His left arm and his left leg are paralysed. We don't know what he can understand.'

Tommy walked across to the chair and stroked his father's still abundant shock of white hair. More like father to son than son to father. But that's the way all our parental relationships change in the end, Jo thought to herself.

'Do we, Dad, eh?' he murmured, his voice suddenly soft and ripe with affection. Then he patted the old man's hand, but still Sam did not react.

Swiftly Tommy retreated to Jo's side. 'Right, that's all you're getting,' he said, as he ushered her out into the hallway again. 'I wanted you to see that,' he went on, once he had closed the living-room door behind them. 'We've kept Sam's condition a secret. That's why you can't print anything. Dad would hate people to know that he had become a dribbling wreck. I mean, he's still Sam the Man. As long as he's alive he'll always be that.' Tommy spoke with quiet pride, reverence even.

Against her better judgement Jo found that she was moved. 'I am very sorry, Tommy,' she said. And in a strange way she meant it, too. She had no illusions about the villainy of Sam O'Donnell or what a nasty piece of work he could be, but there had always been something special about him. He had been big in every way, a character, one of the last of a dying breed. She knew better than to romanticise his sort but with Sam you just couldn't help doing so just a bit.

Tommy was not interested. 'I didn't show you Dad to get your sympathy,' he told her. 'I wanted you to see what you've done, you and that bastard Fielding. You got that new trial staged against Jimbo and that was what did it. No doubt about it. Dad adored Jimbo. All that DNA stuff. He couldn't take it. He was ill, really, right from when it all started again. He had a very slight stroke just before the hearing at Okehampton, that's why you've seen him using a stick since then. But he was all right, in his head anyway, until after Jimbo disappeared. Then he had another stroke. And it was a big one. It was all just too much for him.'

Joanna felt suddenly irritated. 'Tommy, you can hardly blame me and Mike Fielding. If you have to blame anybody you should blame your brother.'

Tommy shook his head stubbornly. Joanna knew that he was a bright, intelligent man, everyone knew of his determination to legitimise the O'Donnell family and how hard he had already worked towards it. The fresh prosecution against his brother couldn't have helped with that. But apparently, in common with so many of these East End villains, when it came to family Tommy had all the old blind spots. 'There was no call for it all to be dragged out again,' he said frostily. 'It was history. And it didn't do anybody any good, did it? Not Angela Phillips's family and not us. We've not only lost Jimbo, we've as good as lost Dad because of it too. He's out of it. The only mercy is we don't even think he knows Jimbo's dead.'

'Tommy, Angela Phillips died in the most horrific circumstances possible,' Joanna responded tetchily, throwing caution to the wind. 'Your brother killed her. The DNA proved it and if it had been available twenty years ago Jimbo would have gone down then. That's what the new trial was about, that's why it was all 'dragged out', as you put it, again. And if it weren't for some bloody stupid anomaly of the law he would have been locked up and he wouldn't be dead. He'd be safely behind bars. Where he belonged. He was a murderer and a rapist. You must accept that. I reckon your father did in the end and that's probably what made him ill.'

'I accept nothing. Jimbo's dead, that's all I know. And he was my brother.'

'Look, do you mind if I ask you some questions while I am here?' she ventured recklessly.

'Yes, I fucking well do,' he stormed at her. Then he repeated his earlier remark, but his voice was much louder and angrier now. 'I just wanted you to see what you did to my father. And now you've seen it — get out.' He didn't take a step towards her. He said nothing that was specifically threatening. He didn't need to. You don't argue with an angry O'Donnell.

She opened the door to the house herself, shut it quietly behind her and hurried to her car, parked down the street.

When she put the key in the ignition she noticed that her hand was shaking.

* * *

Back in the office, she worked on her column through the afternoon. Just after five Paul called through and told her his deputy was editing that night. 'I'm taking an early cut,' he said. 'If you're clear, how about an evening at home? Maybe phone for a pizza or something.'

Joanna was pleasantly surprised. The *Comet* operated a system of duty editors at night. Either Paul, his deputy, or one of three assistant editors edited each night, staying in the office until well after the foreigns dropped, often until one in the morning and sometimes later. But Paul was a hands-on editor, as almost all of the good ones were. Except on Fridays, which was designated as a family evening, he would rarely leave Canary Wharf until

394

ten or eleven even when somebody else was officially editing. She agreed with alacrity and told him she would give him a lift home if he liked and he could give his driver the night off.

They left the office soon after seven, the traffic was as amenable as it ever is at that time, and they made it to Richmond in just over an hour and a quarter. Paul was companionable enough, if a little distant. But she was used to that. It was the way things were. Indeed, he spent most of the journey home talking to the night desk on his mobile phone. That was the way things were, too. Always.

At home he settled down with Emily at the computer in her bedroom while Joanna made drinks and ordered a pizza. Emily was always excited to have Paul home and inclined to monopolise his time when he was there. Joanna didn't blame her. She saw little enough of the father she idolised. The pizza arrived and all three sat down at the kitchen table together. That was rare enough, too, which was why Emily had been allowed to stay up and eat later than usual.

Paul teased her gently once or twice about the purple hair and Jo suspected from their daughter's rather sheepish reaction that she might already be regretting whatever whim or peer pressure had led her into yesterday's drastic hairdo. Paul had the knack of handling Emily, of bringing her round almost always to his way of thinking. He was very good with her, always had been. Indeed, they were like peas in a pod. Emily was a real chip off the old block. Joanna was inordinately proud of her, even if she did sometimes fear that she was old beyond her years. Apart from when it came to that hair!

In spite of the teasing Jo could tell how much their daughter was enjoying the family supper and vowed to try to make it happen more often. Paul promised to take her swimming at the weekend and Emily went to bed happily, although still reluctantly, around 9.45 p.m. Joanna poured the remains of the bottle of red wine she had earlier opened into her and Paul's glasses, and asked him if he would like her to open another.

'In a minute,' he said. 'I want to talk to you. I've been waiting for us to have some time alone.'

She noticed that he was looking very serious. She had already stood up and was halfway to the wine rack in the corner. She turned around and walked back to the table. 'Well?'

'You should know that I am aware that you are once again having an affair with Mike Fielding,' Paul announced in an expressionless voice.

Joanna sat down with a bit of a bump. That was the last thing she had expected to hear. Her first instinct was to lie. 'I don't know what you're talking about . . . ' she began.

Her husband interrupted her. 'Don't insult my intelligence, Joanna,' he told her. 'I said I know. I know about the hotel in Southampton Row; I know that he spent every night with you when you were covering the Shifter Brown hearing in Exeter; I even know about your sleazy trip down to Taunton to the motorway motel. If you would like any more details I can assure you that I do have them.'

She realised at once that he must have had her followed. It was somehow typical of Paul that he could do that over an extended period and actually be able to say nothing, just live with what was going on, until he was ready to make a move. Any normal man would have confronted her long ago, she thought. She had often, by way of attempting to justify her affair, blamed Paul's absence of passion, his calculating businesslike approach to all aspects of his life and his complete lack of spontaneity, for leading her into another man's arms. She knew, of course, that was really no justification for her behaviour. She didn't speak.

Apparently he did not expect her to.

'It goes without saying that you end this affair immediately,' he went on. 'If you do not I will divorce you. Naturally you will lose your job. You will also lose your daughter. I will get custody, I promise you. You may well get access of some kind but I will make sure that it is as little as possible. And I will do my absolute best to turn Emily against you. For ever. I do not envisage that would be too difficult.'

He opened his briefcase, which had been at his feet by the table, and took out a large manila envelope. He waved it at her. 'This is a very full and detailed account of your recent activities. I think if I showed it to our daughter she would make up her own mind, don't you?'

Joanna felt very cold. She believed absolutely that he would and could do all he said, including showing such a dreadful dossier to his only child. She knew just how ruthless he could be when it came to getting his own way. And yes, she also knew that Emily would be quite capable of forming her own judgement of her mother's behaviour and that it would be a damning one. Emily loved her mother, but she was her father's daughter. Nonetheless, she told him, 'I can't believe you'd do that.'

'Yes you can and do, Joanna.' He emptied some of the contents of the envelope on to the table. There were even photographs of her and Fielding entering the Taunton motel, albeit separately, and together both entering and leaving the Southampton Row place. She didn't give her husband the satisfaction of picking them up for a closer look, but as far as she could see there were none of her and Fielding actually in bed. Paul and his representative had mercifully drawn the line at that, it seemed.

'You have too good a life to allow it to be spoiled,' he went on. 'And it will be spoiled, totally, if you don't do as I tell you. You will be swapping all that you have, all that we have, for life with a failed, near-alcoholic, mid-rank copper. I do not actually think you have any idea what that would be like, Joanna.'

That made Joanna wince. The description of Fielding was accurate enough. She supposed she probably didn't have any idea what it would be like to live out in the sticks on a very limited income with a disappointed and often angry man who habitually drowned his miseries in alcohol. Nor was she ever likely to — not even without Paul's ultimatum, as it happened. That was the final irony. At the end of the day she doubted if Fielding would ever have tried to make a life with her, in any circumstances. Such small likelihood as there had been of them being properly together had ended almost twenty years before. And after their last confrontation over her trying to hack into his laptop, there had been barely a chance of the affair continuing, even without external intervention. Strange that Paul had decided to make his move at that moment.

'I'm sorry, Paul,' she said. 'I really didn't mean for any of this to happen.'

'And you think that makes it all right,' he said flatly.

'No, of course I don't.'

'You've let me down, your daughter down and yourself down. Do you realise that?'

She nodded. She wished he wouldn't lecture her but she supposed she deserved it. And he was right, of course. Cool. Logical. Controlled as ever. He sounded more as if he were admonishing a member of staff for some professional misdemeanour or negotiating a business deal than confronting his wife with infidelity. He showed absolutely no emotion at all. But then, he never did.

'Look, Paul, I think it's over anyway between Mike and . . . ' she began to explain.

'You think?' He raised his voice almost imperceptibly. 'Joanna, I will give you twenty-four hours in which to assure me that you *know* it is over. If you cannot do that then I shall ask you to leave this house and I shall start divorce proceedings immediately. The decision is yours. But do not for one moment think that you can carry on cheating on me. I shall know at once.'

She didn't doubt it. And she couldn't understand how she had thought she would ever get away with it in the first place. Not with Paul. He was just too clever. Too astute. She supposed the truth was that she hadn't thought at all.

Paul had started speaking again. 'I shall sleep in the spare bedroom tonight,' he told her almost conversationally.

She found herself once again comparing him with Fielding, that infuriating, emotionally confusing man whom, she had to admit, she had probably half loved for over twenty years. Fielding would have screamed and shouted, ranted and raved, wept, maybe even hit her. He had never actually done that but she had seen his temper, always suspected him capable of violence if sufficiently provoked. He would have confronted her, probably while drunk, the moment he had any suspicion that she had cheated on him. He would have been irrational and illogical and very, very human. He was always that. Human.

Her husband, on the other hand, seemed to be as cold and as matter-of-fact as ever. His behaviour towards her indicated on one level that he loved her very much. The very fact that he was fighting to keep her in the way that he was, that he would be prepared even to keep her in the circumstances, demonstrated that, she supposed. And yet, as ever, there was something about the way he went about things which was barely human at all. Jo would have preferred an explosive no-holds-barred row. Much preferred that. Come to think of it, they had never had one of those throughout their marriage.

She felt overwhelmed with a deep, abiding sorrow. She couldn't help questioning Paul's motives, which was terrible. After all, she was the one at fault. Paul wouldn't want a scandal, of course. His impending knighthood was almost certainly a factor in his determination to keep her.

Her head ached. She did feel guilty about having deceived Paul, but not as guilty as she suspected she should. She did not even know whether she still loved him. In fact, she was not sure whether she had ever loved him, not really, certainly not in the way in which she had loved Fielding. But her husband had left her with no choice. 'It's all right, Paul, I don't need twenty-four hours,' she said. 'I will end it tomorrow.'

* * *

He watched her leave the room and head upstairs for bed, then he went to the drinks cupboard and poured himself a stiff whisky, which he carried into the garden, shutting and locking the kitchen door behind him. He walked across the lawn, past the copse of young fruit trees, to a small wooden shed at the far end. The night was brightly moonlit and he was able to see his way quite clearly. Inside the shed, however, it was pitch-black. A single electric light bulb hung from the wood-panelled ceiling, but he did not switch it on. He did not need to, and he welcomed the blackness which enveloped him when he closed the door. Paul knew where everything was in this shed. It was as orderly as everything in his mind, in his office, in his home, indeed in his life. The mower was to the left, alongside a couple of neatly folded garden chairs and on the right, carefully stacked, were sacks of fertiliser, plant pots and all manner of other gardening paraphernalia. He felt his way to the little wooden stool he kept in the right-hand corner and sat down.

He was as far away from his house and from the neighbouring houses as it was possible to be. The shed was solid, made of two skins of wood and without windows. He could not be seen and it was reasonable to assume that he could not be heard. He took a sip of his whisky, then lowered his glass to the floor. He threw back his head and let out a kind of howl of anguish. With it came the tears.

He wept and howled, and howled and wept, his arms wrapped round his torso as if he were hugging himself, until he ached from the sheer physical effort of the sobs which racked his body. The tears coursed down his face, burning hot. His throat hurt. But he could not stop, not until he had allowed all the anguish that was inside him to be released.

It was not the first time he had used the shed for this purpose, creeping there in the dead of night. But this was the worst, the very worst.

It was almost twenty minutes before he felt the spasms begin to lessen.

Eventually the howling ceased and so did the tears. When he gave in to these outbursts it was the only time in his life that he did not have total control. He reached down with a trembling hand for the whisky and took a deep drink.

He was not sure he felt any better. How could he, with the knowledge he now had of what Joanna had done? But he was at last beginning to calm down. He wished he had been able to tell her, in the depths of his despair, how much she had hurt him. But that wasn't his way. His sister, with whom he had long ceased to have any contact, had once informed him that he was emotionally dysfunctional. Maybe he was. But it was more than that. How could he tell Joanna how much she meant to him? How could he, when he knew that he felt so much more for her than she had ever felt for him? He had no illusions. He had been able to make everything happen for him and Joanna. Everything except make her love him. The way he loved her.

He finished the whisky, rose from the stool, left the shed, locking it carefully behind him, and walked back to the house.

He would carry on as usual, of course. He also had too much to lose. Joanna remained the perfect wife for him, from the outside at any rate, as long as she behaved. And he knew he could make sure that she did so. Then there were both their careers. And, most vital, the knighthood. As Joanna had suspected, he didn't intend to let anything queer his pitch there.

Life was never perfect, but he rather liked the idea that his appeared to be.

Most importantly, he could not imagine even existing without Joanna at his side.

By the time Paul Potter had unlocked and opened the kitchen door and stepped inside his house the episode of the garden shed was over. The moment had passed. It was almost as if it had not happened.

18

Exactly one week later Pam Smythe, nearly bursting with excitement, rushed through the *Comet*'s big open-plan news-room to Joanna's desk by the far window. 'Mike Fielding's been nicked for fixing Jimbo O'Donnell's murder,' she yelled.

Joanna felt as if she'd been slammed against a wall. The shock was numbing. Neither her body nor her brain could function for a few seconds. She was incapable of speech.

The news editor didn't seem to notice Jo's stunned expression. Pam barely paused for breath. 'I just don't believe it,' she enthused. 'Christ! What an amazing story. This one is never going to die down. The police have put out a statement on PA. Arrested on suspicion of conspiracy to murder, that's the official form. We need all the help you can give us, Jo.'

Still Joanna said nothing. She remained unable to.

'Jo?' There was just a note of puzzlement in Pam's voice now.

Joanna managed a nod. Could Fielding really be a murderer? Even when she had been trying to hack into her lover's laptop, checking him out, had she actually believed that he could have done such a thing? Certainly when he had confronted her she had felt merely foolish and disloyal. Her hands were trembling. She clasped them tightly together underneath her desk as she struggled to maintain control.

'Right,' Pam Smythe continued. 'Can you get on to Mallett? We've got the new Devon area man going round to Fielding's family house.'

With a huge effort of will Joanna forced herself at least to appear to react and function like the experienced professional journalist she was supposed to be. 'Of course, Pam,' she said. 'I'm on it.'

She immediately picked up her phone and pretended to dial a number until the other woman turned away and hurried back to her position at the head of the news desk. Then Jo replaced the phone and slumped back in her chair. Jesus! So had her half-formed suspicions been right all along? She hadn't seriously considered it again since that disastrous last meeting with Fielding in the Southampton Row hotel and her even more disastrous confrontation with Paul the following day. She had tried a couple of times to contact Fielding since then, leaving messages both on his mobile and on his voice mail at Middlemoor. It had been her intention to follow through her promise to Paul and to tell Mike that their affair must end. Neither call had been returned, and she had come to the conclusion that Fielding had meant exactly what he had said in that dreadful hotel room and that their relationship was over without her having to do anything at all about it.

'There's no point in carrying on, Jo, is there?' She remembered his words well enough, but now she wondered if there had been more to his silence than just that.

All she could do, however, was to go through the motions professionally and do as the news editor

405

had asked. Although she didn't expect to get much joy from Todd Mallett. One thing Pam Smythe had in common with all the news editors she'd ever known was a selective memory. Pam seemed already totally to have forgotten, or more likely had just chosen to appear as if she had, the breakdown in any workable relationship between Jo and the senior police officer she was expected to contact. A typical desk reaction, that. But she should be grateful for small mercies, she supposed. At least she hadn't been asked to visit Mrs Fielding. She was pretty sure that nobody in the office had had any idea about the resumption of her affair with Fielding after all these years. Indeed, they might have giggled about the *Private Eye* story, but she didn't think there was anybody much around who even remembered that there had ever been an affair. Pam Smythe had certainly given no such indication.

She picked up her phone again and, in spite of her sincere belief that the man disliked and distrusted her, attempted to call Todd Mallett as she had agreed she would. Unsurprisingly, he was not taking press calls. Not from her, anyway.

The following morning Fielding was formally charged at Exeter and Womford Magistrates' Court in Exeter, and remanded in custody at the city prison. Yet another twist in the tail. Shifter Brown, the man he had allegedly hired to commit a brutal murder, was, of course, still being held in the same jail.

Later that day it was again Tim Jones who came up with the background. Not for the first time Jo found herself thinking what an excellent reporter young Tim was. 'The rubber heel boys hacked into Fielding's laptop and uncovered a heap of deleted e-mail correspondence between 'contractor' and 'enforcer',' the *Comet*'s crime correspondent told her excitedly.

'Apparently Todd Mallett got an anonymous call from someone claiming to be 'an associate' of Shifter, saying Shifter suspected all along that Mike Fielding had hired him. Shifter denied it to the wall, but then he would, wouldn't he? Todd Mallett's the old-fashioned sort, of course, particularly when it comes to a bent copper. He'd always stick to procedure with the public, he's a by-the-book man, but for Mallett cops come under different rules. And anyway there's always been bad blood between him and Fielding, hasn't there? Mallett didn't hang about getting a warrant or anything like that, just walked over to Fielding's desk out at Middlemoor, apparently, picked up his laptop and said, 'Right sunshine, we'd best have a look in this and clear things up once and for all.'

'Every force has its super-hackers now, computer-born crimes are becoming more and more commonplace. Apparently it didn't take 'em long to find those hidden files.'

'And what did Shifter say then?'

''Never seen 'em before in my life, guv.' You know Shifter. What else would you expect? That's his code, isn't it? Wouldn't point the finger even at a copper. Although word is he finds it highly amusing that Mike Fielding's been banged up. But one way and another he's no help at all.'

Neither would he be. Particularly not with a

police officer in the frame. Joanna thought for a moment. So much didn't quite add up.

'Shifter did say he was paid fifteen grand for topping Jimbo,' she said eventually. 'Mike Fielding wouldn't have that kind of cash going spare.'

The young man shrugged. 'Maybe doing Jimbo was so important to him he borrowed, got himself a second mortgage or something. Nobody seems to know yet, but chances are it will come out eventually. In any case there's plenty of other possibilities. You know Fielding's reputation. He's always sailed close to the wind. Maybe some toe-rag owed him, or there's a face paying him bundles to keep his mouth shut. Coppers can always get cash, Jo, if they're bent enough, can't they?'

She winced. She had never thought that Fielding was bent. Overeager. So sharp he could cut himself and frequently did — but actually bent enough to take backhanders from criminals? Surely not. But maybe she'd really never known Mike at all. She made herself concentrate on the job in hand.

Like her, she thought, it was unlikely that Todd Mallett had actually believed Fielding had hired Shifter, not even when he commandeered his laptop, but Mike had already been publicly accused, albeit by the O'Donnells, of doing so. It must have been as obvious to Mallett as it had been to Joanna that in view of the way in which Shifter had been hired and paid, the clues could still be lurking on somebody's hard drive somewhere. Maybe Fielding was guilty and, not for the first time in his life, had not been quite so clever as he thought he had. Joanna was more confused than ever. All she knew for certain was that she had to do her best to find out the truth. Did Fielding really do it? Could he have been calculated enough to hire a contract killer?

As soon as Tim left her she wrote to Mike at Exeter prison. It was a brief, carefully worded letter fundamentally expressing her sorrow at his predicament and requesting that he would let her visit him.

Paul had so far avoided talking to her about the Fielding development, which suited Jo totally. The editor was relying on Tim Jones for day-to-day handling of the story and left it to Pam Smythe to liaise with Jo. But that night at home there was a discernible tension between Jo and her husband. The extraordinary sequence of events which for almost two days they had both been unwilling or unable to discuss was obviously to the forefront of both their minds.

Paul played jazz even louder than usual and Joanna did her best not to let it show that anything at all was bothering her. Eventually, just before bedtime, Paul enquired casually, 'What do you think of your boyfriend now, then?'

Joanna thought that was a fairly cheap remark, both unworthy of Paul and unusual for him. 'I don't know what to think, and he's not my boyfriend. I gave you my word.'

'You gave me your word nineteen years ago when we got married, Joanna.'

'What happened between Mike Fielding and me is over for good and nothing like it will ever happen again, Paul. There's no more I can say to you.'

'That will have to be enough, then.' He spoke in a

409

rather faraway manner. However, she was used to this distance in him. He was colder than usual, but theirs had never been exactly a warm cosy relationship.

⋆　⋆　⋆

Four days later she received a visiting order to see Fielding. She took it straight to Paul in his office. She had always intended to do this. She accepted now that there was no way she could see the disgraced policeman without Paul knowing. Not ever again, probably. In or out of jail. So she might as well be up front about it.

'Why do you want to do this?' he asked in a level voice.

'Two reasons,' she responded. 'First, I want to tell Mike to his face that it's over between us regardless of the outcome of his prosecution. I tried to phone him before he was arrested but I never got through. Second, professional reasons, of course. He's not going to talk to any other journalist, is he? And I honestly believe I will learn the truth if I see him.'

Her husband studied her silently for a moment or two. 'I don't want you to see him,' he said eventually.

'I can hardly fuck him in prison, can I?' she burst out.

His eyes clouded over.

'Look, Paul. I haven't come here to ask your permission. I am going to see Mike. I told you I wouldn't deceive you any more and I am keeping my word. I will never see Fielding again after this.

But I am quite determined to do so this final time. I've given you my reasons. If you want to make something of it, you can, but I hope you will accept it.'

'I could stop you.' The usual cool voice. The usual unfathomable look.

'No, you can't, actually,' she said, trying to sound equally cool. 'You can start those damned divorce proceedings if you like, as you threatened you would, although I hope you won't, but you can't stop me.'

She left his office then, without waiting for a reply. She was pretty sure he wouldn't divorce her. He would put up with this. After all, he had put up with far more. He wanted to keep her. He had fought for her. He could have done it in a more human fashion, of course, but Paul was Paul. In a way she was more than ever aware of the power she had over him. She also knew she must never abuse it again. But she could use it. And that was what she had just done. She had been honest, she had been direct and she had forced him to accept something he didn't like.

Knowing Paul, though, she thought with just a flicker of amusement as she walked back to her desk, he would have started by now to consider the professional aspects of her planned prison visit. It would put the *Comet* well ahead of the game, no doubt about it. And Paul would like that very much indeed. No doubt about that either.

★   ★   ★

Two o'clock in the afternoon, the arranged time on the appointed day for Joanna's visit, had seemed a

411

long time coming to Fielding. He was angry with himself for looking forward to seeing her so much. He felt let down by her, as indeed he felt let down by all of them. He was on remand so he was wearing his own clothes. That at least was something. He wouldn't have wanted her to see him in prison drabs. He hoped that nobody would see him in those, ever, but things were pretty bleak right now.

He didn't have a mirror in his cell, which was all for the best, probably. He knew he looked dreadful.

Eventually they came for him. She was already sitting at one of those tables in the visiting room. Her turn to wait. But just for a few minutes, he supposed. He wished he didn't react the way he did whenever he saw her. His heart leapt. And his body? Well, nobody, not ever, had had the effect on him that Joanna Bartlett had. When they had begun their affair again after all those years he had never thought it would still be like that, at least not quite so extreme.

He saw her glance up as they opened the door and he stepped into the room. She looked good. But then she almost always did. She had never been pretty. Striking, yes. Pretty, no. But she had aged well. She had good bone structure and fine skin. Her body was good, too. She worked at that and it showed. He couldn't see much of it — she was wearing a loose linen jacket over a cotton shirt buttoned to the neck — but he had learned over the last few months just how good it was. By God he had. His belly muscles tightened slightly at the thought. She could pass for ten years younger than she was, he thought, which was more than he ever would again. Certainly after coping with all of this — if he did cope with it.

He saw the expression of shock that flickered across her face when she first saw him, and then how rapidly she recovered herself. He knew he looked grey and haggard. That famous prison pallor he had so often seen, which developed so astonishingly quickly.

'Thank you for seeing me,' she said as he approached her. She did not get up.

He did not attempt to kiss her, not even to touch her hand. Instead he swiftly sat down opposite her. 'You know I can never resist.' He actually tried to sound jaunty, he didn't quite know why, but in any case he failed dismally.

'Paul knows.' She blurted out the words, as if she hadn't intended to begin their conversation like this, but had not been able to stop herself.

He raised his eyebrows. 'And?' he asked.

'He told me that if I carried on seeing you he would divorce me, sack me and turn Emily against me. He would, too. And don't think he couldn't.'

'I'm sure he could. So what are you doing here?'

'I told him I couldn't fuck you in the visiting room of Exeter prison.'

He managed a wry half-smile. 'Anything else?'

'I also told him that it would be to the advantage of his bloody newspaper. That you wouldn't be talking to any other journalists and in any case I would be more likely than anybody else to get the truth from you.'

He shook his head almost sorrowfully. He was supposed to have been the ruthless, dedicated career policeman, although that seemed almost like another world now. But Joanna? She was a real piece of work. She never forgot that she was a journalist, not for a second, and her husband, Mike felt quite sure, was of the same stock only more so. 'You two are incredible, you know,' he said.

She didn't seem to understand. She was, as ever, he thought, far too wrapped up in her own curious world. 'What do you mean?'

'If you really don't know, Jo, then there's no point in my even trying to explain.'

She shook her head in a puzzled sort of way. 'Look, we don't have very long. I do need to know the truth, Mike. For myself. Bugger the paper.'

He studied her quizzically. Bugger the paper, he just didn't believe. Not from her. Not from any of them, really, but particularly not from Joanna Bartlett. Hack through and through. Weaned on hot metal. 'I told you before, if you need to ask me that question, then I don't know what we were all about, ever,' he informed her. And he felt the anger growing inside him. As usual he became angry with her more quickly than with anybody else. It was like that when you really cared for someone. It was for him anyway. 'You've already confronted me once,' he snapped at her. 'You tried to hack into my computer yourself. You've made it quite clear that you believe I am capable of this. That's your problem, not mine.'

'I just want to know what I am supposed to believe . . . '

'Do you?' He was seething inside now, barely able to keep his temper in control. 'You could start by asking yourself an intelligent question for a change. They found all that crap on my laptop and charged me on the strength of it. I've no doubt you know all about that unless you've changed beyond recognition. So why didn't I chuck the damned machine? Throw it out with the rubbish, toss it into the sea at the dead of night at Exmouth or Dawlish Warren? Um? Ask yourself that. Which is more than anybody else will do, it seems. Even Shifter had the sense to trash his rig. Do you really think I would have kept a laptop containing files which could prove that I put out a murder contract, for God's sake?'

'Are you saying you've been set up?'

'I don't know, Jo. What do you think? Do you still think?'

'Of course I do . . . '

'Right, then think about this. Not only have I been set up but could you conceive for one moment I would have been remanded in custody over this if I weren't a copper? At least I'd be out on bail. What they've got on me is never going to stand up in court and the way they got it stinks. Can you imagine the outcry if fucking Todd Mallett had come marching into your office and commandeered your laptop?'

'Well, yes,' she began. 'But you are a policeman and maybe the rules are supposed to be the same but I suppose . . . '

He interrupted her abruptly. 'You'd better go, Jo. I'm sick of you and your half-spoken accusations. Just go.'

With one hand he beckoned to a prison officer and with the other he waved her away.

She knew better than to argue. She just stood up silently, turned and walked away from him, head bowed, glancing back at him over her shoulder only when he called out to her.

'Are you sure you didn't get into my computer that evening at the hotel, Jo? You're good, aren't you? You're fast. Maybe you had time after all . . . ' And it had given him some satisfaction to see the shocked expression on her face before he rose wearily from his chair and headed for the door leading back to his cell. The way things were inside his head right now, sometimes it was almost a relief to be locked up.

★　　★　　★

Jo stared after him for a few seconds. What did he mean? Did he suspect that she had tampered with his laptop, planted the incriminating files? She was more confused than ever. And her emotions were playing ping-pong with each other again. She felt the damned tears he could always arouse more quickly than anyone pricking. How was it he could still do this to her, even when some of the things he had said to her displayed nothing more than contempt? It was bewildering.

Hurrying through the prison gates, she bumped into a small, plumpish, red-haired woman on the way in. Jo had been walking with her head down, trying to hide the tears which were by then starting to run down her face. The collision was entirely her fault. She had not been looking where she was going and she had walked straight into the other woman.

416

Looking up, stumbling her apologies, she recognised with a start that she was Fielding's wife. She had seen her photograph, on his desk that first time they were together and even in his wallet. It always seemed to fall out every time he removed his credit cards. Her colouring was distinctive, that bright-red hair which Jo, with a sharp stab of incongruous jealousy, thought was probably still totally natural, the freckles.

Ruth Fielding looked her full in the face. She had bags under her eyes and an understandable weariness about her. She was no longer anywhere near as pretty as she had been in the photographs. She showed absolutely no sign of recognition. ''S all right,' she mumbled and said 'sorry' herself, the way the English do, even when they are not remotely to blame for whatever it is they are apologising for, then shuffled on through the gates.

Joanna had always suspected that Mike had never told his wife about her, despite all those convoluted stories about Ruth's breakdown and their daughter's despair. All of it, even the dying mother-in-law, was probably a load of nonsense. She had always half suspected that was probably the case but confirmation was nonetheless painful. Ruth Fielding had almost certainly never even been aware of her existence, she thought, never known of the affair which her husband had frequently claimed was the most important relationship in his life, more so, even, than his marriage.

Jo was high-profile, pictured regularly in her own paper, occasionally on TV, and had been so long before the notoriety she had gained through the part she played along with Fielding in bringing O'Donnell to trial in that ill-fated private prosecution. She and Fielding had even been pictured together in more than one newspaper, not to mention the innuendoes published in *Private Eye*. If Mrs Fielding had the slightest inkling that Jo and her husband had had an affair, then Joanna felt sure the woman would have had her features indelibly printed on her mind. After all, she had recognised Mike's wife quickly enough, even though she had never met her.

She walked slowly towards her car, turning her thoughts back to the events of the last few minutes. What did it all mean? Could Mike really have been framed? He was never short of confidence. His argument about the laptop was deeply flawed. Maybe he had believed he had removed all traces from it and that it was safe. She reminded herself again of how even the love-bug hackers had been traced. Mike had always been inclined to be overly confident. If that was the case yet again then he had had no reason to destroy his computer. Jo still didn't know what to believe. And that was a nice touch he had added at the end, hinting that maybe she had played a part in framing him. She didn't think he really thought that, but you never knew with Mike.

One way and another she hadn't learned very much; indeed, much less than she had hoped for and, in fact, had actually expected. Bugger all, to be honest. The visit had not given her what she had sought in any direction. She was no nearer the truth than she had been before she had seen Fielding. She couldn't write anything, of course, until the trial was over, but he had told her nothing that would ever make much in the way of copy. Accused man says he's been set up. Hold the front page.

Her mind strayed to their personal feelings towards each other. Jo wondered if his display of disappointed outrage could be yet another sort of excuse, another way of avoiding even the possibility of any kind of real permanent commitment.

She had told Paul that she had made her decision, that she would end her relationship with Fielding and stay with her husband. And she had meant it, every word of it, even before Fielding had been arrested. Paul had been right. She had too much to lose.

But if Fielding were still a free man, if he had ever pressed her to be with him full time in such a way that she had been able to believe it — well, she just didn't know how she might have reacted. In spite of everything. Even including her daughter.

God, it was mad. But then, when it came to Mike Fielding she was quite barking. Always had been. Mixed up. Out of control.

She unlocked her car door and slumped in the driver's seat motionless for a few moments, willing the tears to stop. Eventually they did and she started the engine.

There was no point in rushing back to the office. Instead, she drove, rather slowly for her, home to Richmond. She didn't phone. Not the news desk. Not Paul. Not anyone. She had nothing to tell them, really. She chose the A303 rather than the M5 and M4. She didn't feel like belting along at ninety miles an hour the way she usually did, invariably exceeding the motorway speed limit with a kind of studied nonchalance. She got stuck behind a succession of trucks and caravans on the bits of the A303 that were still just two- and three-lane, but she didn't mind. She stopped at Stonehenge. The sun was just setting and the mysterious prehistoric monument, its giant pillars of stone commanding the sweeping landscape of Salisbury Plain, looked wonderful in the evening light. She parked in the car park, bought coffee from the snack bar and walked out across the access road, where she leaned on the fence and just took in the atmosphere of the ancient place for a little while. Delaying her return, really. God knew, she could do with a few mystic vibes.

At home she and Emily watched a video together. Some teen romance movie. Emily was getting to be disconcertingly into those kinds of pictures. Jo was so preoccupied that she hardly took in at all what the film was about let alone its title or whichever current teen idol it featured. Once it finally ended she agreed without protest that her daughter could stay up much later than usual in order to see her father at least briefly. The presence of a third person seemed like a jolly good idea anyway.

When eventually they were alone she gave Paul an edited account of what had occurred that day. At first, as if by unspoken mutual consent, they discussed only the professional aspects of her meeting with Fielding.

Eventually Paul broached the personal side. 'So did you tell him it was all over between you?'

'Yes,' she said quietly. She hadn't, of course, not in as many words, but it amounted to the same thing. It was all over, she had no doubt about that. Whether she liked it or not, in fact.

'So you really have come to your senses?'

She wanted to slap him. The man could be so smugly arrogant. And always so cool. But she didn't have the strength for argument and in any case he was impossible to argue with. He didn't know how. 'Yes,' she said again.

If he thought her reactions curiously monosyllabic, he passed no remark. 'Good,' he said. 'Then I suggest we never speak of it again.'

★   ★   ★

Meanwhile Tommy O'Donnell gave the impression of being thoroughly smug. Interviewed by the *Daily Mail* — he still wouldn't touch the *Comet*, of course — he made it quite clear just how delighted he was by Mike Fielding's arrest. Whether or not the policeman really was guilty of hiring a man to kill his elder brother, which in any case the *Mail* dared not go into, seemed almost irrelevant, Jo thought when she read the piece.

The Phillips family also made no secret of their satisfaction at Fielding's incarceration. 'This man was more than anybody else responsible for O'Donnell's first trial going wrong and what is happening to him is a kind of justice,' said Rob Phillips in the *Daily Mirror*, and he continued in an interview which skated the edge of the sub judice laws: 'We've always believed Fielding is capable of being just as evil as any of the villains he deals with every day. If he was responsible for

421

James O'Donnell's death, then I and my family can only be grateful to him for that. But he deserves to suffer, too. He has caused us endless heartache.'

★ ★ ★

Joanna managed to arrange another jail visit with Shifter Brown. It seemed curious to think that Mike was in the same prison, maybe in a cell just yards away from the visiting room. And seeing Shifter got her no further than had her visit there to her former lover. 'Could it really have been Fielding who hired you?' she asked him.

'I dunno,' he replied unhelpfully.

'But what do you think, Shifter?'

'I've given up thinking, doll. You do when you're banged up in here.'

'OK, Shifter, but what about the e-mails? They showed them to you, didn't they? Will you tell me honestly whether they were genuine or not? You'd remember the wording surely?'

'Listen, girl, I already told the Old Bill I've never seen 'em before — 'course, they know I probably wouldn't tell them if I had, would I?' Shifter grinned. He seemed to be almost enjoying himself. 'Anyway, the filth always believe what they want to believe. Like a lot of bleeding cannibals, too, when it's one of their own, aren't they? Look. I like you, Joey doll, but I've given you your story. Our deal's done and dusted. I'm not saying any more. I'd never have told you what I did if it wasn't for my little princesses, would I?'

'Just one thing — and I know its for the umpteenth time. Do you really not know who put the contract out? Have you really not got a clue? You wouldn't be winding us all up, would you?'

'Now would I do that, babe?' Shifter replied. And he treated her to a big, juicy wink, just like he had in the restaurant all that time ago.

'For God's sake, Shifter,' said Joanna, throwing her eyes heavenwards in exasperation.

Shifter smiled benignly.

A Shifter Brown wind-up in order to gain some cash for his family had always been a possibility, of course. He could have come up with the e-mail wheeze just in order to have a story to sell which did not break his precious code of never grassing. But was he that inventive? And could he really have been capable of planting the entire e-mail dialogue which had been found on Mike's laptop?

Jo was confused. Bewildered. Consumed with agonising doubts.

She and Mike had shared a mutual obsession with the dreadful death of Angela Phillips. If Mike really had hired Shifter to kill Angela's murderer she wondered when he had made that decision. And if he had confided in her she wondered what she would have done.

Would she have supported him? Would she have stopped him?

She didn't know. She had no answers to anything. Not any more. And neither, it seemed, did anyone else. Except, perhaps, Mike Fielding.

She hated the very thought. But she feared she might have to come to accept it.

19

Then it all changed again. This time it was Tim Jones who told Joanna about the new development, calling her on her mobile early one evening while she was driving Emily to a school friend's birthday party. 'They've found this diary written by Tommy O'Donnell's daughter,' he reported. 'It seems her Uncle Jimbo was a nonce, as well as everything else. He'd been abusing the kid for years and she'd written it all down.'

Joanna swerved to avoid a bicycle. She had reacted slowly to the cyclist, suddenly not concentrating properly on her driving. She was aware of Emily stiffening in the passenger seat beside her and put a reassuring hand on her knee. She was also instantly aware of the huge significance of what she had just heard. 'Tell me exactly what has happened and how,' she instructed Tim, struggling to sound calm and in control.

'The police got another anonymous tip-off,' the young crime man continued. 'They searched Tommy's home and struck gold.'

'And Tommy?'

'Nobody can find him. Already helping the police with their inquiries, I reckon. But neither Scotland Yard nor anyone else will confirm anything yet.'

'So nothing official. How did you find all this out?'

'I picked it up from a mate at the Yard, the place

is crawling with rumours.'

'Rumours, Tim? How hard is it?'

'As nails, Jo. My source is that solid.'

He had little more to tell her. There was little more she needed to know. Motive alone never convicted anyone. But, God, what a motive this was. She had not really been able to imagine that an O'Donnell would ever turn on one of his own — until now.

Just as she had been forcing herself to accept that the man who had been so much a part of her life was guilty of arranging a murder, this latest bombshell had dropped. Perhaps Mike Fielding had been framed. Perhaps he was telling the truth after all.

★　★　★

The murder of Jimbo O'Donnell was Todd Mallett's case and the detective superintendent considered that everything pertaining to the dead man was his territory. So it was Todd who had obtained a search warrant and led the team which descended on Tommy O'Donnell's home. Todd didn't like anonymous tips. And this was the second he had felt obliged to act upon concerning the O'Donnell case. It now seemed increasingly likely, however, that the first one, leading to the files lurking in Mike Fielding's computer, could prove to have been an embarrassing red herring. Like Joanna, Todd began to wonder if Fielding might indeed have been the victim of an elaborate computer frame-up, just as he had always claimed.

Computers were playing their part again, in more ways than one. But then they always seemed to nowadays. The tip had come in the form of a letter, written in Word 97, printed on an Epsom Laser printer. About as anonymous as you can get. Gone were the days when you could match up typed words and letters with the distinctive keys of individual typewriters. The postmark had been central London.

'Go into Tommy O'Donnell's kid's computer,' the anonymous tipster had suggested. 'You'll find her diary. Her dad did.'

They had, too, in the recycle bin. Barely hidden at all. The date indicated that it had been put there after her death. Months after her death. But just days before James Martin O'Donnell had disappeared.

Todd had actually wondered if Caroline's computer would still be at her home. However the girl's room, with its teen rock idol posters on the walls and CDs in untidy piles on a shelf, had looked to have been exactly how she must have left it when she had decided to kill herself — even down to a pair of jeans and a T-shirt casually discarded on the bed. Todd had heard that Tommy O'Donnell and his wife continued to keep the room as a kind of shrine to their dead daughter, it was pretty much common knowledge, but he found the reality eerily disconcerting.

He was grateful, however, that the diary had still been retained. It made fascinating reading.

There had been mystery surrounding Caroline's death from the beginning in Todd's opinion. He had never bought the exam-fever story. The O'Donnells were not that sort of family. They might be villains but they were down to earth, and they loved their children. Tommy O'Donnell believed in education, wanted to take the family legit and into the future, yet it was hard to accept the perceived wisdom that he would have driven his daughter so hard that she did not want to carry on living.

But abuse by her uncle. Harm coming from within this close-knit family. That was different.

The diary, written from when Caroline was eleven until shortly before her death, chronicled in detail the systematic sexual abuse meted out to her by her Uncle Jimmy. It shed a whole new light on why a thirteen-year-old girl should be distraught enough to take her own life. It was quite harrowing.

Uncle Jimmy was looking after me while Dad and Mum went to the club. He came into my bedroom and got into bed with me. He kept kissing and cuddling me and asking me if I liked it and telling me this would be our secret. I didn't like it, but he wouldn't stop.

Another entry read:

He kept pushing himself against me and he tried to get his willy into me between my legs. It hurt. But he wouldn't stop.

I don't know why I am writing this down. I can't tell anybody. I feel dirty. I am so ashamed.

Shame. Amazing how the children in child abuse cases so often felt they should be ashamed. This was something paedophiles played upon, of course.

Todd shuddered at the thought of what the little girl had gone through. He did not doubt the authenticity of the diary for one moment. He had worked in child protection. He had taken statements, even seen diaries like this before. It was not that unusual for children to want to write these things down even when they felt unable to talk to anybody about what was happening to them. Maybe it was a kind of release. These sad tragic outpourings were stamped with the unmistakable ring of truth.

The policeman did not doubt either that Tommy would also have instantly accepted the truth of the diaries. Jimbo's sexual preferences were always suspect. Throughout his life stories had abounded about his perverted sexual activities. There had been the earlier rape conviction and then the Angela Phillips case. However, it had always suited the O'Donnells to cover up for Jimbo, to keep up the pretence that he was a wronged man. Sam might actually have believed that. Todd didn't reckon Tommy ever had. But it would certainly not have occurred to any of them that Jimbo would ever bring his unpleasant perversions into the family and abuse his own niece. After all, the O'Donnells took care of their own.

Sam himself, of course, was out of the frame. The old gang boss had finally died just after Mike Fielding had been arrested, but Todd knew that Sam had been incapacitated by a series of strokes for months before that. The O'Donnells had kept it quiet for as long as they could, but eventually the news leaked. Sam the Man's death, when it came, was what Todd's mother would have called 'a happy release' and they gave him one of those extraordinary traditional gangster funerals like the Krays'. A horse-drawn carriage carried his coffin through the streets of London and as many people gathered to pay their last respects as would to say farewell to royalty. More, possibly, nowadays, thought Todd wryly.

Which left Tommy the undisputed head of the O'Donnell clan.

Todd found it very easy to put himself in Tommy O'Donnell's shoes, to imagine the man's reaction on reading his daughter's diary. Todd had kids, bright, well-adjusted, happy young people who, as far as he knew, had never had to endure anything like this. They were alive, moreover. Todd could imagine only too well what Tommy's feelings must have been.

Todd was a law-abiding, solid citizen. A police officer. But he knew he would have wanted to kill anybody who had harmed his children like this. And if that person were his own brother then his anger would have been even more terrible. Tommy O'Donnell's brother had done unspeakable things to Tommy's daughter. And the girl had been so traumatised by it that she had killed herself.

Todd was quite sure that Tommy O'Donnell would have happily killed his brother with his bare hands. That would probably have been his first instinctive coherent thought. But, like his father, Tommy understood the importance of keeping his hands clean. Tommy's second instinct would have been to seek terminal revenge while protecting himself and the rest of his family. And nobody knew better how to do that than an O'Donnell. Not only would Tommy not have done the deed himself, but he would not have wanted to use a regular O'Donnell enforcer. He would definitely have hired an outsider.

There was considerable significance, too, in the date the diary had been deposited into the recycling bin — just a week before Jimbo had gone missing. Tommy would have made his plan by then, coolly worked out what he was going to have done to the brother who had so terribly betrayed him.

The more of the diary Todd read the more he became convinced that Tommy had hired Shifter. But there was, of course, absolutely no proof that he had done so and neither was there likely to be. He did wonder who, apart from Tommy himself, would have known about the diary to report its existence to the police. But even villains had confidants, he supposed. And sometimes allegiances changed. Another possibility was that whoever appeared to be pointing an anonymous finger at Tommy was actually trying to do Fielding a favour. Somebody close to Tommy who owed Fielding, perhaps. After all, Todd knew the odds were against even being able to charge Tommy with anything, let alone successfully try him. Nonetheless, he brought him in for questioning.

'Yeah, I found the diary, course I did,' he said. 'And once I'd read it I sent it straight to the recycling bin. I didn't want the missus to see it, did I?'

Tommy made his admission freely and immediately — as far as it went. Todd was not surprised. After all, the computer's record of the date on which the document had last been read would have made it nonsensical for him to deny that he, or at least one of his family, had found it. And in any case Tommy knew that he did not need to deny it. If there was anybody who understood about circumstantial evidence, it was an O'Donnell. Particularly this O'Donnell.

After that it was downhill all the way. The interview with Tommy turned out to be as much of a waste of time as Todd had feared it would be.

'Mr Mallett, I can't describe how I felt when I found Caroline's diary,' said Tommy. His voice cracked a bit as he spoke and Todd did not doubt for a second that his emotions were one hundred per cent genuine. 'I'd probably never have found it cos she had the file tucked away among her homework. Essays, and maths tests and stuff, and then . . . then . . . this horrible thing. But there was a printout, you see. It was among her school books. I look through them occasionally. I couldn't believe I'd missed it before. And then, when I read it, well. Do you know I actually thought it was a story at first? But it wasn't.

'The truth is I hated Jimbo enough to kill him. Yes, I did. But I didn't do it. I didn't hire Shifter. I'd only just found the diary when Jimbo disappeared. I was trying to work out what to do about it. OK, I wanted to hurt him badly. But there was Dad to think about and the rest of the family. Poor Caroline was dead. I couldn't help her. I was just working it

431

out — then Jimbo was topped. It was nothing to do with me. Honestly.'

Todd did not believe a word of it. The whole episode had the O'Donnell stamp all over it. Revenge. Rough justice. That was the code they lived by. But Todd couldn't prove a thing and he knew it.

However, the obvious implication remained — that Fielding was probably innocent after all and that his protestations that he had been set up might indeed be true.

Fielding's case was further helped by a computer expert called in by his defence lawyer who questioned the validity of the e-mail evidence discovered by the police hackers, pointing out that it was totally feasible to send a virus into a computer memory which could plant all kinds of files there. It was technically quite possible that the e-mail drafts could have been fraudulently placed.

Finally the father of a twelve-year-old-boy in Scotland, apparently even more of a computer whizz than most twelve-year-olds, contacted his local police station. It seemed that the boy had discovered intriguing files buried in the memory of the second-hand hard drive his father had bought him from Glasgow's famous Burrowlands computer market.

These included e-mail correspondence between 'contractor' and 'enforcer'.

None of the e-mails was the same as the ones found on Fielding's laptop. Nothing matched at all except the user names. Even the language employed was different. Police hackers were able to trace the origin of the 'contractor' e-mails. They had been sent, as Shifter had originally predicted, from another cyber café. And there, once again, the trail ended.

The case against Fielding began to look very weak indeed. A full police report was submitted to the Crown Prosecution Service who promptly applied to Exeter and Wonford Magistrates' Court to discontinue all charges in view of the changes in circumstances.

Mike Fielding was at once freed from jail.

★ ★ ★

Joanna followed the progress of events closely. Tim's contact at the Yard turned out to be as good as he had promised and the young crime reporter acquired far more detailed information than was ever officially released, and indeed far more than could be printed.

Joanna was greatly relieved when the charges against Fielding were dropped. But she found she didn't know how to deal with it when he called her twice on the day after his release and once more the day after that. On all three occasions she avoided his calls and failed to return them. But, maybe because she reckoned she owed him an apology, maybe because she was curious, or even because she still cared in spite of everything, she did eventually call him a week or so later. 'I'm so glad you are free, and I am so sorry I doubted you,' she told him at once.

Fielding's heart lurched. He was so pleased to hear from her. He had feared he might never see her again. And regardless of all that he had said when she had visited him in prison, he wanted to see her very much indeed. He accepted her apologies. It still hurt, but not as much as being unable to be with her any more would hurt.

'I suppose it must have been Tommy, mustn't it?' she asked.

'Oh, yes,' he replied. 'Tommy always had a low opinion of his brother, you know. He wasn't fooled like his father was. I've no doubt he thought Jimbo was a despicable human being. Although he might not have realised Jimbo was a paedophile, Tommy's got the old-fashioned villain's abhorrence of all sex crimes. He would have hated what Jimbo did. But that wouldn't have been enough, of course. Family was different. When he discovered that Jimbo had been abusing his daughter, driven her to suicide probably, his Caroline, the apple of his eye and the whole O'Donnell clan — he'd never let Jimbo get away with that. Never. He couldn't. It would go entirely against his nature.'

'You don't think there's any doubt, then?'

'Nope. But I'll be astonished if it's ever proved. Tommy knows how to cover his tracks. He's had enough practice.'

'Could he have framed you, do you think?'

'He could have. He doesn't like me, but I don't think it would have occurred to him that he needed a scapegoat. And I'm not sure that O'Donnell is that clever. He's bright enough, but whoever did me would have to be very clever indeed and a real computer whizz. Mind you, I reckon Tommy would probably have known where to find the right person for the job.' He paused, then added mischievously, 'Someone a bit like you, Jo, really.'

'Don't start that again, Mike. Apart from anything else I don't have that kind of knowledge and you know it.'

'No. I'm kidding. I just keep going over and over in my mind who might have done it.'

'Any ideas?'

'Nothing definite,' he admitted. 'I've made a few enemies in my time. There'd be quite a list of people who'd like to see me done up like a kipper. How many of 'em would be capable of doing it, though, is something else.'

'So what do you think . . . '

He interrupted her. 'Jo, when I called I didn't want to talk about all this, particularly. I've just got to live with it now if I want any sort of future. And that's what I wanted to talk about. My future. Our future. Us.'

'I didn't think there was an 'us' any more.' Her voice sounded distant.

'There could be.'

His temper had cooled, of course. He wanted to see her again. It was always her he had dreamed about in prison. Always her in his thoughts when he woke up in the mornings with an erection, or half a one more often than not nowadays. It had really knocked the stuffing out of him, all this, in every possible way. He couldn't explain how he felt. He couldn't explain how mercurial those feelings were either. Maybe it was because the strength and longevity of his desire for her frightened him. One minute he never

435

wanted to see her again and the next he felt that life wasn't worth living without her. He couldn't regret that it had all started with her again, there had been too much pleasure involved, even a little bit of joy. But so much bloody pain too. That seemed to be inevitable for them.

'Sometimes I think you and me will always be an 'us',' he carried on. 'I was angry with you because you didn't believe in me, and particularly when I was in the clink that was very important to me. But it hasn't affected my feelings for you.'

'Mike, your feelings change with the wind, I should have learned that twenty-odd years ago.'

Had she read his mind, he wondered. He couldn't argue with her. He was well aware that she spoke the truth.

'I met your wife when I was leaving the prison.'

'Ah.'

'She never even knew about you and me, did she?'

Typically he avoided the question. 'Look, can we at least meet and talk?'

'I doubt it. Talking has never been our strong suit, has it?' she said, her voice heavy.

No, he thought. They never had time to talk much. Sex and their jobs. That had always been their bond. But it must have been more than that to have lasted all that time, to have been resurrected so easily.

'We could try. If we are going to end this for good I really don't want us to do it on the bloody phone.'

He heard her sigh. 'Mike, there's no point. Anyway, I don't dare. For all I know Paul's still having me followed. If you and I even met he'd find out, I'm sure of it, and if he did he'd divorce me. He's told me so and I believe him absolutely. He won't put up with it again.'

'And would that be such a disaster, then?'

'Mike, don't be ridiculous. I have so much to lose. Including my daughter.'

'Since when has your daughter been so damned important to you?'

'Mike, that's a terrible thing to say. Of course she's important to me.'

'Really? More important than your job and that flash house and maybe being Lady bloody Potter?'

He didn't know why he was saying these things. The last thing he wanted to do was alienate her. He wanted to try again and yet he knew he was also doing his damnedest to destroy any chance of that. He was tying himself up in knots. Why was it so often like that with her?

When she replied he thought there was a slight quaver in her voice but she spoke very patiently, as if addressing a wayward child. 'Mike, I don't think you listen to yourself sometimes. In any case it doesn't make any difference. It really is over for us now. It has to be.'

'Why, so you can stay with a man you don't love just because he's a rich cunt?'

He knew he had shouted the last words. He had meant to be vicious but even as he yelled into the telephone he regretted it. Almost at once he began to stumble an apology.

It was too late.

There was a click as he opened his mouth to speak again and he ended up whispering the word 'sorry' into a buzzing receiver.

She had hung up on him.

★ ★ ★

Joanna sat on the edge of the bed in the cream and white bedroom of her Richmond home, staring numbly at the telephone she had just been using. It was typical of Mike to flare up like that. Nonetheless, she was stunned. She had never told him that she didn't love Paul and in any case it wasn't as simple as that. It was to Fielding, of course. He always saw other people's actions in black and white even though his own were invariably anything but.

Joanna had ensured that she was alone in the house before she made the call and she was very glad of that. It was just before six o'clock in the evening. Emily was staying the night at a friend's. The au pair was also out. Paul wouldn't be home for hours.

So Jo could weep in private, weep for the end of the love affair of her life. It was the end. She had no intention of going back on her word. But God, it hurt and Mike's words had hurt more than anything she could imagine. Far more, she thought, than he would ever suspect. She still did not think he truly realised just how strong an effect everything he said and did had on her.

There was no future for them. Maybe there had never been a chance of one. They carried so much baggage now it was impossible. Angela Phillips. Jimbo and Tommy O'Donnell. Shifter Brown. So many images flitted through her mind whenever she thought of Mike. Which was still most of the time. And yet the pair of them were eternally plagued by doubts. In every direction. Their lives together, inasmuch as they had ever been together, tainted with suspicion and betrayal.

Mike Fielding and Joanna Bartlett. An unlikely coupling caught up in a tangled web that was all too often of their own making.

She accepted absolutely now that Mike had not hired Shifter and that he had been framed. But she still didn't trust him. How could she? She could never be sure of anything about him. He was so unlike Paul in that. You could always be sure of Paul.

She knew damned well that if she had gone along with him on the phone, told him what she suspected he had, at that moment at any rate, wanted to hear, told him she'd leave Paul, her daughter, everything to be with him, by the next day he'd probably have changed his mind.

She knew she had made the right decision. She just knew it. It was the only decision. But that didn't make it any easier.

The tears came freely pouring down her cheeks. She'd done a lot of crying lately. But it never seemed to help.

She flung herself full-length on the bed and buried her face in the pillows. An era had ended for good. It was over. And so at last was the case of Angela Phillips and James Martin O'Donnell.

Even in her misery it occurred to her that there had finally been a kind of rough justice.

20

After Joanna had hung up on him Fielding, predictably enough, went to the pub. He knew he should try to forget Jo. She was just too dangerous for him. And it looked as she was in any case giving him little choice.

Mike was still mystified as to how those e-mails had got on to his laptop. And he still had no idea who had framed him so effectively. He assumed it must have been one of the many police colleagues he had crossed over the years, some of whom he could quite believe disliked him far more than most villains had ever done.

And then the police had discovered Caroline O'Donnell's diary, which started all their doubts. Though there was no mystery about that, of course. Fielding himself had been responsible for the tip-off. He had told his wife to write the letter which alerted Todd Mallett. He had told her exactly what to say, and how to type the letter and where to post it from in order to provide virtually no clues to its origin. Ruth had been confused and had asked a lot of questions he'd had trouble answering. But, as usual, in the end she had done his bidding.

Of course, only Fielding knew there wasn't a word of truth in the diary. He had written it himself, on the dead girl's computer sitting in that bedroom which her family had kept as a shrine. He had done it while her parents were on holiday. Down on the

Costa del Crime, naturally. It hadn't been difficult to break into the O'Donnell home. They didn't go in for a great deal of security. They didn't need to. It would be a brave villain who would do their house. And in any case Fielding was good at breaking into places, having a look round, retreating without leaving a sign. It takes one to catch one, he thought with a wry smile. The old adage again.

He knew he'd done a good enough job on the diary to make it appear convincingly authentic. That had been a doddle for him. He'd done his five years in child protection. He'd heard kids talking about being abused by their uncles, and their mother's boyfriends, and yes, their fathers and grandfathers. He'd taken statements, he'd read childish outpourings. They quite often wrote stuff down, these poor mixed-up, mistreated kids. He knew how they sounded, the way they wrote stuff, the words they used and the words they didn't because they couldn't bring themselves to, or maybe because they didn't even know them.

He'd typed it out laboriously on Caroline's computer, hidden it in a homework file, but not too well and, for good measure, he'd printed the diary and left it half sticking out of a book. He knew Tommy and his wife spent time in this room, paying a sort of homage to her. You could see that's what they did from the very look of the place. He'd done his utmost to leave the diary somewhere he felt pretty sure it would be discovered, but where it was possible that both mother and father had missed it previously. That had been the most difficult part of the job. But apparently he had managed it.

Tommy must have wondered who had tipped off the police about the diary, of course. Mike realised how unlikely it was that he would have told anyone about it. He wouldn't have wanted the world to know about what he believed his brother had done, he just would have wanted to sort it. But the O'Donnells had plenty of enemies, and Tommy might well have thought it could have been somebody Sam had crossed years ago, who'd done some snooping. Or perhaps he'd believed that Caroline must have confided in another kid, a school friend who'd eventually owned up to what she knew. Kids did things like that.

Fielding had been surprised when he'd learned that Tommy had used e-mail to arrange the contract. But then he'd recognised the sense of it. It had allowed Tommy to distance himself and his family from the crime. Tommy was clever and no doubt quite knowledgeable enough about the Net to realise that an Excite address on e-mails sent and received at a cyber café would give him total anonymity. Swiss bank accounts all round had taken care of the payments he'd made to Shifter, of course, and that had really been Tommy's style. As Shifter genuinely hadn't known who had hired him, Tommy needn't actually have made the second payment. But Fielding wasn't surprised that he had. If Tommy O'Donnell made a deal he kept it. That was part of the code.

Fielding smiled. He had not killed James Martin O'Donnell. Nor had he hired the man who did. But he had been responsible all right. He had made quite sure that Tommy would not allow his brother to live. James O'Donnell, guilty of the worst crime he had ever known. Guilty of leaving poor bloody Angela Phillips to die alone, violated, disfigured, racked with pain, to be found by a policeman who had thought he had seen it all. A policeman so tough he didn't get moved by dead bodies. Until he saw that one. Jimbo O'Donnell, guilty as hell of all that and guilty also of wrecking what had once been the most important thing in Mike Fielding's life — apart from Joanna Bartlett. His career.

There wasn't much left for Mike to smile about. But the thought of Jimbo O'Donnell lying dead in a hole in the ground with his cock in his mouth, that would always make him smile. That and the fact that he still had a pension.

He ordered another large whisky. Then, when he had drunk enough to numb the pain, he decided he might as well go home to his wife. As usual. Who knows, he thought, hauling himself uncertainly upright from his bar stool, perhaps that's what he would have ended up doing eventually regardless of Joanna. It was, after all, what he had always done.

Fielding would not, however, be returning to the Devon and Exeter Constabulary. How could he? He had been cleared. His record remained unblemished. Officially. An early retirement deal safeguarding his thirty-year pension — there was only about a year still to go now — had been organised.

His wife had always wanted to retire to Spain. Some place she'd fallen in love with on the Costa Blanca. They'd never be able to afford the more southerly Costa del Sol where all the rich villains were. Maybe he would give Ruth something she wanted for once. Yes, that's what he'd do, he thought, oozing drunken benevolence.

He made his way a little unsteadily through the pub door and out on to the pavement. The fresh air hit him like a blow in the face. He staggered, recovering himself with all the acumen of a professional drunk. Anyway, there was this barmaid he'd got to know over on the Costa a few years back . . .

★   ★   ★

A month or so later Joanna woke once more from a largely alcohol-induced sleep with no discernible hangover. You didn't get them when you were in the habit of drinking as much as she had begun to. She feared she was picking up Fielding's habit. Mike had not attempted to get in touch with her since she had hung up on him. And she was determined never to contact him again. Sometimes she couldn't even believe she had allowed, even encouraged, the resumption of their affair. Now she just wanted to put Mike out of her mind. For ever. But trying to forget him wasn't proving easy. In fact, it wasn't easy to forget any of it.

She reflected on how many lives had been touched by the death of Angela Phillips and all that had happened since.

Most affected of all, of course — if you didn't count the O'Donnells and she preferred not to — were the Phillips family. She had, however, been glad to learn through the *Comet*'s new Devon man that the family had sold part of their land, close to Okehampton apparently, for building development. Planning permission had been given, against the odds on the edge of Dartmoor, because of the need for new homes in the area. Big money was involved, which probably meant that the family would be able to save the remains of their farm, even after the disastrous private court case against O'Donnell and the *Comet* reneging on their deal.

She'd heard that Todd Mallett had finally closed down his investigation into Jimbo O'Donnell's murder and Shifter Brown's involvement — and the police never did that with an unsolved killing, even a partially unsolved one, unless they were damned sure they knew the truth but could do nothing about it. They obviously didn't think they were ever going to prove anything against Tommy O'Donnell and that didn't surprise Jo a bit.

Paul, typically, carried on as if nothing had happened. More or less. The previous week, however, he had axed her column. She assumed it was a kind of punishment and had told him so. That had been a mistake, of course. Her husband didn't like confrontation or indignation. Emotional outbursts never got you anywhere with him. 'Don't be ridiculous, Jo, it's what's called an editorial decision,' he had told her. 'There is no place for that kind of journalism in the tabloid world any more. It's old-fashioned and you know it. You must realise how out of place 'Sword of Justice' is in the *Comet*, and has been for some time.'

She did realise that, of course. That didn't mean she liked it any the more. Paul had said she would remain an assistant editor, that he'd find a new role for her, but she really couldn't see that working out. Her disappointment was far more than just for herself, however. She thought it a tragedy that all the great tabloid traditions were being eroded. The British popular papers she had once been so proud to represent were nowadays often not much different from America's supermarket tabloids: just full of throwaway trash. She thought it was a shame. And so, she had always believed, did Paul, whom she had admired for at least appearing to try to walk the tightrope between the kind of journalistic standards now almost invariably ignored and the demands of the modern mass market. She was no longer even so sure of that.

Nonetheless she knew she had little choice but to settle for what she'd got. Which was a hell of a lot more than most people had, after all. Paul had been right. And Fielding, too, in an awful sort of way. She liked her lifestyle, she had got used to the luxury home and even Paul's chauffeur-driven car, to never having to worry about money. She also loved her daughter desperately, even if she had yet to develop the kind of mother-daughter relationship she felt she should have with Emily.

She wasn't happy, of course. All the old demons had been released. She would not forget Fielding no matter how hard she tried. Not ever. Or Angela Phillips, come to that. All of it would be with her always. And alcohol only ever provided temporary amnesia.

She resolved to cut down on the drinking and to rebuild her life. More than anything else she would concentrate on her family in future. The rest of it was over.

As part of this new resolution Jo made a huge fuss of her daughter over breakfast, drove her to school and promised she would be at home waiting when Emily returned in the afternoon. 'And at the weekend we'll do some shopping together, buy you some new clothes, and then maybe go to the cinema,' she went on. 'You can chose the film, Em. Would you like that?'

'Oh, yeah! That would be great, Mum,' replied Emily, with a level of enthusiasm which quite took Joanna by surprise.

Maybe, if she made a real effort, things would work out after all, she thought.

Marginally cheered, she later set off for St Bride's in Fleet Street, the famous journalists' church, for a memorial service for Andy McKane, who had died at the age of sixty-one of sclerosis of the liver. Which was exactly how she'd end up if she didn't watch it, Jo reflected wryly.

McKane may have been a fearful old sexist, but he had also been an excellent news editor and a fundamentally good-hearted guy, beneath his bombastic chauvinism. In any case the memorial service provided a nowadays rare get-together for old Fleet Street hacks. Certainly she found she was looking forward to the diversion.

The turnout was extensive and across the board, as she would have expected for Andy. After the service there was the usual wake in El Vino's wine bar during which, in spite of her morning resolution, Jo drank far more house champagne than

447

she had intended to. By the time she decided, three hours or so later, that she really must leave if she were to have any chance of keeping her promise to Emily, she was feeling quite mellow.

Then she bumped into Frank Manners. Literally. The old crime hack who had once caused her such trouble turned abruptly away from the bar just as Jo was heading for the door and they collided. She hadn't seen him since his enforced early retirement deal nineteen years earlier now and Manners, who must have reached his late seventies, looked to be in far better fettle than he deserved. His complexion was a little more florid, which might in any event have been down to his obviously well-oiled state, but other than that he had changed astonishingly little.

'Good God, it's the golden girl,' he bellowed. 'Got any other poor sod sacked lately?'

A slight hush fell in their part of the bar. Manners's attitude hadn't changed either, she thought. Why did he have to be such a bastard? He must have known he'd been asking for trouble after what he'd done all those years ago, surely. Remembering the shock and distress of it, the anger washed over her. 'If you've got something to say, Frank, say it straight,' she snapped. 'If you hadn't taken to making bloody poisonous anonymous phone calls you'd have kept your job for as long as you wanted it, and you know it!'

Frank stared at her in slack-mouthed bewilderment. 'Have you finally gone totally and utterly barking mad, woman?' he enquired. 'I haven't got the faintest idea what the fuck you're talking about.'

She opened her mouth to make a suitably cutting

reply. Something in his expression and in the way that he had spoken stopped her in her tracks. Suddenly she knew, with terrible devastating clarity, that he was telling the truth. She pushed past him, desperate to get away from the crush of noisy drinkers.

Outside she took deep breaths of the autumn air. Her brain was spinning. There was an all too clear alternative to the various assumptions she had made so long ago about Manners, which had just never occurred to her before. Now it seemed glaringly obvious. And she was horrified.

'Oh, my God,' she thought. 'Paul!'

* * *

For the rest of the afternoon and evening Joanna operated on autopilot. She travelled home to Richmond in a kind of daze, somehow managing both to arrive there as promised before Emily and to go through the normal motions of family life. She cooked them both a meal and forced herself to sit down and eat with her daughter whose chief topic of conversation was Saturday's planned shopping trip and how her life would be ruined unless, as well as new clothes, her mother bought her yet another trendy new computer game, which of course absolutely everybody else at school already had.

Joanna, totally preoccupied, found she kept drifting off, but after a while a thought struck her. 'You like playing computer games, and going on the Net and stuff with your dad, don't you, Em?'

'Oh, yeah.' Her daughter's face lit up. 'He's brilliant.'

'Is he really?'

'Oh, yeah. Dad can do anything on a computer.'

'Anything?'

'Pretty well. Alice Rivers's father's a real geek and he doesn't know half as much as Dad.'

'Bit of a super-hacker, is he then, your dad?'

Emily looked doubtful. 'He said I wasn't to tell,' she said.

'Tell what? I can keep a secret.'

Emily still looked doubtful.

'Anyway, if it's your father's secret I expect I know it already.'

Joanna had the grace to feel ashamed of herself. Not only was she pumping her daughter for information about her father, but she was also playing on Emily's special relationship with him. She thought there was a fair chance that Emily would not be able to resist demonstrating that Paul confided more in her than in his wife. And she was right.

'Once he let me watch him hack into the *Daily Mirror*,' Emily blurted out.

Jo tried not to let her surprise show. 'Ah,' she said non-committally.

'It took him a long time and he said he couldn't get into the whole system but he was actually able to look at some of their stories for the next day. It was awesome.' Emily's eyes shone with pride.

'Awesome,' agreed Jo absently, foreboding growing with everything her daughter told her.

After Emily had eventually gone to bed, Jo

decided, in spite of her resolution, that she needed another drink. She poured herself her usual half-tumbler or so of Scotch and then, thinking better of it, emptied two-thirds of it back into the bottle. She carried her glass into the living room, dimmed the lights and sat very still on the big, squashy black sofa, waiting for Paul to come home. She needed to think.

She had never before talked much about computer skills with either her husband or her child. Jo was able enough, but her interest in computers was strictly limited to their use as a tool of her trade. She'd had no idea Paul was as adept as Emily had suggested. It had never occurred to her before to ask. And she had only done so now because of her chance meeting with Frank Manners earlier in the day, what she felt she had learned from it and the thoughts to which that revelation had led her.

Frank's reaction had convinced her totally that he had not been responsible for those poisonous phone calls and her suspicions had somehow switched instantly to Paul. But could he really have made those awful calls to Chris, deliberately setting out to wreck her first marriage, later even pretending that he had received an anonymous call himself? Was he that manipulative, that wicked? If so, could he also be responsible for much more than that?

After a while she heard Paul's chauffeur-driven car pull up outside and a few seconds later his key turned in the lock. He didn't seem surprised to see her sitting in near-darkness. He glanced pointedly at her drink. She guessed he thought she was drunk again. Actually, she had barely touched her glass and, in spite of all the champagne at the wake that afternoon, she had never felt more sober.

'Emily all right?' he enquired casually, as he too poured himself a whisky. A small one with lots of water.

She nodded. 'Went to bed an hour or so ago. She was telling me what a whizz-kid you are with computers. I had no idea.'

He sat down in an armchair opposite her, putting the whisky bottle on the low table between them, and shot her a quizzical look.

Oh, God, she hadn't meant to blurt out anything like that. She'd no intention of confronting him. Not yet, anyway. The last time she had allowed her behaviour to be governed by crazy suspicions it had led to the awful hotel room confrontation with Mike Fielding, the very thought of which still made her cringe.

'You've never shown any interest,' he told her reasonably. 'In any case, no doubt Emily was exaggerating.'

'She said you can hack into the *Daily Mirror*?'

'Oh, yeah.' He grinned easily. 'I got lucky one night. Impressed Em no end. But I couldn't get to any of the important stuff, of course, that was far too well protected, just the pre-print.'

That meant non-newsy features and service pages like travel and motoring. She had no idea whether or not he was playing it down, but even what he was admitting to impressed Joanna just as much as it had her daughter.

She let it pass.

'How was the memorial service?' he enquired

452

after a bit. 'I was sorry I couldn't get away today. McKane could be a pain in the arse but he was a fine newspaperman.'

Joanna nodded. 'It went well enough. Good turnout. I saw Frank Manners there.'

Off she went again. She hadn't really meant to start on that either, but now that she had she knew she was not going to be able to stop. 'He accused me of getting him sacked.'

Paul laughed lightly. 'Well, to coin a famous phrase, he would, wouldn't he?'

'The subject of those moody phone calls came up. He denied all knowledge.'

'And he would do that, too, wouldn't he?' Paul repeated.

'I suppose so,' she agreed meekly.

He studied her thoughtfully. 'Don't let that old bastard get to you after all these years,' he told her. 'I think you'd better have another drink.' He picked up the whisky bottle and poured a hefty measure into her glass, filling it almost to the brim. Well, she supposed that was the way she had been drinking lately, but he didn't usually encourage her like this.

She thought she had better back off before she talked herself into a corner. After all, she didn't really know what to believe about anything any more. 'I'm tired, I think I'll go on up,' she said eventually.

★ ★ ★

Paul watched Joanna leave the room and head for the stairs, taking the nearly full glass of whisky with

453

her. He was uneasy. Those remarks about his computer skills and the moody phone calls had been distinctly pointed. What was going on in her head, he wondered anxiously.

She was drinking too much, of course, but usually she didn't let it show. He believed that she would pull herself together sooner or later. She was that sort of woman. The important thing was that she was back in line.

He would have preferred just to have been able to wave a magic wand and make Joanna love him so much she wouldn't even have wanted to rekindle her old affair with Fielding. He would have settled just for being able to make her see how very much he loved her. He had no idea why he had never been able to do even that, but he knew that he hadn't.

At least she understood now that he was not prepared to lose her. Men like him didn't take kindly to losing what they had won with hard work and diligent application. For Paul, the same went for his marriage and his wife as for his job. His world, both at home and at work, would carry on, now, just as it had always done. That was all he had ever wanted, that and to ensure that his prospect of being knighted, almost certainly in the new year's honours list the following January he had been led to believe, would not be affected by some unseemly scandal.

He didn't believe that he would face any further problems from Joanna, even though Fielding had been freed. Or at least, he hadn't until this evening.

Paul had never been remotely under suspicion of organising the e-mail frame-up, as he had known he would not be. For a start nobody, not even Joanna, understood the strength of his motivation. And, of course, no one had ever realised quite how adept he was with computers and with working the Net. It was one of the secrets of his success in newspapers. He could hack into the memories of other people's computers and hence into their lives, and even into other newspapers, with surprising frequency. His only mistake had been to show off to his daughter. He basked in her pride in him. How he wished his wife would love him half as much and as unconditionally as he was sure his daughter did. He shouldn't ever have revealed so much of his skill to Emily, of course. He just hoped that Joanna had believed him when he had played down his abilities and achievements. He couldn't be sure whether she had or not, but even Emily had no idea just how good he really was.

What he had done was complex but certainly not impossible, particularly if you had a leaning in that direction. All the software you needed, and the instructions, were available to anybody, free on the Net. It was called LINUX — a robust, fully featured operating system with a mind-blowing hacking capacity. All you had to do was download it and understand it — then you could make it do pretty much anything you wanted. Even Paul didn't understand the half of it. He wondered if anybody did except the brilliant software technicians who had written the programme. But he had managed to decipher and understand enough for his purposes.

With the help of LINUX he had written a virus, which he had lodged in Mike Fielding's computer by attaching it to an inconsequential e-mail. The virus installed the phoney e-mail files, at the same time hiding them from view by burying them deep in the computer's memory. The phoney e-mails left no footprints because they were only ever files within the virus and the e-mail Paul had attached the virus to was, of course, untraceable — despatched from yet another Excite address, set up and operated from a second-hand laptop.

It wasn't just East End villains who knew about computer markets and the advantages of their stock. Even before the love-bug hackers had been caught through the codes inside their Microsoft software, Paul had taken no chances. He kept his street-market-acquired laptop locked in a box in a dark corner of the garden shed that was his own secret retreat.

Paul had so far been quite pleased with himself in the circumstances. He supposed it would have been overly optimistic to have expected his ruse to result in Fielding actually being convicted for a crime he had not committed. He'd settled for knowing that he'd wreaked havoc in the policeman's life, just the way Fielding had wreaked havoc in his. He'd rather the policeman had been convicted, of course, sent down for good. But his plan had proved effective enough. It had ended Fielding's career and been the final nail in the coffin of the detective's affair with Joanna. Actually, he'd been quite content to settle for that — and for getting Joanna back.

But now he was not quite sure of her again. For a moment, as they had sat together earlier, he had thought she had been going to level some kind of accusation at him. He couldn't be certain, but he reckoned he ought to play safe. Joanna must never know what he had done. That would ruin everything.

He finished his drink, put the empty glass in the sink in the kitchen and left the house through the kitchen door. As he headed across the lawn, he glanced behind him up at the window of the bedroom he and Jo shared. The light had been switched off. He'd had an ulterior motive in pouring her that extra large Scotch. She was certain to be deep into a whisky-induced sleep by now. Nothing was going to wake her for several hours.

At the bottom of the garden he unlocked the shed. The second-hand laptop was still safe in its usual hiding place. He knew he ought to have disposed of it before now and wasn't quite sure why he hadn't. A kind of arrogance, he supposed. He had always been so far ahead of the game he hadn't felt the need to abide by the normal rules. But Joanna had rattled his confidence somewhat and he was going to take no more risks.

He picked up the laptop, all its various software and connecting bits, and carried the lot back into the house cradled in his arms. He closed and locked the kitchen door behind him, walked through the house to the front and put the pile on the hall table while he opened the door to the cupboard alongside and rummaged around for the holdall he knew was there somewhere. When he'd found it he transferred everything into it and left the house through the front door as quietly as possible, setting off on foot down the hill. He had considered using either Jo's car or his own, locked in the garage, but he didn't know where her keys were and opening up the garage could well make enough noise to wake even Joanna. No more risks. That was his new rule. He'd walk. After all, the river wasn't far away.

★　★　★

Less than a minute later Joanna slipped out of the house behind him.

She hadn't drunk the huge whisky Paul had poured for her. She hadn't wanted it. Neither had she wanted to sleep. She had just wanted to be alone to carry on thinking. She had switched off the bedroom lights and sat, still fully clothed, in the chair by the window overlooking the garden.

It was a clear, starry night and anyway it never got properly dark in London or the suburbs. She had seen Paul padding across the lawn, disappearing past the fruit trees into the dense shrubby area at the bottom of the garden. At first she took little notice, he quite frequently went into the garden when he came home at night. She had no idea what he did down there and had never given it much thought until now. She certainly had no idea of any of the uses he had for the garden shed. He just told her that he enjoyed the fresh night air after a day cooped up in an air-conditioned building and that had always seemed perfectly reasonable. But watching idly as he reappeared, walking back across the lawn towards the house just a few minutes later, she saw that he was carrying something in his arms, although the light was too dim for her to see what it was.

She heard him lock up the back of the house and make his way through to the front, then open the hall cupboard and start rummaging about. On impulse, she made her way as silently as possible out through the already ajar bedroom door to the top of the stairs. Looking down, she could clearly see an unfamiliar laptop computer on the hall table. She backed away on to the landing as Paul emerged from the cupboard clutching a holdall and, peeping cautiously through the banisters, she watched him load the little computer into the bag, sling it over his shoulder and leave the house.

Again acting on impulse, she decided to follow him, hardly believing what she was doing. It was almost one o'clock on an autumn night; there were hardly any other pedestrians about and very little traffic. She was wearing only jeans and a cotton shirt, as she hadn't waited to grab a coat or a jacket. She shivered in the cool air and was careful to keep well back as Paul made his way down Richmond Hill and into Hill Rise past their favourite Chinese restaurant. Then he turned smartly left towards the river and set off purposefully across Richmond Bridge. Jo ducked into a convenient doorway, realising she would have to wait until he had crossed over before following him if she was to have any chance of avoiding being seen.

But halfway over the bridge Paul paused, glancing briefly around him as if checking there was nobody nearby. Then he moved closer to the bridge wall. His back was towards Jo. The street lighting on the bridge was not as bright as it might have been and Jo's angle of sight was all wrong. From the doorway she could not quite see what he was doing. She moved out on to the pavement and took a few cautious steps forward in order to get a better view. As she did so, she saw Paul remove the holdall from his shoulder and in one fluent movement toss it into the River Thames.

Joanna gasped and only just stopped herself crying out. She supposed this was what she had been half expecting. It was also what she had been dreading. She went into shock.

Her husband stood for just a few seconds longer, looking down at the water, then turned round and began to walk briskly back towards her. At that moment a car swung over the bridge, its headlights fully illuminating Jo. She felt like a rabbit trapped by a lamper. She just couldn't move. She froze.

Paul's stride faltered. She knew he must have seen her, must have realised that she had followed him and what she had witnessed.

Her body was starting to work again. She found she could move her legs, now, and took a step backwards. Paul was still approaching, more slowly, his arms stretched out towards her. She spun round and took off at a run, not up Richmond Hill towards the home she shared with this man she didn't want near her, the house where their daughter slept unaware, but off to the left along the main street through the town. She didn't know where she was going. She barely cared. Her body might be functioning once more, but her brain was numb.

'Jo, Jo, wait . . . '

She heard him call after her. She ran all the harder.